W9-AZB-677

My Last Lament

Also by James William Brown

BLOOD DANCE

My Last Lament

James William Brown

BERKLEY
New York

BERKLEY
An imprint of Penguin Random House LLC
375 Hudson Street, New York, New York 10014

Material from this book has appeared in other forms in *Narrative* magazine and *Fiction International*.

Library of Congress Cataloging-in-Publication Data

Names: Brown, James William, 1942– author.
Title: My last lament / James William Brown.
Description: First edition. | New York : Berkley Books, 2017.
Identifiers: LCCN 2016004357 (print) | LCCN 2016017033 (ebook) | ISBN 9780399583407 (hardcover) | ISBN 9780399583414 (ebook)
Classification: LCC PS3552.R68566 M9 2017 (print) | LCC PS3552.R68566 (ebook) | DDC 813/.54—dc23
LC record available at https://lccn.loc.gov/2016004357

International edition ISBN: 9780399586804

First Edition: April 2017

Printed in the United States of America
1 3 5 7 9 10 8 6 4 2

Cover design and illustration by Adam Auerbach
Book design by Tiffany Estreicher

For Jane *always*,
and to the memory of
Mary Dodds Szasz

Time will explain it all. He is a talker, and needs no questioning before he speaks.

—Euripides,
Aeolus

CASSETTE 1 ✦ Side 1

Now **let me** see, how do I turn this thing on? Oh. Maybe it *is* on. There's a red light, anyway, a little fiery eye in this dark kitchen. I guess I speak into this bit—hello, hello in there. One-two-three-four. I'm just going to rewind and play that back to make sure I'm doing it right, seeing as how all machines are out to humiliate me. Technology means putting a cassette into a recorder and that's *it* for me, no comments, please. Okay, everything's okay, though I would never guess that's how I must sound to others, old and croaky, like a geriatric frog.

Well, then, where to begin? My name's Aliki and I'm the last professional lamenter in this village of ours in the northeast of Greece. That's right, a composer of dirge-poems, called *mirologia*, chanted at wakes and such. Well, actually, I don't really compose them. I seem to fall into a kind of state and they really compose themselves and just pour through me like a long sigh. Maybe they're not even poems, more like chants. It's an old village custom, one long practiced by crones like me, though, as I say, I'm the last in these parts. And the dead I chant about, well, they seem to *linger* around me whether I like it or not—you'll see what I mean. The dead never seem to finish with us, or is it we who never finish with them?

When someone from one of the old families dies around here, the relatives ask me to lament. It's not exactly grieving they want, just the marking of a life. The lament can be grand or small and not necessarily sad. The family wants to feel they've honored the dead in the traditional way before they trundle the body off to the church with that new, young priest, Father Yerasimos. Of course the younger families skip me and go straight to him and I bear them no ill will. I'm here for those who need me and in return they give me whatever they have on hand—a few eggs, olives, cheese, a day-old loaf of bread. Some are more generous than others, but I accept what's offered and don't complain. No one has much cash these days, thanks to the blunders and outright thievery of our governments these last years, not to mention those moralistic neighbors to the north. Well, I don't need much; time has made me small. That's what the years do—shrink you down by plucking away those you love one by one and eventually even your memories of them. In the end, there's a lot less of you.

I dress only in black, once the custom for widows and crones. It's still my custom. My head scarf too is black and when I go out, I draw the corner of it across my nose and mouth to hide my bad teeth. I look like a storybook witch. The girl I was on the day the Germans executed my father wouldn't recognize the crone I've become.

Speaking of my father, I saw him again this morning standing in my back garden. He fished a cigarette out of the shirt pocket next to the blackened bullet holes in his chest and lit up. There wasn't much point in telling him that smoking is bad for him as he's been dead for more than fifty years. So there he was, saying again between puffs that things over there were not much different from here. Of course I'm not sure I believe in an *over there*, but when the dead turn up, you have to give them the benefit of the doubt.

We stand around all the time talking politics, he said. *Everyone speaks at once, interrupting and yelling, and nobody agrees on anything. It's just like life.*

It was back in '43 that the Germans executed him along with two other village men. Made them stand next to the stone wall under the plane tree in the *plateia* and shot them down, just like that. It's still there, that wall; I think of him every time I pass it.

There isn't even a decent kafeneion *here for a good cup of coffee. We're trying to circulate a petition about it, but no one can agree on the wording. And there's nobody to give it to. Doesn't seem to be anyone in charge.*

"But what about the saints," I always ask, "or the Holy Family?"

We've never seen any of them. But there's probably a bureaucracy full of incompetents somewhere. He took another drag on his cigarette, leaned back and blew a perfect smoke ring. *Also just like life.*

That was no surprise. Who can believe in all those sour faces in church icons? When we were wasting away back in the forties, they hadn't helped us at all. So what were they *for*?

He paused and then said, *Go back to sleep, my child.*

"But I'm awake, standing here on the back steps watching you smoke your lungs out."

Oh, well, he said. *Sleeping, waking—what's the difference?* Then he was gone.

There is this about the dead: they're so light. They slip in and out of our world with no effort whatsoever. By contrast, we seem heavy, dragging our lives along behind us like an old sack of stones.

Oh, now wait, what's that clicking noise? Maybe if I push this button? Really, I hope we're not going to be plagued with stops and starts. This recorder and these cassettes were left here by a Greek-American scholar who came to see me a few months ago. An earnest young woman from an American university, doing research on rural lament practices, or so she said.

You see, when you're the last of a line of just about anything, people will come to study you as if you're a donkey that can salute the flag. How do you *feel* about it, they want to know. At my age there's so much to feel *about*, one way or another. It's a mystery to me how one chunk of memory gets stuck to another from years earlier and finally adds up to something different from the last time you remembered it.

Anyway, this scholar, an *ethnographer*, she called herself, was a pretty little thing, though her blond hair looked as if she'd taken an eggbeater to it and then glued it all in place. She had these tiny glasses that she had to push up her little bit of a nose as she talked about recording all my laments. She asked questions about a lamenter's *otherness* and something called *the poetics of social commentary*. What could I say? I just looked at her while she ran on about *high voicing versus low voicing* and a lot of other things I've never heard of. We were sitting in the kitchen—as I am now—and out the window I could see my neighbor, old Stavros, pitchforking hay into his donkey cart. A breeze blew the hay every which way, but what landed in the cart looked a lot like my visitor's hair. I could see that my silence was making her uneasy; I was probably not turning out to be the kind of subject she'd been looking for, poor little thing. She kept patting her head as if to make sure it was still perched on her tiny neck, then pushing her glasses up her nose again.

"As we know, death is the passage from the inside to the outside," she said. Her Greek was good even with that flat American accent, though I had no idea what she was talking about. Seeing my blank expression, she asked, "Wouldn't you say?"

"I've never thought about it," I said. "Is it something about yourself or your family you're trying to tell me? Do you need my services? For this you've come so far?"

No, no, she said, flustered, it was just her area of study, *Mediterranean ethnography*. She was trying to get established, publish some original field research. She'd already interviewed some lamenters who mostly wail and weep, as she said, and others who sing or call out the deeds of the dead person. But she hadn't talked to anyone about dirge-poems.

"Has anyone else interviewed you?" she asked.

"Not unless you count those TV people who came all the way from Athens. And then there was that newspaperman from Thessaloniki. But no one from a university, not 'til now."

She seemed relieved and said she wanted me to lament into this gadget she had, a thing she held in her hands and worked with her thumbs. It seemed to give her a lot of trouble because, she said, our village was tucked down in this valley on the other side of the mountain. Though she was interested in the fact that isolation has kept our ways mostly unchanged, we seemed to be too remote for her gadget.

We're not remote here, I told her. *Remote* is always somewhere else, a place where you're not. And I don't know why anyone would carry around something to aggravate them the way that thing did her.

"And I can't just turn laments on and off," I said, "like the kitchen tap."

"Oh, yes, of course. I'm sorry—I did think of that. I was hoping you'd record yourself when you're in, well, the right frame of mind."

I didn't want to go into it, but in fact my neighbor and old childhood friend, Zephyra, was (and still is) moving toward her end in her house just along the road. Poor thing, what a thin little life she's had. There will be lamenting enough in a while.

Then the scholar reached into her briefcase as she said that she'd thought our remoteness might be a problem so she'd also brought this battery-operated recorder and cassettes that she'd leave with me. I didn't say I'd use them and I didn't say I wouldn't. She'd traveled a long way to find me, after all, so I thanked her for coming and gave her a jar of our good village honey as I sent her on her way, saying she should visit again sometime soon. We may have lost our wits, but we still have our manners. She said she'd be in touch.

And really, that was it. She hasn't returned and it's been months, so who knows if she will? Not many people find their way to our village even once, not to mention twice. Her recorder and blank cassettes have been sitting here and sometimes I think they're whispering to me, *Tell me how you feel.*

What I feel is that time will only snatch away more of me before long. So finally I think I'm going to do some telling, but not only about lamenting. I'd like to unspool what's happened in the order it once had and get back to that other time, a time of secrets. But it feels odd now, me sitting here talking about myself to myself. So here's what I think I'll do—I'm going to imagine you listening, my American scholar, though I know so little about you. Well, I'm sorry about those comments I made about your hair and such. I'd go back and erase them, but I'm not sure how to do that. So if you'll forgive me, I'll just move along, pretending you're interested in my life and times, not just my laments. Well, you *are*, aren't you? And of course you're young so I don't know how much you know about the war and what came after. I hear they don't teach much history in your country, but can that be true? It's hard to believe that here, where we can never get out from under our glorious past or stop measuring it against our much poorer present. Anyway, I'll stitch in some facts here and there.

But I should also tell you that we may get interrupted from time to time because of my poor friend Zephyra. She's held on longer than anyone expected, but she's into her final days at last.

Oh, now the clicking of this machine has stopped. So, onward.

I was talking about those stolen squash, I think. Oh, no, I hadn't even got to that. I'd better start further back. Well, it was 1943 and the Germans had been here for a while. The Italians had come through first, but then the Germans took over. My father always said that the fact they were in our village at all was probably some bureaucratic mistake. They were mostly in Athens and the islands but not much on the mainland, which was largely occupied by the Italians. Had a spelling error been made by a clerk who'd confused the village name with that of some more strategic place? The Germans certainly weren't here for the charcoal our area produces. It's made from the nearby grove of resinous pines, once owned by my grandfather. His son, my father, was the last charcoal maker in his line. It was difficult work. Being the last of a line seems to be a family trait. From the smoke in the smoldering process, his skin was walnut-dark and his clothes picked up the unmistakable smell of resin. The men in my family have always had that particular mixture of scents—a piney, smoky maleness.

But the charcoal making stopped during the war along with everything else. The Germans had taken our crops, our livestock, our olive oil to feed themselves. They even shot the larks out of the sky and roasted them. As a result, we had little to eat except for the greens we could dig up from the mountainside. So we had almost no energy or will. We moved in slow motion. Nearly four years they'd been here by then and I'd just turned fourteen.

The Italians had invaded first from the north, not so far from here, back in October of '40. Some of our own village boys died there along the Albanian border, may the earth rest lightly on them, while trying to hold off the macaroni-eaters. And our troops did actually manage that for a few brave months, with the help of British, Australian and New Zealand troops. But by the following April, Hitler had come to Mussolini's rescue and in the end the two of them divided us up like a pair of wolves devouring the same sheep. Our government and royal family fled to Cairo, leaving us to the wolves. We in areas that went to the Germans envied the other areas because we'd heard that the macaroni-eaters were not so bad. In fact, they were a bit like us, ignoring rules and regulations, always trying to wring a bit of pleasure from life, even in wartime. But the Germans, bah, they didn't leave us so much as a loaf of bread.

At night we dreamed of food, of Paschal lamb roasted over charcoal, fragrant egg-lemon soup, sheep's yogurt with thyme-flower honey, delicate little meatballs infused with mint and parsley. I was obsessed with thoughts of sweets; tortured by the vision of almond cookies dusted with powdered sugar.

With little energy, I did everything the way my father told me to, but slowly, slowly, never running or shouting. "Imagine you're dancing on the last night of Carnival," he said, "and each step must be just so. Don't move without pausing first. Then be slow and careful."

The day he died, I was stepping carefully down our main street on the way to my friend Takis's house, past some German soldiers standing at attention near the stone wall in the *plateia*, just there by the old plane tree that was nearly dead from drought. A few villagers stood to one side, being held back by other soldiers, watching something and all talking at once. I threaded my way through them until I could see that my father was standing with two other men at the wall. Stepping as precisely as I could, I tried to walk over to him so he would see that I was doing as he'd asked. But one of the soldiers came over and pushed me back. It was then that I saw my father notice me. He looked aghast.

"Go home, Aliki!" he shouted. "Go now!" And to one of the village women he shouted, "Chrysoula, take my daughter!"

I realized that the woman nearby, who'd pulled her apron up to her face and was weeping into it, was my friend Takis's mother, Chrysoula. She let go of her apron, grabbed my hand and started to lead me away, still weeping. But I looked back just as the German soldiers raised their rifles, which made sounds like toy guns: *pop, pop, pop*. My father's cap flew off as he pitched over backward. Puffs of smoke flew up into the tree and its dry leaves rasped against each other.

At first it didn't occur to me that he'd been killed. There'd been other executions in the village, I learned later, but my father had protected me from that knowledge. Happening upon this one by chance, I didn't realize at first that my father's fall was connected to the popping sound.

It had all begun with those squash that I mentioned before, secret squash. The fields had been stripped, but there was a gully below one of them, not quite visible unless you knew just where it was. So my father and the others were picking by night and hoarding the secret produce in a root cellar. From time to time we ate one and, oh, I can't tell you what the taste of squash cooked golden was like in such times. Just that buttery smell. I can't eat it at all now because the memory is too piercing. Well, anyway, someone had informed the German officer in charge of the area, Colonel Esterhaus. The life of a secret in the village is not long even today, and back then people were willing to debase themselves for the prospect of food.

Oh, I don't even cry about it anymore. I'm like an old sponge left out in the sun, dry as cardboard. At the time, I couldn't cry because I didn't believe what everyone told me, that the dead, including my father, were truly gone. I stopped arguing with adults about this and closed my mouth. When you don't respond, people tend to leave you alone. I couldn't bring myself to speak for months.

After my father's burial, I was taken in by Chrysoula, the woman who'd tried to take me away from the execution. There was nowhere else for me. My mother had hated village life, my father told me, and ran off to Athens years earlier. I never knew more than that. He seldom mentioned his runaway wife and I had only faint memories of her. It was one of the mysteries of my childhood. She was my mother, after all—hadn't she loved me enough to stay? After I lost her and then my father too, Chrysoula and Takis became my second family.

"Such a good man, your father," Chrysoula would say, her eyes brimming. "We were all so fond of him." Before the war Chrysoula had been a shapely woman with lively eyes much admired by the village men. But by the time I moved into her house, she'd become a shadow of herself inside her old dresses, which by then were several sizes too large. Her eyes, though, still held their light. "You'll be here with Takis and me," she said, "so it will seem that part of your father is here too."

Takis didn't care that I wouldn't open my mouth to speak. He talked enough for both of us. The house was small so he and I had to share a room, even a bed. He was ten and both of us were too young to know much about what grown-ups did in bed. We played cards by candlelight at night on the floor or bed, slapping them down noisily. It was Takis who taught me how to cheat by sliding a card into my sleeve or under my bottom. Then he'd call me *cheater* or *gangster*. And we'd throw our cards in each other's faces. It was the best part of the game. Finally, we'd topple over into bed saying good night to the gecko that lived in a crack in the wall.

Takis had nicknamed his own feet Mr. Shepherd and Mrs. Shepherd. He'd waggle them out of the thin blanket and make up conversations.

"I've lost the flock again, Mrs. Shepherd," Takis would say in a deep voice, wiggling the toes of his right foot.

"Oh, dear, Mr. Shepherd," he'd answer in a falsetto, wagging his left foot in a frenzy. "Was it the wolves this time?"

"Ate every last one. We'll have nothing for Easter."

"We could eat the baby."

"Mrs. Shepherd!"

Chrysoula would stick her head in the door and tell us that was enough. She'd tuck us in, saying, "Keep each other warm, my little geese."

Orion marched across the sky above the house those winter nights as frost etched itself on our window. Lying there with Takis breathing softly beside me, I knew there was this one big thing we shared: the mystery of how our fathers could be there one day and not the next or ever again. I just couldn't accept death. The old villagers said that souls of the dead hung around after their funerals for about ninety days, reluctant to leave, trying on their old shoes and taking pinches of their favorite meals right out of the pot. Sometimes I heard my father in the wind through the pine trees, in the water splashing in the lion fountain nearby, in the cries of birds passing over the village on their way south to Africa. He'd taken to complaining a lot and he's done that ever since. *Where are my tools?* he'd ask. *I can't do anything without tools.* I didn't understand why he needed them.

I thought about telling Takis this, but no words would come and anyway Takis didn't like to hear anything about fathers. His own wasn't around and no one ever mentioned him anymore. But I remembered my father saying that there'd been something wrong in the mind of Takis's father, that he'd imagined things. He'd thought the whole village was set against him and picked fights for no reason. Then he and Chrysoula had gone away for a while and she came back without him.

We woke each morning to the sound of Chrysoula's voice calling out the window to other women around the lion fountain. Houses had no running water then so women came to the fountain to fill their jugs and pails from the stream that poured out of the lion's marble mouth. Of course they also stood around and gossiped. Chrysoula's house was closest to the fountain so she presided.

"Good morning, my beautifully ugly neighbors," she would call out her kitchen window to the other women. "What's bothering you today?"

Of course everyone knew everyone else's troubles because they were mostly the same: hunger and heartache and isolation, endless worry about how to stay alive and keep out of the way of the Germans. This aged everyone; even young women looked almost as old as crones. But they picked up Chrysoula's cue.

"Ugly we may be, but at least we're clean," one said. "We so seldom see you taking water into your house."

"It's true," Chrysoula said. "I only clean with bleach. It's so much better for washing your husbands' drool off my front steps after they beg me to open my door to them at night."

There were shrieks of laughter, which set off spasmodic coughing because many of the women were ill. One called out, "So *that's* where they were!"

"And we thought they were doing their business in the outhouse," yelled another.

"It's almost the same thing, isn't it?" a third one asked.

More shrieks and hoots of laughter.

"Too bad your own husband can't satisfy you, Chrysoula," someone called out. "You couldn't even keep him at home, could you? No wonder you try to lure our men."

Chrysoula always sidestepped any reference to her husband. "No one needs to lure *your* husbands, my dears. One look at any of you is enough."

"Oh, we curse our fates not to be born beautiful like Princess Chrysoula," someone said. In fact, Chrysoula was as scrawny and worn looking as any of them, as all could clearly see.

But they began calling out, "Health to the beautiful Princess Chrysoula!"

"Health and life to the great beauty!"

"If only we looked like her, we could keep our husbands in our beds."

They could go for an hour or more like this, some of the women finally sitting or lying on the ground, exhausted from laughing and insulting each other. After a while, a pair of German soldiers would arrive to investigate the noise and break up the crowd, pushing the women to their feet with the butts of their rifles. The Germans didn't know Greek, of course, so the women would talk about them.

"That one has the forehead of a monkey!"

"And look at the other's low-slung bottom. As pretty as any girl's."

"He thinks so too. Look how he walks as if he's just longing for a pat or a pinch."

"Or something more."

Their wheezy laughter would trail off into the village lanes. Well, you can see where I got my early training as a crone. But most of the soldiers were just boys, really. They should have been behind school desks, not out here being hated by everyone. Sometimes they chose teams and played soccer matches, ordering us to come and watch. We'd stand in silence as they whooped around a field, scrambling after a ball. Once they requisitioned a couple of our donkeys and raced the beasts across a field so they could place bets on them. Anything to pass the time in what must have seemed to them a dull place.

I didn't understand war at all—it meant that foreigners took over your country, stole your food, watched you starve and shot you for the sake of a few squash. But *why*? It didn't make any sense. What we didn't understand at the time was that the real prize for the Germans was our island of Crete with its strategic airfields and harbors sitting right there in the middle of the Mediterranean offering easy access to North Africa and the Middle East. But for us here in the village cut off from the world, finding a moldy potato to eat meant another day's survival, maybe even a chance to squeeze a grain or two of pleasure out of whatever we could so as not to shrivel up inside. We're all like that here; we know how to get around anything with a laugh, a wisecrack, a little foolishness. It's our ancient gift, even when trapped. Of course the soldiers were as trapped as we were. They lacked our gift, but on the other hand, they had the guns. Boys with guns—the old story of war.

Takis liked the way the soldiers marched. He pretended to carry a rifle as he imitated their goose step.

"Stop that!" his mother would say. "I won't have a German in my house, even a small one."

Most mornings he was either impossible to wake at all or else he hopped up full of questions that had perched in his sleeping mind like owls. Shaking me awake, he'd ask, "Why don't the stars fall on our heads?" Or, "When I jump up, why don't I come down in some other village?"

I had no answers for him; I still couldn't bring myself to speak.

But there were other days when he sulked around, kicking the furniture and scowling at everyone. I took him to see the charcoal pits where my father had worked, just outside the village. He liked it there because, as he said, the pine trees talked to him.

"They want to teach me to fly so I can drop bombs on the Germans." He cocked his head near the trunk of a pine and said, "I'm sorry, Aliki, but they don't want to teach you."

I shrugged and walked away. Takis lost interest in the pines and followed. There were no piles of dried logs anymore as the Germans had taken those for firewood. But there was a lot of bark on the ground. I pointed to where my father and the other men had stacked logs in conical piles with an airhole down the center. Acting it all out for Takis, I showed how they covered the wood with dirt and then dropped hot coals into the airhole.

"Why the dirt?" he asked. "Weren't they trying to burn the wood?"

That was just what they didn't want to happen. But I didn't know how to make that clear without language. My father always said that if fire broke out, everything was ruined because the wood would burn down to ash. But if it only smoldered, over time it would reduce to charcoal. Sometimes the pile of wood started to catch fire and he'd have to jump on it, throwing on more dirt to put it out. I'd seen him do that once, a kind of crazy dance on top of the pile in all that smoke, flinging fistfuls of dirt at places where little flames were licking out.

I danced around for Takis and threw dirt every which way until he flopped onto the ground and rolled around laughing. When he laughed, there seemed to be nothing in the world except his enjoyment. Here was this half-starved, skinny boy—what did he have to laugh about? For that matter, what did any of us? The women at the fountain, Chrysoula, even the Germans didn't look too happy to be stuck here while they were losing the war everywhere else—or at least that was what we heard on the shortwave radio late at night.

It was illegal to have an unregistered radio and the punishment for owning one was death. But Chrysoula managed to conceal this one somehow. I don't think there were many shortwave radios in Greece then. It had been sent to Chrysoula by a cousin who'd emigrated to your America years before the war. We knew so little about that place then—there were no movies, no newsreels in our area and we seldom saw newspapers. What we did know was that your Mr. Roosevelt had sent all those Yanks to help us out in Europe and the radio told us the Yanks and other Allies were winning the war. And of course the radio itself—big and shiny with the word ZENITH on it—came from there. So I imagined America as a place of such radios, one for every man, woman and child. The Land of Big Radios.

But when I listened to the radio, sometimes I thought I could hear my father speaking just behind the voice of the news announcer, still asking me questions. They were so specific: Had he left the lid off the tin of kerosene in the basement? Had I found the eggs from the hen that had wandered into the woods? Where were the saw and ax he'd used on the pine logs?

The dead leave the earth, old villagers said, but can't get rid of the dailiness of their lives on it. They worry about dripping taps or debts unpaid or crops left standing in the fields. They're not interested in the big things like war or poverty or happiness or the loss of it. But if the roof in the stable has a leak, they'll worry it to death and beyond. If I asked my father something that I thought the dead would know, like what his life had been all about anyway, he always said that my question was too simple and the answer too complicated.

Oh, wait, there's someone at the door. How do I turn this thing off?

Back again. It was just a neighbor talking about old Zephyra down the road. Remember I said she was dying? Well, she may die at any moment from the many things that ail her and there's nothing to be done, sadly. We used to walk to school together back before the Germans came, but even then Zephyra was such a beaten-down little thing, bossed around by her busybody mother who was always sniffing out everyone's secrets. Little Zephyra was as plain and quiet as a turnip. She asked me one day if she could come live with my father and me. "I can clean and cook," she said. "Oh, please, Aliki, can I?" It was an odd thing for someone my own age to suggest, but I think she was afraid of her mother. Zephyra always looked so sad when the schoolday ended and she had to go home.

After I moved into Chrysoula's house, Zephyra stopped speaking to me, as if she thought I'd chosen Takis as my friend instead of her. Takis noticed this, asking me about that girl who crossed to the other side of the road when she saw us coming. And to think that Zephyra's name comes from the ancient god of the west wind, Zephyrus, but there wasn't even a trace of a breeze in her spirit. And of course she never lived down that business of the goat stealing, but I'm not going to get started on that. Nothing like the nearness of death to dig up the not-quite-buried past.

I'm getting off track here. Better replay a little of this. Oh, I see, all right, my father on the radio, yes, I heard him, or at least I thought I did. It comforted me to know he wasn't completely gone. He was around *somewhere*. I'd go over to our old house, perched on the side of the hill at the edge of the village. It had been empty since I'd moved in with Takis and his mother. But I could feel my father's presence in the house. Once I thought I saw his shirttail disappearing around the corner, but when I went into the next room, there was no one there. Climbing down the ladder beneath the trapdoor in the kitchen floor, I would come into what once had been a stable on the lower level, what we called the basement. There was the kerosene tin just as my father had said, without its lid. And I found the missing saw and ax. But I never found the hen in the woods or her eggs.

Chrysoula said there used to be wild chickens around the area, hens and roosters that escaped and set up housekeeping in the lower branches of the pines. They left their eggs all over the place and they were much better tasting than the usual kind. Over time, the chickens taught themselves to fly and you could see flocks of them in the morning sky. They stopped clucking and developed their own song—"You know what I mean," Chrysoula said. "Loo, loo, loo, loo, loo, loo."

Takis and I had never heard anything like that. But Chrysoula would say whatever crossed her mind when asked a question, and she didn't seem to care if anyone believed her. She had a reputation in the village for giving curious advice to those who came to her with problems. Back before the war, a neighbor woman told her that she'd been unable to decide whether or not to sell her house and move to the nearby town after her husband's death. Chrysoula had advised, "The carpet slipper of life doesn't accept or deny what is written on the last hats of the old blood."

The neighbor pondered this for several days and decided not to sell her house.

But Chrysoula had no comment on the matter of the partisans in our area who were sabotaging Germans, blowing up their tanks, mowing them down in lonely mountain passes, slitting the throats of their sentries at night. There were several groups of partisans and we'd heard some of their names, all important sounding. *National Liberation Front*, *People's Liberation Party*, *National Social Liberation*, *National Republican League*. But they broke down mostly into two kinds, communists and royalists. I wasn't sure what exactly communists were, but I knew that the royalists were supporters of our king in exile in Cairo. The communists and royalists had their own little war going with each other while they were snatching territory back from the Germans. And like the Germans, they demanded food from us.

In a place on the other side of the mountains, villagers had given supplies to one of the partisan groups. What else could they have done? If they hadn't helped, they would have been accused of collaborating with the Germans and shot as traitors. In this case, a village informer told the Germans. As punishment, German soldiers lined up all the village men in the *plateia* and shot them. Then they herded the women and children into the village church and set it on fire. When they tried to escape the flames, they too were shot.

But we'd heard that in areas the partisans controlled, they were as ruthless as the Germans they'd driven out. All this made us feel helpless, like flies trapped in a bottle. To fight that sense of helplessness—which can kill you—we had to come up with our own solutions. Chrysoula had decided on one without telling Takis or me.

She'd started going over to my father's house regularly, saying that she needed to make some repairs. A shutter in the kitchen had come loose and was banging in the wind. Rain had poured down the chimney, bringing soot with it, making a mess on the hearth. On the roof, some tiles had been broken by a fallen branch. The house wasn't her problem to deal with, but she told me, "Sometime, when all this is over and the Germans have gone home, this house will be your dowry. We must keep it worthy."

Dowry? I hadn't thought of such a thing. It seemed that my second family would just go on as it was. I wasn't able to think far ahead. The few young men in the village had gone off to the Albanian front to fight Mussolini when he invaded from the north. Some had been not much older than I and none had returned. And who needed a husband anyway? Not Chrysoula, it seemed.

I went with her one day and inside the house she made a lot of noise, grabbing a broom and banging around in a big show of cleaning. Then she hammered on the broken shutter and even crawled out onto the roof to examine the cracked tiles. After a while, she sent me back to the fountain for a pail of water so she could scrub down the hearth and the kitchen floor.

But when I got to the fountain, I saw the German officer in charge of our village, Colonel Esterhaus, at the front door of Chrysoula's house. I froze because this was the man who would have been responsible for the order to execute my father and the other two men. I hadn't seen him this close before. Thin, with fair hair and a rosy complexion, he'd brought along his translator, our old schoolmaster, Petros, who knew some German. Whenever they had something to say to us, the Germans brought him along like a puppy on a leash. It was said that his family was given favors of food for his service. He stood there in the doorway, nearly bald and squinting through spectacles with one cracked lens as he listened to Colonel Esterhaus trying to talk to Takis. Petros noticed me and waved me over.

Crouching down, the colonel looked directly into Takis's eyes as he spoke. Takis was always impressed with uniforms so he'd drawn himself up and was saluting the colonel. Petros told us that the colonel said he had a son of his own at home outside Hamburg just about Takis's age. The colonel saluted Takis in return, then laughed and ruffled his hair.

What the colonel had come to see us about was my father's house, now my own, Petros said. On behalf of the Führer, the Reich was requisitioning it for military use. It was empty, so soldiers were to be housed there, effective immediately. I looked into the face of the colonel. I remember it as an ordinary sort of face, a bit flushed, a bit worried. It was not the face of a monster but just that of a busy man, carrying out duties, a man who missed his son. Yet from the mouth in that ordinary face had come an order for execution. And having killed my father, the colonel was now taking my father's house.

Suddenly it was as if I'd stuck my finger in a light socket and the jolt, working its way up and out, made me shake my head: *no.* Fear widened Petros's eyes. But I couldn't stop shaking my head. I tried to speak, but nothing came out, so with the toe of my shoe I scratched *no* in the dust. Petros stepped between the colonel and me, covering the word with his shoes and putting his hands on my shoulders.

"Child, he's not asking," he said, voice wavering. "He's telling."

The colonel, whose face had remained expressionless, said something more to Petros, who translated that the colonel intended to inspect the house shortly and if everything was suitable, the soldiers would move in later that day. Then he and the colonel left.

I couldn't move for what seemed a long time but probably wasn't. Then I went as limp as a noodle and reached for Takis as support.

"Do you know where Mother is?" he said. "I'm hungry."

I remembered Chrysoula was alone in the house. Fearing that the colonel might find her there before we could warn her, I grabbed Takis's hand and stumbled along, ordering my legs to run, run. I was half dragging Takis, who cried out that I was hurting his arm. When we got to the house, we couldn't find her at first. From below, we heard muffled voices. Opening the trapdoor in the floor of the kitchen, I started down the ladder with Takis behind me. I was startled to see Chrysoula with a middle-aged woman and a young man. They certainly hadn't been there the last time I'd come. And they certainly weren't from the village. Partisans? There was no time to wonder. I prodded Takis to tell his mother what had just happened. He missed the point, telling her that the colonel said he had a son ". . . just like me." I was hopping up and down with impatience, shaking my head then shaking Takis and gesturing at the house above and around us until he said, "Oh, that . . ." and finally got it all out.

Chrysoula clapped a hand over her mouth. There was silence as everyone took in the information. Removing her hand, she asked, "When will they come?"

"Maybe now . . . ?" Takis said.

I looked at the two strangers and realized that they were better dressed than village people, though their clothes were rumpled and dirty. A mother and her teenage son, I guessed. There was a resemblance, the same gray eyes and dark hair. He looked older than I was though not much. They couldn't very well be partisans who lived in caves or ravines in the mountains. A pair of suitcases and some articles of clothing were lying about. So the two of them had been living there awhile. That didn't seem possible in our occupied village where the Germans knew nearly everything that was going on. But there they were!

Without a word, we flew around grabbing up their belongings and stuffing them back into the suitcases while Chrysoula all but shoved the pair of visitors out a window at ground level. She told them to run down the slope to the field below the village and hide in the gully there, the very one where my father had picked the squash. Just as soon as she'd done so, we heard from upstairs the tread of boots coming in the front door. To this day, I can't imagine a sound more terrifying.

The first one down the ladder was Colonel Esterhaus. He and another officer stood staring at us, then said something in German, probably asking why we were there. Chrysoula must have assumed the same thing because she said we were cleaning the house. To make them understand, she made circular motions with her hands as if polishing something and then pretended to sweep the floor with an invisible broom. I started to tremble with fear, all electricity gone. Did the Germans shoot girls? I had no doubt of it.

They looked blank at first, then moved forward together and seized Chrysoula by each arm, forcing her up the steps toward the kitchen. She swore at them, telling them to go to the devil and leave a respectable woman alone but she also shouted at Takis, "Run, run get Petros—I don't know what I'm accused of!"

Takis and I climbed out the window after they'd gone and ran to the schoolmaster's house. Petros was just about to settle into a nap. "What, they need me again? What sperm of the dog they are!"

Chrysoula was with the Germans most of the day. The poor woman came home that evening, limping and carrying her shoes. Some of the village women gathered at the lion fountain as she leaned against her doorway.

"Well, praise God," she said. "I straightened them out!"

One of the women said it looked as if it was Chrysoula who'd been straightened out. Her face was bruised and streaked from tears, her hair in tangles, her dress torn. The other women agreed and nodded together, clucking tongues in sympathy. I went to Chrysoula, took her hand and pressed it to my heart.

"Oh, don't worry, Aliki. They were sure I'd done something," Chrysoula went on, "but they had no idea what it was, the fools."

She told how they'd slapped her repeatedly, questioning her about partisans. She insisted she was just a housewife, how was she to know about such things? Petros had vouched for her, saying he'd known her all his life. She was a good woman who'd taken in the orphaned child of the charcoal maker.

"They didn't care," Chrysoula said. "They pulled my shoes off and beat my feet and legs with a stick. But I made so much noise, putting a curse on them that their pricks should wither and fall off."

The women laughed and one, an old wisewoman, the mother of our present one, said she'd burn some herbs in front of the icon of St. Athanassios, he who'd spent so much of life suffering in exile, to make the curse come to pass.

Finally, Colonel Esterhaus had seemed to grow tired of the noise Chrysoula was making and told her that this was just a warning and that they'd be watching her.

"What's there to watch?" Chrysoula asked the women. They looked at one another but said nothing.

The next day, the mother and son moved into the basement of Chrysoula's house, which was in the same place in her house as in my father's, down a trapdoor ladder. But unlike my father's house, Chrysoula's was placed in such a way that from the outside it appeared to have just the single above-ground story. Chrysoula had put a thin rug over the trapdoor to conceal it in the kitchen. She pulled the rug back to open the door. But she'd attached a piece of twine to the outer edge of the rug, and she tugged the twine after her when she was the last person to go down the ladder. So the rug was pulled back into place as the trapdoor closed.

When I drew a question mark in the air and pointed downstairs, Chrysoula told me only that they were city people. Refugees, she said. I didn't know what that meant so I drew another question mark.

"People who have to leave their homes and need to hide for a while," she said quickly as she turned away from me before she could see me ask again. "Don't be so curious. Now go play with Takis. I'd like you to make sure he keeps his mouth shut tight. No one must know. *No one.* Outside the house, these people don't exist. If only Takis were as silent as you."

But what did it mean to be a refugee? I wondered. I didn't want to think what was likely to happen if the Germans found out about them. Why did refugees have to come here anyway? And why was Chrysoula taking them in? There had to be something unusual about our visitors, some secret, and, after thinking about it, I guessed that they must be spies. I'd heard about spies on the shortwave radio and was excited to think that we were living in the same house with two of them. And they had to be important ones, didn't they, or why else would Chrysoula have taken such a risk?

I wouldn't let her alone about it. Following her around, I drew question marks on a dusty windowpane, on a bar of soap, in a plate of boiled greens.

"What do you want me to say, Aliki? Stop asking." But when I'd made a big enough nuisance of myself, she said simply, "Sometimes you have to do something not to feel helpless. I don't know how else to explain it."

Once Takis realized there was someone downstairs, there was no stopping him from pushing the rug aside and scooting down to see our visitors. I heard him warning them, "Be careful of the ghost down here. His name is Dimos and he has orange hair and eats dirt."

I joined him. "She doesn't talk," Takis told them about me. "But she's my friend."

"We saw you at the other house," the woman said. Though they'd spent the night in the gully, they still looked more like people out of the magazines we'd seen now and then before the war. "I'm Sophia," the woman said, "and this is my son, Stelios." He glanced at me from under thickly fringed eyelashes, then looked quickly away. "He's shy," she added.

A shy spy? But I knew nothing about city people and I don't think anyone in the village had ever been to Athens except my mother and Takis's father, who'd never returned. It seemed nearly as distant and foreign as the Land of Big Radios, where everyone wanted to go because Chrysoula's cousin had become rich enough to send the shiny Zenith to Chrysoula. In magazine photographs, city people always looked in a hurry, moving across streets in a mob while traffic waited. Or flowing like rivers in and out of sports stadiums. What did they know about villages like ours where people made charcoal or harvested flax in the fields? There was no bank here, no pharmacy or doctor. The only law enforcement was that of a field policeman, who made sure no boundary stones were moved between fields unless he'd been paid not to notice. It was many miles to the nearest hospital or regional court of law on unpaved roads that were often deep in mud all winter.

But right there, in Chrysoula's house, were two people from the outside world. Spies, refugees, how could you tell? And how had they managed to find us? And did they play cards?—that was Takis's main interest. Stelios did. At first Takis seemed wary of the gangly young man with the bashful smile. But Takis covered it by trying to boss him around.

"Sit there," he told him, pointing to a grubby corner of the basement. "They're my cards so I get to shuffle and deal."

Stelios just smiled and sat down cross-legged on the floor.

I thought Sophia was lovely even though she looked tired and uncomfortable in the dirty basement. She had a quick smile and kept thanking me for letting her and her son stay in our house. I tried to act out the fact that this was Chrysoula's house, not mine. But I only seemed to confuse her. For the first time since my father had died, I wanted to talk. But all I could do was open and close my mouth like a fish. When words began to form in my throat, a great sadness came over me and I wanted to weep.

With two more people to feed, Chrysoula needed help. Wandering the mountainside behind the village, she and I pulled up wild greens, mostly dandelions, which we'd boil and eat with vinegar. Other women were there too, including my little friend Zephyra—the one who's now so ill—and her mother, all slowly searching the rocky ground for anything that might be edible. I waved to Zephyra, who pretended not to see me.

"Ah, so little today," her mother said, glancing over to see how Chrysoula and I were doing.

Chrysoula was showing me how to use a spoon to dig up the bulbs of wild hyacinths. "We can pickle them. Along with wild onions and garlic. Look, more over there."

"Where?" the other women asked, rushing to where Chrysoula had pointed. They shoved one another to get the best spot for digging.

Chrysoula laughed, saying, "Look, Aliki, the old cats are all chasing the same mouse."

Zephyra's mother hissed back at her, "Take care of your own mice that they don't get us *all* caught!"

Chrysoula took my hand and we walked away from the others. Zephyra's mother was certainly referring to our visitors downstairs.

Already news of their existence must have spread somehow, but how many villagers knew? If Zephyra's gossipy mother had worked it out, then the others probably also knew. To shelter anyone endangered everyone. I glanced at Chrysoula to see if she felt the fear as I did, but her face showed no emotion.

"I know a ravine where we might find some striped snails," she told me, marching along. "We can make *salingaria vrasta* with lots of thyme. Very tasty. I'll collect the snails; you pick the thyme."

That night, she put the snails in an earthenware jug with the thyme so they would feed all night and have the flavor of the herb when cooked. From the room where Takis and I slept next door, I could hear them. They'd crawl partway up the jug, trying to get out, lose traction and fall back down. Their shells would make a little *click* when they hit the bottom of the jug. Just as I'd be about to fall asleep, there'd be another *click*. And then another. They couldn't escape and they couldn't stop trying. My mind clouded over then as Takis's and my breathing slowed and we slipped together into the dark shell of sleep.

Sophia and Stelios had never eaten country food like boiled snails or pickled bulbs. So the next evening in the basement lit by candles, Chrysoula tried to demonstrate. "You hold it like this," she said, positioning the opening of a snail in front of her lips. "And then you suck and suck until the tasty creature just pops into your mouth." She made loud slurping noises and chewed vigorously. "Like that. And then you have one of these little vinegary bulbs, so nice and crunchy."

Sophia looked dubious but Stelios dipped into the pot and followed Chrysoula's instructions. "They're good," he said. "Thank you for your kindness."

He was always polite and at first spoke in a more formal way than we were used to. Or maybe it was that he got rather tongue-tied, as when the day before he'd asked me if I liked to read. "Books, I mean, or, well, you know, well, I guess you don't have a library here, I mean, well, do you? Read, I mean?"

I didn't. I knew how to read and write a little, but when the village became occupied Petros had closed the school and locked up the textbooks. Who would want to read those old things anyway? There weren't any other books in the village that I knew of and most villagers couldn't read at all.

Sophia was having trouble with the snails and bulbs. Although she maintained a pleasant enough expression as she put the shell to her lips, I guessed that sucking a snail out of its shell was not something she'd ever expected to do.

Takis was little help, saying, "No, no, you have to suck really hard, like this." He slurped at length. Sophia clapped a hand over her mouth and hurried upstairs.

"Stop that, Takis," Chrysoula said.

"What did I do?"

Stelios explained that his mother had stomach problems. "It's been worse since my father and uncle . . ."

Chrysoula shook her head for him to stop, but he didn't seem to see her in the dim light.

". . . were taken away."

"Who took them?" Takis asked.

"Let him eat his dinner," Chrysoula said. "And you tend to yours."

No one said anything for a minute or so until Takis blurted out, "But where'd they go?"

Stelios spoke haltingly at first, but his shyness seemed to drop away as he went on. Chrysoula looked alarmed, but she didn't stop him again. What he was saying didn't make much sense to me then—how there'd been a lot of family discussion about whether his father and uncle should go to the central synagogue in Athens to register because the German-appointed mayor had demanded it. I didn't know what a synagogue was then. And register for what?

"Most were too afraid. But, uh, my father and uncle thought, well, what if they didn't? What might happen?" After registering, they and other men were herded into trucks and driven away. When the news reached Stelios and his mother, they threw a few belongings and some gold sovereigns into suitcases and fled the city.

"My father thought we might all have to, you know, get away eventually," Stelios said. "So he had a plan, I mean a contact in a band of partisans on the mountain." He and his mother had walked partway up Mt. Hymettus to meet the contact, who'd sheltered them for a few days and relieved them of most of their sovereigns.

"We moved from village to village. So many times we've moved—a cave, a stable, a schoolroom. Each time we had to pay someone. There were different groups, but they all charged something and called it a tax to support their work." His voice caught in his throat. "It's been hard for Mother." But there seemed to be a partisan grapevine and because of it, they'd been brought to the empty house of the charcoal maker in this village. "You know the rest."

Actually, what I didn't know was vast. I'd had little religious instruction since the school shut down and couldn't remember what was meant by the word *Jew*—a word not yet spoken that night. And in places like our village, even grown-ups didn't fully understand what was happening outside. In time, it would become known that Greek Jews had been rounded up, especially in the city of Thessaloniki, north of here, but also in Athens, stripped of their belongings and sent north to the concentration camps. Some, like Stelios and his mother, fled to the countryside where villagers took them in.

But all I knew then was that Sophia and Stelios were just Greeks like the rest of us, weren't they? Or were they also spies along with the father and uncle? Was that really why they'd been taken away? I wondered how to ask this without words as I glanced at the plate of discarded shells and thought again of the snails climbing the sides of the jug, forever falling back, *click*.

"I don't understand anything," Takis said.

"It's not for you to understand," Chrysoula said. "Just forget it and go get ready for bed." When he'd gone, she asked Stelios, "Your father and uncle? You've heard nothing?"

"No, no. My mother, she recites an old Hebrew prayer for their safe return. It helps her a little, I think."

"And you?"

"I'm not a believer. I can only hope . . ."

What was the prayer, I wondered, and what did it mean that it was *Hebrew*? For that matter, what was it that Stelios didn't believe?

"I'm so sorry," Sophia said, returning. "Just a bit of indigestion. What were you saying, Stelios?"

"I was telling them about the partisans, Mother. How we gave them some of our sovereigns and they got us here."

"Oh, yes. We're so lucky to have found you."

They still had a few sovereigns and she offered to give one to Chrysoula, saying that if there was any way to use it for provisions, they'd be pleased to help. "You have so little for yourselves, much less for two more."

Chrysoula refused politely, but not for long. Gold was the only thing that mattered then. Paper currency had become nearly worthless—a pillowcase full of thousand-drachma notes wouldn't buy so much as a kilo of salt. In the cities, I heard later, people would trade things such as a grand piano or Persian carpets for just a few kilos of rice or olive oil. But our village was not far from the coast and it was known that the small fishing boats called caïques were making illegal runs to some of the islands and even the Turkish coast. People there didn't have much either, but the fishermen traded for anything they could get and brought it back for sale at exorbitant prices. It was possible to buy a few things such as flour, rice and olive oil, even the occasional fish or two, if you could pay the inflated prices. Somehow these things were smuggled into the village—perhaps with payoffs to the Germans, who could say?

"I am so embarrassed," Chrysoula said. "Hospitality is a matter of pride in my family. But what can we do in such times?"

So at last we were able to make bread, which, dipped in olive oil, kept us going. And sometimes there were small fish to be eaten with rice. Now, if only we could keep the other villagers from finding out. There was no question of sharing our small good fortune. If luck had come to a different house, that family would have done the same. And secrecy, we found, added a flavor all its own.

CASSETTE 1 • Side 2

Sorry about the interruption. I have to remember to watch the little reel before it spins itself out. And while I was turning over the cassette, the neighbors came again about Zephyra, who'd been asking for me, they said. And making strange noises. The doctor and Father Yerasimos had come and gone; there was nothing more they could do. When I got there, Zephyra was sitting up in bed, but her face, well, it had gone all pinched and narrow. Difficult to see in it the girl I'd known so long ago. When I asked how she was, she began to make this sound, "Maaahhh, maaahhh." I didn't know what it meant and told her who I was. Her expression slowly changed as she seemed to recognize me. Her eyes filled and she took my hands in hers as she tried to form words.

"Not . . . my fault," she said with difficulty and then said it again. Before I could ask what wasn't her fault, she slipped back into making that sound again, "Maaahhh," like a sheep or goat. This went on for several minutes and I could see her struggling to get it under control. Who can understand what pieces of a life float past the inner eye of the dying?

She let go of my hands and seemed to drift for a bit after that, but then her expression narrowed again and she made that same sound,

"Maaahhh, maaahhh." And I realized that with her face all pinched like that and what with her long nose, she'd actually taken on almost a goatish look. I might not have thought it if she hadn't gone on making the sound, which she did ever more loudly. "Maaaaahhhhh, maaaaah-hhhh, maaaaahhhhh." And then, well, this is hard to believe, but she actually started to bleat the way a kid does when it gets separated from the rest of the herd. She pawed at the bedclothes.

It wasn't the first I'd seen of such things. Living so closely with animals as many of us do here means that the creatures seem to get right into our souls. Why, old Yannis, may the earth rest lightly on him, used to blame his donkey whenever the early rains washed out his flax crop. He'd fly into a rage and beat the poor creature, until one day he actually beat it to death. Then a couple of years later when Yannis himself was meeting his own hour, he sat up in bed hee-hawing just like that dying donkey. Deeds can come back to you before you die; they won't let your soul escape. But what did it mean in Zephyra's case?

"Calm yourself, Zephyra," I said, trying to pat her hand, but she went on pawing the bedclothes. I told the women gathered outside her house that they'd better send for the old wisewoman, Aphrodite, from the next village to come and wave her burned herbs and icons over Zephyra. Even if no one believed in such things much anymore, something had to be tried to relieve Zephyra of this misery so she could die easily.

"Her soul can't get free," I told them. "Something's holding it back."

I saw them later leading Aphrodite past my house on her way to Zephyra's. They'd brought her over from her village, I supposed, but as always I wondered what it is about wisewomen that they have to look so wretched. Aphrodite—and what a name for her—always looks as if she's dressed in two or three threadbare rugs, silly woman. And she can't have washed her hair in years. But she, like me, is the last of her kind in these parts; so the village puts up with us. She's not so well herself. I could hear her coughing and wheezing as she went past the house. Of course if Father Yerasimos hears that Aphrodite's around, he'll be there trying to drive her away, as if his holy water and incense are superior to her icons and smelly herbs. Priests, doctors and wisewomen—if one doesn't work, just try another. But it's the lamenter who gets the last word.

Now see, all this has made me lose track again. Have I mentioned the notepad I'd taken to carrying around Chrysoula's house? I don't know where I'd found such a thing—writing paper wasn't easy to come by back then. Maybe one of the Germans had tossed it out. Anyway, I could write down questions I wanted to ask and pass them to others. When I showed Chrysoula that I'd written about our visitors, *Who are they really?* she just said again that they were Athenian refugees who had to hide until the war was over. *Spies?* I wrote.

"Oh, dear, no. They're Jews." I drew a question mark. "Oh, yes, of course. You wouldn't have met any Jews before. Well, they're just like anyone else."

So why do they hide from the Germans?

She looked out the kitchen window. A spring wind was spinning the last dead leaves of winter. "You know, Aliki, I'm not really sure. Such awful things happen in a war. It gives an excuse for all kinds of hidden poisons to work their way out."

While I was wondering over this, the card games between Takis and Stelios had turned into drawn-out contests by candlelight. Stelios tried to stop Takis from cheating.

"A card just went into your sleeve, Takis. I mean, there's no point to the game if you do that."

"What card?" Takis asked, taking another and putting it on top of his head, then sticking out his tongue. "They're my cards, anyhow."

"Oh, Takis," Stelios said, "what are we going to do with you, little monkey?"

Takis hopped up and loped around the room, simian-style, scratching himself. Anything to entertain Stelios. In time, he would even stop trying to cheat him at cards. His loyalty and affection were shifting. Maybe Takis had noticed that Stelios was paying more attention to me, less to him.

Takis began treating me in an offhand way lately, saying even in my hearing, "Look how stupid she is—she can't even talk."

The hurt would heat up my face and Stelios would look embarrassed. Chrysoula would send Takis to his room. When he wasn't around, Stelios would tell me about books he'd read, such as *The Count of Monte Cristo*. He made the count, Edward Dantès, sound so real, as if he was someone you might actually know. Stelios promised to get me a copy one day so I could read for myself what the count wrote in his letter to his friend Maximilian, who thought his great love had died.

"I don't remember it exactly," Stelios said, "but it's something about how there's neither happiness nor misery in the world. I mean, it's all in the way you think about something, what it adds up to at the time. And only someone, uh, someone who's felt the deepest grief can experience the greatest happiness." He said the words with such belief, almost as if he'd written them himself. I was impressed but not sure that I understood. I suppose I'd been happy before the war, but it wasn't something I'd ever thought about. It was only after the Germans came that the—I don't know what—the *glow* just went out of everything. But Stelios seemed to be saying something more complicated. I'd have to think about it.

Sophia passed the time by borrowing sewing things from Chrysoula and patching clothing, theirs and ours. She had a slight tremor in both hands and so made little progress, but she stayed with the task even in the dim light. Sometimes she sang softly as she worked, an Irish folk song she'd heard on the radio years before.

Oh, I wish that we were geese,
Night and morn, night and morn.
Oh, I wish that we were geese,
For they fly and take their ease,
And they live their lives in peace,
Eating corn, eating corn.

It was such a sad song. I could only guess at her fear for her husband and brother-in-law. And there was the life together they'd all lost.

I asked on my pad, *Why are the Germans taking the Jews out of Greece?*

Sophia looked startled. "Oh, my child," she said as her left eyelid developed a rapid twitch, "I wish I knew the answer to that. I suppose they need someone to blame for the misery in the world."

"That's not it, Mother," Stelios said quickly. "They need labor for their war factories. All their men are off fighting."

From the way he said it, not looking at his mother, I suspected that he didn't quite believe what he was saying. He was trying to calm her. There was an awkward silence. To fill it and change the subject, I scribbled on my pad, *What's it like to live in the city?*

Sophia looked relieved as she read this easier question to answer. "Well, Aliki, when you've lived in a place all your life, you don't really think about what it's like. It's just what you know." She sighed.

What do people do in the evenings?

"Let's see, well, before the war, if the weather was good, we'd often go for a stroll in the National Gardens." She described dusty lanes lined with oleanders, orange trees and cypresses, where peacocks wandered and nightingales sang in the spring. There were ornamental ponds with goldfish and ducks. Near the big Zappeion Exhibition Hall, where international exhibitions were held, there was an outdoor café. "At night it becomes a cabaret with singers and comedians. Alexis, my husband, always loves anything funny."

She stopped speaking and her eyelid fluttered again. She rubbed it with her finger until it stopped. But then it started again. "Do you know what else is near the Zappeion?" she asked, trying to ignore it. "The wonderful shadow theater of Karagiozis."

I drew a big question mark on my notebook.

"You don't know about the shadow puppets?" Stelios asked. "One day you and Takis will come to Athens and we'll take you to see them."

"Yes," his mother said. "It's a kind of theater for children. Well, really, for everyone." The main puppet, Karagiozis, was a poor Greek who lived under Turkish rule, she explained, during the time of the Ottoman Empire, which occupied Greece for four hundred years before the revolution that drove them out. A wily underdog, Karagiozis played the fool in order to outwit the rulers.

Like us with the Germans? I wrote.

"Well, yes, I suppose, in a way." Shadow theater started in Egypt long ago. Then it spread through Asia and the Middle East, into Turkey and the Balkans.

"Here," Stelios said, "let me show you what he looks like." He took my notebook and pencil and drew a hunchbacked man with a big nose and one arm longer than the other. His clothes were ragged and patched and his feet bare. Stelios drew quickly and well, making sketch after sketch in which Karagiozis was dressed as a sea captain or a doctor or a fisherman. He also drew the sultan, the enemy of Karagiozis, a plump man in a robe and turban.

"The characters are moved on poles behind a lighted screen. You see them all as shadows." He took a shirt his mother was mending, put a candle behind it and cupped his hand into the shape of a bird's head so its shadow appeared on the other side of the shirt. Stelios's father had once given him a small shadow theater with ready-made puppets for New Year's and Stelios sometimes put on shows for friends. "But simple ones, not like the complicated plays at the Zappeion." The plays always opened with music provided at home by Yannoula, the family housekeeper, who played the squeeze box, a kind of small accordion.

"She's wonderful," he said. "Her music is as good as at the Zappeion."

Takis clapped his hands and said, "Let's do it. Let's make the Karagiozis!"

Sophia said, "Hmm, that's an idea. Well, you know, I suppose we could do a little play. You know a lot of the stories, Stelios, and it might help pass the time. But what would we make the figures from? They're usually leather or cardboard."

Takis went to find his mother; surely she would know a way. But at first Chrysoula didn't think it was a good idea. We heard her tell him, "In these times you want to play theater? You will make a lot of noise and get us all shot."

"Bang!" Takis said. "Bang, you're dead."

"And you're a foolish cabbage. Now let me think."

Later that day Chrysoula came downstairs and said, "Well, what about pine bark? Isn't there a lot of it over by your father's old charcoal pits, Aliki? It's thin and flaky. Could you use that to make the characters? It would be easy to cut."

Stelios wasn't sure if bark would work, but Takis and I went out with a basket to gather some. If anyone asked what we were doing, we were to say that we were going to dry the bark for kindling. While we were gathering it, Takis said that one of the pines was speaking to him. He pointed to the biggest of them, the one with branches so low they swept the ground. I gave him a skeptical glance.

"It says that Stelios likes me better than you," he said softly, looking away from me. This was clearly Takis's own wishful thinking.

I wrote, *How would a tree know?*

"They know everything."

I had nothing to say to this so we went on picking up bark in silence. After a while, Takis asked me to do my dance again, imitating the men throwing dirt on the cones of stacked logs to keep them from bursting into flame. It was the first time he'd been really friendly to me for a while. He even did the dance with me and we chased each other around, throwing dirt, until Takis tripped and fell and couldn't get up from the ground, he was laughing so much.

"You're the dirtiest thing in the world," he said.

I dumped the basket of pine bark on his head. He looked so startled and funny that I lost control. Takis saw the stream shoot down my leg and that set him off again.

When we got back to the house, he had to tell everyone, the snitch. "That's enough, Takis," Chrysoula said. "You can't talk about Aliki that way. You must be her protector, like a brother. It's time to start acting like a man."

After that, I would see him trying to draw himself up, as if holding himself straight would make him taller and more manly. I caught him standing on a box so he could see himself in the mirror as he tried on a hat his father had left behind. It was huge on him; its brim rested on his ears. Holding it just so at an angle, he then turned it the other way. I went over and pulled it all the way down over his ears and then, with my fingers, showed how he could push eyeholes through the cloth.

"Who asked you?" he said, snatching the hat off his head and tossing it on the floor. He stuck a finger in his mouth, puffed out his cheek and pulled the finger out fast to make a noise like farting. One of his favorite tricks.

I applauded, raising my eyebrows as if to say how very grown up he was acting.

"Ha, *you're* the one who wet yourself."

Then he made more farting noises. Clearly he had a ways to go to manhood. For me, the thought of my becoming an older version of myself was troubling. What would happen to the person I already was?

Would it disappear inside the older one? I wanted to grow up, but I didn't want to let go of what I meant when I thought *I* or *me.* I wondered about this late at night, lying there listening to Takis's breathing. Did Stelios ever think about such things?

But he seemed mostly interested in the bark, which he sorted through and arranged in piles by size and shape. "I think I'll do the play *Karagiozis the Baker*, so this lumpy piece will be good. It looks like a chef's hat on top." He chose a wide piece for the fat sultan and two others for villagers. With the knife and scissors Chrysoula gave him, he carved the figures.

"Stelios has always been artistic," his mother said.

"No, I'm not," he said. "I'm not much good. I mean, I just like it, that's all. Papa says it's all homework avoidance anyway. He wants me to be a civil engineer like him, but I don't know; I just want to read and . . ." Stelios caught himself, glanced at his mother and stopped speaking.

I didn't look at her because I knew the mention of her husband would cause the twitch in Sophia's eyelid. Stelios worked on, still and concentrated. Karagiozis emerged from the bark as a hunched-over man, bald and with a big nose. His body was curved like the bark. Out of paper Stelios cut a long arm for Karagiozis and pinned it to his bark body so the arm could be moved back and forth as the figure gestured while speaking. On the smooth side of the bark, Stelios drew features: heavy eyebrows and a droopy mouth. Karagiozis wore a loose shirt and baggy Turkish trousers. His feet were bare.

Takis and I wanted to help Stelios, but Chrysoula kept sending us out on errands. If we spent all our time inside, the neighbors might get suspicious. And that year, the winter of '43 gave way to the summer of '44 without much of spring. The piercing scents of narcissi and cyclamen had faded fast and already the bloodred anemones were giving up their petals to a breeze. We picked herbs so Chrysoula could make infusions to strengthen Sophia: sage and sweet chamomile for medicinal tea, valerian root for the treatment of nerves and fevers. And some other root, mallow, I think it was, to thin the blood, Chrysoula said, "Because winter makes your blood thick and gooey. It slows the brain."

My brain seemed fine. I took in what the shortwave radio told of the victories of the Red Army chasing the Germans back from their failed invasion of Russia, advancing toward the Balkans. If they got to the northern border of Greece, our occupiers would be trapped. Surely they would leave before then. It also looked like Italy next door might surrender to your Land of Big Radios and other Allies before long.

There were really no set scripts for the plays, Stelios told us. The puppeteers just carried the stories in their heads and made up lines as they went along. Sometimes they wove in events and people of the place and time of the performance. Using an old bedsheet for a screen, he tacked it to the rafters so that it hung from there to the floor. Behind it, he lit candles. The bark figures had been attached to some old bamboo poles he'd found in a corner of the basement. With these, he would make the characters walk or jump or dance. On the other side of the screen, we would see only their shadows.

When he was ready to present *Karagiozis the Baker*, Stelios had us all sit in front of the screen. We waited there in the near dark with candles glowing as if we were cavemen gathered around the fire, hoping for a tale.

"There's supposed to be a singer or musician," he called to us from behind the screen. "But we don't have Yannoula to play the squeeze box. So it will only be me and I can't carry a tune."

"Of course you can," his mother said. And then to us, "I don't know why he's being so modest."

There was the sound of two pans being slammed together like muted cymbals and the shadow of our hero, Karagiozis the baker, was there on the screen, leaping and chanting.

Trin, trin, trin,
What a mess I'm in.
They call me a baker
But I'm really a faker.
Trin, trin, trin,
What a mess I'm in.

When Stelios ran out of words, he hummed or just sang *thrum thrum thrum*, over and over again while Karagiozis bounced across the screen. Takis was delighted, shouting, "Mr. Karagiozis, I'm here. I'm Takis."

Chrysoula hushed him, but Sophia said that it was all right for the audience to talk to the characters or make comments. It happened all the time at the shows at the Zappeion.

"Ah, Mr. Takis," Karagiozis said, bowing deeply, "you're looking very clever this evening so I know you'll understand my problem. I've talked myself into the job of a baker. But what do I know of baking? Cakes, bread, they might as well be rocks."

There was another clash of pans. A fat villager appeared stage right and told Karagiozis that he'd killed a fine goose to offer to guests at his house. Like most villagers, he had no oven at home so would Karagiozis bake it in the bakery oven? He must be careful not to burn it.

"Bah!" Karagiozis said. "I do not burn what I bake. Give me the goose." When the man had gone, Karagiozis said to the audience, "Burn it I will not, but eat it—that my three poor sons and wife will do!"

Then another customer brought Karagiozis a casserole of potatoes and tomatoes flavored with garlic and rosemary. Karagiozis said again, "Burn it I will not!" But when the customer had gone, he turned to the audience. "How perfectly it will go with the goose!"

Enter the sultan. He'd smelled everything cooking and commanded Karagiozis to send it all to the palace when it was ready. "But what will I tell my customers?" Karagiozis asked. "They'll complain to you that I'm a thief and you'll have me hanged."

"Don't be a fool, Karagiozis," the sultan said. "Tell them anything you want. If you don't bring me the goose, then I *will* have you hanged."

"You want everything, even the stewed potatoes and tomatoes?"

"No, *you* eat them; I'll just take the goose. When your customers come to me, I'll shut them up fast enough."

After he'd gone, Karagiozis turned to the audience. "I lie, but he lies even bigger!" Taking the goose and the stew from the oven, he carried them to his own hut on the other side of the screen. "Oh, Karagiozis," we heard Stelios say in a high-pitched voice as the wife, "so delicious this is!"

When the first customer returned for his goose, Karagiozis told him, "Such a miracle we've had! The goose left the baking pan and flapped out of the oven. I tried to catch her but she flew out the door."

"The plucked and stuffed goose?"

"The very one."

"It flew away?"

"Just like that!"

The customer began to beat Karagiozis, calling out, "Liar! Thief!" Before he had finished, the second customer came for his potato and tomato stew.

"Such a miracle," Karagiozis said. "The potatoes didn't get along with the tomatoes and they got into a brawl. They leaped out of the pan and chased each other out the door."

"They ran out the door? Potatoes? Tomatoes?"

"Just like that."

Then the second customer began to beat Karagiozis too. The sultan arrived, asking, "What's all this?" Karagiozis had tricked them, the customers claimed, repeating what Karagiozis had told them about the goose and the stew. But the sultan said they were wrong. "The miracle was foretold by prophets: A roast goose will come to life and fly away. Potatoes and tomatoes will argue and chase each other." When the customers cried out that this wasn't possible, the sultan claimed they doubted the word of holy prophets and ordered the guards to take them away and beat them.

"Now," he said to Karagiozis when they had gone, "where's the goose?"

"Goose? What goose?"

"The one we lied about in front of your customer."

"A lie? You mean it was a lie? It wasn't a miracle? It wasn't prophesied?"

"Bring me the goose!"

"It flew away. You said so yourself, and it was prophesied. You have said this in front of everyone."

The sultan roared, "Aye, you've tricked me again. You're a liar and a swindler. And one day you will go too far and I will trap you." He turned to us in the audience. "One day, Takis over there will not find you so funny, right, Takis?"

Takis clapped and then we all clapped.

"Such days will come for us all," Karagiozis said. "And that is the end of tonight's play." Both characters bowed as we applauded.

Stelios peeked around the screen. "Thank you, thank you. Now, would anyone like my autograph?"

"He's such a ham," his mother said. "Not so modest now."

Actually, the play seemed kind of like village life though without the boring parts. But what struck me then was Stelios himself, how cleverly he'd put this all together and out of nothing—bark and a bedsheet and his own talents.

Will you teach me? I wrote on my pad.

"Teach you to . . . ?"

Do the voices and control the puppets and learn the plays.

"Me too!" Takis said, hopping from one foot to the other. Jumping in front of me, he grabbed my notepad and threw it to the floor. "Teach me, not her!"

"Hey, Takis. That's not nice," Stelios said, bending to pick up the pad. "But I'll teach you both." He took the pencil from me and drew a little grinning Karagiozis face on the pad, then handed it back to me.

And so it began. I didn't really understand it then, but in some way I sensed that Stelios was a path I might take. I had no idea where it might lead or if there would be any possibility of return. And though I didn't know it then, the yearning to return to someone, or somewhere, was to shadow my life.

CASSETTE 2 • Side 1

Well, I'll need to gather myself up for Zephyra's wake tonight. It was her death that the neighbors came to tell me; you probably heard them pounding on the door before I turned the machine off. Too much trouble to find my place on that cassette so I'm just starting a new one here.

Poor Zephyra, may the earth rest lightly on her. She died shortly after Aphrodite had finished her chants and bustled off in her rugs. She must have brought Zephyra some final relief, allowing her soul to fly into the wind she was named for.

There aren't any relatives nearby as Zephyra's husband, Kostas, died years ago. And good riddance to him, that man who let it be known that he was marrying her in spite of her enormous nose. She suffered from this all her life. The village women predicted in Zephyra's childhood that she'd never marry because of "a nose bigger than her dowry." And when, years later, the men of her family persuaded old Kostas to marry her after he'd had his way with her, she took revenge by telling the women that his *cucumber* was far smaller than her nose. Ah, life— the indignities it forces on us without a scrap of pity.

There was a son but he left for the Land of Big Radios after his father's death. Your country is so big that he just seemed to get swallowed up. We have no idea where he is. So it was up to the other village women to wash and perfume the body before dressing it in its grave clothes. Now, that's not something I like to do, as such intimate knowledge of the dead may interfere with my ability to create a lament, though I've never understood why. I'll need a pair of her shoes, I reminded the others, if I'm to mourn for her. I don't know the why of this either, but putting on the shoes of the dead seems to stir up some sense of who they've been. When I'm in their shoes, the dead seem to rise up through my legs all the way into my head and behind my eyelids. Then, with no effort at all, the words come out of my mouth. Of course Zephyra's shoes won't fit. That's often the way. It's not my fault I have such big feet. But I'll only have to squeeze them into her shoes for a few minutes at the wake.

Before I get ready for that, there's just enough time to tell you more about Stelios teaching us shadow puppetry in the downstairs of Chrysoula's house. That was around the time when the Allies were taking Italy. From what we heard on the Zenith, Yanks from the Land of Big Radios had been all over Italy for months, using it as a point from which to bomb the Greek military base occupied by Germans at Tatoi, north of Athens. What had happened to Mussolini? It wouldn't be until after the liberation of Greece that we'd see the newsreels of Il Duce and his mistress hanging by their heels in a public square filled with laughing Italians. The camera caught one grinning man leaning over the edge of the roof where the bodies were hanging, just touching the dictator's shoe and looking so proud of himself. Ah, what we won't do for a bit of notoriety. It would not be the last opportunity for such dismal fame in that grim decade.

Sometimes at night we thought we could hear the muffled shudder of distant bombing. With all the talk about it, we didn't at first think it was unusual when Takis announced he had a bomb inside him. "Shh, shh," he'd say, a warning finger on his lips, "don't make it explode." It seemed most likely to do so whenever he couldn't get his own way. Pushing Stelios to teach him the craft of shadow puppetry, he'd say, ". . . or else my bomb might blow up."

Stelios, who was going to teach both of us anyway, said, "Ooh, I'm afraid."

"If you go on talking like that," Chrysoula told Takis, "you're the one who'll get bombed, and by me."

If the Germans in our village had heard about the Allied bombing, they didn't show it. But there did seem to be a general loosening up, as if they were trying to enjoy themselves before going home to defeat. There was to be another donkey race, we were told, another way for the soldiers to make money off each other, there being nothing left to take from us. The same two donkeys used in the previous race were requisitioned again and Petros came house to house to tell us that we were all commanded to be the audience. Such a joke, we said to each other, as we trudged off to the field. Why did they need us standing there stone-faced, with rifles aimed at us by guards? Did they think they were doing us a favor maybe, giving us a bit of entertainment after they'd taken most of our food? It was impossible for us to understand them. But Chrysoula and I agreed that at least we'd have a story to tell Stelios and Sophia when we came home. So, along with Takis and the other villagers, we lined up under the olive trees at the edge of the field.

"Look," Takis said, pointing at Zephyra and her mother not far from us. "There's that girl who doesn't like us. The one with the big nose." He thumbed his nose at her and Zephyra turned red before ducking behind her mother, who glared in our direction.

"Stop that," Chrysoula said. "Just stand here quietly until the race starts."

"I want to race too!" Takis said. "Can I? Can I?" He ran around his mother in circles until she grabbed him by the shoulders and held him still in front of her. Pointing to Colonel Esterhaus on the other side of the field, Takis said, "I'll ask *him*. He'll let me."

"No, you won't. Stand still," Chrysoula said.

Hot weather was upon us already and the Germans who were going to race had taken off their shirts. With their sunburned faces and white, muscular chests, they seemed a different species from our scrawny selves. Near the colonel, a soldier was collecting money from others.

As usual, the first pair of soldiers had trouble adjusting to the hard wooden saddles we use here. They were made for fieldwork, not for the thrust and grind of racing. The soldiers got on them, then off to make fidgety adjustments, then on again.

"Their bottoms will be as red as their faces," someone said.

"There'll be no buggering in the barracks tonight!" another called out.

The donkeys themselves looked puzzled. They're amiable and intelligent creatures when treated well, but no one expects them to move fast. When the colonel shot a pistol in the air, the two soldiers flapped their legs against the flanks of their donkeys. One went in a circle while the other walked straight ahead, then came to a stop halfway across the field. The first soldier managed to maneuver his donkey out of the circle and it trotted in a leisurely way up to the other donkey before stopping. Then both animals lowered their heads and munched some weeds.

Their riders flapped legs and reins while shouting, but the donkeys took no notice. On the other side of the field, the soldiers who'd wagered money were also shouting. Suddenly the first donkey ambled forward and trotted to the edge of the field, passing the swastika flag that meant it had won.

Takis was squirming to get away from his mother. "Me next!" he cried out. "Me now."

In the second race, the colonel himself was on one of the donkeys. But it kept twisting its head around in an attempt to bite him. He jerked the reins to turn the donkey's head, but this made the donkey go in circles while continuing to snap at its rider.

Takis shrieked with laughter and we all laughed too at the whirligig of animal and man. The faster the donkey danced in circles, the more we laughed.

Suddenly it stopped its dance, shook its head and trotted in our direction, still with the colonel trying to control it. We quit laughing. He managed to bring it to a stop just in front of our little group, where Takis drew himself up and saluted.

Colonel Esterhaus grinned and saluted back, then reached down and grabbed Takis under the arms, swinging him up onto the saddle in front of him. He shook the reins and this time the donkey obeyed, trotting across the field toward the flag. Takis continued to salute all the way and the other soldiers cheered and applauded.

We didn't cheer. Chrysoula marched after them and when she caught up with the donkey, she reached up and demanded of the colonel, "Give me my child!"

"No!" Takis said, clinging to the colonel.

"Give him to me!"

The colonel looked at her. Possibly he remembered that this was the woman they'd interrogated, the woman who'd been in the wrong house at the wrong time on the day it had been requisitioned. But whatever he was thinking, he gently pried Takis away from himself and lifted him down to Chrysoula.

"No!" Takis screamed, and he tried to pull away from his mother, grabbing hold of the colonel's leg. This startled the donkey and it jerked its head around and brayed at length. It was a great barrage of noise, as if the rusted hinge of a massive door were being worked back and forth until it gave way at last. Takis let go, giving himself over to his mother. Then the colonel dismounted and led the donkey away.

And that was the end of it. Or so we thought. Once home, I heard Chrysoula giving Takis a lecture punctuated by swats to his bottom with her big wooden spoon.

"The bomb!" he shrieked. "You'll make it explode."

Takis was no different the next day, insisting that Stelios teach him the puppets or he'd be bombed. Stelios ignored him, telling both of us, "Make up whatever lines you want, but in each scene something must happen that moves the tale forward." He showed us how that was true for *Karagiozis the Baker*. Over the next month or so we learned the plots for *Karagiozis the Senator*, *Karagiozis the Prophet*, *Karagiozis and the Ghost* and *Karagiozis the Doctor*. Stelios also taught us how to make sound effects and manipulate the puppets in their turns and leaps and attacks.

Takis carved a lumpy little puppet which he named after himself, and he made up his own play called *Karagiozis and Takis*, starring Takis. He rehearsed it in a low voice in a corner, telling us over his shoulder that it was "probably the best play ever and you'll hate me because you'll wish you'd thought it up instead of me." But when he performed it for us, there wasn't much more than the Takis and Karagiozis puppets hitting and yelling at each other. It concluded with a song called "Takis, the King of the Puppets."

Takis is right,
Takis is bright.
No one tells him to stuff it,
'Cause he's the King of the Puppets.

"I don't think Karagiozis would agree," Stelios said afterward.

Takis flared up. "In *my* play, Karagiozis agrees."

"If there's a king of the puppets, it's Karagiozis himself. Your play was a good start. But it turned into all anger and hitting. It's important to tell a story."

"You know what? You're just stupid is what."

"Takis, don't be so aggressive," Chrysoula said. "You sound like a German again."

"Yes, yes!" he said, goose-stepping around the room and carrying an invisible rifle. He pointed it at Stelios, saying, "Pow, you're dead!"

"And enough of that too," Chrysoula said. "Up to your room."

Takis started to cry. He went over to the wall and hit it with his fists. "I have a bomb inside me," he said. "A big, red bomb."

"I'll make something else red if you don't stop that," Chrysoula said, taking him by the arm and pulling him after her up the ladder. Poor Takis. I could see that he was behaving this way out of jealousy of Stelios, but there wasn't much I could do about it. I felt disloyal in paying more attention to Stelios than Takis, but there wasn't much I could do about that either.

While she was upstairs, I noticed how pale Stelios and his mother were becoming. Staying in the dark basement all day and night with no sun or fresh air had not been good for them. Sophia had developed a bad cough and Stelios had lost weight. Although Chrysoula kept feeding Sophia her herbal infusions, they didn't seem to be helping.

I wanted to get Stelios out of the house for a walk in the hills with me. Convincing myself that this would do him good, I was also longing to show him my special places, the trails and animal tracks and the big rock that looked like a giant tortoise. Would Stelios like the kinds of things I liked? What if he didn't? The thought worried me, but I wasn't sure it mattered. The important thing was for us to be alone for once, to breathe free together, away from the supervision of Chrysoula and Sophia.

But did I dare? Although the Germans would never see us up there, we had to get there first. They'd been in the village so long that our faces were all familiar to them so Stelios would really stand out if he were so much as glimpsed. There was also the problem of his city clothes, which would make him stand out from other village men. So that afternoon while everyone else was napping, I borrowed some things from an old trunk that must have belonged to Takis's father. Baggy pants, a faded shirt and a cap like the ones old men wear to pass the time talking and fingering their strings of beads. I wrote Stelios a note asking him to put these things on and pull the cap down over his forehead because we were going out. When I went downstairs to give him the note and clothes, he was working on some new puppets for a new play he'd told us about. Sophia was napping on a cot in the corner.

When he'd read my note, Stelios looked at me, alarmed. He didn't seem to understand. I wrote out where I wanted to take him and what I wanted to show him. I hoped he could read it in spite of my awful spelling and badly shaped letters.

"It's too dangerous," he whispered so as not to wake his mother. He reminded me that he hadn't been outside since the day he and his mother had moved in months before. He was right, but once I've made a plan, it's hard for me to let go of it, even if I can guess possible consequences. It's always been one of my failings, I suppose. I put the cap on his head and pulled it down so he could barely see. Then I held up a mirror. We both laughed. When he'd put on the rest of the clothes, he could have been any village man if you didn't look too closely. I wrote that the villagers were all inside at this time for their afternoon naps and there were never any soldiers around.

We crept upstairs and I peeked out the door. After making sure there was no one around, I signaled for Stelios to follow me. I ran and he ran after me. We were soon in the pine grove where the charcoal had been made. It was a warm, almost hot day. I felt the sun spreading through my body as we climbed out of the pine grove and made our way along a rocky ridge overlooking the village and valley. From there we could see the hillsides below green with thyme and oregano, the olive trees that rippled in the breeze as the undersides of their leaves flashed silver in the sun. Above us, a pair of hawks glided in intersecting loops beneath a spine of clouds. I led Stelios farther along the ridge to show him the leafy crevice where I'd once found some poor baby hares abandoned and dead. Their little skeletons were still there, the delicate seashells of their skulls, the spray of tiny rib bones against tufts of fur the mother hare would have pulled from herself for the nest.

While we were kneeling beside each other I found myself overwhelmed with a little burst of joy, the exhilaration of our freedom from the house, the sparkling day and our place in it. Without thinking, I turned quickly and put my lips on his. His eyes widened with surprise, but he kissed me back, gently at first, then harder. It was as if we were drawing in each other's breath, our tongues touching, our teeth knocking together, heartbeats speeding. We drew apart, dazed, and looked at each other as though seeing ourselves for the first time. Color had risen in his cheeks.

"Well . . ." he said and laughed a little.

My face had grown so hot that I felt like the flame of a candle. I opened my mouth to speak but had no words. As always when I came close to speaking, a wave of sadness washed through me and I saw my father again, his cap flying off, the popping of the guns. But for the first time since then, I felt almost as if I'd begun to return to something I'd lost. The feeling was strong, as if I'd been drifting since his death. My eyes filled and brimmed over.

"What is it, Aliki? Tell me. Please."

But I couldn't. The time for speaking was coming, though I didn't know it, but it wasn't there yet. Stelios brushed the tears off my cheeks and took my hand. We stood up and started our walk back to the village.

"Don't worry," he said, taking my hand. "It doesn't matter. What matters is that we'll be friends forever now."

He didn't say anything else all the way back. He walked along running his hands through the heads of tall grasses that brushed our legs. I wondered what he was thinking; I was having trouble keeping track of my own thoughts. There was something in me that suspected I'd planned the whole outing with the kiss in mind. Well, not in mind, exactly, but sort of lurking around the edges. Another part of me said it had just been a matter of the moment. That seemed equally true. But a third part said, well, really, who cares? The important thing was that I felt different and I supposed he did too. But what was the difference and what did it mean?

We'd spent more time away than I'd been aware of and, lost in thought, I hadn't remembered that the village would be coming alive again as afternoon shaded into evening. When we were nearly down the path that brought us back, we could see old Theodoros with his donkey cart half-full of hay near the *plateia* and our priest hurrying out of the church in his vestments, a sign that someone was probably dying. If those two were up and about, soldiers would be too. The village was waking up.

We stopped and pressed ourselves against the wall of a roadside shed and, when no one was around, darted from house to house. We ducked under grape arbors at the sides of houses and then hid ourselves in a huge, red-flowering bougainvillea that grew over the house next to Chrysoula's. We were just about to dash to her door when it opened and the colonel came out, followed by the officer who'd been with him that day in my father's house, and Petros. Stelios and I froze and glanced at each other, our eyes wide. Petros said something we couldn't make out over his shoulder to Chrysoula, who was standing in the doorway. We stood quite still, willing the bees in the bougainvillea away from our faces, but one did land on my cheek. I almost screamed, but Stelios flicked it away with his finger. When the three men had turned the corner of the house, we counted slowly to ten, then ran to the door.

Chrysoula let out a shriek as we flew inside. She quickly clapped a hand over her mouth and slammed the door shut behind us. *"Theo mou!"* she said. "Where did you two come from? If you'd jumped in here before they left, just minutes ago . . ." She trailed off as she pulled the hem of her apron up to wipe her eyes. It took her a minute to get control. When she did, she looked at us as if she couldn't decide whether to embrace us or kill us. Stelios started to ask about the colonel at the same time that Chrysoula demanded to know why Stelios had been outside the house.

"Whose idea was it?" she asked, looking at me. She'd never been angry with me before and had never talked to me in such a tone. The heat rushed into my face and she rightly took it as a sign of guilt. "So it *was* your idea? I thought so. And *you*," she said to Stelios, "you're older than Aliki and should have better judgment. You nearly gave your mother a heart attack when she realized you weren't in the house." She looked him up and down, saying, "And where exactly did you come by those clothes?"

"I'll explain. But first, please tell us why the colonel . . . ?"

"I'm afraid something awful has happened. One of those old village hens has done some squawking—and I think I know which one it was. Before I'm done with her she'll be laying eggs!"

The woman had evidently told the colonel that there'd been more food in this house than elsewhere and he wanted to know if it was true and where we were getting it. Luckily there wasn't much at hand at the moment; there hadn't been a fisherman's caïque come through for a while—who knows why?—so the black market faucet was turned off. There was nothing for him to see aside from the greens and bulbs we'd gathered.

"But he had a good look around my kitchen, pointing out that hoarding food was punishable by death. As if I hadn't noticed what they did to your father, Aliki."

Chrysoula had leaned against the kitchen table, trying to appear calm while the other officer searched the rest of the rooms, tapping on the walls to find hollow spaces. Takis had goose-stepped around the colonel, saluting him, trying hard to impress. The colonel let him try on his hat.

"What a creature that man is. He would have shot me without a thought if he'd turned up so much as a tin of beans. But Takis just makes him melt." She took a deep breath, shaking her head, but then said to Stelios, "I was waiting to make sure they were really gone before going down to explain to your mother, the poor woman. First you disappear and then she hears all this going on above her head." Stelios went to the kitchen, where we could hear him pushing aside the rug to climb downstairs.

"Now, Aliki, let's sit down. I'm exhausted." We went into the front room and sat on chairs beside the old wood-burning stove, cold at that time of year. Chrysoula looked distracted then seemed to notice the stove for the first time. "I need to replace this when the war is over," she said, patting it. "The vent pipe is rusted and won't get us through another winter."

She fell silent for a long minute. Then she looked at me and sighed. "You have no mother to look after you, Aliki, so you're my responsibility. But I haven't done much of a job of it if you thought it was a good idea to persuade Stelios to leave the house. If he'd been noticed, it could have been the end of all of us. Didn't you understand that?" She glanced out the window and added, "And that's not even to mention that it also isn't right for you to be out alone with any boy."

My throat constricted as she said I'd become a little headstrong lately and she'd been meaning to speak to me about that and about my spending so much time with Stelios. But there was much to worry about these dangerous days, especially with Takis always being so difficult, that she hadn't been careful enough.

"That's my fault," she said. "I blame myself completely. Your dear father, may the earth rest lightly on him, wouldn't be happy with me."

She wanted to know everything that had happened—what had come over me and everything Stelios had done. I couldn't remember where I'd left my pad and pencil so I tried to point in the direction we'd gone and show her that all we'd done was walk and talk.

"You're not allowed out of the house at all anymore," she said. "I'm not sure I can trust you again. And don't you know that a village girl is nothing without her good reputation? She must always guard it against the clucking tongues of the village."

She talked about the war winding down and how Stelios and his mother would probably return to Athens around the time our village boys who'd been prisoners of war returned here. I'd become a young lady of property—it was unusual for someone my age already to have a house of her own as dowry. More importantly, I had my good character and reputation, much more valuable than any piece of property. I'd be able to make a good marriage but only if I was careful.

She reached out to touch my hair. "You're a bit young still, but it's not too early to take precautions about your good name. I need to ask you something: have you noticed any bleeding between your legs?"

I didn't know what she was talking about. I drew a question mark in the air.

"Well, when it happens the first time, you're not to worry about it. Come tell me and I'll show you how to manage. It just means your body is old enough to have babies." She saw my confusion and said, "Oh, my dear, it's hard to be young when most everything is still a mystery, isn't it? I'd almost forgotten what it was like until you came into my life. And you know, I don't think I've ever told you, but I'm so glad you did." She took my hands in hers. "You're very dear to me, Aliki. It's as if you were my own daughter. *Just the same.* And we're going to have lots of long talks from now on."

Was this what having a mother meant? It made me feel cared for in a way I'd only felt with my father. Though he was a loving man, no one would have called him motherly in the way Chrysoula now seemed to me. She took her hands away and asked me if I knew how babies were made. I shook my head. Of course, living as we did near fields with animals, I'd seen the way they behaved. But silly fool that I was, it hadn't seemed possible that people would act that way too. When she explained, I was aghast. I went to find my writing pad and when I had it, I wrote that what she'd told me sounded disgusting and that Stelios would never do anything like that.

"What men will and will not do is a very big subject, I'm afraid. We'll need to talk more about that. But for now, I've probably said enough. You just think about it and when you have questions, ask me. Meanwhile, I'm going to set up a bed for you in my room. You're too old to be sharing with Takis."

But marriage? I scribbled down. *How do you know when? And who? How do you ever know that?*

"Oh, you'll know. But all I can tell you now is what my mother told me long ago. You may not be able to marry the one you love. So learn to love the one you marry. It'll work out better in the end."

I wasn't quite able to take that in. I drew a question mark on my pad.

"Yes, I know, Aliki. It probably sounds as strange to you now as it did to me then. But don't worry about it. Sometimes ideas that seem so odd at first go away for a while. Then one day they walk back into your head and sit down just as comfortably as if they've been there all along. You'll see."

We had a tense evening with all of us sitting in the basement listening to the shortwave, which continued to talk about the Soviets pushing the Germans back to Europe. If the ones in Greece didn't leave soon, they'd definitely be cut off at the northern border and trapped here. With the Allies then all over Italy, and British victories in North Africa, there'd be little possibility of escape.

But the voice of the newscaster seemed to fade from time to time when I thought I heard my father talking again in the background. No one else in the room could hear him becoming more urgent, asking if he'd left an ax in the woods or maybe a hammer. They were borrowed from old Damien, the carpenter, and would have to be returned, he insisted. Was it just my longing for him that was turning into words he might have said? Or was there some kind of border area in life, like the margins on either side of a page, where the dead lived alongside us? If that was true, what did he think of Stelios?

After Chrysoula put Takis to bed, she and Sophia started a quiet conversation in the far corner of the basement. I couldn't make out what they were saying, but Stelios was nearby, listening and saying nothing. I caught his eye and asked with my own eyes what was happening. He came over and sat beside me.

"Mother thinks that, uh, she and I should leave. It's too dangerous for you all to have us here in the house any longer."

The events of the day, especially the fact that Stelios and I might have come home when the colonel was here, had convinced her. And she, like Chrysoula, was angry that the two of us had behaved so foolishly. As she talked to Chrysoula, Sophia looked pale and distraught and it was clear that she'd been weeping. She'd told Chrysoula that the village informant was not likely to give up and there might be more than one.

"Mother wants me to help her make our way into the hills. Beyond where you and I were this afternoon, I mean. She hopes we can find another partisan group who'll help us the way the others did when we left Athens and came here. We still have a little money left. I mean, they always want money."

The thought of his leaving and the role I'd played in it made me feel ill. A wave of nausea shook me. *But what do you think?* I wrote.

"Mother's too weak for the climb into the hills. I've already told her that. And what are the chances of our finding a sympathetic group to help us? I think Chrysoula is saying the same thing. And that the Germans are *finito*."

He drew a finger across his throat. They'd start pulling out any day now. And Chrysoula had also pointed out Sophia's health. With her persistent and worsening cough, which had left her weak and listless, how far would she get in the mountains, even with Stelios to help her?

"About this afternoon," he said to me, "don't blame yourself. Chrysoula was right about my being older and I should have been more responsible. But whatever happened, we both wanted it, didn't we? And we were lucky, so lucky. Maybe that's a good sign. Maybe Chrysoula is right and this will all be over next week."

Chrysoula and Sophia had stopped talking but it wasn't clear that anything had been decided. Or if it had been, they weren't telling us yet. Chrysoula asked Stelios how his new play was coming along.

"We could use a diversion, I think," she said.

"It isn't completely new," he said. "There's an old one called *Karagiozis and the Seven Beasts* and I'm adapting it. There'll only be one beast with four heads. You'll see why. I'll work on it some more and show you tomorrow night."

The next night we gathered in the candlelit room, waiting. I looked hard at Stelios before he disappeared behind the white screen. Could what Chrysoula had told me about what men did with women be true even of him? I wasn't sure what to think; it made me a little queasy.

Just before the play was to begin, Takis stomped down the ladder and sat. Earlier he'd said he didn't want to see the play because he was sure it would be stupid. But there he was, sitting with us in the half-light.

In the opening scene, Karagiozis danced and sang.

Trin, trin, trin,
What a mess we're in.
The beast is at the door,
Soon we'll be no more.
Trin, trin, trin,
What a mess we're in.

The sultan appeared and told Karagiozis that it was time to rid the village of the great four-headed beast. Handing him some coins, he said, "Go throughout the village and announce that whoever kills the great beast will win the eternal friendship of the lovely but silent Aliki."

Everyone looked at me. I flushed with pleasure and some embarrassment. I suppose Stelios wouldn't have worked my name in if we hadn't had our walk together. So something must have felt different for him too, as I'd suspected.

Next, Karagiozis met the puppet that Takis had named after himself. "That's my puppet," the real Takis said. "Who said you could use it?"

"Ah, Mr. Takis," Karagiozis said to both Takis and his puppet, "will you help me? Will you help our village?"

"Ye-e-esss," Takis said, dragging out the word with reluctance.

"We must make an announcement," Karagiozis said. He told the Takis puppet what to say and they agreed to split up so they could cover the village more quickly. They crisscrossed the screen, shouting, "Hear ye, hear ye! Whoever kills the beast with four heads wins the eternal friendship of the silent Aliki."

I was to be the prize? Was the play a little valentine Stelios was sending me? A villager came along and said he would do it, he would kill the beast. Did the villager have any coins on him? Karagiozis asked. "The beast has magnets in his mouth and will draw you in for a meal if your pockets are full of coins." The villager thanked Karagiozis and gave him his money.

Enter the beast with four heads. In fact, it was a swastika carved out of bark like the other puppets. On each of the four arms was a paper cut-out monster head with open mouth and waggling tongue. Stelios had attached the swastika loosely to one of the bamboo poles so it could rotate as it moved. The beast roared and whirled toward the villager, entangling him and dragging him offstage screaming.

Sophia and Chrysoula looked at each other. Sophia called out, "Really, Stelios, I don't think this is funny at all. Couldn't you . . . ?"

"What a monster!" Takis called out. "Takis will bomb the monster! Let Takis do it."

Other villagers volunteered. With each one, Karagiozis cheated him of his money first, then the whirling swastika came for the villager.

"Yaaaaaaay!" Takis yelled.

"It's only a play, Takis," Chrysoula said.

"Eh, Stelios," Takis called out, "let Takis kill the monster!"

A new character appeared. From his gangly tallness, we saw that it was a caricature of Stelios himself.

"For the fair Aliki and for the good of all mankind," Stelios said in his own voice, "I will do the deed!"

Enter the monster again, spinning and growling. It went first for Karagiozis. But the Stelios puppet collided with the swastika, ripping off two of its paper heads. It collapsed, bellowing.

Takis jumped to his feet. "No, no, Takis should bomb the monster!"

"Sit down, Takis," Chrysoula said. "Stop interrupting."

"Let Takis bomb the monster!"

"Just be patient," Stelios called from behind the screen.

"I hate this play," Takis said. "It's stupid. Mine was better."

"Then don't watch it," his mother said. "Go to bed." Takis climbed upstairs.

Sophia told Stelios to stop the play. "It's too upsetting."

He peered over the top of the screen. "There's more to come about Takis. I'm not leaving him out. I mean, he comes to help me and together we kill the beast and win Aliki's friendship."

"Another time, dear," Sophia said.

But there wasn't to be one. Chrysoula and Sophia were talking about Takis and probably didn't hear what I heard: the front door upstairs opening and Takis's footsteps leaving the house. I was helping Stelios gather everything from the play and he was saying how Takis's jealousy had ruined the evening. How much time passed? I've never been able to remember. Stelios handed me the swastika monster and I was looking at how carefully it had been made. Our fingers touched on the puppet and I felt the same little surge of joy I'd had on our walk before I kissed him.

There was a hammering at the door upstairs, then boots thumped through to the kitchen. With a shock, I realized the obvious—that Takis probably hadn't pulled the rug back across the trapdoor before he went out. Down the ladder came Colonel Esterhaus and some of his men, who spread themselves out in front of us. At first they just stood there looking at us, especially at Stelios and his mother. And at the swastika puppet Stelios and I were holding. We'd gone completely still and I saw the color drain out of Stelios's face. What would the colonel have understood of all this? Whatever it was, he barked a command to his men, who began to herd us together and push us one by one up the ladder to the main floor and toward the front door. Sophia stumbled and fell to the floor coughing. I helped her to her feet, but we were both shaking so badly that if one of the soldiers hadn't pushed us with the butt of his rifle, we would both have collapsed together. Outside, Takis was crouched beside the fountain. When he saw his mother, he ran to her, but she asked him what he'd been doing.

"Get back inside," she ordered. Instead, Takis threw himself at the colonel, seizing his leg. The colonel pushed him away and he fell to the ground. Neighbors were pouring out of their houses.

"Chrysoula, what is it?"

"What has happened?"

"And who are *they*?" someone asked, pointing to Stelios and his mother.

More soldiers were there now with rifles, ordering the neighbors back into their houses. A few did go in but not all. Some of the same old women who gathered regularly at the fountain to trade insults with Chrysoula stayed and one of them began a low hiss at the Germans—the old sound meant to shame someone for an unspeakable act. The other women joined her and the hissing grew in size and repetition. It was a strange, frightening sound and the soldiers clearly didn't know what to make of it. But the women, who would have been more cautious only a few weeks before, were probably worn out and fed up with the loss of sons and grandsons, with eating grass and even dirt. The war was nearly finished and the Germans defeated, so the women continued hissing and hissing.

Then one of them spat out the words *Your shame!* The soldiers wouldn't have understood or even cared what the women were saying or that this carried power in our language. But the disdain in the words was unmistakable. It became a chant. *Dropee sas! Dropee sas! Dropee sas!*

Who threw a stone? Who threw another? Just pebbles, no doubt; the street was full of them and soon whole handfuls were hitting the soldiers' faces. At first they tried to avoid the stones, ducking and turning, but there was no escape; the women were relentless and some of the soldiers' faces were bleeding. An order was shouted and the soldiers began to shoot.

In the chaos—screams and shots and everyone running from the rifles, escaping into side streets and lanes—I tried to run, but someone grabbed my hand and pulled me down behind the fountain, where the wounded lay on the ground moaning. In a few minutes the shooting stopped, but there was the sound of a lot of running back and forth. Soon smoke was everywhere and I realized that houses were being torched. But why? Just in retaliation for the stone throwing?

We heard later that things like this had happened in other places just before the Germans pulled out. Nasty farewell gifts? Perhaps the soldiers would have done such things here anyway, with or without the stones. But if the women hadn't acted as they did, what would have happened to those of us brought up from the basement? We would never know the answers to these questions and we would never stop wondering.

I saw it was Stelios who'd taken my hand and was pulling me away, asking, "Did you see my mother? I lost her when the shooting started."

I hadn't and I'd also lost track of Chrysoula and Takis. We were running from footsteps behind us, but whether they were soldiers or other villagers, we never knew. At the edge of the village, we stumbled into the ditch where my father had stolen the squash, where Stelios and his mother had originally hidden. We lay there for most of the night. It sounded as if the soldiers were going from house to house, setting them on fire and shooting anyone who tried to stop them. Screams rose up from the village along with the shouting of the soldiers and smoke from the burning houses. Stelios beat the ground with his fists and cried out, "She's dead, I know it." I covered his mouth with my hands to stifle the sound.

"Don't," I heard myself say quietly. "We'll find her."

Words had finally come from my mouth. The new disaster had released the hold of my father's death. But I spoke in the cracked voice of an old woman, the voice that has stayed with me all these years, this voice of a crone. I don't know why, any more than I know why once I had a father and Stelios a mother and then we didn't. Or why once there was a village and then there wasn't.

With all the shouting and screaming, Stelios didn't seem to notice that I'd spoken. There was also a new noise, one of engines starting up, and the sight of headlights moving away from the village. Were the Germans leaving at last?

Early the next morning when everything was so quiet that the village seemed deserted, we crept back. Several houses were still on fire, including Chrysoula's, but where was she? Bodies were everywhere, but there were no soldiers. We stepped over people I'd known all my life—the carpenter my father had once borrowed the ax from, women who came to the lion fountain.

And then we saw them—Chrysoula and Sophia. They were propped up against the wall of a house, almost as if they'd been sitting there having a companionable chat. Their eyes were still open, their faces expressionless. Kneeling in front of them, Stelios reached out and shook his mother's shoulder lightly, as if to awaken her.

I closed Chrysoula's eyes, this good woman who'd cared for me as a daughter. Sitting beside her, I stroked her hair and thought of the long talks she'd mentioned that now we'd never have. "Talk to me," I said, though I knew she would never do so again. "Oh, please." Around us, the few remaining villagers alive searched for their dead, wailing and tearing their hair. But where were the Germans? And where was Takis?

Stelios was holding his mother and rocking her, muttering words of the song she used to sing, ". . . For they fly and take their ease . . ."

I don't know how we managed the next few days. It was as if weights were strapped to my head and limbs and even the slightest movement in mind or body required effort beyond my strength. But effort had to be made. I somehow took my grief and just put it away, pushed it into a little room in my mind and shut the door. It was the only thing I could do in order to get through one day and then another. This wasn't entirely new for me. I realized I'd done something like it after my father's death in order to bear the weight of what had happened . . . I know now that time lessens these things as if it takes pity on us when death does not.

Men from an unharmed village nearby came to help us prepare our dead for burial. From them we heard that the Germans were leaving the countryside everywhere, in fact evacuating the whole country. Ordinarily, we would have celebrated, but instead Stelios and I had to rely on these men to help us bring the bodies of his mother and Chrysoula to my father's house. It was one of the few that hadn't been burned, because, we supposed, the colonel had requisitioned it. Now it was empty.

Placing broad planks between two pairs of chairs, we laid out Sophia and Chrysoula with candles at their heads and feet. I sat with them all night while Stelios paced. He'd stop and stroke his mother's hair, saying, "You were right—we should have gone. We'd be far away by now and none of this would have happened. How will I tell Papa when he comes back?"

I wept for Chrysoula and Sophia but especially for Stelios, as there was no knowing if his father would ever return. Looking at the two women, I couldn't help thinking, *They're dead, but we're alive.* I felt ashamed of the thought. But then I heard my father's voice saying, *It's all random, Aliki, who lives and who dies. There's no sense to it.*

I wasn't sure what was happening to me, but I felt a kind of wave rise through me, into my chest and then my head, and I just seemed to swoon away. I saw myself entering a room of shadows. On the other side was a door just a bit open with a dim amber light spilling out. I had the feeling there was some truth beyond everything I'd ever known beyond that door. If only I could get it fully open. I tried to move closer, but it seemed my feet were as heavy as blocks of cement. I heard a sound that I would realize later was my own voice. But I couldn't make out any words. They went on for what must have been a long time. When they finished, I was filled with a sense of well-being, almost of calm.

Through it, I heard Stelios say, "Aliki, you've been speaking!"

"I have?"

"So you have a voice after all. But it's scratchy like an old lady's."

"What did I say?"

"I didn't really understand. Something about the earth eating the young and old, mothers of children and the fathers too. I mean, there were lots of sounds that weren't words, sort of like, *oo loo loo.*"

"Oh, the sound that Chrysoula said the flying chickens make."

"What?"

"Just something she said once."

The door opened and a few neighbors came in, the only survivors, all in black. Who was lamenting? they asked. Would she lament for their dead too?

So that was what I had been doing—lamenting. But I was too exhausted for any more and fell asleep there on the floor.

The mass funeral and burial of the dead took most of the next day. So many new graves had to be dug, so many coffins made. We wouldn't have been able to manage it without the help of the other village. Our priest had survived, but other area priests came to help him as there were more dead than living. And it was said that some villagers had fled when the shooting started and hadn't returned. I saw Zephyra and her mother walking among the coffins, crossing themselves whenever the priests did. Zephyra's mother and the few surviving women were talking about what had happened, how it had all come to pass. I felt them staring at me. But where was Takis?

After the dead had all been buried, I saw him for the first time since the events of that night. Crouched at the edge of the cemetery, he was watching, filthy and wild-eyed. When I went over to him, he looked like a dog that expects to be beaten. I held out my hand, but his eyes were so crazy I wasn't sure he knew who I was. I tried to think what Chrysoula would have done. On a hunch, I turned as if to walk away, then wheeled back around and slapped his face twice. He sobbed and, after a few minutes of this, let me lead him back to the house.

Stelios looked at Takis with incomprehension. Finally Stelios said, "You couldn't be there for your own mother's burial?" Takis didn't reply. Stelios seemed to take in the fact that Takis had become someone other than the boy we'd known. He exchanged a glance with me but turned back to Takis. "And how did you happen to be in the street already when we were all brought out? What had you been up to?"

Takis flew at him, clamping his jaws on Stelios's right leg. Stelios cried out and tried to slap Takis off but instead lost his balance and fell over Takis onto the floor.

"Get him off me!" Stelios called and I ran to the kitchen, grabbed some bottled water left by the Germans and threw it in Takis's face.

He let go, and I pulled him across the floor while Stelios held his leg and moaned. "What's wrong with him?"

"Takis, Takis," I said, shaking him by the shoulders. His eyes were glazed and he trembled all over. I asked Stelios to help me get him onto one of the cots left by the Germans.

"Are you serious?" he said. "I'm not going near him."

At first I thought Takis had lost his mind out of grief for his mother. They'd killed her in front of him, after all. I managed to hoist him onto the cot and pulled an army blanket over him. This seemed to calm him. He finally turned his face away from us and, amazingly, considering all that had happened, his breathing slipped into the rhythm of sleep. With twine from the kitchen, I tied his ankles together.

Stelios sat on the floor with his pants leg rolled up, examining the bite mark. There was a clear imprint of Takis's teeth. The skin had been broken and blood was seeping out. I helped Stelios clean the wound and wrap a dry cloth around it.

"You should probably stay off it for now," I said. "Lie down on one of the other cots, why don't you? Here, I'll pull one over."

"As far from him as possible."

I pulled two cots next to each other with a small space in between. Then I jumbled all the others in a great pile between us and Takis. If he tried to get to us in the night, he'd fall over the pile and wake us.

Stelios and I lay side by side. He reached across and held my hand until he fell asleep and let go.

I drifted through the night, asking myself the answers to the questions Stelios had asked Takis. I remembered hearing his footsteps upstairs as he left the house. I could guess what had happened, but I pushed it away. The pressing matter was, what would we do with him now? He could be a danger to us and probably was also one to himself. And more importantly, how were we to live? The Germans were gone, but the village was mostly a smoldering ruin. And there was bound to be blaming for what had brought the Germans out that night. I remembered Zephyra's mother and the others staring at me in the cemetery. It was time to go.

In the morning, Stelios and I peered over the pile of cots at Takis, who was peering back. Some small awareness had returned to his gaze. I asked him how he was.

"I don't know," he said in a monotone. "My jaw. It hurts."

"Not as much as my leg hurts," Stelios said.

The reference was lost on Takis. He glanced around the room. "Where are we? Whose house is this?"

"It's my father's house," I said.

"You can *talk*, Aliki. You're talking."

"Yes."

"But you don't sound like you used to. Has Mother heard you? She'll be glad."

Stelios and I exchanged glances. He was about to say something, but I rolled my eyes at him. "What exactly do you remember of the last two days?" I asked Takis.

"I don't know."

"I don't believe you," Stelios said.

"It's the bomb. Maybe it went bang."

"There's no such thing."

"*Something* went bang."

"You could say that."

Takis started to weep.

"Enough," I said. I told them that we needed to get out of there to someplace where there'd be real food. If the Germans were pulling out all over the country, then they might already be gone from Athens. There was nothing to keep us in the village. Did Stelios have a key to his parents' house in Athens? He said we wouldn't need one because there was a spare in the courtyard of the Athens house. And the housekeeper, old

Yannoula, was living there, looking after the place. She wasn't Jewish so she hadn't fled with him and his mother.

"But I don't know if she's definitely still there. Anything could have happened."

We needed to survive until we could figure out what to do next. Or until Stelios's father came back, if he ever did. My own father's house would always be here in the village if we needed it.

Stelios shook his head. "I don't seem to be able to think at all now. I just keep seeing my mother's face everywhere I look." He glanced at Takis and asked what we would do with *him*. Takis had stopped weeping but still seemed glazed.

"He has to come with us," I said. "We can't leave him here to starve."

"Why not? I can think of a few good reasons."

"Chrysoula wouldn't have wanted us to abandon Takis. And certainly not in the state he's in. I'll look after him and keep him from bothering you." I surprised myself with the authority in my new old-lady voice. Stelios wasn't pleased, but I could see he understood how determined I was.

"Do you think we'd walk to Athens?" he asked. "It's a long way and I don't know if I can even walk across the room."

"Try."

He limped around the room. But to go far, he'd need a cane or crutch of some kind. I untied Takis's ankles and helped him to wash up a bit.

As we left the blackened village, Stelios broke a board from a fence and used it for a walking stick. Takis kept his eyes ahead and didn't appear to be taking in much. Even when we passed the cemetery, he looked neither right nor left. Stelios and I glanced at the mounds of raw earth but the sight made us both come unstrung. We turned away, our faces wet, and hurried after Takis, who'd moved on without us.

The road was full of ruts made by the departing German tanks and trucks and we walked in them slowly so Stelios could keep up. At one point, Takis asked over his shoulder, "What's wrong with your leg?"

"Go to hell," Stelios muttered.

After a while, we passed the next village, the one whose men had helped us bury our dead. Flags were flying and villagers were shooting off guns in celebration. Banners were strung across the road and tied to olive trees on either side. "Long live free Greece!"

An old man with a donkey cart offered us a ride, saying, "God has enough to spare." Was it a general comment or was he talking about himself? The three of us sat in the back, our legs dangling off the end, with me in the middle separating Takis and Stelios. We rode for a long time without speaking. Then a group of four or five boys, half-starved and in ragged clothes, crept from behind a boulder. They stared as we went by. Farther along, three girls about my age came up behind the cart and asked if we had anything to eat. I had a single packet of the leathery German rations left and tossed it to them. As it hit the ground they fell on it, fighting each other to tear off the wrapper.

We didn't know it at the time, but there were bands of such children all over the country. War had left many orphans and they roamed the countryside in packs.

"Where are you going?" one called up at us.

"Athens," I answered.

"It's worse there. People starving in the streets. Don't go."

"We have to."

"Don't go."

But others said, "Take us with you!" and ran alongside the cart.

"They're like wild dogs," the old man said. "My wife, she tried to help them, even took a couple into our house. But they stole anything they could. And then others showed up. You know what they say—if you lie down with dogs, you catch their fleas. I drove them off."

A little later, we passed a rocky outcrop far above us with a monastery on top. They had plenty of food there, the old man said,

". . . the greedy bastards." The monks dropped rocks on anyone who tried to climb up to the walls. "One day, though, they'll have to pay. Every sheep will hang by its own foot on the butcher's hook, as they say."

For most of the day, we bounced on the hard boards of the wagon. Stelios stared into the distance behind us and from time to time wiped his eyes. Takis held on to the side of the wagon and kept his face turned away from ours. I tried not to look at either of them, tried to empty my mind and make it ready. For what? I didn't know. After my father's burial, Chrysoula told me that the death of someone you love was like a deep cut with a sharp knife. "The real pain," she said, "comes later when the wound is cold."

The old man asked me where we were going and why, but I just said Athens. It seemed to me that what had happened to the three of us back in the village had to be secret. It made us different from everyone else and I wouldn't have known how to explain it anyway. We passed through many towns, sometimes sleeping fitfully on the hard wood, as day became night then day again. The old man stopped at the side of the road for a nap now and then, but soon slapped the donkey's rump, urging him on. Finally late one afternoon he stopped in the Athenian suburb of Halandri. The streets were full of townspeople waiting to see the British troops, the first Allied forces in Greece, pass through on their way to Athens. People had carried Oriental carpets into the street and scattered flower petals and laurel leaves to welcome the troops. Without a word, Takis clambered down from the cart and wandered off into the crowd. I called after him, but he disappeared. I couldn't just let him go so I helped Stelios down from the cart and the old man said, "Be brave, and remember—he who slaps his own face should not cry out!"

"What's that supposed to mean?" Stelios asked. "He has a saying for everything whether it fits or not."

"Do you know where we are? Is it far to your house?"

"Quite a ways. We'll need another ride."

We made our way through the crowd and climbed up onto the

base of a statue of a hero of the War of Independence. From there we watched the British jeeps approach. Flowers and laurel branches rained down on them from the cheering crowds. The smiling and waving soldiers were up to their chests in tributes from the towns they'd already passed through. Jeep after jeep went by, but the crowd never ran out of enthusiasm. People surged toward the jeeps and some ran alongside, trying to touch individual soldiers. A young woman caught up with one jeep and passed the soldiers a pitcher of cold water. Someone else offered up a beaker of red wine. A man held up a sign in English: PLEASE TO MARRY MY DAUGHTERS PLEASE!

Then we saw Takis. He was trying to run with the jeeps but kept falling behind. One of the soldiers reached down and pulled him up. There he sat, our Takis, amid flowers and leaves on the lap of one of the British soldiers. He lifted Takis's arm and helped him wave to the crowds. Takis quickly caught on and waved hard, as if he had personally brought about the liberation of Greece. Well, I thought, he's exchanged the Germans for the British. I called out to him, but he didn't look our way.

"He won't know how to find us in Athens," I said.

"Good," Stelios said.

"Where will he go? How will he survive?"

Stelios didn't reply and we climbed down from the statue. People were getting into cars and trucks to follow the British jeeps into Athens. We found room in the back of a truck where people were embracing each other and singing the national anthem.

. . . from the graves of our slain,
Shall thy valour prevail,
As we greet thee again,
Hail, Liberty! Hail!

It was as if we were all friends, part of a huge family. The outlying towns seemed to run into each other, one after another, until a sign told us we'd entered Athens and a huge hill right in the middle of the city came into view. A cheer went up and I recognized the Parthenon from postage stamps and drachma notes. But I'd had so little schooling that I really didn't understand what it was. I asked Stelios if that was where the king had lived before the Germans came. He just laughed.

The buildings were so tall and didn't look at all damaged. Stelios said there'd been no house-to-house fighting when Greece surrendered to the Germans so most buildings were intact. But they'd taken most all the food, as they'd done elsewhere, and promptly shot both looters and people who'd defaced walls with anti-German slogans.

The streets were full of people embracing and kissing as all the bells in the city rang. When the truck could go no farther, near a place that Stelios said was Parliament, we all climbed down. He took my hand and pulled me along through the crowd, up a wide avenue where electric trolleys—I'd never seen one before—were stranded like islands in a sea of people. We climbed a hill into the area called Kolonaki, where flags were draped from all the balconies of the houses and apartment buildings. People in a square were shouting and waving flags.

Opening a gate just off the square, Stelios led me into a shady courtyard. There was a fountain and orange trees so I couldn't see the house well.

"It's all right!" he said. "It looks just the same. We're *home*, Aliki!"

From under a stone bench, Stelios took a key and unlocked a door. Inside, the house was narrow but tall. I'd never been in a house with more than one story. This one went up and up, with a marble staircase coiling right through the center and rooms opening off each side. Stelios ran up the stairs, calling out, "Yannoula, Yannoula! I'm home."

I wandered into a parlor with a chandelier, something else I'd never seen, that threw sparkles of light over the red plush sofas and paintings in gilded frames. I wanted to see more, but I was so exhausted that I wondered if I was already dreaming. I sat down on one of the sofas and fell asleep at once.

Hours later, someone nudged me awake and I thought it was Chrysoula. But it was an old woman in black. She passed me a mug of something steaming—bean soup. Oh, the smell of it, garlic and onions and—could it be? Chicken broth! To use a chicken for broth in those times, well, it was almost a criminal act, but I was grateful for the crime. A bay leaf floated on the surface like a tiny arrow pointing at me.

CASSETTE 2 • Side 2

Excuse my hoarseness. My throat's still sore from the wake last night. Such a gathering—all the women of the village were there, at least those of us who can still walk and talk. At the far side of Zephyra's parlor, her wooden coffin was supported on chair seats, with the tall brass candlesticks from the church at head and foot. Even from across the room you could make out the Nose.

I went up to the coffin and wept for Zephyra, for all of us, damaged as we are, who must bear our damage through and out of this world. The women who'd prepared Zephyra for burial had come across a stash of bottles of raki under her bed. I hope, in life, they gave her some comfort, after all. And they would give us some too before the evening was out.

A pair of Zephyra's shoes had been placed for me on the floor in front of the coffin. Taking my own off, I slipped into hers. Well, no, *slipped* is not the word. Forced my feet inside, ouch. I could barely keep my balance and teetered over Zephyra's body so close I could smell the lemon soap they'd used to wash her. The other women began to wail and call out messages for Zephyra to carry to their relatives on the other side.

"Can you ask Mother where she hid the family wedding shawl? Could she send a sign? Our Frosini needs it for the ceremony."

"I can't find the bag of gold sovereigns that Manos left under the floorboards in the work shed. Did he spend it all?"

"Tell Kostas that his brother is still trying to cheat me out of the potato field."

The cries came faster, along with one higher voice calling out, "For death is the camel, the dark camel that kneels at every door." We keened and shouted curses on God for taking the living from us. What do we really own, after all, but our bodies and memories? Then the surge of Zephyra started up through my legs and into my chest. In the room of shadows, I moved toward the partly opened door, but when I reached it, my own voice filled the room, saying something I couldn't follow as the amber light faded and the door was gone.

As I came to I saw that I was on a sofa with the others gathered around me waving spirits of ammonia under my nose and telling me to calm myself. Such eloquence, they said; I'd honored Zephyra with my lament. What had I chanted? Something like this, they told me:

I was Zephyra,
Named for the wind.
But my life fell as rain on hard summer soil,
Cooling not even the sweet basil by the gate,
Not even the goats that ate it
When they'd finished with my soul.
I was Zephyra,
Named for the wind.
But cursed with a mother, a husband and son,
Loving neither my hands nor heart,
Not even the food from my hearth
That they ate without thanks.
I was Zephyra,
Named for the wind.

On and on I'd gone. It made me weep for her sad life. Never mind, the women said, passing me a glass of raki so we could drink to Zephyra's life. We drank some and then we drank some more. The raki filled our tired bones and pulled us to our feet. With knees creaking and other joints complaining, we took each other's hands and danced through the house in a line, singing.

In darkest midnight
Comes a knock on my door,
But no one is there.
Who can it be? What does he want of me?
In this life of webs,
Why has he come?

"O-pah!" we called out, turning and twisting until we threw off our grief and trampled our fear that there would be no one to grieve for us as we grieved for Zephyra. Most of us have outlived our families, if we ever had them. After my father was executed, I'd taken Chrysoula and Takis as my family. And after Chrysoula, my next new family began, I suppose, that first morning in Stelios's house in Athens.

When I came downstairs from the room up under the eaves that the housekeeper, Yannoula, had shown me to the night before, Stelios was waiting for me in the hall. He'd slicked down his hair and put on a dark suit and tie. I was startled to see what a handsome young man he'd turned into overnight.

"Are you yourself?" I asked.

"The very same. Just in my city clothes, that's all. Yannoula will find some for you."

The plan for the day was to see if we could find anything to trade for food. Yannoula had been getting by with a small vegetable garden in the courtyard, where she also kept a few chickens for their eggs. She'd also exchanged some of the furniture in the unused bedrooms for pasta, rice and olive oil. But supplies were running low and now there were three of us to feed. At least the neighborhood had been relatively safe because many of the foreign embassies were there.

Stelios asked me to come with him into his parents' bedroom and I was alarmed at first, remembering what Chrysoula had said about men. "I had to tell Yannoula about Mother last night," he said, showing me inside. My alarm disappeared as I looked at the enormous blue canopy over the bed. I'd never seen such a thing. Was it in case rain leaked through the ceiling? No, just decoration, he said. I opened the double glass doors and walked onto a balcony overlooking the orange trees in the courtyard. Stelios came after me, saying, "I told Yannoula while she was cleaning my leg wound. Now she's too upset to leave her room."

She'd worked for the family for years and was more like a friend of Sophia's than an employee. She hadn't said much as she led me up the stairs the night before, except that Stelios had already gone to bed in his room on the second floor. When she'd given me some clean towels and said good night, I saw that although she dressed in black like a village crone, she had a sweet though deeply creased face, probably once pretty. Stelios himself had been further saddened by the telling of his mother's fate. His eyes were moist as he opened a drawer of the dresser and took out her jewelry box.

"By rights this all belongs to my father now," he said, opening the box and taking out a gold hat pin in the shape of a tiny tiger with ruby eyes. "But I think he'd understand." Sophia hadn't been a flashy woman, but her husband had given her a few good pieces: a necklace of pink amethysts, some gold bracelets and a few rings set with sparkly stones. A cousin of his father's might be able to help us, Stelios said. Unless the cousin had also been taken away by the Germans.

When we left the house, Stelios was walking better with only a slight limp. We passed groups of police patrolling near embassies. But some blocks away from the neighborhood, in a poorer area, we almost stumbled over the corpse of an old man in pajamas. Stelios said the bodies of those who'd starved to death were put outside for a cart to take them to the municipal mortuary. There were no more coffins and few men to dig graves. This had been true even before he and his mother had fled the city. The man's jaw had dropped down, giving him a surprised look. I couldn't bring myself to step over him, but Stelios took my hand and helped me around him.

Most of the shops we passed were closed or burned out. Banks were boarded up and people were sleeping in doorways or public squares. The cheering crowds of the day before were gone and our footsteps sounded loud in the empty streets. In a section full of warehouses and closed antique shops, Stelios told me to wait while he went up to a second-floor office.

Standing on the sidewalk, I realized that we were just below the hill I'd seen the day before as we entered the city. Partway up the rocky slope, immense fortification walls surrounded the top. I couldn't see the Parthenon or anything else from there but I wondered how anyone had ever built walls so huge and high. And for what purpose? Below it, on almost the same level as the city streets, was an area of ruined marble buildings, broken columns rising above the weeds. I was going to ask Stelios, but when he returned after a while, his face was gray.

"He took it all," he said, "all of Mother's things." He was carrying two burlap bags, one full of rice, the other containing a ten-liter tin of olive oil.

"Is that all they were worth?"

"This is what I got. What something's worth these days is whatever you can get for it."

He handed me the sack of rice, the lighter of the two, and we started home. A pair of jeeps driven by British soldiers roared past and I told Stelios that I didn't understand why the British were here. Were they going to run the country now?

"Do I know?" he asked, more sharply than I would have expected. Then he said he'd learned something else from his father's cousin. It was the fact of the labor camps where Greek Jews had been sent in Poland and Germany. Tens of thousands had been taken from Greece—the actual numbers wouldn't be known until much later. But at that time, the International Red Cross in Geneva had no record of them, including almost the entire Jewish population of Thessaloniki in the north, more than forty thousand people.

"They've disappeared off the earth. Papa and Uncle Nikos with them." I was lagging behind him and he looked back at me, his face still gray. I asked about the cousin he'd just been with and Stelios said some friends here in the city had hidden him and his family in their house. So he hadn't gone to the synagogue to register with the others.

I still didn't understand why anyone had been taken in the first place. I was about to ask Stelios, when I heard rapid footsteps behind me and someone grabbed hold of the sack of rice and tried to pull it away. A man in rags with a pinched face and wild eyes. I pulled back, but he shouted at me to give it to him.

"For my children," he said. "Three of them without food."

Stelios turned and swung the bag with the heavy tin of olive oil, hitting him in the face. Blood spurted from his nose and splattered onto me.

"Please, just a little," the man begged. "Only a little."

"Run!" Stelios shouted. And we did run as best we could with the heavy sacks. I didn't think my legs would hold me up, but somehow they did. The man dropped farther behind. When I looked over my shoulder, he was standing beside a wall, weeping, his face covered in blood.

"Can't we give him some?" I asked.

"No. Hold the sack close to your body, like this," Stelios said, demonstrating with his own. "So no one can grab it."

"I'm going to give him some."

Without stopping, I reached into the bag and scooped up a handful of rice, then threw it over my shoulder. And one more. Glancing back, I saw the man on his knees trying to brush the rice into little piles he could scoop up.

"Stop it!" Stelios said. "Others may see you. They'll be all over us."

But we made it back to the house without more trouble. Old Yannoula opened the door, her eyes swollen from weeping. She looked at us without speaking and then turned away. That evening Stelios and I sat at either end of the table in the yellow dining room over the rice and boiled greens that Yannoula had made. On the walls were paintings I didn't understand: human beings or flowers made out of cubes and triangles. Stelios seemed bowed down by the weight of his thoughts. It was hard for me to imagine the boy who walked out with me in the hills beyond the village. I felt cut off from him so, trying to find something to say, I asked Stelios about the huge walls I'd seen, and the ruins.

"Oh, that's right," he said softly, "you don't know much about Athens."

He left the room and returned with a guidebook. He said he was sorry, but he didn't feel much like talking and was going to bed. I took the book with me to my room. But there were too many hard words for me. In the center of the book were a lot of photographs of places in the area I recognized but also some of the National Gardens, much as Sophia had described them.

The next day, I asked Stelios if he'd take me there. We waited until evening when the shadow theater would be operating—if it still existed. The gardens were not far from the house so we walked over to the entrance near the Parliament building. But as Stelios said, everything had changed. Trees and bushes had been stripped bare by hungry Athenians, some of whom were living there in flimsy shelters made of cardboard or tin roofing material. Paths still rambled among the streams and pools. But the ducks and goldfish were long gone.

"Mother wouldn't recognize it," Stelios said. "I'm glad she can't see it. This was one of her favorite places."

I remembered Sophia saying how much her husband liked the cabarets nearby. And I wondered again why he and the others had been taken by the Germans. I asked Stelios.

He sighed and said, "It's an old racial hatred." He stared straight ahead as we walked. His father had told him that Jews in Greece were Sephardic, which meant that they'd come originally from Spain hundreds of years earlier, escaping persecution there. People like Jews, people without a homeland, were often not accepted elsewhere. "But here in Greece there's been no problem. If you're Greek, that's all that matters. I was born here and my parents before me. No one has ever taken us for anything but Greek."

His father's cousin had told him it wasn't only Jews the Germans took but Gypsies, Muslims, mentally or physically sick people, communists, socialists, people with police records. If any had children, they were taken too.

"I mean, really anyone they didn't like."

A breeze whirled circles of dust on the path up ahead. Across it ran a gang of ragged boys chasing a scrawny cat. I didn't want to think what they would do when they caught it. We walked along in silence until we heard laughter and applause in the distance, a few chords of accordion music. I took his hand and we walked in that direction.

"The Germans are gone," I said. "They can't hurt anyone now, can they?"

"But the people they took, where are they? And not just the ones they took to the camps but the laborers they also abducted?"

The Greek puppet government set up by the Germans had formed Security Battalions, local men willing to do anything for food and uniforms. They carried out what came to be called *bloccos*. Along with the Germans, the Security Battalions would move into a poor section of Athens and, with megaphones, command all the men of the area into the central square. Wearing black bags with eyeholes over their heads to hide their identity, the men of Security Battalions moved among the men, pointing out any suspected of being communists or anyone else likely to be dissenters of any kind. Most of these were shot immediately. But many others were rounded up to be sent to Germany as laborers in the war factories of the Reich.

"They can't *all* just be permanently gone," Stelios said. "How can thousands of people just disappear?"

I had no idea; it was incomprehensible. But nearly everything had been so since the awfulness of the failed Italian invasion followed by the German one. There was no way to take it all in or make sense of it. Sense had left the world, it seemed, and taken these thousands of lost people with it. But Germany had been defeated. So surely some of the missing people would be able to make their way home again. That was what we had to believe, I thought, just as we rounded a corner at the edge of the gardens. I recognized the Zappeion Exhibition Hall with its great semicircle of columns from the guidebook photos. In front there was another group of ragged children and adults looking at a screen stretched between two of the columns. I was surprised that the colors and features of Karagiozis and the sultan showed through the screen, which must have been of thinner cloth than the old bedsheet we'd used in the village.

"You're a villain!" the sultan said.

"And you're a sultan," Karagiozis replied. "Sultan and villain—they have the same meaning."

The shadows on the screen were huge compared to the little ones we'd had in the village. Stelios and I stopped and looked at each other, both of us remembering the last night of the puppets in the village. But that memory hurt too much so I reminded him that he'd promised to take me here one day after the war.

"Yes," he said. "You and Takis."

As if saying his name somehow conjured him up, there Takis was, sitting on the shoulders of a soldier in a British uniform near the back of the little audience. I was shocked to see him there behaving like any ordinary little boy after all that had happened. He was concentrating on the play and hadn't seen us. I pointed him out to Stelios.

"My God, the little monster himself," he said. Takis had on a British uniform way too big for him, with rolled-up pants and shirtsleeves. He rocked back and forth clapping and laughing as the soldier reached up with both hands to steady him.

"Takis!" I called out, but he didn't hear me over the laughter of the audience. "I'm going over to talk to him."

"Why?"

I didn't know how to explain, but I said maybe it was something to do with all those nights matching my breathing to Takis's before kicking off into the darkness. We had breathed as one as if we shared the same breath. He was of my village, of my second family. "And we still don't know exactly what happened," I said.

"Are you sure about that?" Stelios asked, letting go of my hand and walking away.

The soldier supporting Takis seemed to notice me making my way through the crowd toward them before Takis did. A tall blond man with green eyes, he smiled down at me. I didn't know any English so I spoke directly to Takis.

"How are you, Takis?" When he looked down at me, all the laughter went out of his face. "Where've you been?"

"Who are you?" he asked.

"Oh, Takis, stop it. What's happened to you? I was worried."

"I don't know you."

His face was blank, a mask of indifference. He turned back to the action on the stage, ignoring me. The soldier smiled at me again, uncertainly. He could have been the one who'd taken Takis into the jeep in Halandri, but I wasn't sure. Lifting Takis off his shoulders, he set him on the ground in front of me.

"Oh, Aliki, it's you," Takis said, pretending surprise. "I didn't recognize you."

"I'll bet. Where've you been?" I heard my voice go up and realized how angry I'd been that he'd just run off. Chrysoula would have wanted me to look after him. The times were still dangerous; a boy on his own wasn't safe.

"I've been with him." He nodded at the soldier behind him. "Sergeant Whitfield. He's teaching me English. They all are."

"They . . . ?"

"At the barracks."

I wasn't sure what that was exactly, but it didn't seem a good place for a small boy on his own. His arms and legs stuck out of the uniform like sticks. "Are you getting enough to eat? Do you have a clean place to sleep?"

He laughed. "Do you?" He stuck out his tongue.

Onstage the sultan was beating Karagiozis with a club, shouting, "You have swindled me again." There was a ripple of laughter from the children that swelled into shrieks as the beating went on. Takis said something else, but I didn't catch it. Then the sergeant knelt down beside Takis and me and spoke in painfully simple Greek.

"Many children we have. They are orphans we think. What we can to do? Family? You are in his family?"

"No. Yes. Well, sort of. We're from the same village." I could see he hadn't really understood. I asked Takis where the British barracks were and he pulled a small notebook from the sergeant's shirt pocket and drew a simple diagram of the area called Kaisariani.

"I'll come find you," I told him.

"What for?" he asked.

"Someone has to look out for you now that your mother is . . ." I hadn't meant to stop there but I did. His eyes narrowed. I said, "Now that she's not around."

"What happened? Something happened, didn't it?"

"But you were there, Takis. Don't you remember how the German colonel . . . ?" Another burst of laughter interrupted me.

"I can't remember," Takis shouted over it. "I don't know."

"The colonel and his soldiers came to the house . . ."

"It's bad, isn't it? What happened? Don't tell me." He clapped his hands over his ears.

"Takis, just let me . . ."

"Don't tell," he said again. "Don't ever tell." Then he said something in English to the sergeant, who lifted him back onto his shoulders. Takis stared at the shadows on the screen as if I were no longer there.

"You come see us," the sergeant said to me. "Is strange boy. Good him to have friend."

I wondered what Takis had done, for the sergeant to call him a strange boy. Whatever it was, he seemed to me what he'd always been, confused and a little lost. I wanted to protect him. On the screen, the sultan was chasing Karagiozis, followed by a pair of villagers who were trying to beat the sultan while he was beating Karagiozis. The children in the audience were wild with laughter as the shadows chased each other off the screen. The puppet master came from behind the screen for a bow, then passed among the parents with a basket. Some put a few coins in it. One left a half loaf of bread. Takis and Sergeant Whitfield had gone.

When I got back to the house, I asked Stelios to show me the little puppet theater he'd said his father had given him. He took me into his bedroom, where the theater and puppets were set up in a corner. Sports pennants hung on the walls and signed photographs of his favorite soccer players were everywhere. There were shelves of books on the walls too, probably one containing *The Count of Monte Cristo*. I remembered Stelios telling me something about grief and happiness in that book, but I couldn't remember exactly what he'd said.

We knelt on the floor and he showed me how the theater worked. Though it was smaller than the one in the Zappeion, it seemed better made, with painted puppets of real leather with movable limbs.

"I have a plan," I said. "Take your stage and screen outside and put on the plays. You know the stories. I can help. There must be other squares and parks beside the Zappeion."

"Oh, Aliki, haven't we had enough of puppets?"

"Wouldn't it be possible to earn enough to feed ourselves and Yannoula?" We couldn't just sit there watching our supply of food dwindle. The rice and oil wouldn't last forever.

"Why don't you ask your friend Takis to do it with you?" he said, standing up. "Did the little crazy one have anything to say for himself?"

I got to my feet, ignoring the edge in Stelios's voice, and told him about Takis and the sergeant and the barracks. "I don't think Takis understands what happened to his mother."

"And *my* mother? What about *her*?" His voice thickened and he couldn't go on for a few seconds but then added, "He's probably forgotten about her too."

"I haven't."

"*He* brought the soldiers that night. We were all in the basement but Takis was outside, angry and jealous. It's not hard to figure out."

It wasn't. But I couldn't really take in the awfulness of it. I kept thinking of the colonel ruffling Takis's hair that day in front of Chrysoula's house. And she'd said he'd done so again only the day before when he'd followed up on an informant's tale that she was hoarding black market food. And who'd told him that? Would an angry boy have been able to take the colonel by the hand and lead him and his men to the house? Was it possible, especially considering the Germans had been on the verge of leaving the village, leaving Greece, pulling out? Why would they have cared at that point what was happening in Chrysoula's house, or cared that a boy was angry about something he couldn't explain?

"Whatever happened," I said, "it's been wiped out of Takis's mind. I really don't think he knows anymore. Maybe it's gone someplace deep inside, a place he can't find."

“Is that possible?”

“I don’t know.”

We didn’t talk about it any more that day. Or at all over the next few weeks. I wanted to go see Takis, but I didn’t know what to say to him. I kept on talking to Stelios about using the shadow puppets to get a little income. He said that we still had his parents’ artwork to sell, about a half dozen paintings. And then there was the remaining furniture. But so many others in Athens were doing the same thing that dealers were glutted with such merchandise. Still, when food got low, Stelios negotiated what he could. The house grew emptier and our voices echoed in the dining room.

“If not the shadow puppets,” I said, “then what?”

“I don’t know where we’d perform. No one’s heard of us and . . .”

“There are lots of parks and *plateias*.” The area wasn’t yet as militarized as it would soon become. “I can make some posters and put them up for neighborhood children the day before a performance.”

He ran his hands through his hair and paced around the dining room. “It’s just that when I think of puppets,” he said, “I remember the two of us standing there with one in our hands when the soldiers burst in.”

I thought how Takis had buried his memories and Stelios was haunted by his. I was somewhere in between, fighting to keep myself from sliding in either direction. Trying to push my own bleak feelings to one side, I thought I’d just have to get to them later because someone had to plan ahead, find a way to get us through whatever lay ahead. So I nagged.

“Look how many were in the audience at the Zappeion,” I said.

“The puppet master there is famous,” Stelios said.

“He wasn’t always. He had to start somewhere.”

“I don’t want to talk about it.”

“You have a flair for puppetry. We all saw it in the basement of Chrysoula’s house. There were good nights before the bad one, Stelios. You held us together in the dark.”

I suggested that we try to put on *Karagiozis the Baker* again. I could do the voices of Karagiozis's wife and some of the villagers. He'd do Karagiozis and the sultan. And why not here in Kolonaki? It looked to me if there was any money to be had, this was the place. All those white marble buildings.

"It's too close to the Zappeion," Stelios said. "I can't compete with the puppet master there."

He took me to a small park in Pangrati near the end of the trolley line. There were two outdoor cafés nearby. One was closed, but at the other the audience could get refreshments. We stood, looking at an open space where the stage and screen could go.

After a while he said, "We can try it. See if it works out."

"Yes, just to see."

"No need to say it in that satisfied way."

"Who, me?"

"It's an experiment. We'll see how it goes."

"Of course. See how it goes."

The next day, I made posters advertising the play to be performed in three days' time and tacked them to trees in the park and to the sides of houses and apartment buildings nearby. At home, we rehearsed. As we did so, Stelios started to lose himself in the work.

"What we could do," he said the day before the performance, "is to have Yannoula sing and play the squeeze box before the play starts." We were in the living room packing the puppets and screen into a suitcase to carry them to the park. "She was a professional singer when she was young. I mean, music halls and clubs, that kind of thing. And it's traditional to have music before a performance."

I couldn't imagine Yannoula, all in black, singing to an audience of mostly children. But Stelios brought her into the room and explained what we were going to do.

"Oh, no, I couldn't," she said. "It's been years since I sang." She giggled and covered her yellow teeth with her hand.

"Sing something for Aliki," Stelios said. "That one you used to sing before my plays."

"I don't remember it."

"Of course you do. I remember some of it." He sang in a voice much deeper than his speaking one.

Red twine braided fine,
tightly wound around a wheel . . .

"Oh, that," she said and joined him. Then Stelios went silent and Yannoula went on by herself, clasping her hands in front of her as she sang.

Set the wheel a-spinning, do,
and I'll spin a tale or two,
for all this happy company.
And may your time pass pleasantly.

Her voice was quavery but there was a sweetness in it. When she finished, I applauded.

"What do you think?" Stelios asked.

"Oh, please do it, Yannoula," I said. "And play the squeeze box too."

"No," she said, eyes cast down. "I don't want to. It was wonderful those days, singing and dancing in the musical reviews at the old Astir theater in Piraeus. But it's two husbands later and another time now. And, with just hearing about my poor Sophia, well, I'm not up to it."

But the next evening, as we were ready to leave the house with the suitcase, she came down the stairs in a long green dress. It was too big, probably made for a better-fed version of herself. And she'd put on some lipstick—a little red heart shape in the middle of her thin lips.

"A person can change her mind," she said. She was carrying a case that I guessed contained the squeeze box.

As the sun went down in the park in Pangrati, we lit kerosene lamps behind the screen and set out the puppets. People in the café nearby pointed us out to each other and a few children with their mothers dragged their café chairs nearer. There were only about eight or nine, but they were enough. Yannoula stood in front of the screen and began.

"Red twine braided fine . . ." From behind the screen, we heard more people gathering. Yannoula sang the song through twice and when she finished there was scattered applause. Stelios and I began the play, our first together.

Our audience was quiet at the beginning. At least, I thought, no babies were crying, no one whining to go home. When Karagiozis told the villager that the plucked goose had jumped out of the pan and flown away, the children laughed so much that we had to pause and wait for them to stop. And when he said that the tomatoes and potatoes had run away too, the same thing happened. From then on everything seemed to work. How easy it was to make children laugh in times that were not at all funny. At the end, Stelios had the sultan chase Karagiozis around the stage, hitting him while Karagiozis yelled, "Ouch, ouch, ouch, ouch!"

Stelios and I stood up behind the screen to take our bows in the applause and Yannoula kissed us both, leaving little lipsticky heart prints on our cheeks. Our audience began to trail away and Stelios remembered about the collection basket. He dropped some coins in it so people would get the idea and caught up with the departing audience. Carrying the Karagiozis puppet, he called out in his voice, "Who will help a poor starving actor?"

Not many, as it turned out. A few dropped some bills into the basket. But with the devaluation of the drachma when the economy collapsed during the occupation, even a thousand-drachma note was barely enough for a cup of coffee.

"Only that?" Karagiozis shouted. "You shame my mother, my father, the king of Greece and the patriarch of Constantinople!"

Some laughed, but no one gave any more. Stelios came back dejected. He flicked through the thousand-drachma bills and said, "Not even enough for a meal."

We were repacking the suitcase when the manager of the café came over and thanked us. A twitchy man named Theo with a dirty apron and red face, he said his customers had stayed longer and ordered more drinks and snacks because of our performance. Would we do it again in a few days? A longer play maybe?

"The longer the play, the more orders," he said. "I can't pay. But after each performance, you can eat and drink what you like. Within reason."

Yannoula and I were delighted. A meal every night!

But Stelios said, "What do you mean you can't pay? Your customers must pay something."

"Ah, the times, the times," Theo said, tapping the side of his head and then his nose. "Many of the customers are my relatives, so what can I do? I give them credit." He and his relatives were from the island of Crete, where, as he said, blood was stronger than money.

"Your café was nearly full tonight. All of them, relatives?"

"Most. Well, about half, but they bring their friends."

But some must pay, Stelios told him, or it wouldn't be possible for Theo to stay in business. Theo said they often brought him belongings from home or maybe things they'd stolen, who could say? Some came with suitcases of cash, enough for a few drinks. One had given a valuable ancient coin to settle an old bill; another, a good piece of jewelry.

"We'll need ten percent of whatever you take in," Stelios said.

Theo blanched and stepped back. "Do you think I'm a fool?"

He and Stelios went back and forth. There was a lot of hand waving and declarations of poverty on both sides. Finally Theo walked away. Stelios followed him and when he returned a while later, he told us that Theo would give three percent of anything that could be divided up.

"How did you manage that?" I asked.

"I told him we were going to perform at that other café over there. Then we'd see how many customers he had. I looked over at the boarded-up café.

"But it's closed," I said.

"I told him the owner had offered to reopen if we would perform there."

We were to stage another show two days later, but we had to come up with a longer play. Stelios thought we might try *Karagiozis the Senator* and began to explain it to me scene by scene. I was quietly pleased that my plan was working.

This time, the audience was bigger. We repeated the play the next night and then in the following week did another new one. Over the next few weeks, we were able to break away from our old diet of rice and olive oil. News of the once well-known Yannoula had apparently spread and she developed a small following of elderly gentlemen who waited for her after the show.

"I have no time for them," she said. "I have to think about my new career. And you too," she told me. "It's time to do something about your clothes," Yannoula said. "You've grown too tall for that little-girl dress."

She took me into her room at the back of the house, which had an old-lady smell of dried flowers and stale cologne. There she opened a battered trunk of costumes from her theater days. It also contained street clothes from another time, before Yannoula had been widowed, she said. I'd never seen anything like them. In front of a full-length mirror, she held up one dress after another, but most were either too large or too fancy and all were dated. They looked silly on me, plain little thing that I was, somewhere on the far side of pretty but not completely homely. Yannoula saw the expression on my face.

"Never mind," she said, "everything can be fixed. You have expressive eyes, but your hair—oh, yes, we must do something about that."

In the theater, she told me, audiences expected to see entertainers who looked better than themselves. It was especially true in times like these, "when everyone looks and feels so drab," she said. "People want a little sparkle."

"But I'm behind the screen."

"They see you at the end when you stand up. And anyway, in the theater one should always be *ready* to be seen."

She scissored much of my long hair and, using a sticky liquid, set the rest so that when dried, it became a mop of jiggly curls. Then she cobbled together a few outfits: a long one of shiny red material, then a pale blue, drapey thing with puffed sleeves. And a couple of other, plainer ones. When I looked in the mirror, my reflection reminded me of that cartoon character I'd seen on movie posters downtown, Betty Boop. One thing was certain, though: I didn't look like a skinny village girl anymore.

Stelios was stunned when I came downstairs. For the first time since those earliest days, he spoke with a stammer. "Aliki, you don't—don't—don't . . . look like yourself. More like, I mean, someone out of a movie."

"Betty Boop?"

"Who? Uh, well, not ex-exactly. But I wouldn't have recognized you."

I felt the color rise in my cheeks. So this was the effect of a new look? Not that our next audience noticed. Before we could begin the performance, an argument started inside the café. It sounded like two men insulting each other's politics at first, but soon others joined in. Tables were pushed over and bottles smashed. Someone drew a pistol and there were shots. We threw our things into the suitcase and fled home. The next day Stelios went to see what had happened, but the café was closed and the area cordoned off. Theo was not around.

Such things and worse were happening all over Athens. No one group seemed to take control after the liberation. We'd heard that the prewar prime minister and some of his old government had returned from their exile in Cairo. They'd been escorted by the British and supported by the royalist faction—the Republican League—though the king himself hadn't returned. But the communist-based National Liberation Front and its military wing were in control of large parts of the country, including some sections of Athens, and considered themselves the rightful government. We felt fairly safe in our embassy neighborhood, protected by British forces and Greek police. But we heard that People's Committees had been set up by the communist groups to try anyone suspected of collaborating with the Germans, especially members of the Security Battalions who'd taken part in the *bloccos*. In the morning, even in Kolonaki, there were sometimes bodies in the street and not just of people who'd starved to death. Down the block from us, a man was found hanged from a plane tree.

With few functioning newspapers and not much on local radio, we had to rely on word of mouth to find out which groups had taken control of which neighborhoods outside our own. I missed Chrysoula's big Zenith, partly for the news but also because without it, I no longer heard my father's voice. Was he still fretting over his misplaced ax and hammer or saw? Would I ever hear from him again? I hoped so, but I needn't have worried.

And was it safe for us to continue performing anywhere else in the city? We couldn't find out for certain. Yannoula was especially put out by this.

"Just when I've returned to the stage," she said. "All right, the small stage. All right, the *very* small stage."

We gave one last Athens performance nearby in Kolonaki Square. But partway through the play, a pair of Greek policemen along with a British soldier showed up and started to interrogate audience members, looking for any parents who might belong to People's Committees. The performance had to stop while individuals in the audience were questioned. It seemed unlikely that People's Committee members would attend a puppet show or, even if they did, admit their affiliation. But one or two people were led away. Then I realized that the British soldier was the one who'd been with Takis at the Zappeion, Sergeant Whitfield. I'd told him that I would come see Takis, but with all the work for the performances, I hadn't done it. I still worried about him every day and felt bad about not going to see him.

Stelios had started packing things up because those in the audience who hadn't been questioned were leaving quietly. I went over to the sergeant after he'd finished talking to a young woman, but he didn't recognize me. Those new curls! So I said Takis's name to him and this he seemed to understand. He called to one of the policemen, who knew some English, to come translate for us. The policeman gave me a little bow and said he was glad to be of service to the young lady. No one had ever called me that before and I supposed it was the result of Yannoula's efforts. His dark Greek looks with chiseled nose and chin were as striking as Sergeant Whitfield's blondness. The sergeant said something to the policeman in English and he translated.

"He wants you to take this Takis away from the barracks, please. And the others, if you can help us to place them."

There were about fifty war orphans there, the policeman explained, and the British were going to have to turn them all over to the International Red Cross if no one would claim them here. No one knew for sure what would happen to them, but they were likely to be placed in orphanages in other countries where the fighting had ended. These were the other boys he'd mentioned at the Zappeion, I supposed. But their situation had changed. The sergeant said something else and the policeman translated that there'd been complaints from residents near the barracks about Takis specifically.

"They found him naked," the policeman said. "Wandering around their back gardens, talking to himself." When he was brought back to the barracks, Takis said that the nearby trees had told him to take off his clothes. And the roots of the trees whispered about underground tunnels beneath the field of tents that made up the barracks.

Sergeant Whitfield twirled his finger beside his head. *"Trellos,"* the policeman said.

Running around naked certainly sounded crazy enough, but it was new behavior for Takis, as far as I knew. Talking to trees was more familiar ground. He'd once claimed the village pines wanted to teach him to fly. Was the sergeant certain it was Takis in question? He nodded.

"Tell the sergeant I'll come talk to Takis," I said. "But I don't know what I can do."

"Can't you take him away? Find another place for him? He's not a bad boy. Just, you know, *trellos*. He needs a doctor, treatment. We can't take responsibility."

I said again that I didn't know what I could do. But I would try. The policeman told me to use Sergeant Whitfield's name to get past the sentry. He apologized for ruining our performance.

Stelios and I walked home together; Yannoula had gone on ahead. Why had I been talking with the two military men? he asked. Didn't I know that the police were known to have their own death squads just as bad as the People's Committees? It was dangerous to come to the attention of either side.

"Someone," he said, "one of the ancients, I don't remember which, wrote, 'When the buffalo fight in the marsh, it's the frogs who pay.' I think we frogs better stay out of the way. No more performances for now."

I took a deep breath and told him that Takis might be sent to a foreign orphanage. We couldn't let that happen to him.

"Why not?" he said. "It might be the best thing. He could have a new life."

"A new life in an orphanage?"

"Maybe someone would adopt him."

"He wouldn't speak the language."

"He'd learn it if he had to."

A cold wind slapped into us and sent leaves chattering around our feet. It was already late November. The cold winter rains would be coming down on all of us before long, including those boys up in Kaisariani. "Look, Stelios," I said, "Chrysoula took me in when I had no place to go. And you and your mother. Now we're safe, but her son isn't."

Stelios didn't say anything for a few minutes.

When he finally did answer me, he said, "Well, speaking of his mother and mine, have you so quickly put their deaths behind you?" He asked this calmly, but his voice was hard. "Don't forget that when I asked Takis about his part in it, he answered by *biting* me. I mean, I still have the marks." He touched his leg as we walked. "And then he ran away the next day. So what makes you think he'd want to be with us—and that's what *you* want, isn't it?—even if *we* wanted him too? And there's also Yannoula to think of. Would she want Takis in the house? I've told her how it was he came to attack me."

Stelios was right; there was no getting away from it. I said that of course I hadn't forgotten any of what happened in the village. I could never forget. But in spite of everything, I needed to protect Takis, even if mostly from himself, for now, anyway. I owed that much to Chrysoula.

"I keep thinking that she's watching us," I said, "and watching Takis and . . ."

"You have a good heart, Aliki," Stelios said, as we went through the gate into the courtyard in front of the house. "Take care that it doesn't ruin you and the rest of us too."

I started to say something. I can't remember what because he stopped me with his mouth on mine. It happened quickly and was over just as fast. He stepped back, looking as if he'd surprised even himself, just as Yannoula opened the door. He hurried inside the house ahead of me, leaving me staring at Yannoula with the heat of his sudden kiss spread all over my face.

"Well," Yannoula said. "Well."

The next morning, a Sunday, I left the house early. Neither Stelios nor Yannoula was up so I made my way out of Kolonaki and across Vassilisis Sophias Avenue. The air was crisp and filled with the scent of chestnuts that vendors had been grilling on their street corner braziers the last few weeks. I hadn't slept much the night before, trying to decide what to do. Stelios's kiss had made me light-headed and, as I lay awake, it put Takis right out of my mind. I thought of what Chrysoula had said about men and I started to think about what married couples might likely do with each other at night. I'd flung the covers off, even though the room was cold. When I'd cooled down a bit, I was embarrassed by my thoughts and how I'd completely forgotten about Takis. I resolved to set out early the next morning.

In the street, I buttoned my coat, one of Yannoula's old ones, and held my handbag close to me as I walked into the Pangrati section of the city. From a balcony above, I heard someone call down to me. I couldn't make out the words, but he pointed in the direction I was going—a warning of some kind—but I couldn't turn back, couldn't risk losing Takis to a foreign orphanage. I wasn't sure what neighborhoods in that area were controlled by which armed groups. But I went on. There was a street sign about a monastery and cemetery at Kaisariani, pointing uphill in the eastern foothills of Mt. Hymettus.

As I rounded a corner, I saw the street ahead was blocked by a barricade of wooden sawhorses. Behind it was a single man with a machine gun. He looked as if he hadn't seen me yet. I stood still, wondering if I should run into one of the side streets. But he turned, saw me and ordered me to halt.

"I *am* halted," I said.

"You can't come into this area. What's your business?"

"I'm looking for the monastery at Kaisariani."

He came over to me. "And why would that be?" he asked, looking me up and down, grinning. He was just a boy with the faint trace of a mustache. He wore old army fatigues, but the insignias had been ripped off so there was no way of telling which group he was with. "You're going to pray with the monks, I suppose?"

"There's a cemetery there."

"You visit the dead a lot, do you? I've never seen you through here before." He took my handbag and rummaged in it. He asked me where I lived and when I'd told him, he stooped down and looked directly into my eyes, as if to find out if I was telling the truth. I didn't flinch or look away. Then he gave back my handbag, but as I took it from him, he slipped his hand up under my skirt and tried to slide his fingers inside my underwear. I shrieked and jumped away. "My regards to the dead!" he called after me as I raced up the hill, my face still aflame with anger.

The barracks turned out to be just a field of tents up above the monastery. I asked the sentry for Sergeant Whitfield and was told he wasn't there so I said he'd asked me to visit the boy named Takis. The guard told me to wait. When he came out, Takis was still dressed in a British uniform too big for him.

"Aliki!" he said. He had an uncertain smile, which quickly disappeared. "You look different. What happened to your hair?"

"It's changed."

"I'll say."

There was an awkward silence, then I asked how he was and he said, "I probably look different too. Like a British soldier, right?" He snapped his right hand to his forehead in a smart salute.

"You look the same as you did at the Zappeion, a boy in a uniform too big for him."

"And you still have that old-woman voice. I'd forgotten it. Say something else."

"I need to talk to you."

"Oh?" He glanced around as if looking for a way out. Then he scraped his shoe along the ground and looked down at it. I said I'd talked with Sergeant Whitfield and he'd told me about the International Red Cross taking orphans away. Takis said he already knew all about that. But he liked it here and wasn't going to leave.

"They can't make me," he said.

"I'm sure they can. It's not just you. There are a lot of others, aren't there? Where do you all live?"

"Tents. Over there." He pointed at a rocky meadow to our right. I could see a group of boys kicking a soccer ball and yelling.

"Winter's coming," I said. "You can't be outside in the rain and wind."

"The soldiers are."

"That's different. They're grown men. And they don't want the responsibility for you all. You could get sick. Who'll look after you?"

He shrugged and slumped his shoulders and looked at his shoe again. He'd lost the spark he'd had in the village, I thought. The lively, noisy boy he'd been there had been replaced by this sad, stubborn one who had no real place anywhere. I said he'd need a place to be if he was going to remain in Greece. What would he think about joining Stelios and me at his parents' house?

"Stelios?" He frowned. "You're living in *his* house?" I nodded and the frown became a sneer. "I guess he's your *boyfriend* now."

Ah, I thought, that old jealousy was still burning away. And was Stelios really my boyfriend? What did that mean? In the village, parents arranged everything for a young couple, who were never alone until their lives were planned out by their families. And here I was living in the same house with Stelios, who definitely wasn't a relative. What would Chrysoula have thought?

"We're not alone in the house," I said. "There's an older woman, a housekeeper who looks after us." I blushed at having to justify myself to him. What did he know about these things anyway? I told him how to find the house and repeated that British soldiers were going to send him and the other boys away before long. He had to find somewhere to stay. If not with Stelios and me, then where?

"What do you care?" he asked.

"It'll be safer for all of us if we stick together."

He turned away from me, looking at a nearby mulberry tree as if expecting it to advise him.

I said, "I'm sure your mother would want that."

He wheeled around. "Ah, now I know why you're here. You want to talk about . . ." He broke off, maybe realizing how loud he'd become, and looked around. "Go away," he said.

"Look, Takis . . ." I stepped toward him.

"Just go away." He was nearly shouting. "It wasn't my fault."

"*What* wasn't your fault?"

"Whatever happened."

"And that was . . . ?"

"I can't remember. I can't get to it."

"Do you remember the German colonel? How it was he came to the house that last night and . . . ?"

"Oh," he said, sneering again, "I see what you want. You want to turn me in as a collaborator."

"What?"

"Just because I talked to him sometimes. That German. But he couldn't understand me. So what?" He spat on the ground, an adult gesture, something he'd picked up from the soldiers, no doubt. "You know what they do with collaborators."

"But you're not one."

"I remember wanting to punish Stelios. His stupid play. And he was always talking to you." He paused and seemed to wait for the effect of this on me. I thought maybe we were getting somewhere, though I wasn't sure where that was and kept my face blank. Then he added, "When I get angry, the part of my brain that's red takes over the part that's white."

I didn't know what to say to that.

"I have a bad brain, that's all." He sucked in his breath, looked down at the ground and said, "You'd better leave me alone."

"I can't. I'm sorry, but I can't."

"Go away. Don't come back." He started walking toward the boys who were kicking the ball in the meadow. I was losing him.

I called out, "Sergeant Whitfield says you walk around naked, and that you talk to trees. Do you think they'll let that go on? Don't you understand? They'll put you away, Takis."

He stopped and stood still. His shoulders were shaking slightly. I went over and put my arm around him. When he'd got control he said, "Can't we go back, Aliki, back to the village to the way things were before? Before we left, even before Stelios and his mother came? It wasn't so bad then, was it? Remember how you wrote notes all the time and wouldn't speak? But I understood you and we played cards and . . ."

I held him until he stopped talking. He stood in my arms silently another moment then broke free and ran off toward the boys in the meadow. I started after him, then stopped. I watched until he joined them and I could no longer make out one from another, just boys running. I started after him, but something inside me said, *Let him go. He's dangerous.* Standing there with one foot in front of the other, I felt stalled between my desire to save him from an orphanage and Stelios's certainty that bringing him into the house was a dangerous idea. Most of what Takis had just said to me seemed to line up with Stelios's point of view.

I turned back, divided and worried, so much so that I didn't notice I wasn't going down the hill the way I'd come up. I was on an unfamiliar, deserted street. Turning one way then another, I had little idea of where I was. At the curb, three scrawny dogs were nosing a pile of rags that might have been a person. I ran past and one dog chased after me. Running faster, I tripped and skidded to my knees on the cobblestone street. The dog stopped, baring its teeth. Then a pair of hands reached down, grabbed the dog by its neck and snapped it. It barely had time to yelp. My rescuer was tall with an enormous black beard and two belts of ammunition across his chest.

"What are you doing in this street?" he asked. "Visiting the British?" He was joined by another man, a smaller version of himself. They didn't look at all like the one I'd met on the way up. I guessed they were another group entirely, maybe the sort that worked for the People's Committees.

"No," I lied. "I'm the cleaning girl for Mrs. Longos up the hill. Just trying to get home when that dog attacked." I don't know, even now, where that story came from. But I suppose it was the beginning of a reaction that would last me all my life: when in a corner, say or do something, *anything.*

"You're not dressed like a cleaning girl," he said, looking me over. "And there aren't many around here who could afford one."

He helped me to my feet. We were at the open end of a barricade made of furniture dragged out of houses. Sofas were stacked on top of beds and dining room tables. Rolled-up carpets had been thrown over a jumble of chairs. On top of a cabinet with smashed glass doors sat a painting of a three-masted ship in a harbor at sunset.

The first man asked the other if he knew anyone named Longos in the area. The man shrugged. I noticed a sign above a closed greengrocer's shop across the street and said, "Her husband used to be the greengrocer. Over there."

They looked at each other and said something I couldn't catch. Then the big one turned back to me and said, "We think you're carrying messages from the British base up there. Who would suspect a girl, yes? I think maybe we should shoot you."

He smiled when he said it, but his eyes were flat, dead. My scraped knees started to shake. I tried to keep my voice steady. "I don't know anything about that. My father's waiting for me. He's not well and I don't want to worry him."

I don't know if this gained me much ground, but they took my handbag and told me to wait over by the barricade of furniture. My knees were shaking so badly I could barely stand so I pulled a chair off the pile, sat down and rubbed them. In the next half hour, several other men arrived and talked excitedly with the first two. They turned to look at me from time to time but seemed to lose interest as conversations became arguments with lots of shouting and hands slicing the air. It was hard to follow, with words I didn't know, like *proletariat class struggle* or something like that. At least no one was paying attention to me. So finally I stood up and simply walked around the open end of the barricade. Looking back, I saw that they were all still arguing.

I ran down the hill and back to Kolonaki, where I realized that they hadn't given back my handbag. But it seemed a small loss and as I slipped back into the house, I thought with relief that at least I'd escaped the buffalo in the marsh. For now.

CASSETTE 3 • Side 1

We buried Zephyra the day before yesterday, may the earth rest lightly on her. The men carried her coffin on their shoulders through the cemetery gates while we women stood on either side making bird noises to ward off bad spirits.

Once inside, I nodded to the graves of those I've loved. I'll lie next to them one of these days, but who will be left to lament for the lamenter? Not the other women, who lack the—What should I call it?—the inner eye and ear to take in what has not been seen or spoken. Still, they were kind enough to give me a nice shoulder of lamb for my services at the wake, though I would have lamented for nothing. I stewed the lamb with chopped spring onions, romaine and dill and planned to finish it off with an egg-lemon sauce made from the broth, all in Zephyra's honor. As I was stirring it, I thought of her the last time I saw her, that sound she made as she pawed the bedclothes. I turned the flame down to a simmer and put a lid on the pot. Then I set out for the next village to see Aphrodite, our wisewoman, who was the last to be with Zephyra.

Aphrodite's house—if it could be called that—was outside the village, standing by itself in a meadow. It was just a stone hut of the kind shepherds use for temporary shelter in bad weather. The door was ajar and inside I could see a small fire burning in a grate in a corner, though the day was warm. As my eyes adjusted to the dark inside, I made out bunches of herbs hung so thickly from the ceiling that I had to stoop to enter. The walls were covered in icons. I called out her name. A pile of rugs in another corner stirred. Aphrodite sat up and blinked.

"Is someone there?" she asked. The light was behind me so I told her who I was. She got to her feet and came closer, peering into my face. "Ah, that one," she said. "Am I dead yet? Did you come for a pair of my shoes?"

"I'm not here to lament," I said.

"Oh? They say that when you arrive, death is at hand."

"They say the same of you."

She giggled and threw her hands in the air. "What can we do? We are like sisters. We prepare the way."

We were not exactly competitors, but we've always stayed out of each other's paths. Aphrodite deals with healing, charms and curses, telling the future by throwing smooth stones on the floor and reading their patterns. Or acting as a go-between when villagers need the favors of saints. I'm not saying these things were nonsense, but they weren't of much use to me. And to fewer and fewer villagers as the years turned, but of course that was true of lamenting too. Aphrodite served the living and I the dying or their relatives. But sometimes her services and mine overlapped near that space between life and death. So it had been with Zephyra.

Aphrodite took my arm and pulled me farther inside. On the dirt floor were clumps of white feathers here and there, as if a chicken had recently been plucked. She motioned me to a low stool on one side of a table and she sat down opposite. From the nearness of her, I understood that there must be no place in the hut for her to wash. Or maybe there was little inclination? Her hair was matted and her skin looked gray. She opened her mouth to say something but started coughing so hard she couldn't speak. When she got control, she wiped her mouth with the corner of the rug draped around her shoulders and stared at me as if she'd only just noticed I was there.

"It's about Zephyra, isn't it?" she asked.

"How do you know?"

"How do I know anything? How do *you*?"

I couldn't answer that so I started to tell her how Zephyra had acted the last time I saw her, but Aphrodite cut me off.

"Yes, yes, I know. She was the same with me."

"What did it mean?"

"What did *what* mean?"

"The noises."

"Is that all that's bothering you? I can tell you about it, but little else. I keep the secrets of the dying, you know."

During the time of the Germans, Aphrodite said, Zephyra's mother made a goatskin disguise for her daughter. Zephyra wasn't much bigger than a young kid herself so her mother fitted the skin over her and tied the leg bits to Zephyra's own legs and arms with twine.

"Like a costume for Carnival," Aphrodite said.

"But no one celebrated Carnival in those years."

"That's right, you were there in that same village then, weren't you?" She paused and scratched herself roughly around the waist. "The charcoal maker's daughter, taken in by Chrysoula. We heard of you all even over here. You and your secret guests."

There were few still alive in the village who even remembered those events. I don't know why I hadn't thought about it before, but of course Aphrodite, who looked older than God, was probably around my age. But I was startled to know that news of Sophia and Stelios had traveled even to this village.

"Did everybody know?" I asked.

"Some did. Some didn't."

Before I could ask who knew exactly, she began coughing again, just a little at first, then a spasm overwhelmed her in terrible heaves. I reached across to hold her shoulders until it passed.

"What are you doing about this cough?" I asked.

"I am in *his* care." She pointed at one of the icons on the wall. "St. Athanassios. Don't worry about me." She adjusted her shoulder rug and said, "What everyone knew about your village was Zephyra and the goats. Nothing like that happened here."

Aphrodite paused and picked a chicken feather off the rug around her shoulders. She studied it carefully as if she'd never seen one before. She showed no interest in continuing to speak. I took some coins from my pocket and slid them across the table, saying as I did so that here was something for a few candles to light in front of the icon of St. Athanassios. Aphrodite glanced at the coins, then covered them with her hand.

"Everyone was starving," she said. "Well, you remember how it was. But the Germans had some goats in a pen. They'd taken them from Manos, the goatherd. Was that his name? No, Christos? Anyhow, Zephyra's mother would send her among the goats late at night in her disguise and on all fours. The goats could smell one of their own on her so they weren't startled or noisy. You know how goats are. Skittish."

She wrinkled her face and sniffed about as if she were a goat testing the air. For a second she reminded me of Zephyra as I'd last seen her.

"Well, Zephyra would slide a rope around the neck of one and lead it to her house, where her mother would slit its throat and skin it. They had plenty to eat when others had none."

Except for us, I thought. Sophia's gold sovereigns and the black market food they bought had kept us alive. But it hadn't taken the

Germans long to realize the goats were disappearing faster than they could eat them, Aphrodite said. They could count, after all. So a guard was posted and that stopped Zephyra's stealing. Soon she and her mother were back to eating snails and grass like the rest of the village.

I tried to imagine little Zephyra in a goatskin coaxing an actual goat along the street. It must have been terrifying for her; the Germans were brutal to anyone caught stealing, even children. In a village in the next valley over, they'd beaten a boy to death with the butts of their rifles for stealing potatoes off one of their trucks although the year's crop had been seized from the villagers there in the first place. And what could be said of Zephyra's mother that she risked her daughter's life that way? Poor Zephyra must have carried the experience all the way to her deathbed. In the cloudiness of her last days, the sound of goats intruded on her own dying. I've seen before how a mind near death fixes on an event known only to it.

Aphrodite pulled the coins toward her and said nothing more.

At home, beating the egg-lemon sauce for my lamb, I reflected on how village secrets always come out in time. But here was this velvety piece of lamb in its tart sauce to remind me of the comfort of food and the degrading acts people could be brought to by the lack of it.

In Athens, food hadn't suddenly appeared just because the war was over. That winter—what was the year, '44, I think—was to be one of the worst. But we did get some good news when Stelios received a hand-delivered message from the owner of a café along the waterfront in the Piraeus harbor to the south of Athens. He'd somehow heard about our performances in Pangrati and sent a message offering ten percent of each evening's take plus ticket sales—no more passing a basket—if we would perform *The Hero Katsondonis* at his café. The long play was one of "the heroics," usually performed over three successive evenings. Stelios had seen it several times and believed he could work out the story in two parts and teach it to me. Of course Piraeus was a long way, through dangerous neighborhoods, but the café owner had offered to send a car for us. That he could afford this meant that he ran a much more profitable café than Theo's in Pangrati.

The message had come while I'd been off seeing Takis. When I came in, Stelios and Yannoula were in the dining room talking about making the new puppets we'd need for the performance.

"Katsondonis has a big mustache like this," Stelios was saying, sketching on a pad. "And he wears the warrior's *fustanella*." He roughed in the white pleated skirt that had been part of the military uniform of revolutionary officers.

I wanted to tell Stelios where I'd been, but I knew he wouldn't like it. If I told him how Takis had behaved, that would put an end to the possibility of his joining us, if it existed at all. But how could we let Takis go with people who'd never understand what was going on inside him? Not that I had any idea about that, but I knew he had a place full of sickness inside. If we could all stay together, maybe it would go away as he grew up, or we could find someone who knew about these things. But how much time did we have? Sergeant Whitfield hadn't said when the removal of the orphans would begin.

When Stelios was working on a play, he almost seemed to forget himself; almost seemed happy. When he told me about the message from Piraeus, he talked about Captain Katsondonis, who'd been a folk hero of the War of Independence that ended the Turkish occupation of Greece in the nineteenth century. Originally a shepherd, Katsondonis led an uprising. But a Greek priest betrayed him for a single gold sovereign.

"The Turks executed him with sledgehammers," Stelios said, raising his arms in the air as if he were holding one of the hammers. "They broke all his bones on an anvil!" He slammed his arms down in front of him with a shout: "Sperm of the devil!"

I jumped and what was left of my intent to talk to him about Takis evaporated. Sometimes Stelios was so forceful that he startled me. In the last scene of the play, the spirit of Greece, in the form of a winged young man crowned with laurel, descended and claimed Katsondonis for History.

Over the next few days, Yannoula practiced the melancholy songs from the play.

"Are they sad enough?" she asked. "I think I need to sound more tearful."

The play was indeed sad, full of Turks (always dastardly) and Greeks (always brave). I had several vocal roles, primarily that of Angeliki, Greek wife of the hero—"They have boiled my father-in-law in oil, the villains!" And that of the Turkish ruler, Ali Pasha—"I will smash your ankles and scatter them on the road!" I loved learning all this patriotic history. We'd had some of it in school before the war, but it was never as exciting as Stelios made it. I was looking forward to our first performance but even more to riding to Piraeus in a big car.

But the car was actually small, heavily dented and so covered with dust and dirt that you could barely make out its liverish color. The driver was a burly man in a stained undershirt who introduced himself as Michaelis. When he heard that I'd never been to Piraeus and Stelios and Yannoula hadn't seen it for years, he talked all the way.

"This whole area," he said, waving his arm out the window as we passed through a run-down neighborhood, "it's controlled by guerrillas from the so-called National Liberation Front. Communists. Liberate us from what? Stupidity and poverty?" Farther on, in a better area, he said, "There's Republican League around here—you can smell them."

"So who's worse, left or right?" Stelios asked.

"From what I hear, whoever is in charge in any area—they're tyrants then and there. But it all changes and the next one is worse than the last. What a joke!"

"Maybe you should run the government yourself."

"Maybe we all should. That's what's wrong with this place—we *all* think we're the government. You've got the police, the British and the royalists on one side trying to get the king back and splintered communist and socialist groups on the other. And they all think *they're* the government. Bah, a curse on them all!"

He was getting out, he told us, emigrating to Canada. He had a cousin who ran a restaurant there, Spyros, his name was, who was going to make him a partner.

"But it's cold there, isn't it?" Yannoula said.

"Yes, yes, I know, and I *hate* the cold. I was in the army up on the Albanian front, trying to hold back the macaroni-eaters. Now *that* was cold. Hands had to be amputated. Feet. Outside the medical tent there was a big pile of hands and feet. And for what? I ask you. The Nazis came to the aid of the Italians and drove us back anyway. You know the rest."

There was silence in the car until Michaelis dropped us at the café in a central *plateia* that was crowded with people who'd come for our performance. Among them were several armed guerrillas with machine gun belts across their chests. They looked like the ones who'd stopped me on the way back from seeing Takis, but we were far from there. In the play, when Katsondonis and his warriors took their oath to free their homeland from the Turks or ". . . filled with honor's bullets, together upon the earth we'll fall!" the armed men stood up and sang the national anthem.

In the second act, Stelios did the voice of Katsondonis's son, who says to his mother (me), when they hear distant shooting, "Listen, Mother, listen, they're fighting."

Then I responded, "Yes, my child, but *who* is fighting?"

The guerrillas in the audience cried out, "We are!" and everyone applauded, drowning out the next lines. The audience was entering the play. It was going to be a long performance. After it finished, the owner showed us to rooms above the café as it was too far to get back to Kolonaki and return for the concluding performance the next night. Yannoula and I shared a room and Stelios was down the hall. Yannoula had brought a large beaker of wine back to the room and was getting through it, sitting on the bed opposite mine. She said she'd be sleeping in her clothes and told me to do the same.

"Bedbugs," she said. "These ports, they're always full of them. The foreign sailors, they're the ones that bring them. I used to sing in reviews at the Astir music hall just over there," she said, pointing out the window, "and sailors came to the shows. They always left their crawly little friends behind."

The reviews had featured many acts: comedians, trained animals, magicians, ventriloquists. They had changed regularly, but Yannoula had been a permanent feature. "I was famous, you know. Not *really* famous, but enough for it to be fun. And not only for my voice!"

She winked. She told me the prime minister had once come to the theater wearing dark glasses so as not to be recognized. And after the performance, she'd received a huge spray of expensive orchids from an anonymous gentleman.

"Oh, I had so many beautiful gowns, you can't imagine. The red ones always suited me best, you know, with my high coloring." She turned her head just so as if to show me, but without makeup, her skin had the papery whiteness of someone long out of the sun. While she talked, we could hear intermittent gunfire from another part of the port.

"Listen to them out there," she said. "Now that we don't have the Germans to kill us, we have to do it ourselves. That Michaelis is right, of course, but we don't all have relatives in Canada. And anyhow, someday this will all be over and we'll be glad we're not freezing in Toronto."

When things calmed down Stelios would likely be called to do his national service, she said; he'd been too young to fight in the north where Michaelis had been, thanks to God. But we weren't going to let Stelios go, were we? "We'll hide him. Or, wait, we could dress him up as a girl. Like Achilles." She said that Achilles's mother had disguised him as a girl and hidden him on the island of Skyros to evade the Trojan War. "Brave Achilles, just imagine, in skirts. But Odysseus found him out and tricked him into joining the forces. Did you know that?"

I didn't know anything, I said, and told her about the village school closing.

"Get Stelios to teach you. He told me that about Achilles. Smart boy, our Stelios." She'd noticed the way he'd been looking at me, she said, especially that night she'd opened the courtyard door and he'd rushed inside. I felt myself blushing. "Oh, I'm embarrassing you," she said. "I'm as blunt as a battleship sometimes."

She handed me a glass of the wine and told me to go ahead and try it; it wasn't going to hurt me. "You have to learn to drink sometime." The wine tasted strongly of resin, but I got it down and the glass was quickly refilled. After a bit I didn't notice the taste so much. Yannoula was telling me how naughty she'd been in her theater days.

"Here's a little secret: I dyed my hair. Not that on my head, which was as black as midnight. No, I mean down there, on my what-do-you-call-it. With the help of a little peroxide and a toothbrush, I was blond below and black on top. Let me tell you, it drove the men wild!"

Seeing me blushing again, she apologized. "I keep forgetting how young you are, Aliki. You act so much older. Well, everyone's an adult these days. Some are just shorter than others."

What she really wanted to know, she said, was who was this boy who'd bitten Stelios back in the village? And what had really happened there? What Stelios had told her hadn't quite made sense; he'd been so angry he could barely get it all out. Her Sophia, really her dearest friend even though her employer, was dead; that was all she'd understood.

I wasn't sure where to begin. I said that Takis had probably brought the soldiers that night because he was jealous. He seemed crazy enough to do such a thing, though he had no memory of it and denied it. Chrysoula's house had been under suspicion before that and someone had been informing on her. But it was the village women throwing pebbles at the Germans that brought on the shooting that killed both women and many other villagers. Takis, out of his mind from the death of his mother, had attacked Stelios. He needed help and there was no one to give it, no one to love him. Except me. And I was letting him down.

"What a story! Letting him down? Because of him, my dear Sophia and the others are dead!"

"Maybe."

When I explained about the orphanage, she said, "Oh, dear, how awful. But if he really is so disturbed it might be for the best. Where's this base he's at?" I told her the route I'd taken. "*Theo mou*, Aliki. By yourself you did this?"

"I couldn't bring myself to tell Stelios. I want to get Takis out of there. I think . . . I think he could live with us."

"*Really?* Is that a good idea?"

"I don't know. I can't just abandon him." My voice quavered and my vision blurred. "I can't."

Yannoula came over to sit beside me and put her arm around my shoulders.

"Let me think about this. It's far more complicated than I realized. I could have a word with Stelios, I suppose. But I'm not sure what I'd say."

"He's stubborn."

"Oh, well. Two women, one stubborn man. It's the history of the world. Let me think about all this." She moved back to her bed and finished the wine in silence. Then she yawned and said, "Right now I think I've got an appointment with some bedbugs."

She climbed into bed fully clothed. I got into the other bed. Through the room's single window the lights of the city had died down and high above in the night sky the stars were like salt shaken from a giant saltcellar. But they seemed to sway. Or was I the one swaying from the wine?

The gunfire continued and was still going on by the time of our performance the next evening. It grew closer as the play unfolded. When Katsondonis was saying good-bye to his wife, a few people in the audience got up and left. Further along, others did the same. Afraid we'd lose the whole audience and have to return their money, we tried to speak our lines faster. Stelios raced through one of the hero's final speeches.

I say good-bye to you, tall hills, and to you, rocks on high.
You are my witnesses and must to all proclaim
That with a few soldiers, I put thousands to flight.

An explosion nearby was followed by the tremendous noise of what seemed to be a collapsing building. A group of men with rifles charged past the screen, shouting, "Death to fascism!" They disappeared inside the ruined apartment block. By then our audience was gone.

Michaelis took us back to Kolonaki but by an indirect route through side streets and lanes. When we asked why, he said that the day before, December 3, there'd been a demonstration organized by communist groups in front of Parliament in the very place where, only months before, crowds had celebrated the liberation. It was to protest the fact that the British, along with the old government and the Athens police, had demanded that members of the groups turn in their weapons.

"The police got scared—probably thought it was some kind of takeover—and stupidly fired into the crowd. What idiots! Blood everywhere, more than thirty dead and a hundred or more wounded. Now mobs are attacking police stations all over the city. And the British, they're trying to protect the police, the fools."

Right on cue we turned into a *plateia* not far from the house and nearly collided with a British tank coming straight at us. Michaelis tried to back out, but we were blocked from behind by another tank.

He shouted out the window in English at no one in particular, "What you want, to kill me? Or better I should do it myself to save you the trouble?"

But the tanks weren't interested in us. The one behind moved forward and Michaelis was able to back out, turn around and, in a few minutes, rush through the deserted streets. We were home. "Go inside, lock your doors," Michaelis said. "Don't go out even if you're starving." Stelios invited him to come inside and stay until it was safe to drive back to Piraeus.

"And when will that be, the year after next?" He was gone before Stelios could insist.

The fighting continued the rest of the month. Our neighborhood remained under British control and we were advised not to leave the house except to run a few close-to-home errands. We had enough money from our Piraeus performances to buy the few supplies we needed. To go anywhere else, people had to pass military checkpoints. Anyone who crossed back and forth regularly was suspected of being a spy and could be shot on the spot. We could hear gunfire in spurts from other neighborhoods nearby. Some of the worst fighting was up near the Kaisariani area, we heard. So when Yannoula tried to discuss Takis with Stelios, whether or not to have him in the house wasn't the point anymore. There was no chance of getting safely up to the British base by then. And, as Stelios said, probably the orphans had already been sent abroad.

It was my fault, I thought; my own indecision was to blame. I should have gone after Takis that day. Stelios might have given in if I'd just shown up with Takis. I was certain I could have looked after him and kept him from exploding again. But it was too late.

I lost all appetite and energy. Even the news that the British were bringing in more troops barely registered. Stelios told Yannoula and me that he'd heard that Winston Churchill himself was here, determined not to see the city fall to communist hands. He was directing the British forces from the steps of the Grande Bretagne Hotel in Syntagma Square. I didn't care. On Christmas Day, I went to bed and didn't want to get up. For days I drifted and dreamed and slept and drifted again. Yannoula brought me soup and helped me to the bathroom, where I threw it up.

The place of laments—I recognized it when I drifted into it. Oh, this again, I thought, the door partway open, the light from behind it. What did this place want of me? I sensed no laments. But there were other dead there now. First my father, who didn't ask me about his missing tools. Did he know I wasn't in the village anymore? He was still complaining that there wasn't a decent *kafeneion* where a body could sit with friends, bothering a string of beads. *What's the point of being eternally dead if you can't even get a good cup of coffee?* Someone was circulating another petition, but he didn't expect much to come of it. *Around here, no one ever learns anything. Everyone's as stupid as the day they got here.*

Chrysoula was there too and welcomed me the traditional way, saying, *It is good that you have come*, and I gave the formal response, "It is good that I have found you." She handed me a glass of cool water and some preserved cherries on a spoon. But then she went back to comforting Sophia, who was walking back and forth across the room, pulling her hair, now white, and shrieking. Her husband, Alexis, had still not turned up, Chrysoula said, and they didn't know what to think. *Is he with you?* she asked me. *Did he come home?* Before I could answer, a hot wind rushed up from nowhere, pushing us all against the wall. Sophia's hair fanned out like a helmet. *Have a snail,* Chrysoula said to no one in particular. *They're so tasty.* "What about Takis?" I asked. *Not here, not here,* she said. *He's with you. Treat him like a brother always.*

From far away, I heard Yannoula. "It's that boy she's grieving for," she said to someone as she helped me out of bed to the bathroom and back again. I drifted off again and then a while after that—hours? days?—I felt myself lifted and I smelled the scent of lemon soap, felt warm water rush over me, or was it rain outside the window?

"It's New Year's Eve," Yannoula said, beside my bed. "It's almost 1945." She was wearing a long apron with wet splotches. "I gave you a bath. Hope you don't mind. Best to greet the new year clean." She was holding a bottle of yellow liqueur. "Here, drink this." She tipped it to my mouth. "A little treat for New Year's." It smelled like honeysuckle and its sweetness made my teeth ache. She helped me dress and go downstairs.

In the parlor, Stelios was cranking up an old Victrola and putting a record on it when he turned and saw me. "Ah, you're better," he said, crossing the room to put his arms around me. "We've been so worried."

He smelled faintly of the honeysuckle liqueur. A waltz started up on the Victrola and he tried to lead me into it but I was too weak and didn't know how to dance anyway. He got me to one of the remaining chairs, saying that I hadn't heard the rumors of a possible cease-fire. Churchill had flown to Athens on Christmas Eve and had been negotiating with the local leaders at the Grande Bretagne Hotel downtown. And already the fighting had lessened a bit in anticipation of an agreement expected soon. I realized then that the sound outside was just heavy rain, not gunfire.

"All over the city," Stelios said, "people are starting to go out and around again."

"I was able to do a little trading," Yannoula said. "Just a few things for a little celebration." She took off her wet apron, revealing that she was wearing one of her old gowns, faded yellow, with a train. Pouring more of the liqueur for herself and Stelios, she offered me some, but I turned it down, still feeling a little dazed. Stelios pulled her into a waltz and they whirled around the room, Yannoula talking all the while.

"My second husband, Manolis," she said, "used to take me dancing at this wonderful place for New Year's. Out in Voula, it was, overlooking the water. It had everything—dancing, drinking, gambling. Manolis liked to play cards so he was at it all night, the old fool."

She told us how she'd run into some old friends from the theater. It had been years since she'd left the stage so they'd started drinking toasts and trading stories. This had gone on until dawn and by the time the sun appeared, they were all drunk, falling over each other, shrieking with laughter. The manager and waiters stood around yawning. It was bad manners and bad business to ask them to leave. It might have brought a year of bad luck.

"Then Manolis appeared and said he'd lost everything—the house, the car, everything. In one night our lives changed utterly. Just imagine."

"What did you do?" Stelios asked, stumbling on Yannoula's train as he spun her around.

"Moved in with relatives, but it killed Manolis. In six months, he was dead. Just willed himself to die, you know, from the shame of it all. He wasn't a bad man, but he had his demons, like all men. Gambling was the worst. What was I to do? That's when I answered Sophia's ad for a housekeeper. The very next day after the funeral. I certainly never thought . . ."

The lights blinked once and then went out. The music distorted as the record slowed and stopped.

"This keeps happening," Stelios said. "Wires down everywhere and no one to repair them."

"If you can feel your way to the dining room," Yannoula said, "there are candles. And I've made a little New Year's meal."

Stelios and I held hands and felt our way along the walls. Yannoula had lit candles in a candelabra in the middle of the dining room table. On a platter, herbed rice had been molded into an odd shape.

"A goose!" she said. "In honor of Karagiozis. Let's eat it before it runs off with the potatoes and tomatoes. Then we can cut the New Year's cake and see who gets the lucky coin." The cake was a sad business, flat on one side and a bit burned because the flour you got these days, Yannoula said, was like sand.

Just as we were sitting down, there was a pounding at the front door. We sat still, looking at each other in the flickering light. Before the cease-fire, a knock on the door after dark might mean anything. Had that really changed? Stelios took a candle out of the candelabra and left the room. Yannoula and I heard muffled conversation and returning footsteps.

Standing in the dining room doorway with Stelios was what looked like a dripping tent under a large British Army hat. An arm appeared from a slit in the side and took off the hat, revealing the head of a very wet Takis. He was in what must have been an army rain poncho, which dragged on the floor and dripped from all sides.

No one said anything for a long moment. Then Yannoula raised her glass of liqueur and said, "Happy New Year."

I walked unsteadily to Takis, knelt and put my arms around him, pressing my face against his wet neck. "You're here," I said. "You're safe."

"You're crying on my neck," he said.

"Yannoula, this is Takis. He's from my village."

"Really? I've heard a lot about you, Mr. Takis."

Takis winced, then said, "But I haven't heard anything about you."

"Well, we'll have to work on that, won't we? But first you must take off your wet things." She bustled over to him, yards of her gown trailing after. Grabbing one edge of the poncho and signaling me to take the other, we pulled it over his head. He was still in the too-big uniform with rolled-up sleeves and trousers.

"What am I doing here?" he asked.

"Yes, well," Stelios said, "that *is* the question, isn't it?"

"Have a drink," Yannoula said. "It's very warming."

She wobbled back to the table, poured a glassful and took it to Takis. He had a sip.

"Yuck."

"We're all waiting to know," Stelios said. "Why *are* you here?"

"I escaped."

"What does that mean?"

"Actually, I didn't really escape. I just walked out. No one cared."

"Come sit down, Takis," I said. Yannoula and I led him to the table.

"What's that?" He pointed at the rice goose, which had begun to lose its shape.

"Have some," Yannoula said. "Let's all have some."

We ate in silence. Then I asked Takis how he'd found us and if he'd had any trouble getting there. None at all, he said, there were no neighborhood patrols anymore; you could go anywhere. He'd remembered my directions.

"But why now, Takis?" I asked. "After all the trouble you gave me that day, what made you come now?"

"What trouble?" Stelios said. "What day?"

I explained to Stelios that I'd been to see Takis a month or so before, but he hadn't wanted to come away with me. Stelios took in this information with a frown.

"They stopped deporting us during the hard fighting. But it's started up again. I had to go *somewhere* or be shipped out. They don't want us around, not now that they've found the graves."

The British had tried to keep it from the orphans on the base, but word got out, Takis told us. The first mass grave was not that far from the British base in the foothills above Athens, row after row of bodies, men and women of all ages. The British soldiers had come back to the camp, talking about the horror of it, and had been overheard. After the riots of December 3, the People's Committees had rounded up their enemies all over the city, some accused of being collaborators, including men from the Security Battalions who'd staged the *bloccos* with the

Germans. But many were just ordinary citizens possibly subject to old grudges, not always political. Some had been tortured and all had been shot and hastily buried in trenches on the slopes of Mt. Hymettus, just behind Athens. There would turn out to be in all nine mass grave sites discovered there.

"I heard they put out one man's eyes with their thumbs," Takis said. "Do you know what eyes look like outside their sockets? Like runny eggs. That's what they said."

We put our forks down. Takis went on eating. Stelios left the room.

"He hates me," Takis said.

"Stelios has always been such a good boy," Yannoula said. "I'm sure he doesn't hate anyone."

"I didn't want to come here. But everyone says awful things happen to the Red Cross orphans." He started to cry, then went to the door of the room and grabbed his wet poncho. I went after him.

"You can't go," I said.

"I shouldn't have come."

"Stay. I'll talk to Stelios."

"It won't make any difference." His shoulders were trembling.

"It'll be all right."

He cried even harder and sobbed, "I want my mother. I don't know what happened to her."

Yannoula came after us and said to me, "Here, let me hold the child."

I went to find Stelios, who was upstairs in his room. He was sitting on the edge of his bed, head in hands. I sat down beside him. After a minute, he sighed and, without looking at me, said, "What next?" I didn't say anything. "What are we to do? Send him into the streets? What bothers me is that he talks about these things as if he were talking about, oh, I don't know, the weather. And that's not all that bothers me."

"He's seen more than any child should ever see."

"Yes, well, haven't we all?" He turned to me and said with annoyance, "Why didn't you tell me you'd been to see him? I mean, I sort of thought you might, after that sergeant told you about the Red Cross and foreign orphanages. But I also thought you'd tell me if you did go."

"I wanted to tell you. But I . . . lost my courage. Sometimes your anger startles me. And then I blamed myself when I thought we'd lost him." I paused and then said there was something else he should know and told him about Takis running around naked, talking to trees.

"*Theo mou!* He should be locked up."

"You can't mean that. He's just a child."

"Like no other."

"Well, yes."

Stelios stood up and walked around his room, looking at the sports pennants in bright primary colors on his walls. "I don't know why I still have these. They don't mean anything to me anymore." He pulled out the tacks that held one to the wall and let it slide to the floor. "Who cares now which team won what game? That was part of another world."

His tone was hard. He moved from one pennant to another, pulling out tacks until the floor was littered with the sporting colors of the past. Then he turned to me and said, "If he's going to stay, he'll have to be confined to the house. We can't trust him outside."

"I'll look after him."

"Are you really up to that?" His tone softened. "You've just gone through some kind of, I don't know, collapse."

"Yannoula will help."

"Look, I can't ever forget what happened in the village, you know that. I'll try to push it to one side for now since we all have to live in the same house. But I don't guarantee it'll stay there."

"I know, Stelios. It's not as if I've forgotten either."

I went to him and held him, laying my head on his shoulder.

When we went downstairs, we saw that Yannoula had cut a slice of cake for Takis. No doubt she'd intentionally cut the part with the lucky New Year's coin. He held it up just as the lights came back on.

"Look! Yannoula says I'll have a lucky year."

We didn't say anything.

Yannoula gave Takis a room down the hall from mine on the top floor. The next day she found some of Stelios's boyhood clothes for him and dressed him to look like a proper schoolboy. I explained to her why we needed to keep him inside unless one of us was with him.

"He did that?" she said. "With no clothes on? A little discipline, that's what he needs. Then he'll remember how to behave."

What Takis would and would not remember was more complicated than she knew. But he seemed to take to Yannoula, holding her hand or even crawling into her lap so she could tell him a story. For a while he seemed to have turned back into the little boy he'd been when I'd moved into his mother's house. But when I thought of how crazily he'd acted at the British base, I was uneasy about this new change.

Late the next night he slipped into my room. "I can't sleep," he said, hopping on top of the bedcovers and sticking out his feet. He wiggled his right foot and said in Mr. Shepherd's voice, "What's for dinner?"

"Takis, we're too old for this," I said.

"Oh, my dear Mr. Shepherd," he said in Mrs. Shepherd's voice, "there's nothing at all. We'll have to eat the furniture. I'll have the floor lamp. Will you have an armchair?"

"Oh, stop it, Takis. I need to talk to you."

He fingered the edge of the blanket, crumpling it up then smoothing it out. He couldn't go outside without one of us along, I told him.

"Why?"

"You know. You can't take your clothes off the way you did near the base."

"I don't remember much about that," he said, crumpling up the blanket again.

"Sometimes you scare me."

"I'm sorry, Aliki. I don't know why I do what I do. Words fly out of my mouth and I don't know where they come from. I scare myself."

He climbed out of bed and went to the window where the leaves of a tall eucalyptus were beating against the glass in the wind.

"Why do you talk to trees?"

"I don't talk to *them*," he said. "They talk to me."

"Isn't it like calling your feet Mr. and Mrs. Shepherd? It's silly fun, but they're still only feet."

"No, no, trees *do* talk to me."

"Saying what, exactly?"

"They told me to take off my clothes."

"Why would they want you to do that?"

"How would I know? I remember being cold in someone's garden and I couldn't find my way out. I got scratched all over. Stupid, that's what it was, stupid."

"What other things do they tell you to do?"

"I don't always remember afterward."

He climbed back onto the bed and waggled his feet again.

"Stop that," I said. "We're having a serious conversation."

"You're no fun anymore. When did you get so serious?"

"I think you know. It happened in the village."

His reaction was immediate, expression darkening as he jumped off the bed and went out the door. I called after him, but there was only the sound of his footsteps hurrying down the hall and the bang of his door.

When I came downstairs the next morning, Stelios was in the library, a room at the side of the staircase with floor-to-ceiling shelves of books. He was pulling books off the shelves and stacking them on the floor. "I hate to see these go," he said. "But we don't have much left to sell. Would you like any of these? Yannoula said something about my helping you read."

Was there a dictionary I could use to look up words from the Athens guidebook he'd given me? He pulled one off a low shelf, but it was so heavy I could barely hold it. I flipped through its pages and thought of the millions of words that I mostly didn't know. Where should I start?

"See what you think of this," Stelios said. He pulled a volume off the shelf, blew off the dust and handed it to me: *The Iliad*.

"What's it about?"

"Greeks at war."

"We can see that by looking out the window, can't we?"

"This is different. Or maybe not. It's about the Trojan War, you know, the Mycenian Greeks attacking Troy to avenge the abduction of Helen."

I'd never heard of this Helen or the Mycenians and wondered if this was something that had just happened and they'd already got it into a book. He saw that I was puzzled and explained that Paris, a Trojan prince, had kidnapped the wife of the king of Sparta, Menelaus, with whom he'd been staying as guest, and had taken her off to Troy. The Greeks fought the Trojans for ten years to get her back. *The Iliad* told all about it.

"But actually it's about *everything*," he said. "Listen, listen to this. Wait, just let me find it." He flipped through clumps of pages until he found what he wanted and read out this:

As is the generation of leaves, so is that of humanity.
The wind scatters the leaves on the ground but the live timber
burgeons with leaves again in the season of Spring returning.
So one generation of men will grow while another dies.

"Do you like it?" Stelios asked.

"Yes, yes. I've never heard anything like that. Read some more."

"Let me find something." As he turned the pages this time, things slipped out and fell to the floor. I bent to pick them up: dried leaves, a photograph of a soccer team, yellowed newspaper clippings.

"Don't, don't," he said. "I'll get them."

By then we were both on our knees, bumping heads, laughing. "I save things," he said, "just things I like, and keep them in the pages. They're really nothing." He gathered them up and inserted them back in the pages, looking embarrassed.

"Will you show them to me one day?"

"Oh, they're just foolish mostly."

We got to our feet and he put *The Iliad* back on the shelf without reading anything else.

"What about that book you told me about in the village?" I asked.

He found a copy of *The Count of Monte Cristo*, but it was almost as big as the dictionary. I said I remembered him telling me how someone in the book said that happiness and misery are really the same. But it couldn't be true, could it?

"Look at all we've been through," I said, "some of each, and they weren't the same at all."

"I think it's more that they're relative, Aliki. What we call happiness or misery might be something else to other people."

I could understand that, but as I thought about it, I was bothered. "If that's so, how would we know what's true about anything? It would just be one person's idea against another's, wouldn't it?"

"Ah, you're a philosopher. That's a good question and a lot of people have thought about it, starting with someone called Socrates."

He took from a shelf a copy of Plato's *Republic*. I put down *The Count of Monte Cristo* and took the *Republic* from him. It wasn't as thick as *The Count*, but the print inside was tiny.

"Aren't there any pictures?" I asked.

Stelios sighed.

"The guidebook has lots of pictures and that helps me figure out some of the meaning. If you could help me with the hard words, Stelios . . ."

"All right. Why don't I read to you while you follow along word by word? Just a little each day. Then you can try to read it back to me and I'll explain whatever you want. How would that be?"

I'd left the guidebook upstairs, but he found one about the history of Athens with lots of pictures, some even in color. We sat down on the floor side by side and held the book between us as he read slowly out loud, but then he paused and said, "Oh." I looked up and saw Takis standing in the doorway.

"What are you doing?" he asked.

"Learning to read better," I said.

There was an uncomfortable moment as the three of us stared at each other without speaking. Takis's eyes flashed briefly, but then he looked down and scraped his shoe along the floor. "You look funny, the two of you on the floor there like that."

"And you look much better," I said to break the tension. Yannoula had cut his hair and dressed him in a sailor outfit from Stelios's childhood.

"I look like a monkey," he said.

"No, you don't. Monkeys are more handsome."

"Ha-ha." He looked at the staircase curving up to the next two floors. "This is *some* house. What do you do here all day?" We told him about our Karagiozis performances, but he winced and turned away at the mention of them.

"Because of Karagiozis, we eat," Stelios said. "We should do more performances now that the shooting has stopped." Takis said nothing. "Look, Takis, would you like to read with us?"

"I can't."

"You could learn along with Aliki."

"Isn't there anything else to do?"

"There's a backgammon set around here someplace. And a deck of cards."

Takis made a face and left. Stelios sighed again. We went on with our reading.

Through the next weeks, we read a few pages every day and I filled a notebook with new words. Stelios was patient with me, adding his own details about the city, which was slowly coming to life around us: where the blind violinist played so sweetly in a park, which lottery ticket seller was the luckiest, how to find the *kafeneion* where the old men still smoked hookahs—a kind of water pipe—in the evening. We went for walks now that it was safe, past buildings pockmarked with bullet holes or in streets that had been reduced to rubble by British tanks. Police and British troops seemed to be everywhere, telling pedestrians where they could and could not go. We were grateful for the end of local fighting, but as Stelios put it, the British troops were "acting as if they owned the place." Along with the royalist government, they were determined to retake parts of the country in communist hands. Athens was an island of relative calm and the actual islands, in their isolation, were not so bad.

On our walks, Stelios stopped at cafés to ask if they would like to have shadow puppet performances there, and though many said yes, few were willing to pay anything. One proprietor even wanted us to pay *him* for the use of his café.

Sometimes we took Takis with us, trying never to let him out of our sight, but even so, he trailed behind and sometimes disappeared. We had to circle back to find him.

"Here, you walk in front," Stelios told him.

But if we stopped to talk to a café owner or look at a bookstall, he was off again, forcing us to search. I had to do my balancing act, trying to make Takis feel part of our lives without exasperating Stelios.

Most days Takis stayed home with Yannoula. He helped her shop, cook and clean while she told him stories from her life. At least, I supposed that was what they were doing.

His dark looks at dinnertime worried me. I wasn't sure if he was glaring at Stelios or at me or at both of us. Our walks together were among the happiest times Stelios and I had ever had, just looking at everything and talking about it all, sitting in a park. Yannoula seemed to trust us together in a way Chrysoula never would have done and I felt so safe with Stelios, as if I'd returned home. We probably glowed when we came home and Takis clearly noticed. The closer Stelios and I became, the more sullen and brooding Takis was, answering questions with a grunt or a shrug. Was he sinking again? Was some gravitational pull drawing him down into a shadow world?

Yannoula would try to cheer him up, asking him about life in the village. What was it really like? She was just a city girl, she said, and had no idea about village life.

"I hated it there," he said.

"Oh, Takis, you did not," I said. "Remember the good times we had—me showing you how my father made charcoal and how much you laughed at me and . . ."

"I hated it."

Then one day he ran off. He'd been sitting with Yannoula in the library. Stelios and I had gone for one of our walks. When we returned, she met us at the door.

"I don't know what made me ask him," she said. "I just wanted to know what happened to Sophia and his mother, what really happened, you know, from his point of view. I asked him why it was that the Germans came to his mother's house when they did. He got up and walked out of the room without a word. I went after him but he'd gone. That was hours ago."

He was not back by nightfall. I searched the neighborhood but found no trace. Stelios tried the National Gardens because I thought Takis might be where there were trees. But he wasn't. Stelios went as far as Theo's café in Pangrati and stopped there to see if it had reopened. But neighbors said Theo had moved his family back to Crete during the worst of the street fighting in Athens. He'd opened a café there in Heraklion, the capital of the island. When Stelios came back, he said he was going to write Theo that day to ask if he had work for us. No local cafés had shown interest and there was still too much street fighting around Piraeus for us to consider performing there again. We'd sold most of the items of value in the house and were running out of money again. We had to have a new plan.

"That's all you can think of," Yannoula said, "with our Takis still missing?" Her eyes were red. "It's my fault. I shouldn't have been so nosy."

I tried to tell her again that something was wrong with Takis, something we couldn't understand, and he couldn't talk about anything that happened that night. She must never ask him again.

"All he needs is a mother," she said. "He's just young and confused. We were all that way once."

Stelios rolled his eyes at me. "I'll look for him again tomorrow," he said. "I don't know what else to do."

There was nowhere to report a missing child then, but two days later a woman named Nurse Papadakis phoned from a clinic in the suburb of Kifissia to say that Takis was there and he'd given her this number. He'd been found naked and half-drowned in a fishpond in the back garden of a villa near the clinic.

When Stelios and I got to the clinic, we saw that it was itself an old villa of fading and crumbling pink plaster. There was a spray of bullet holes across the archway above the front door. All the windows were shuttered. We pounded on the door for some time before it was opened by a stout woman in a smudged apron who said she was Nurse

Papadakis. She motioned us into the foyer. We had to shout who we were because in another room a woman was singing the national anthem at the top of her voice and someone else was shrieking about her mother-in-law, whom she called, "that whore." A pair of old men in their underwear marched into the foyer, saluted us and marched out again.

I'd never been to any sort of clinic and wasn't even sure what it was for. I asked Nurse Papadakis.

"It's for those who've lost their minds," she said. "Or never had them to begin with."

As we were to discover, there was almost no treatment for mental problems at that time. People who were thought to be crazy were locked up and that was that. Nurse Papadakis led us through what had once been the parlor of the house. It was now filled with single beds in rows. Standing on one of them was the singer of the anthem, who was still in full voice. Other patients were sleeping, talking to themselves or playing cards. Perhaps some of these were staff, but it was difficult to tell them from patients. Nurse Papadakis said that most of the patients were hopeless, beyond anyone's reach.

"But your friend Takis, he's young so he may grow out of it."

"Out of *what*?" Stelios asked.

"Whatever it is that's wrong with him."

"And that is . . . ?"

"We know so little of the mind," Nurse Papadakis said. "But young people do often get better. Of course they need to be purged regularly." Stelios and I exchanged glances. "All of these people . . ." she said, waving at those sleeping on cots as we passed through the dining room, "they have regular purges. They can't expect to get better without them."

"That's the only treatment?" Stelios asked, astonished.

"There's laudanum, of course, so calming. Sleeping elixirs, aspirin . . ." Nothing else had been available since the end of the war. She wasn't prepared to give extensive treatment at the clinic in any case; most people were only there temporarily until they were claimed by families. If that didn't happen, they were sent to a place for long-term patients in the town of Dafni, southwest of Athens. I didn't like to think what that might be like.

"Most of these patients, they'll be gone by this time next month," she said. "But there'll be new arrivals. It's the times, you know, they make people lose their minds."

"I'd like to speak to the doctor in charge," Stelios said.

"Oh, he only stops by twice a week and this isn't his day. He has other clinics to see to. Next week on Tuesday, you could see him then."

She was leading us up to what must have once been a grand staircase, saying that the owners of the property where Takis had been found thought he'd drowned in their fishpond, but when they pulled him out he was sputtering. Covered with scratches and insect bites, he wouldn't say who he was except that he was Karagiozis, King of the Puppets. Once he'd arrived and had been purged, he'd "loosened up," as Nurse Papadakis said, and he'd given her our phone number.

"Now he's better," she said. "Can hold an ordinary conversation, if he wants to. But that's the way with some of them. They're perfectly ordinary until suddenly they aren't." That didn't seem much of a diagnosis to me. But Takis's behavior confirmed what Sergeant Whitfield had said about Takis wandering naked in other people's gardens. I didn't understand it and didn't know what, if anything, could be done about it.

The nurse led us up another, narrower flight of stairs, telling us that she'd put Takis in a locked room to keep him from wandering. She unlocked a door and on a cot against the far wall was Takis, covered by a blanket. "I'll leave you with him," she said. "If you're taking him home today, please remember there's a fee for his stay here."

I went to Takis and shook his shoulder gently. He woke up and stared at me with a flat, expressionless gaze, which slowly turned to terror. He pulled me to him and said, "That woman with the rubber tubes, keep her away from me."

"We're taking you home," I said.

"What happened, Takis?" Stelios asked.

But Takis started to wave his hand in front of his face, as if brushing away cobwebs. I rubbed his feet, which were red and swollen. He was naked under the blanket and I asked if there was anything he could wear for the trip home. He didn't know where he'd left his clothes, he said. Stelios went to see if we could borrow something from Nurse Papadakis.

"Can you walk?" I asked, helping him to his feet, which were obviously sore. But he managed to hobble around the room while leaning on me. He said he was sorry to be so much trouble.

"It was the wind. It told me to run." I asked how he'd come to Kifissia, but he wasn't sure, maybe someone had given him a ride. There'd been a man in a truck, he thought, who'd taken him into a pine grove somewhere, but the breeze in the pine boughs also told him to run. He came to a garden wall, climbed over it and slept under bushes. In the morning he was hungry and was trying to catch goldfish in the pond when he became dizzy and fell in. That was all he remembered except for Nurse Papadakis and her terrible tube.

"Do you know what she does with it? Where she *puts* it?"

Stelios came back with a pile of old clothes. "Horrible woman," he said. "You wouldn't believe what she charged me."

When we had Takis dressed, we helped him walk to the only tram that was still running from the suburb to central Athens. At home, Yannoula asked no questions but gathered Takis into her arms and took him to the bathroom to treat his scratches and bites.

"What if he does this again?" Stelios asked me in the library. "We can't keep track of him every hour of the day."

"But most of the time he's all right. It's just when he gets so jealous of you or when the subject of what happened that night comes up."

"He gets in between *us*, Aliki. You know that, don't you?"

"Yes, yes, I do. I'll look after him better."

"But it'll happen again. Sooner or later you'll have to make a decision about him." He ran his hand down the spine of a book, pulled it partway out, then shook his head and pushed it back.

"What do you mean?" I asked.

"You can't look after him all his life," Stelios said, pulling me to him. "You might have, well, someone else to look after."

Was he talking about himself? I didn't think Stelios needed looking after. He usually seemed so confident. Had it come to a choice between him and Takis?

"Can't we be a family?" I said. "We *are* a family."

"Don't you want a family of your own one day?"

"You mean if we ever get to lead a normal life, whatever that is? I don't know. Besides, I'm too young to worry about that. So are you."

"Try looking in the mirror, Aliki. There's more to you than you know."

I wasn't sure what he meant. And then I was. The heat rose in my face and I remembered how Chrysoula had been so upset that day I took Stelios up into the hills above the village and we were alone there. Now there was only Yannoula to supervise us, but she was so easily distracted and generally unconcerned about where Stelios and I went and what we did. It frightened me a little. Or maybe I was frightened of myself, the way I kept noticing the dark shadow of a beard on Stelios's face and the strength in his arm when he took mine as we crossed a busy avenue. I would feel almost feverish suddenly, as if I was melting. I'd pull away, fanning my face with my hand. He hadn't kissed me since that night at the front door, but I felt as if it had happened only minutes before.

"Remember how before the war people married," he said, "and had children and went to school or work? It was just life. Now it seems almost a dream beyond reach. But it won't always be that way. Neither of us has family now so we can make our own decisions about these matters."

What matters? He was getting way ahead of me. Or was he? He seemed to be assuming we'd marry one day and have children. The thought flowed over me and I felt its warmth, as if he'd just wrapped me in the softest blanket on a winter night.

"Do you mean . . . ?" I asked.

"Yes."

We walked into each other's arms and stayed there without speaking for what seemed a long time. And then we were laughing and talking and being altogether silly whenever his mouth wasn't on mine. But that wasn't often.

"Just look at us," I said, standing back finally.

"Just look." He turned me around to face a mirror above his bureau, where I saw two disheveled people wearing decidedly foolish grins. We looked and looked until I saw his grin start to fade.

"And that's why," he said in a more serious tone, "as I've said, that sooner or later you'll have to decide about Takis."

I understood, but that was too far off for me to grasp. I just wasn't going to think about it then.

How to keep Takis inside, that was the question, I reminded Stelios. In the days that followed, Yannoula began making sure Takis never left a room without her knowing it. He didn't seem to remember what she'd said to upset him before he ran off. She referred to it as just one of his *spells* and now that she knew what brought them on, she was certain she could prevent them. Takis had reverted to a little boy again, holding her hand and asking her to tell him stories. He ignored Stelios as much as possible. He clearly sensed the new bond between Stelios and me but was trying not to show it.

Our lives changed quickly after Theo phoned Stelios from Crete to say that we should come at once. He had a new *kafeneion* with room for our screen and there was plenty of business because "there's no stopping these Cretans from having a good time even when the sky is falling." There was still guerrilla activity around the island and sometimes even in the cities, he told Stelios, but it would be safe for us. He owed us money from our last disastrous performance in Pangrati, which had ended in gunfire. So he'd reimburse us our fares there and give us six percent of each evening's café take in addition to the proceeds from ticket sales.

"What an offer!" Stelios said when he'd put down the phone in the parlor. "And I've got some ideas for new plays. I want to put us, all of us, in as characters, along with Karagiozis . . ."

"I'm too old," Yannoula said. "I can't go dragging myself around from place to place, warbling like an old hen." She sat down on the red sofa and considered for a moment. "But I've heard that Cretans are wonderful people, with the souls of artistes."

Stelios insisted that she come. Traveling on our own without an adult might attract attention. There was also the question of Takis. He said he didn't want anything to do with shadow puppets anymore. Stelios said he could sell the tickets.

"Why would I want to?" Takis asked.

"You need to contribute if you're going to stay with us."

"Who says I want to stay with you?"

"You can't remain here alone. Someone has to look after you."

"Yannoula and I can stay here together. Can't we, Yannoula?"

Yannoula looked uncertain. She shifted on the sofa, crossed her legs and then uncrossed them. It was one thing to be protective of Takis when we were all around, she was probably thinking. But the prospect of taking sole responsibility for him might be something else entirely, especially after he'd run away and ended up in that awful clinic. There was no question in my mind that we all needed to stay together and Crete would be a new beginning.

"Look, Takis," I said, "if you stay here, you could end up in that clinic again. Or some other place like that. Do you want that?"

"You're threatening me. That's not nice."

I felt a flash of anger and thought, oh, all right, do what you want. I'm not your mother. Then I saw Chrysoula's face in my mind and kept my mouth closed.

"Now see here, Takis," Stelios said with barely controlled irritation, "I can't let you stay here in the house by yourself. You're too young and the situation outside is still too unstable. So if you stay, where will you go and what will you do for money? You wouldn't survive on the streets. You really don't have a choice but to come with us." He paused and sighed, then said in a kinder tone, "And it might be a chance for you and me to get along a little better." I was surprised to hear Stelios say this but grateful to him. He walked to the stairs and started up them. Over his shoulder he said, "Think about it, Takis. But not for long because we need to get organized."

Takis had turned pale and looked as if he might start to cry. I felt for him, though I knew Stelios was right and admired him for being so direct.

"We should take care of each other," I said, trying to smooth things out a bit. "Like a family. Stelios, when are we supposed to leave?"

"As soon as possible," he called back from partway up the stairs. "Theo is already scheduling performances for later this week."

"Then, Takis, you'll need a suitcase. Stelios, are you packing the puppets? I'll break down the stage into the valises." Yannoula and Takis looked at me, surprised at my tone. But there was much to be done, plans to be made. "Yannoula, you'll come, all right?" I said. "And Takis?"

He didn't say anything. But he suddenly ran to the bottom of the stairs and shouted up, "*If* I come, *you* can't tell me what to do, Stelios. I won't take it from you. Only from Aliki."

Stelios stopped on the landing and shouted back, "Fine with me! What makes you think I care what you do anyway?"

Yannoula stood up, saying, "Oh, stop it, both of you." But she too went to the bottom of the stairs and said, "Stelios, I've been thinking—what about your father? What if he comes back and finds no one here?"

We were all probably wondering the same thing: how likely was it that he'd be back? The truth about the camps was beginning to be known then, especially Auschwitz-Birkenau, where most of the Greeks had been sent. It was the first still-functioning camp to be liberated by the Soviets and news of what had taken place there had begun to appear in the papers. At first it was difficult to believe the accounts; they must have been exaggerations, people said. Then the photographs started to appear. Stelios and I had seen some on a newsstand on one of our walks. All the color had drained from his face.

While Yannoula and I started packing, Stelios went to see his father's cousin, the one who'd traded rice and oil for Sophia's jewelry. What they said to each other, Stelios never told us. He was gone most of the day and when he returned, he went to his room and didn't come downstairs until the next morning. He didn't speak about it, and he didn't answer Yannoula's question. But before we left for Piraeus to catch the night ship to Crete the next day, Stelios put an envelope addressed to his father on the hall table. He didn't say what he'd written.

Takis never actually agreed to come, but he'd packed the clothes Yannoula found for him in Stelios's childhood trunk and was ready when the time to go arrived. I wasn't happy about the position he'd maneuvered me into, a kind of go-between with him and Stelios. But either it would work out or it wouldn't, I thought. At least we'd all stayed together and were on our way again.

Neither Takis nor I had ever been on the sea before and the dipping and bowing of the ship that cold mid-February evening of 1945 made us queasy. But the salty sea wind slapped our faces and revived us. Stelios had given me one of his mother's warm wool coats and he'd taken an old tweed jacket that belonged to his father, buttoning it all the way up against the wind. Yannoula wrapped Takis and herself in a brown blanket so that Takis said, brightening, "We look like a great big package."

Earlier that day, a fine red dust had blown up out of Africa and across the sea. Though this happened regularly in summer, it wasn't usual at that time of year. It gave the water a reddish cast and Stelios said maybe that was what was meant in *The Iliad* by the words *wine-dark sea*. He'd brought his copy with him and inside its cover he kept our tickets and Theo's address in Heraklion, where we were to dock the next morning. Takis wanted to know what the book was.

"Oh, read him something, Stelios," I said, trying to build a little bridge between them. "It's a wonderful book, Takis."

"Hmm, let me think what you might like, Takis," Stelios said in a tone of forced goodwill as he thumbed the pages. "Ah, here, let's try this. It's a battle scene."

. . . and Patroclus
came up and stabbed him on the right side of his jaw
and drove the spear through his teeth. Then, gripping the spear
shaft,
he pivoted back and lifted him over the rail
like a fisherman who sits on a jutting boulder
and hauls a tremendous fish out of the sea
at the end of his line, caught on the bright bronze hook:
just so did Patroclus haul him up out of his chariot,
mouth gaping around the spear point, and tossed him down
on his face, and he lay there flopping until life left him.

It was nothing like what he'd read before and I thought it was horrible. Yannoula said, "Really, Stelios, is that something to read to a child?"

But Takis let out a low whistle and said, "That's so gory. I *love* it. Read some more."

Stelios looked up at Takis's face lit with enthusiasm and snapped the book shut, saying, "It's getting too dark to read."

CASSETTE 3 ✦ Side 2

"All this furniture," said one of the women in the parlor of Zephyra's house. "What use is it now?"

"Why is it here when she's not?" asked another.

It's the old custom that after a death, possessions of the deceased not claimed by family or friends must be destroyed. For how is it that a person's belongings have a right to last longer than she does? To look at a kitchen chair when its owner is in her grave is to despise the chair.

So where to begin? First we ran upstairs, lungs heaving, joints popping, and entered the bedroom of Zephyra's long-gone son. She always kept his room as it had been—photos of sports heroes torn from magazines, a backgammon board on a table, a suit of clothes laid out on the bed. We threw the table and game board out the window. They seemed to hang in the air a second or two before smashing to the ground. How good it was to see this, as if they'd been waiting for this final splintering. We moved on—the old wooden chairs, the rickety bureau of thornwood—they too exploded on the hard ground, a single drawer of the bureau sailing into the road in front of the house. The mattress was another matter. It took all of us to heave the musty thing off the bed and out the window. It landed on top of the pile with a burst of straw ticking.

On to the other bedroom. In a small glass case on the wall were the dried wreaths from the wedding of Zephyra and Kostas next to their wedding photograph. They looked as somber as if they'd just been given death sentences. Maybe that's what marriage was for them—who knows what goes on between two people beneath a single roof? They probably wouldn't have chosen each other of their own accord. But choices were few then for families with little to bring to a match. Sometimes actual love follows a marriage contract; sometimes not. I remembered Chrysoula saying you couldn't always marry the one you loved. You had to learn to love the one you married.

Here was the bed where Zephyra died, where I'd last seen her before Aphrodite released her from the hold those goats had on her soul. Taking the bed apart was too much for us so we climbed onto it and jumped up and down, shrieking and hooting for the sheer joy of it, until the bed collapsed. Then we carried the mattress, headboard, endboard and wooden slats to the window, where we tipped them out piece by piece, starting a new pile on that side of the house. When we turned back to the room, we saw an old suitcase that had been under the bed. It was locked and badly disintegrated but heavy enough to contain something. Carrying it downstairs to the kitchen, we forced the lock with a knife. Inside was a red velvet box with a framed photograph of Zephyra's malicious mother. She had that same low brow I remembered, and dark eyes beneath it. What had become of her? I asked. I hadn't seen her since that day in the cemetery just before Stelios, Takis and I left the village.

"She was run out of the village as a collaborator," one said. "She and the schoolmaster. Others too."

Some of the villagers had shaved the heads of the accused, tied them backward on donkeys and led them through the streets while others pelted them with rotten vegetables or emptied the contents of chamber pots on them as they passed under balconies. Most, including Zephyra's mother, had never returned to the village. I could understand all this in the case of poor Petros, though it wasn't his fault that he'd been forced to translate. But Zephyra's mother? What had she done?

The women with me in Zephyra's house had been little girls then, and who tells a child about these things? Children had been kept inside as the collaborators on donkeys passed through the streets. Zephyra would have known the truth about her mother, we assumed, but she'd never spoken about it to anyone, as far as the women knew. And in Zephyra's presence, no one mentioned her mother. Some even said that it may have been Zephyra herself who'd accused her mother. But of what? And was that possible—a child accusing her own mother? Who would believe her? In those first months after the Germans left, accusations had been as thick as wasps in a nest, the women said. If anyone had seen you so much as saying hello to a German, they might accuse you. So in that sense, nearly everyone in the village had been a collaborator, willingly or not. When everyone had accused everyone else, matters could go no further and, in time, died out.

A chill passed through me, remembering the soldiers in my father's house, and thinking of Takis and the colonel. It was good that we'd left the village when we had, before accusations could take wing. None of the adults who'd been there that night—the women who'd thrown the pebbles, the neighbors who'd seen Stelios and Sophia—were still alive or, if they were, their minds had clouded over, and no one talked about it anymore. I wondered if we would ever know the secrets of Zephyra's family. Was she likely to bother me from the other side the way my father was still doing? The dead often have more to say than when they lived just down the street. Would it be that way with Zephyra?

There were a few other things in the velvet box that she'd probably collected as a child: a pile of polished stones, a doll made from a corncob, a necklace strung with uncooked macaroni. And that was it, we thought, putting the box aside, until we noticed some kind of fur on the bottom of the suitcase. It fell apart when we tried to remove it, but, putting the pieces together on the floor, we saw that it had once been the skin of an animal, now dry and cracked. The white-and-black-spotted fur came away when we touched it, but we realized it had been the pelt of a lamb. Or a young kid.

Could it be the very one that Aphrodite said Zephyra's mother had made into a disguise for her daughter? If so, why would Zephyra have kept it all those years? We could make out traces of partly disintegrated twine that could have been used to tie it to her arms and legs. I thought of how it had been there just under the part of the bed where Zephyra slept, where she'd made those goat noises the last day of her life. I told the others about my visit to Aphrodite.

Yes, yes, it was true, they said. Zephyra's mother skinned and butchered each goat Zephyra stole and then boiled hunks of it in a big stew pot. At least, that was what the neighbors saw, alerted by the smell, peering in the windows. They'd tapped on them, pointing to their own mouths, begging for just a bite, nothing special, maybe a bit of brain or tongue, a morsel of hoof meat. But nothing had been given.

We moved the pieces of skin to the kitchen table, saying such are our lives, full of secrets and mysteries. And Zephyra, unlike other dead I'd lamented for, hadn't appeared since her death. Only some did that and she wasn't one of them. So I couldn't ask her. We didn't want to toss the skin out, as it clearly had some meaning beyond itself, though we didn't know what. So we divided up the kitchen utensils, the mortar and pestle, the sieve, the bread bin and the other things. Moving on to the remaining rooms, we found nothing interesting. Zephyra's other furniture was old and little of it was worth saving. The village junk man would take away what we'd thrown outside, the sad piles of shattered furniture, traces of her life. And what would become of the goatskin still there on the kitchen table? We agreed that some things just had to be left to fate.

The ancients thought Fate amounted to three old women, the spinners, measuring out the thread of lives, deciding how long or short each should be. I imagine them to be vinegary old crones like me, sitting in that sacred cave up on Mt. Ida in Crete. Well, I don't believe in them, though it does have to be said that much of whatever fate we four were to make for ourselves was partly woven in the mountains of Crete. Of course we had no idea about this when our ship steamed into the Heraklion harbor on Crete that day. We weren't prepared for the destruction everywhere around us.

You see, although the mainland had surrendered peacefully to the Germans, the island of Crete had not. Bombing had left ruined ships and planes half-submerged in shallow water. As our ship made its way among them, blasting its horn, it dodged enormous cranes fishing out whatever metal could be salvaged.

We were barely down the gangplank when a young policeman not much taller than Takis demanded our names and the purpose of our visit. We were a family of Karagiozis players, Stelios said, but the policeman told us we would have to go to the central police station to have our luggage searched and pay for a permit to perform. He led us around piles of rubble in narrow streets between tall buildings, some laced together by graceful stone arches and trimmed with balconies of metalwork. Takis and I fell behind, stumbling into each other as we stared. The fronts of some buildings had been sheared off by bombs, but next door might be one in perfect condition where a woman on the third-floor balcony watered a potted palm as if nothing had happened.

Up ahead, Yannoula was having trouble matching the brisk pace of the little policeman so Stelios had taken her arm. What she'd said in Athens about being too old to travel had probably been true. She looked and dressed younger than she no doubt was, but I could sense the effort and will in it. She barely resembled the crone in black who'd brought me soup my first night in Athens. "It's so good to be needed," she'd told me one evening before stepping in front of the screen to sing the opening verse. "It changes everything."

At the police station, she perked up in the presence of the handsome young police captain at his desk beneath a framed photo of the king. The captain had a black handlebar mustache and hooded eyes that looked at us without expression. When he asked why we'd come to Heraklion, Stelios started to speak, but Yannoula cut across him, saying, "We're artistes." As if to prove her point, she took out her squeeze box. "You Cretans," she said, "everyone says you have such poetry in your souls. Such music. Such joie de vivre." She began to play and sing.

The daisy told me you don't love me,
petal by petal, can it be true, my sweet?

She smiled and winked at the captain. I'd never seen her so coquettish.

The captain ignored her. But when he noticed me, he swept off his cap and placed it over his heart. I felt my face color up as he stared boldly into my eyes, flashing a smile full of huge teeth.

"You see how it is with Cretans," Yannoula said, annoyed.

Stelios stepped in front of me and asked the captain please to contact Theo and gave the name of the café. The captain sent the short policeman off, but while we waited, he picked up the phone and ordered coffee for us. In only minutes a boy rushed in the door and set up a little table with white cups. We'd just begun to sip, surprised to find it was pure coffee, not watered-down chickory like most those days, when Theo, in a dirty apron and with his face red, arrived.

"Come, come," he said, motioning us to our feet. "I have advertised the first part of *The Hero Katsondonis* for today. You wrote that you know it, yes? We must hurry." He tapped the side of his head as if to emphasize the point and showed the captain the performance permit he'd already obtained. Offering the captain free seats for himself and fellow officers, Theo gave a little bow as he said, "If you will so honor us." The captain stood and bowed back to Theo, then flashed me his toothy smile again.

"Are all Cretans like that?" Stelios asked Theo when we were in the street.

"Like what?" Theo said.

His café was in the old fishing harbor on the other side of a seawall from the main harbor. Pointing out a massive stone fortress, Theo said it had been built centuries earlier when Crete was part of the Venetian empire. I'd never heard of Venetians and was more interested in the hundreds of small fishing boats bobbing in the water there, each with eyes painted on either side of the bow to help it see, Theo said, through darkness or fog. The boats knocked into one another in blasts of wind off the water. Nearby sat fishermen mending their yellow nets or calling out the day's catch to passing townspeople.

At the far side of the harbor was Theo's café. Because of the wind, we set up inside its main room with all its tables and customers. The air was almost blue with the cigarette smoke of the men drinking ouzo or raki. On the walls hung yellowing photographs of Theo's ancestors in suits out of another time. Theo himself waited on tables but went out front from time to time to call out the news that our performance would be starting shortly. In the doorway, Takis was selling tickets, but he'd never learned much arithmetic so Theo had to help him make change. Just before we started, the captain and several other officers took seats at tables near the stage. Then Yannoula stepped out, played a little riff on the squeeze box and sang the opening.

Red twine braided fine,
tightly wound around a wheel.
Set the wheel a-spinning, do,
and I'll spin a tale or two,
for all this happy company.
And may your time pass pleasantly.

Partway through the play, two puppets entered, made in the likeness of Stelios himself and his mother. These must have been what

Stelios was making that night on the ship from Piraeus. I'd dozed off and then woken briefly to see him working away at something. Now they spoke in chorus to the soldier (Karagiozis) outside the cave where Katsondonis was hiding.

SOPHIA AND STELIOS: *We are travelers seeking shelter.*

SOLDIER: *There is none here.*

SOPHIA AND STELIOS: *But isn't that a cave? We could rest there.*

SOLDIER: *It is occupied. Move along.*

SOPHIA AND STELIOS: *Who's inside? Can't we share the shelter?*

SOLDIER: *Move along, I say. You would not be safe here.*

SOPHIA AND STELIOS: *There's little safety for us anywhere. But farewell, friend.*

At the end of the play, when the angel descended to take Katsondonis to heaven, someone in the audience shot a pistol out the front door. And then someone else. We threw ourselves to the ground and accidentally pulled the screen on top of us. But the audience only laughed and Theo helped us to our feet, saying, "They love you; that's how they show it here on Crete."

"Bang!" Takis said, aiming an imaginary rifle at the departing audience. "We love you back."

I asked Stelios about the new puppets.

"Did you like them?" he asked.

"Well, yes, I suppose. I didn't know Karagiozis could play other roles than himself."

"Oh, you mean as the soldier tonight? Well, he's always himself. And everyone else, like a kind of stand-in for the rest of us. But what about the other two?"

"You and your mother? Why were they there?"

"I'm not sure. I'll have to find more for them to do. I mean, I just like the idea of mixing our own stories in with the old ones. It keeps the stories fresh. And Mother and I did once try to hide in a cave before the partisans brought us to your village."

That evening over dinner Theo told us about the battle of Crete. When German paratroopers started to parachute down onto the island after the mainland had been taken, a child in a Heraklion street cried out, "Mama, Mama! Men with umbrellas are falling from the sky!" People rushed out to see and when they understood this was an invasion, they grabbed anything they had: scythes, pitchforks, spades, even kitchen knives.

"They were housewives, priests, farmers, shopkeepers," Theo said, "but they pounced like lions on the Germans as they touched down. Before they could even get untangled from their gear."

Theo lunged forward at the table, pouncing on a plate of salad, scattering its contents. "Sorry, sorry. But you see what I mean. Just imagine it! If only I hadn't been in Athens."

This fierce resistance had gone on for days, aided by Greek troops and the Allies—British, Australian and New Zealander. But it became clear that the sheer number of Germans would prove overwhelming in the end. Most of the Allied troops finally evacuated to Egypt, though a few stayed in the mountains to help the villagers there harass the Germans. Once the invaders were in control, the reprisals began. Entire villages were sacked and burned, the residents massacred.

"Sometimes they went through a whole valley, the Germans, burning all the villages, killing everyone, with no more pity than for chickens or sheep."

But the Germans on the island had been in retreat since before the liberation of the mainland. Those left had been trapped by British and local forces near the city of Chania in the west. And the civil fighting had not been as bad as on the mainland. Theo said that bands of communist guerrillas were still forcing mountain villages to pay tribute. Sometimes at night, guerrillas came down from the mountains to settle old scores from before the war and even to blow up police stations. *"Banditos,"* he said, and he spat on the ground. They even took hostages and demanded ransoms. "As if anyone has anything to give after all these years of fighting."

Takis was taken by the idea of banditos; he was sure they were everywhere. In the days to come, he'd ask, "Do you think *he's* one?" pointing at an old man in a café who looked entirely harmless to me. "Or *him*?"—a grocer stacking oranges outside his shop. At the next performance of *Katsondonis*, Takis was convinced banditos had bought tickets from him and were sitting at the tables among other customers. "I can hear their voices," he said. "They're here somewhere."

Stelios added banditos to the plays over the next six weeks or so. Theo liked this because we presented some of the same plays again and again. So by the end of March, audiences started to thin out. "Don't you have anything new?" Theo kept asking. Stelios said he was working on something, but it wasn't finished. Before long, he'd made puppets of us—Yannoula, Takis, me—and started to work them into existing plays, as if trying them out. We appeared whenever there were supposed to be crowds of people. I wasn't sure what he meant by it since we were the only ones who noticed; to the customers in the café, they would just have been other puppets.

Each morning, we all gathered in the lobby of the boardinghouse where we'd taken rooms, a few blocks from Theo's café. We lived on the second floor of the run-down building. Takis's room faced the street and was next door to mine. Yannoula's was on the other side of mine and next to Stelios. A communal bathroom with wheezy plumbing was at the end of the hall. Downstairs, the lobby was a musty old parlor with faded floral wallpaper, furniture losing its stuffing and stacks of prewar magazines and newspapers. We'd used many of them for my reading practice, so my notebook included words like *appeasement* and *treaty* from the newspapers along with phrases from magazine ads, like *banishes wrinkles overnight.*

Yannoula preferred romantic novels, which she could read perfectly well for herself. But they were hard to find in those days and she joined us in order to keep an eye on Takis.

Our only book was *The Iliad*, contributing *rage*, *elated*, *slaughtered* and *doomed*, among others, and graceful lines that Stelios pointed out and I copied whole: *A thousand watch fires were burning upon the plain.* We didn't really need any other books, he said, because this was all of them rolled into one. Takis said it was stupid for all these men to be fighting and dying just because of a silly woman.

"I mean, she couldn't have been *that* pretty."

"I don't know," Stelios said. "The old men of Troy said it was no wonder that they should endure long years of war for such a woman."

. . . she is dreadfully like an immortal goddess; her beauty
pierces the heart.

"Read that other part again," Takis said, referring to the bit where Patroclus speared the man like a fish. It was one of the many passages of gore in battle that Takis liked. Spears crunching through helmets, heads and limbs lopped off, teeth splaying out of a mouth, innards spilled from a belly wound—all the hideous grit of war intrigued him. But that passage fascinated him more than any other and he badgered Stelios to read it every time we were all together in the lobby.

"Later," Stelios said that day, holding the book for me while I copied the lines about Helen into my notebook. A gull's feather lay in the margin of *The Iliad* like a bookmark. Stelios picked it up and stroked the back of my hand with it as I wrote. He was so close that I could feel the warmth of his breath on my neck. It took some time for me to form the words.

When we looked up, Yannoula and Takis had gone. We didn't see them the rest of the day. Yannoula came to the performance alone.

"He was angry and wanted to go back to the harbor," she said of

Takis. "You know what his anger is like. It comes out of nowhere. When I stopped to talk to one of those nice young fishermen—that little one with the bushy eyebrows—Takis ducked behind a pile of nets and was gone. I've been looking for him all afternoon." Her voice wavered with fear. "It's the second time I've lost him."

She took Takis's place selling tickets and when the performance was finished, the three of us went to the other end of the harbor where she'd last seen him. A few men were sitting on the ground around a lantern under a fern tree, drinking ouzo and mending holes in their nets with wooden needles. Maybe they'd seen Takis, maybe not, they said.

"You mean the boy who's a little bit . . . ?" one of them asked, twirling a finger beside his head. In the light of the lantern his face was leathery and grooved. Stelios said we'd just like to find the boy; did they know where he was?

"Out there," the man said, pointing toward the harbor beyond the Venetian fortress. Takis had borrowed a rowboat from one of them, saying he wanted to get away from the banditos who were everywhere and after him; they'd even got in behind his eyes. The fishermen laughed, but the old one said with anger, "We used to call them *partisans* when they fought the German scum. Now they're *banditos*."

"You loaned a boat to a child at night?" Stelios asked.

"Wasn't night when he took it," the old one said. "He had trouble with the oars at first. But he's probably out there somewhere."

"He has problems," Stelios said.

"Like spells," Yannoula said, "when he doesn't know what he's doing."

The men fell silent. There was only the clicking of their wooden needles and the hissing of the lantern. A winged beetle was flinging itself at the glass, falling back and trying again. Another man spoke but from the far side of the lantern so we couldn't see which one it was.

"My young daughter," he said, "she has problems also, a little light in the head, she is. Some of the local fascists—royalists or police, who knows—they broke into the house when she was alone. Four of them. When they finished enjoying her, they put a small glass up inside. They punched her until it broke."

No one said anything. The beetle hit the lantern again and fell to the ground. "Did you report what they did?" Stelios asked.

"Who to report it to? *They* run the city."

Stelios said it was terrible what had happened to the man's daughter. One day the men who'd done it would have to pay. "But what does it have to do with giving a rowboat to a child?"

"It's just that some of these fascists, police and others, they come to your, uh, entertainments, in the café down there. You're in *their* protection. You and your friends here." He nodded at Yannoula and me.

I thought of Theo giving the captain and his officers free seats whenever they wanted them, and how he offered them drinks and refilled their glasses without charge at intermission. It hadn't occurred to me that this might be protection.

"Anyone can come to the plays," Stelios said.

"Not *anyone*," one of the others said. "It would not be a good idea for just anyone."

"And what kind of man are you, anyhow?" the old one asked Stelios. "Playing with dolls in a café, bah, this is no work for a man today when there's a great struggle going on."

"He's a better man than any of you," Yannoula said, stepping into the circle of light. "Giving a boat to a child, why, you should have your faces slapped."

The men laughed and one called out, "Me first, Grandmother."

"No, not him," said another. "Me first!"

"They're not dolls," Stelios said, "as I'm sure you know. It's shadow theater, the ancient art."

"Art? Ha. Listen to this." The old one chanted a verse and the others joined in, repeating it.

We're going to fight the bankers,
the landlords and the rest.
We'll seal the fate of priests and monks,
those damn bloodsucking pests.

"Now, *that's* art," he said. "You can tell 'cause it rhymes. Better than shadows on a screen."

The beetle had singed its wings and flapped on the ground. "I'm nobody's grandmother," Yannoula said, crushing the beetle under her shoe as she glared at the men. She turned and stalked off with Stelios and me after her.

One of the men called out, "You will find him when you will. But the fish may find him first."

"The *bandito* fish," another called. They laughed.

We searched along the beaches down from the harbor, but it was too dark and we had to give up for the night. It wasn't until the next morning that a washerwoman beating laundry against shoreline rocks noticed a small boy struggling to row himself along the coast. He was standing as he rowed and he was completely naked. The woman called out to a friend on the next rock down, who called out to others, and soon a group of people were watching. Word got back to us at the boardinghouse and by the time we arrived at the beach there was a crowd, including Theo and some of the fishermen from the night before. Takis was rowing in to shore, where the women were all giggling and pointing. One had pulled her apron up over her face.

As Takis stepped out of the boat into the shallows, Stelios took off his shirt and tried to cover him. Ignoring this, Takis splashed past Stelios and pulled the boat ashore. His eyes were glazed when he stopped in front of me. "Listen, Aliki, the fish are singing. Can you hear them?"

Theo helped us take Takis back to the boardinghouse, asking us what was going on with him. We tried to explain that most of the time

Takis was like any other boy. But then he would have one of these spells beyond his and our control.

"You mean he's . . . ?" He twirled his finger next to his ear, a gesture I'd come to hate.

"Not most of the time," I said. "He's been through some terrible things."

"But look, there's a doctor who comes into the café sometimes. I think he works with children. Maybe he can help."

While Theo went to find this doctor, we put Takis to bed. When the doctor arrived he gave Takis an injection, which sent him under for most of the day. I sat with him while Stelios spoke to the doctor at length outside the room and then went away with him. I didn't see Stelios again until the evening performance. After it, I hurried back to check on Takis. He was sitting up in bed, staring straight ahead.

"What's wrong with me?" he asked. "I don't know what's wrong with me."

"Tell me what happened," I said.

"They want me to kill myself. But I don't know why. What did I do to them?"

"Who?"

"The communist banditos."

He started hearing them just after Theo mentioned them at dinner our first night in Heraklion. When we'd all been in the lobby for my reading lesson that morning, he began to hear them even more strongly. "It was when Stelios was stroking your hand, they told me that nobody would ever love me. That I might as well be dead. They were inside the walls in the electrical wires."

"Can you hear them now?"

"No, but they're there, waiting for you to go away. They don't like you."

I wasn't sure what to say. If the voices were part of him, did that mean there was part of him that didn't like me? Which part was I talking to at that moment? I could tell from his tone that there was no point in my trying to reason him out of this. I sat on the bed and put my arms around him, saying that no one wanted to hurt him. He said the voices had told him to come to the harbor and row out to sea and never return. But when he rowed into the bay, he couldn't hear their voices anymore because the fish in the water beneath him were singing a song about the caves and tunnels under the sea floor where they hid from the fishermen's nets. He would be safe there, they said. So he took off his clothes to swim with them. But he'd been too frightened to get into the black water.

I rocked him in my arms and said nothing. We sat like that for quite a while until I could tell from his breathing that he was sliding back into sleep. I went to my room and sat staring at the wall. That was how Stelios found me.

"It's Takis, isn't it?" he asked, taking off his jacket and sitting beside me on the bed. He held me as I'd held Takis and stroked my hair. He said that the doctor had told him that there was a place on the island, a kind of hospital for children with problems. "Of course he'll have to examine Takis once he's calm. But then he'll see if anything can be done."

"Oh, no. It'll be like that clinic in Kifissia."

"We don't know that."

"We can't abandon him. Think of Chrysoula—what would she want?"

"I *am* thinking of her. And how she would probably have had to find a place for him too, had she lived. He needs help, you know, much more than we can give him."

"I don't know about that."

"Think, Aliki, think. He could turn on you or any of us and believe we're out to get him too. He could hurt you."

"He'd never do that."

"And besides, we have to make a life for ourselves."

"Do we? How can we do that? I don't know how to do that."

He didn't say anything but pulled me closer. We sat there quietly for some time just holding each other. He started touching me gently, touching me all over. He loosened my blouse at the waist and slid one hand over my back and the other up my front. I said we should stop, but he said we'd be sweet to each other, touch each other in all the sweet places, here and also here. We wouldn't have to do more than that if I didn't want to. I thought of Chrysoula's warnings, my breath coming in spurts as Stelios asked, does this feel good and how about this too?

"I've never done any of this before," I said.

"Neither have I." We both laughed, nervously at first, and then harder. Our laughter inflamed us and we went at each other again until all our clothes were on the floor. "Look how sweetly we slide together," he said.

The bed was squeaking and banging the wall. We were making a lot of noise for quite a while when, gasping for breath, it hit me that Takis, next door, would certainly hear us. I didn't want to think about that, but I started pushing myself away from Stelios. It was often jealousy that set Takis off and he'd talked about killing himself. What if he'd heard us already?

"We have to stop," I said. I tried to pull Stelios's head off my breast. He paid no attention, as if he was trying to swallow me whole. "We can't do this here."

"We can do anything we think of."

"Takis." I pointed at the wall. "He'll hear."

"Who cares?"

"*We* do. You and I."

Stelios stopped and sat up. He swore, saying what Takis could do to himself.

"But isn't there another place?" I said. "Why not your room? I don't want to stop."

"But *you* stopped us."

"I'm afraid . . ."

"Of . . . ?"

"Of hurting him. He might do something to himself."

"Oh, for God's sake. Can't we do *anything* without him?"

He grabbed his clothes and pulled them on in anger. As he went out the door, he said, "He *has* to go." I heard him stomping down the stairs to the lobby.

I pulled the covers over me and lay there a long while staring at the ceiling. I didn't know what to do and couldn't calm myself. A car or truck backfired in the street once or twice. Dressing quickly, I crept down the hall to Stelios's room, but he wasn't there and his bed hadn't been slept in. Back in the hall, I peered down into the lobby, but it was dark and silent. So I returned to my room and waited for the first light of morning. Retracing my steps then, I saw that nothing had changed. I didn't know what to think.

While I was in the bathroom, Yannoula tapped on the door and said that the doctor was back, waiting in the lobby, and wanted to talk to Stelios and us about Takis. Did I know where Stelios was? I said no, I had no idea. When she'd gone back downstairs, I went to Takis's room. He was sitting up in bed, looking like his ordinary self again. I asked how he felt.

"Better. I'm sorry about yesterday. I make too much trouble all the time."

"Yes, well . . ."

"I don't know how to help myself."

"I know. But look, Takis, have you seen Stelios?"

"He isn't here?"

"We've looked everywhere."

"He must have gone away with those men."

"What? What men?"

"I woke up in the night and was looking out the window and saw him. He was sitting in the empty sidewalk café across the street. Then an old truck full of men drove past. It kept backfiring."

"Oh, Takis, are you sure about this?"

"Maybe they were banditos."

"Oh, be serious. You think they're everywhere."

"They are."

"*Theo mou.* Tell me exactly what you saw. Start from the beginning."

He'd been awakened by some noises. He wasn't sure what they were so he went to the window and saw Stelios come out the front door below and cross the street. The sidewalk café opposite was closed, but he took one of the stacked chairs down and sat on it, doing nothing. After a few minutes, the truck with the men roared past and turned the corner. Takis was about to go back to bed when it returned, drove slowly past Stelios, then stopped and backed up in front of him. It blocked Takis's view, and someone in the bed of the truck began to talk to Stelios.

"And you're sure it was Stelios over there? It was dark out—could you really see?"

"There's a streetlight. And he had on his old jacket, you know, the tweed one he wore on the boat. That one he always wears when it's cool."

"Could you hear what they were saying?"

"No. But when the truck drove away after a while, Stelios wasn't there anymore."

"But why didn't you come tell me? Or Yannoula?"

"No one believes me anymore. And anyway, I thought he'd walked back over here. But I was almost falling asleep standing there so I went back to bed, and when I woke up just now, I wondered if it was a dream."

I stood there beside his bed telling myself that only the previous day Takis had heard fish talking, not to mention banditos in the wires in the lobby walls. Could he have imagined what he'd just told me or, as he said, dreamed it? But there was the fact that usually after he'd come back from one of his spells, his mind was clear for some time. What he'd said didn't sound like his usual imaginings; no one in his story was out to get him, though it did include suspected banditos.

I went downstairs to tell Yannoula what he'd said. She'd sent the doctor away and was standing in the doorway looking up and down the street. When I'd told her, she said, "But how can we believe Takis? Look how he was yesterday. Singing fish!"

"Yes, I know. But somehow this sounds real. And I did hear a truck backfiring too."

"That could mean anything. Maybe Stelios just went over to Theo's."

As we hurried there, she said it was just not possible that Stelios would go away without saying anything. "I *know* him. He could almost be my own son."

I thought of Stelios leaving my room so angrily. If I hadn't stopped him in bed, would he still be here? It was my fault, all of it, and just because I'd worried that Takis might hear. What was wrong with me? I was ruining everything between Stelios and me because of a crazy, jealous little boy I was imagining I could mother. I was going to have to choose and I didn't like the fact that I was being weak and indecisive. I told Yannoula how it was that I'd made Stelios angry the night before. She gave me a hard look, then said it was no wonder he'd walked out. He'd probably gone across the street to cool off.

"But he'd arranged to meet the doctor to talk about a place for Takis this morning," she said. "So how could he go off with the men Takis saw? Did he say anything about loud voices or a struggle?"

"No."

Theo hadn't seen Stelios since the day before. But he dismissed what Takis had said. "That boy, he isn't right in the head, you know. What did the doctor say?" We explained that we hadn't talked to him because of Stelios's disappearance. Theo tapped the side of his head rapidly the way he always did when excited. "Aliki, you know Takis better than anybody. Do you believe he actually saw what he said?"

I thought for a moment, took a deep breath and said, "I think so. Yes, yes, I do."

Theo wiped his hands on his apron. "We'd better talk to the police."

At the station, the captain greeted us like old friends, flashing me his toothy smile and barking at the little policeman, the same one who'd escorted us from the port, to bring chairs for us. "I *love* your Karagiozis," the captain said, picking up the phone and ordering coffee.

Theo said it was about the puppeteer that we'd come. He'd disappeared. The captain put down the phone. We told him what Takis had said.

The captain sighed and picked up a leaflet from his desk. "Have you seen this? We've had planes dropping them all over the island."

I realized I'd seen them blowing around the streets but hadn't picked one up. They told of an amnesty for guerrillas, the captain said. Fighters of any kind could turn themselves in, surrender their weapons and escape prosecution. It wouldn't matter what they'd done or who they were. Many men had already deserted their mountain groups and surrendered, signing a declaration of loyalty to the new government-backed militia. It was a way of winding down hostilities, weakening the opposition to government militia. But who had issued this, Theo asked, the government in Athens?

"No, they would never do such a thing," the captain said. "They just want to kill!" We would hear in time that this would be known as the White Terror, the massacres of communist guerrillas by government and British forces on the mainland. "Here we take a different tactic. As a matter of fact this was *my* idea." He proudly patted a stack of papers on his desk. "Just in the last two weeks, this many have signed."

True, the guerrillas were mostly communists, but, he said, they'd harassed the Germans when they'd been in control, and saved Cretan lives. This was a more sensible way to deal with them.

We didn't understand what that had to do with Stelios. The guerrilla leaders still up in the mountains had to replace the deserters, the captain said, so abductions of men had increased. He patted the stack of papers again. It was the young ones they were after, those who could endure life up there, living in caves, blowing up bridges, charging villagers for protection.

"They took Avgustos, the butcher's son, just a week ago. His mother has lost her mind with grief."

The boy from the café arrived with coffee as the captain said, "Sometimes they use chloroform to knock the ones they take unconscious. They break into pharmacies to get it. If the abducted ones then refuse to take part or try to escape," he said, "they're tortured or even killed."

His face swam and blurred before me. The next thing I felt was water splashed on my own face as I was lying on the ground. For a moment I didn't know where I was or why I'd fallen. But seeing Yannoula bending over me made it all come back. Theo and the captain helped me up and got me into a chair. When I thought of what they might do to Stelios, I felt sick and leaned forward, my head in my hands.

"I mean this kindly," the captain said, "but maybe your friend, he just ran off with a woman. It would be better for him than what we are thinking." He had a sly grin.

"That's certainly not true," Yannoula said. "And not a helpful thing to say."

"No, no, you are right, of course," he said, his grin fading. "There have been others taken. We search for all of them. Don't worry. We'll find him." He gave me another of his smiles, a token of reassurance, I thought, but I had the strong sense that in fact he saw little chance of finding Stelios.

Yannoula told him about the fisherman who'd criticized Stelios for not taking part in the struggle. "Oh, them," the captain said. "I know who you mean. We'll see about them."

But when he stopped by the boardinghouse later that day to question Takis himself, the captain told us those fishermen weren't around anymore. And no one had heard of the daughter who'd supposedly been attacked.

"She doesn't exist," the captain said. "People here, they make up stories."

Who was making up what? How were we to know?

Takis had little to add to what he'd told me. He hadn't heard any kind of struggle, but the noisy engine of the truck had been running all the while. And it backfired again when the truck drove off.

Theo went to the police station daily for the next couple of weeks, but there was no new information. The captain said that either Stelios had gone off to join the guerrillas or he had been forcibly taken by them. The first possibility was not remotely likely, we said, so it had to be the second. Well, the captain told Theo, there'd probably be a breakthrough at any minute. The government militia was more involved on the mainland, where there was a great deal of active fighting, not just the sporadic sniping and abductions as on Crete. So they tended to leave these matters to local police. They'd begun riding the country buses around the island after several were stopped by guerrillas who robbed the passengers and, in some cases, took hostages.

Yannoula stayed in her room and paced. I could hear her weeping at night and I supposed she could hear me. Without Stelios, there were no more performances so we had nothing to interrupt our despair. It hollowed me out until nothing remained but this vast aching. Wandering the streets in the day, I peered at everyone I passed, going into shops and out again, reading every face as if I might find in it some clue, some hope. In the harbor, the fishermen we'd talked to that night were indeed gone. When I asked questions of those still there, they were evasive or looked the other way.

I went through Stelios's things in his room, as if something there might help me understand what had happened. Nothing did, but just sitting on the edge of his bed made me feel closer to him. I came across his copy of *The Iliad* and thumbed through the pages, looking at some of the things he'd saved: the gull feather he'd stroked my hand with the day Takis disappeared, a red ribbon that had been won as third place in an unnamed athletic event, a snapshot of his parents in front of the Zappeion building in the National Gardens, some dried grasses from who knows where. I pressed my nose into the pages, inhaling their dry and dusty scent. Looking at a page with a turned-down corner and a penciled checkmark, I read this:

> *Clanless, lawless, homeless is*
> *he who is in love with civil war,*
> *that brutal, ferocious thing.*

I was sure Stelios was out there somewhere with the lawless and the homeless. But holding his copy of *The Iliad* made me feel closer to him. He'd probably want me to continue with my reading, so that was what I would do, I thought as I pocketed the book. The next step was to find him and I didn't know how we would do that. But we had to. I told Yannoula and Takis this the next morning in the lobby.

"Let's go find the banditos," Takis said. "I'll spear them like fish, like in *The Iliad*!"

"We're not in a book, Takis," Yannoula said.

"Actually," I said, "I've got a plan."

It wasn't a very good one, but just waiting for news would most likely make us crazy. We couldn't stay in the boardinghouse forever. Theo had been helping us with the rent even though we were no longer making money for him at the café. He couldn't be expected to do this much longer.

Yannoula was sitting on the sofa, her eyes swollen, while Takis walked around the room so charged with energy he seemed ready to explode. Because he was the only witness to what had happened, he'd become the center of attention.

"We have to learn to perform without Stelios," I said. "And we have to do it outside Heraklion so we can look for him."

We all knew the plays except for some of the new bits Stelios had added. So it was a matter of reassigning parts and rehearsing for a few days. With my hoarse old-lady voice, I could take some of the men's roles, but Takis would have to do the others. And Yannoula could do the few women in addition to singing the opening. Manipulating the puppets on their poles behind the screen was not all that difficult; I'd done it with Stelios and I could teach Takis. When we were ready, we'd take local buses to towns and villages in the interior and perform for them. The bus terminal was nearby and although the buses were ramshackle, they were still running, and police were on board to protect the passengers.

"We can ask around about him as we take buses from place to place. That's the point of leaving Heraklion. Someone will have seen him or heard of him; I'm sure of it."

Yannoula and Takis just sat there saying nothing. I hadn't expected immediate agreement, but neither had I expected silence.

"If either of you has a different plan," I said, "now's the time for it."

They both spoke at once, Yannoula saying that it was too dangerous outside Heraklion (she was right) and Takis saying he wouldn't be any good as a puppeteer (he was wrong).

"I keep wondering if we should go back to Athens," Yannoula said. "At least we have a place to live there. But I don't want to leave Stelios here, wherever he is."

"We can't go without him," I said.

"But what chance is there of finding him or freeing him? We'll end up abducted ourselves. You can't be serious, Aliki."

Takis perked up. "I could be the bait. If they abducted *me*, I could work from within. I could find him."

"No, no," I said, "they don't take women and children; at least, we haven't heard of any. If we learn anything useful, there are the police on the buses. We can perform from village to village and ask questions as we go. No one will suspect anything of two women and a boy with puppets."

"Let's go!" Takis said.

"It's naïve," Yannoula said, "and ridiculous and dangerous."

"Yes," I said. "It's all of those. And probably more. So let's start working out the plays and packing."

"Now!" Takis shouted.

"I'm not going," Yannoula said. "And the two of you can't go by yourselves. You know that." She sighed and stood up. "I think I need to go upstairs and lie down."

I had to admit that she was probably right, at least about Takis and me traveling alone. We'd stick out all on our own with no adult. Guerrillas might not be interested, but if we made money from performances, others would be. As we were setting up the screen and puppets for our first rehearsal, I said that we'd have to persuade Yannoula.

"We could wait 'til she's asleep," Takis said, "then tie her hands behind her back and put a bag over her head."

I narrowed my eyes at him. He was serious. "Of course," I said, "no one would ever notice a bound woman, her head in a bag, sitting beside us on the bus."

"Well, we could take the bag off once the bus was out of town."

"Oh, stop."

For the next week we rehearsed most of the day most days. Takis was a reluctant puppeteer at first, but I told him what Stelios had once told me, that it was a little bit like being God because you could make the characters do whatever you wanted so long as it was believable to the audience. Then Takis started to have fun with it, taking on the Karagiozis role and that of the sultan. He made up the lines as he went but loosely followed the set plot in general. As he danced the puppets along on their poles behind the screen, he was discovering the other thing Stelios had taught me: shadow puppetry was a lot of fun. When we took breaks, Takis talked excitedly about finding the banditos who'd abducted Stelios, but I knew it was the prospect of the heroic pursuit that excited Takis, not the finding of Stelios himself.

Yannoula watched from the top of the stairs. "You're not fooling me, Aliki," she said. "I know what you're up to."

Theo interrupted us one afternoon, storming into the lobby. "What is this craziness I hear from Yannoula? What do you think, Karagiozis will protect you out there?"

Takis and I tried to explain what we wanted to do, but Theo wouldn't hear of it, at least not on our own and not on public buses. He didn't seem to mind the thought of us leaving Heraklion in general, as the audience for Karagiozis at the café had dwindled. It occurred to me that maybe our problems, first with Takis and now Stelios, had become too much for him. He'd stopped his daily visits to the police station, describing the captain as "useless." Theo wanted nothing more to do with police. We'd come to Crete because of him, but there was probably not much more he could do for us. Except for one last thing.

"You can't travel the way you want, Aliki. It's too dangerous. But look, I have an idea." There was a friend of his, a truck driver named Thanasis, who drove all over the eastern half of the island, buying and selling fruit and vegetables from place to place. He'd had to stop during the occupation after his wife died in the invasion of the island, but he'd started up again. Maybe he would take us with him. He was always complaining how lonely it was on the road.

"Thanasis will be glad of the company. And he's a man, a *big* man. It will be safer for you. I'll talk to him."

Takis and I were waiting in front of the boardinghouse when Thanasis stepped out of his truck the next morning. He was the biggest man I'd ever seen. Not fat, just tall and broad. He could have picked us up and juggled us, if he'd had a mind to. Takis looked up at him in awe.

"You're a tree!" he said.

From behind a graying and shaggy beard, Thanasis said, "And you're a twig." Then he noticed me. "Ah, and who's this sweet plum?"

"My daughter," Yannoula said behind me. I hadn't realized she was there. And there was certainly no mother-daughter resemblance. "And as far as you're concerned," she said to Thanasis, "she might as well be a bitter lemon. But enough of the flora and the fauna."

"Hmm, yes, now I see the resemblance." He winked at me. "May you grow as beautiful as your *mother*." To Yannoula he said, "You'll, of course, sit up front with me. We'll keep each other company."

Yannoula didn't say anything at first but looked him over, head to toe and back. His graying hair and beard framed the deeply creased face of an older man but one who seemed to carry his years lightly. Over the sleeve of his right arm was the narrow black band of mourning. He was taking Yannoula into full consideration too.

"We'll keep our eyes on the road," she said at last.

We could get out in any village or town he passed through and stay there until he returned that way, usually a day or two later. In villages, Thanasis bought produce cheaply from farmers—now in April, lettuces and green onions, leeks, beets, spinach and all the citrus from the past winter—then sold it in towns at slightly higher prices. We could eat what we wanted of it, but could we just give him a few coins now and then to help cover fuel, still so expensive since the end of the war? We could, I said, if people had anything to pay us for Karagiozis.

That evening Yannoula came down the stairs to the lobby, saying, "Well now, my cabbages, I think we should have a sip of something to start our new venture." Clearly she was in a thoroughly revised frame of mind. Sitting down on the old sofa, she brought out a flask from her purse, took the cap off and said, "Respect for elders first." After she'd drunk deeply, she cleared her throat and then passed the flask to Takis.

"What is it?" he said.

"Just try it."

He took a cautious sip, then swallowed and coughed violently. "It's poison!"

"Well, yes. But this one's called brandy." She passed it to me. It burned down into my belly. I liked its sweetness but not its bite, remembering the way the stars swayed after I'd had wine that night in Piraeus.

"Here's to you, Aliki," Yannoula said. "When you get an idea, you certainly stick to it."

Roads outside Heraklion were mostly deep ditches and ruts cut by the German tanks and trucks when they'd all retreated to the western part of the island. Takis and I grasped each other, trying to remain upright as we lurched along. Many of the villages we passed had been burned, but we didn't know what destruction had been done by the Germans and what by guerrillas fighting the government militia or police. Other villages looked untouched, smoke rising from chimneys, sheep grazing on a hillside. Thanasis stopped at these, buying whatever was for sale.

Waiting for him beside his truck in one of the villages, Yannoula said, "Such a lovely man, if you don't mind the smell of garlic."

He sold his first big load of produce in the seaside town of Agios Nikolaos. It was a sleepy little port known mostly for its prison camp, Thanasis said, where captured guerrillas were interrogated and sometimes sentenced to other camps or prisons on remote islands. We saw none of this in the central market area beside the sparkling sea where townspeople bartered with merchants and farmers. I would see the town differently the next time I passed through.

Farther on at Ierapetra, a larger seaside town on the south coast, we decided to stay over and give performances. Thanasis said the town had been attacked by more than a hundred guerrillas a few weeks earlier. They'd raided warehouses for sacks of flour, sugar, rice and pasta and forced local residents to give them blankets and clothing.

Then they'd disappeared back into the mountains. As a result, the town was now heavily patrolled by the militia. Soldiers checked our identities on the outskirts and we saw them standing guard in front of the bank and the city hall.

"You'll be safe," Thanasis said, unloading his oranges and lettuces in the main street, "unless the locals eat you."

"They *do* that?" Takis asked, eyes wide.

"It's just that they're fierce around here. And don't take much to strangers."

As we went around town tacking up posters, we could feel everyone watching us. In cafés or shops, people asked who we were *really*. No matter what we answered, they'd ask why we were *really* there. Takis went into a taverna and described Stelios to several customers on the off chance that he might have been with the guerrillas who'd invaded the town. The customers didn't respond.

"They stared at me and said nothing," Takis said of the men in the taverna. "One man shrugged his shoulders then turned and stared at the wall. *The wall.* As if even that was better than talking to me."

Thanasis vouched for us, telling his customers that we were just traveling players who'd come with him. But in spite of this, neither of the two local cafés would let us set up there. So the first evening, we performed *Karagiozis the Baker* on the half-moon beach that curved around the bay in front of the town. Our audience was small, a few children and their parents who had to sit on piles of fishing nets or overturned boats. This was our first show without Stelios and we were nervous, skidding in the soft sand and muffing our lines. Takis, however, carried the show, handling multiple puppets on poles, changing his voice for each, laughing maniacally as Karagiozis, sneering as the sultan. He seemed to be enjoying himself so much that it was difficult to believe this was the same boy who thought trees and fish talked to him. Even when the balmy April wind gusted off the water and blew out our candles and kerosene lamps, erasing the shadows on the screen, Takis incorporated it into the play until we could get them relit.

KARAGIOZIS: *All is black. I've gone blind. You put a curse on me!*
SULTAN: *The sun is behind a cloud, you fool. Here it is back again.*

Ierapetra had no hotel or boardinghouse, but at the far end of the beach was a smaller version of the Venetian fortress of Heraklion. Facing the sea, its crumbling stone walls would protect us from the sea wind. So there we carried our things when the performance was over and built a small campfire of driftwood to take off the night chill. Yannoula and I bedded down in what had been the fortress courtyard while Takis wandered off to hunt for more driftwood.

"I can't live like this," Yannoula said. "Oof, I'll look like death in the morning. When's Thanasis coming back?"

"Day after tomorrow," I said.

"I'll be dead by then. Too bad. Such a nice man, and a widower too."

He'd told her that his wife had died in the invasion of Crete, one of the many townspeople who attacked the German parachutists as they landed. She and other neighborhood women had rushed out with only kitchen knives as weapons and had been shot. Thanasis was on the road at the time and didn't find out until later. It had been almost four years, but he was still stunned, still wearing the black armband.

"He needs someone to make him laugh," Yannoula said. "All men do. They forget how to laugh at themselves, tramping around in their big boots as if they owned the world. Then life punches a hole in the heart."

Was that what had happened to my father? I wondered. And Stelios too? And what about Chrysoula? Or for that matter, me? I said that it wasn't just men.

"Of course not, my child. My heart's a leaky old sieve by now. But men, well, they need our help because they don't recover as fast as we do, the poor babies. So it's really up to us."

"What is?"

"To put ourselves into their hearts when they're not looking. Do some plastering, so to speak, some patching up. Run up fresh curtains, that kind of thing. They'd never manage it by themselves. Then, just when they start to feel that somehow everything is getting better, but they're not sure why, *there* we are."

I'd never thought of the heart that way, like a run-down house in need of redecoration. Yannoula reminded me a bit of Chrysoula talking about men: *What men will and will not do is a very big subject, I'm afraid.* What men were doing to each other every day in towns and villages across this island surely meant a lot of holes in hearts.

Just as Yannoula was drifting off, Takis came back with more driftwood and built up the fire. He and I lay awake a long time, watching stars.

"Do you ever think of my mother?" he said after a while.

"I was just thinking about her a few minutes ago," I said.

"What were you thinking?"

"About some of the things she used to say. I thought she knew everything."

"I . . . I can't remember her face anymore. I try, but I can't."

I described her face, tone of voice, the funny things she said. If she'd seen the way he'd worked the puppets, she would have been proud.

"When I'm doing them," Takis said, "I don't have to be myself. I'm free. Do you know what I mean?"

"I do. I think the same thing happens to Stelios when he works them."

"Stelios." He paused for a moment then went on. "When he comes back, I won't get to do them anymore, will I?"

"I don't know. We can work something out."

"When I play Karagiozis, I don't have to think about anything else. I don't have to think about my mother and . . ."

He didn't say anything more and after a while I heard him turn on his side away from me. When he was calm like this, I always thought it meant he was getting better, that he'd be all right. But then he always slid back into his own darkness. Would it be different if he could keep working with the puppets?

Word of our performance had apparently gone around because the next night the audience was so big that we had to give two separate shows to accommodate everyone. People had little to pay but brought what they could—a few cigarettes, a bag of lentils or a bit of embroidery from a dowry chest. Some had nothing to spend; but no one was turned away. At the end, I looked from behind the screen at our departing audiences and wondered if anyone would ever help us find Stelios—the old woman in black with the cavernous face, the shopkeeper who laughed at nearly every line, the young shepherd who brought his crook with him and beat it on the ground instead of clapping.

When Thanasis returned the next morning, he drove us farther up to the high plain of Lasithi with its thousands of windmills. Villagers there used the wind power to irrigate the fertile plain, Thanasis said. But because they were at such an altitude, it was still chilly and the sails of most mills were furled. No, no one had seen anyone who matched our description of Stelios, but the villagers were happy to see the fresh produce from the plains down below and offered us simple hospitality, a drinking gourd of resinated wine or a handful of almonds to be cracked with a stone. Easter would come soon in early May. The villagers had been fasting for weeks.

"It's easy enough to fast," Thanasis said, "when there's little to eat anyway."

When he'd traded his fruit and vegetables for bags of local maize flour, he drove us into the foothills near Mt. Dikti. As we rounded a bend leading into a high village, its *plateia* came into view and from the lower branches of a huge plane tree we saw three hanging bodies. There were hoods over their heads, pillowcases actually, but from their clothing they appeared to be two men and a woman. They turned slowly in the breeze. Thanasis started to speed through the village streets, but I beat on the back window of the truck cab and screamed for him to stop.

One of the hanged men was wearing what looked like Stelios's tweed jacket.

CASSETTE 4 • Side 1

Yes, I know, what a place for the cassette to finish. And that was the last of those you left me, my little American scholar. I suppose you thought that was all I'd need for my laments. Of course I'm taking advantage of you a bit, telling so much more than you wanted. But laments are surrounded by life, even though provoked by death. They're not separate from it, because on their own, laments don't make much sense. They've grown out of *my* life as much as out of the lives of the dead.

No one here in the village carries cassettes, certainly not old Stamatis in his one-room shop, though he's got all sorts of batteries and chips for gadgets like the one that you worked with your thumbs. He had to order more cassettes for me and apparently they're hard to find because no one uses them much anymore. *Old technology,* he says, but who's he to talk, still scooping salted cod out of the barrel for his customers, as he has all these decades? Anyway, they've just arrived finally—the cassettes, that is, not the cod—but while I was waiting for them, the forty days passed after Zephyra's wake and funeral so yesterday her memorial service took place.

It started in the church with young Father Yerasimos up front in his brocade robes waving censers around until the clouds of incense sent some of us into spasms of sneezing. Through multiple prayers we sneezed, cupping the flames of our candles that represented our souls. When Zephyra's own soul had received as much repose as our prayers could manage, we moved forward to put our candles in the candelabra in front of the crucifix. But as we stepped up, I sneezed once more, so hard this time that I blew out my little flame and another one. I got the giggles thinking, oh, well, out goes the soul on the breeze of a sneeze. Father Yerasimos gave me such a look.

As we walked behind him to the cemetery where he was to bless Zephyra's grave, I mentioned to the other women that I wanted to visit my father's grave there too. Funny you should mention it, they said, and they told me that during her nights of goat stealing as a child, Zephyra had sometimes seen my father in the shadows alongside the houses, moving from one to another. Oh, he would have been stealing those squash, I said. They looked at each other and smiled. What Zephyra had seen in the time of the Germans, others had known long before, they said. It had been going on for years. One of the women snickered and then the others.

My father was a bee, they told me, gathering nectar. And not from only one flower. They drew their black scarves over their mouths. It wouldn't have done to look amused as we walked to the cemetery. Other villagers stood by the side of the road or on balconies above to watch us pass.

It started long ago, the women said, even before my mother fled the village. What was the *it* exactly that had started? I asked. But I didn't need to hear their answer and none came. Was that why my mother left? I wondered. As a child, I'd worried it was something to do with me, that through some fault or flaw of my own, she hadn't wanted to stay. All at once as I walked beside them in the street, I felt lighter, as if something I'd carried a long time had been lifted, the dark little burden of being unloved by my own mother.

"It went on for many years," one of the women said.

"You've already told me that," I said.

"He went to this one and then that one."

"Oh, please. There can't have been that many unfaithful village wives. Were there no suspicious husbands?"

He'd nearly got himself in trouble a few times, they said, but it hadn't changed his habits. I did remember that he often went out after he'd put me to bed. And sometimes later, waking from a dream, I would hear noises from his bedroom: a cry, a laugh. When I called out, he would rush in to soothe me. But later the noises would start again.

How had he managed to get away with it? Village husbands were not so easily fooled about the virtue of their wives. Of course there were always widows, not to mention unmarried women living on the thin charity of relatives. But would there have been enough of them to keep him as busy as he evidently was? The women had no answer for this, saying only that my father was as clever as he was handsome. It was hard for me to think of him that way; to me he was just my father. I remembered Chrysoula saying what a good man he was. Had hers been one of the houses he'd visited? Well, I'm not going to begrudge them a bit of happiness after all these years, if that's what they had. And I hope it was. Poor Chrysoula—no wonder she was so shattered by his execution. But what about the others? There'd certainly been a lot of wailing at his wake; that I remembered.

As we followed Father Yerasimos through the cemetery gates, I paused just inside at my father's grave with new interest. All that after-death complaining about misplaced tools and not being able to get a good cup of coffee over there—was that all he had on his mind? Or was it just that matters of the *heart*—I use the word loosely—did not carry over to that side? Scanning the other graves from his time, I wondered how many of them held women he'd once held. And where on this earth was the grave that held my mother with her tattered heart?

Father Yerasimos waved more incense at Zephyra's gravesite with its sad funeral flowers long since dried out in the sun. The wind carried off the incense along with his chanted blessing:

. . . give rest to Thy servant Zephyra
in a place of light,
a place of repose . . .

And a place without gossip about my father, I said to myself. And without *goats*.

I didn't wait to eat the boiled wheat and raisin mix, *koliva*, offered in memory of the dead. Walking home alone, I thought of the three dead hanging from the plane tree that day I was describing before the third cassette ran out, one of them Stelios, I thought. Did anyone ever give them a funeral or memorial service or offer *koliva* in their memory? And I remembered what I wanted to finish telling you, for I left you, as well as them, hanging.

Thanasis braked and backed the truck up under the swaying bodies. Takis and I had already climbed down and stood to one side with Yannoula, who was holding me to stop me from shaking. The one in the tweed jacket was Stelios, I was sure of it. As Thanasis climbed into the bed of the truck with a knife, Yannoula turned my face away. I could hear Thanasis sawing through the rope and then the awful thud of the body falling into the truck. I couldn't bear the sound of it and cried out. Yannoula held me tight until Thanasis had pulled the hood off and asked that one of us tell him if this was the Stelios we were looking for.

Takis started forward, but Thanasis said, "No, not you. You're too young."

"I am *not*, and I want to see!"

Yannoula let go of me, telling me to stay put. She walked to the back of the truck, where I heard her give a little cry and then she began to retch. I ran to the truck.

"It's not him," she said. "But don't look. It's horrible." She crossed herself three times. Takis ran around the back of the truck and, before Thanasis could stop him, jumped up to see the body.

"Why is his tongue sticking out?" he said. "And it's all purple, ech!"

"Shut up, Takis," Thanasis said. "Show some respect."

"But, you know," Yannoula said, "that *is* Stelios's jacket. The one that was his father's originally. That cigarette burn on the lapel—his father did that years ago. I tried to mend it for him."

So Stelios must have been in the area and someone had taken his jacket? Because he was dead and had no need of it? Or maybe he'd been forced to give it up? Thanasis put the hood back on the body, jumped down from the truck bed and lifted the body gently in his arms, laying it next to the trunk of the tree. "I can't just leave these others," he said, so he cut them down too and carried their bodies over beside the other one.

Back in the truck, we drove through the center of the village and stopped in front of an old woman in a doorway to ask her what had happened back there. She crossed herself three times and said the government militia had hanged the three, who were "*communistas guerrillas.*" There'd been no trial of any kind and no one from the village knew any of the three. The village just happened to have the best hanging tree in the area.

"Let the crows have them," she said, and she spat on the ground, then crossed herself again. We described Stelios, but she just shrugged and said, "There are many who look like that."

Driving higher into the mountains, we looked out at what I thought Stelios must have seen if he'd been brought here. *Where is he?* I silently asked the craggy slopes we passed. *What have you done with him?* I demanded of the little collections of huts like eagles' nests perched on ledges above steep ravines. None of the villages here had been burned and the men we passed looked as tough and gnarled as mountain pines, their faces burned to leather by sun and wind. Many still dressed in the traditional Cretan way we'd sometimes seen on market day in Heraklion—black head scarves tied into bands around the foreheads, trouser cuffs tucked into jackboots, purple sashes around the waist. Some men had pistols jammed into their sashes.

At these heights gusts of frigid wind flung handfuls of rain into our faces. Pulling my own coat tighter, I thought of Stelios without one. How had his jacket ended up on the hanged man? I could feel again the warmth and weight of his body that night in my room. If only I hadn't made him stop, we'd still be in the boardinghouse, maybe warming each other again under blankets.

Takis and I huddled against the wind and rapped on the window of the cab to ask that we stop soon. It was too chilly for us to go on riding outside and there wasn't enough room in the cab for all four of us. Thanasis called back that we were almost there, but we didn't know where. Shortly after that, we pulled into an open space near a small church that seemed tucked in just under the clouds. As Takis and I climbed down and looked around, we said this had to be the top of the world. It was almost as if we could reach up and touch the clouds scudding past. The wind was sweet with the scent of jasmine. Could it bloom at such a height? How could anyone live here? But plumes of smoke rose from the stone huts that made up most of the village. And a few village men in sashes and headbands came out to the truck.

"Eh, Thanasis," one called out, gesturing at us, "what kind of cabbages have you brought us today?"

"Not ones for boiling," he said, laughing as he unloaded bags of maize flour. The men stared at us with such suspicion that had it not been for Thanasis, to explain about the puppets, who knows what would have happened?

Yannoula tugged down the hem of her skirt and whispered that I was not to meet anyone's eyes. Even so, only the older villagers had heard of Karagiozis, not the women and children, who, when they joined the men, were shy and stood back. After everyone had stared long enough, the children came forward and reached out to touch us, our clothes, our hair and, as we took our things down from the truck, the puppets. We were led to a large stone house to refresh ourselves, as the villagers said, where a crone with stony eyes and yellow teeth sat us down at a long wooden table. She ladled lentil soup out of a cauldron over a hissing fire in a fireplace big enough to roast a whole sheep. Along with the soup she gave us thick slices of coarse bread and quarters of raw onion. The wine she poured was so resinated it might have been steeped in pinecones. But after our cold ride, everything was fragrant and delicious.

Yannoula whispered that she couldn't eat anything because she couldn't stop thinking about the face of that poor hanged man. Thanasis touched her shoulder gently and said it was the same for him, and with the smell of the bodies still in his nostrils, but we all had to eat. It would be insulting not to do so.

"These people have little to give but give it anyway."

As many villagers as could squeeze into the house did so while the others stood outside peering in as we ate, as if expecting us to do it in some strange, new way. Then the questions came from all sides. They rarely saw strangers "from below" and wanted to know: What was it like down there—had the Germans really and truly left, or were they still trapped in the west? Had the Allied troops, Australians and New Zealanders come back, they who'd fought so bravely? A few men of the British special forces had helped the guerrillas harass the Germans here in the mountain passes—but where had those brave British gone? Had the king returned from exile? No one seemed to have a radio up here and there were no newspapers. We answered as we could, Thanasis saying that there was to be a referendum on the monarchy at some point and, depending on which way it went, the king might or might not return.

We had questions of our own. I described Stelios, but no one recognized him from my description. Yes, they'd heard about the hanging of the three in the other village. It was terrible that one was a woman, they said. It wasn't right to hang a woman.

"The others, well, they can go to the devil," said the village elder, a strongly built man with white hair, a beard and a wide mustache that curled up on both sides. His name was Vasili and everyone stopped speaking when he spoke. "We have nothing for guerrillas to take. What will they have of us—our small green olives, so slow to ripen here? Bah! They think they own these mountains." He glanced around the room. "Some say they have relatives *here* in this very room."

There was angry muttering near the door and a few people pushed their way outside. Vasili stared straight ahead while others in the room turned to see who'd left. "And as for the government militia and the police," Vasili said, "who are they really? From what government?" There was more muttering, though this time in approval of what he'd said.

When by evening deep shadows had crept across the village, we set up our screen and lit our lamps in the open space in front of the church. The villagers spread sheepskins on the ground and sat there to watch. Everyone came, from children to crones, and Vasili sat in front. Thanasis had told us that Vasili was known for his formidable memory and could recite the whole of *Erotokritos*, a Cretan epic poem from the seventeenth century, consisting of some ten thousand lines in rhymed couplets. Because of this, we felt nervous putting on our own poor play. But the children were ecstatic; jumping up and down, cheering Karagiozis and booing the sultan. Their reactions made us all work even harder to please them, especially Takis, who was almost as good a puppeteer as Stelios. The children had never seen this kind of thing before or indeed any other entertainment besides church rituals, their parents told us later. When we'd finished, Vasili said, "You honor us with this gift. It lifts the hearts of our children, and that lifts ours too. You must stay here as long as you like."

Thanasis left the next day, saying he wouldn't be back until Good Friday. But before he drove off, Yannoula loitered around the truck watching him load the casks of olive oil he'd bought from the villagers. She kissed him on both cheeks, but he pulled back and waved a quick farewell as he climbed into the cab of the truck. Her eyes had misted over when she turned to us, but she said nothing.

We performed each evening for the next few days and then had a simple meal, usually thin soup and boiled greens, with a different family each night until we had broken bread with many of the villagers. After dinner we listened to stories told late into the night around a fire, tales of long-standing feuds between villages, of a bride abducted at gunpoint, of a wisewoman in the valley who cast spells, of a wolf that got into a house one winter night and made off with a baby. Its bones were found in the spring near the mouth of a cave. While stories were told, the young men of a family stood at the window staring into the night, pistols tucked into belts. Though so far the guerrillas had left this village alone because, it was suspected, they had relatives here. I remembered those who'd left the room the first night when Vasili referred to this.

Each morning the children were bused to a town where they went to the area school, which had reopened. They invited Takis and me to come with them, but I was too embarrassed. I'd wanted to go to school for so long, but now that it was possible, the fact was that I was older and much taller than the others. I would have felt foolish sitting in their class. And I didn't want them to see that, despite my age, I didn't know my multiplication tables or how to spell or what countries sat along the equator. Takis went with the other boys his age, though he said later that all he'd learned was that guerrillas had abducted several men from the town and regularly broke into shops and warehouses at night. The militia had caught a few and taken them back to Heraklion. Any one of them might have been Stelios, it seemed. They all looked alike—beards, boots, ragged clothes, guns—who could tell one from the other? I was losing heart that we'd ever see him again and couldn't stand to imagine life without him. We had planned to live our lives together. Was it possible that our time was already over? Maybe we should go back to Heraklion with Thanasis when he returned and wait there, I thought. I was losing my sense of the safe return that Stelios always gave me. We weren't getting anywhere here in this high village, though the villagers were happy about having us as their guests for Easter week.

"We will teach you our dances," Vasili said. "After we drink the rest of last year's wine."

Yannoula had started helping out in the village store, a one-room place that carried everything from nails and bolts to lentils and soap. It was a gathering place for the old men, who sat on upended barrels, turning their strings of beads over in their hands, telling stories of the war. I preferred the little church, the only place where the electric light was strong enough for reading. Most of the houses had only a dim lightbulb on a cord hanging from the ceiling in the center of one room. And some had no electricity at all. But once I'd turned on the lights in the church, I could take out Stelios's copy of *The Iliad*. Puzzling out new passages and rereading ones I already knew made me feel close to him. Under the cold stares of the saints in their icons, I sounded out the unknown words and guessed meaning from context, as Stelios had taught me. My reward was to catch the sense of a line.

. . . the goddess filled her heart with yearning warm and deep
for her husband long ago, her city and her parents.

I could certainly understand that *yearning warm and deep*. This woman of so long ago, fought over by two armies, had felt something that I too felt sitting there thousands of years later in a mountain church. I looked up from the book and silently asked the saints if they'd felt *sweet longing* too. But maybe it was the absence of it that had given them such disapproving looks. Anyway, they weren't saying.

I couldn't use the church on the day before Good Friday because the women were cleaning it for the coming ceremonies. Yannoula and I stood outside where the boys gathered around Vasili. They wanted to borrow the pistol tucked in the sash around his waist.

"Boys become men before their time," he told Yannoula and me. "All our boys here, they know how to shoot. My brave grandson, Christos, only fourteen years old he was, when he shot and wounded a

German officer right over there in that valley." He pointed to it and then to the cliff above. "And up there is where the officer's comrades took Christos after they'd caught him. Those ill-fated ones—they threw our little hero into the ravine below." He crossed himself three times and said, "And they wouldn't let us go to him for more than a month. By then the animals . . ." He stopped a moment, collected himself and went on. "So now it's not the Germans we fear but some of our own, even from this village." I remembered again how a few villagers had walked out when he'd referred to this the day we'd arrived.

"Teach me," Takis said to Vasili, "teach me to shoot."

Vasili looked down at Takis and said, "Aha, my little warrior, are you old enough to learn?"

"I'm fourteen," Takis said. He would have turned eleven around the time I turned fifteen in the past year.

"Are you indeed?" Vasili said, rolling his eyes at Yannoula and me. But he pulled his own pistol from his sash and said to one of the other boys, a tall lad with a black braided headband, "Here, Mitso, take this and teach our friend something useful."

Yannoula and I exchanged glances of alarm at the thought of Takis armed. Yannoula told Vasili this wasn't a good idea, but he said not to worry; boys needed to know things beyond what women understood. Mitso was a good boy who would look after Takis. We both tried to explain that Takis had many problems, but Vasili said only that this was so with all boys.

"Learning to shoot is a manly thing. We all do it here. It's part of our fate."

Boys with guns, I thought, the same old story. But this might be an even worse one. All afternoon we heard Mitso and the other boys shouting encouragement to Takis as they threw pinecones into the air as targets. They told him not to shoot directly at one but at where it would likely be when the bullet struck. Tying a Cretan bandana around his forehead, they called him a *palikari*, a brave young warrior. Takis puffed out his chest and attempted a manly swagger.

That night, Yannoula and I spread blankets on a pile of hay in the stable behind one of the houses; it was all that particular family had. They'd actually offered us their own beds in the house, saying they would sleep in the stable, but that was taking hospitality too far for us. Their donkey in its corner watched us with a single eye, its other just a blackened hole from a farm accident. Takis was staying with the family of Mitso, the boy who was teaching him to shoot.

"I wish Thanasis would come back," Yannoula said, fussing with her blanket and then warming her hands over our single candle in the neck of a bottle. "Chances are I won't make it through another winter."

"You always say things like that. But you're a tough old bone."

"It would be good to have someone to look after."

"We just met him a while ago."

"At my age, who has time to spare? People who live alone don't live long."

"You're not living alone."

"Not *now*. But you and Stelios, you'll want to make a life of your own eventually. You won't need me."

"But his family house is your home. We could all live there again. That's, of course, if Stelios . . ." I couldn't finish the sentence.

"Of course he is. Alive, I mean. Isn't that what you were going to say?"

"I guess. Yes."

Where are you? I asked him again silently. I felt that he was near, but this was probably only my wanting him to be. Still, it was some small comfort.

"I feel like our life together hasn't even begun yet," I said.

"Oh, it has, trust me. It's here and now; life always is."

"I thought it would start when the fighting is over. When Stelios is back. And when Takis is . . ." I couldn't finish that sentence either.

"I think . . ." Yannoula said, then paused and shifted on her blanket, scratching her legs roughly. "You know what's in this hay, Aliki? *Fleas.* Worse than bedbugs. Wrap yourself up. Leave no inch exposed."

We pulled our blankets around us like cocoons covering even our heads so that only our eyes were exposed, peering at each other in the dim light of the candle and a slice of moon through the window. Then a shadow fell across the moon. A face looked in the window and I screamed.

"No, no, it's all right," a man's voice said. "Just checking on you." The voice was familiar, though we couldn't tell which of the village men it belonged to. "But best to put out your light."

Yannoula blew out the candle and the voice wished us a good night.

"Theo mou!" she said. "You terrified me, Aliki."

"*He* terrified me. I could just see the shape of a head. How was I to know?"

"We're all a little jumpy at night, I guess. At least we know we're being looked after. What good people these are. Imagine that family offering us their beds."

We didn't say anything else for a while as we snuggled down into the hay and tried to get comfortable. "What I was going to say," Yannoula said into the dark, "before the fleas and our visitor, was that I think Takis may always be what he is now."

"What? How do you know?"

"I just feel it. Inside, he'll still be a boy hearing voices. He won't grow out of it even when he grows up."

"That's not possible, is it? Everyone grows up. Everyone changes."

"Outside, yes. But maybe not inside. Long ago they might have thought he was a seer, one who could see what's visible to no one else."

A gust of wind rattled the roof tiles, pushed the latched door open slightly and slammed it shut. We both pulled our blankets tighter around us. "Oof, what a place," Yannoula said. "At least it's too chilly for Takis to wander around without his clothes. In fact, I hope he doesn't start delivering messages from trees while we're here. That old Vasili, I don't know what he'd make of it."

"I hope you're wrong about Takis."

"I hope so too. Either way, he won't have an easy life, that's for certain, and possibly not a long one. But who does anymore? Now, me—I keep getting new beginnings. That's about as much as we can hope for. I thought Thanasis might be another beginning for me, but am *I* one for him—that's the question."

The idea of new love between older people like Yannoula and Thanasis seemed strange to me. It would be a while before I would grasp that the gray-haired and wrinkled need it as much, if not more, than the young.

When Thanasis climbed down from his truck the next morning, he went round the back and pulled down a tarp. Beneath it lay two lambs, cleaned and dressed, ready for roasting. He told us he'd been back to Ierapetra, still heavily protected by militia. The shopkeepers there had bought all his produce because they had to feed the militia stationed there. But there was little cash to pay Thanasis. They'd been doing the traditional butchering of the spring lambs so they'd given him these two instead. They would be the village Easter feast.

"I'm no cook," he said, "but I know how to stuff these with herbs and sew them up. Yannoula, can you help?"

She looked pleased to be asked, but before she could say anything, Vasili stepped forward and said, "We'll all help. It's not enough to feed everyone, but with lots of roasted potatoes and salad greens, there'll be plenty. And with enough wine, who will care? We'll ask Brother Pavlos to bless it all when he comes today." A monk from a nearby monastery, Brother Pavlos was going to help with the Friday and Saturday night services because the village was too small and out of the way to have its own priest.

It was later that I heard that Thanasis had told Vasili there'd been brutal fighting outside one of the villages a ways from Ierapetra. Government militia had killed a number of guerrillas, including one of the leaders known for brutalizing area villages. After he was dead, militia soldiers had severed his head and right hand, impaled them on a pole and carried them through the villages he and his men had terrorized, inviting villagers to spit on them. Thanasis hadn't seen it, but everywhere he went, people were talking. Vasili told only one or two people, but in only an hour or so, everyone in the village seemed to know. Yannoula told me only because she knew I'd hear one way or another.

"Thanasis didn't want you to know because it would make you worry even more about Stelios. But there's no reason to think . . ."

"Oh, God. Oh, God." How hideous it was. How could men do such things to one another? How could they do it to someone like Stelios, who'd never harmed anyone? "One of them was Stelios, wasn't it?"

"Now listen, Aliki, all we know is that someone took his jacket. That's all we know. This new story has nothing . . ."

"Oh, God."

"He's not anywhere near where this happened, I'm sure of it."

"How?"

"I just am."

That evening, dulled by worry, I joined the others around the little church. Takis was there with his new friends and passed beeswax candles to Yannoula and me. Inside, Brother Pavlos, a bony young man so thin you could see the outlines of his skull through his face, sang the Good Friday lamentations in a high, nasal voice. Wrapping the icon of Christ in a white cloth, he placed it in a coffin that the women covered with flower petals. Thanasis and five other men lifted it onto their shoulders and, with Brother Pavlos leading the way in front of the coffin and the rest of us behind, we began our slow procession through the village lanes. Brother Pavlos led the singing as we walked.

Sun and moon together darkened.
Like loyal servants, they wore their
grief, wrapping themselves in darkness
like a shawl.

Earlier that day I'd overheard Vasili talking with Brother Pavlos before the ceremony began, about the beheading of the dead guerrilla.

"It's not the first time," Vasili said. "There've been other cases. On both sides."

"They debase themselves," Brother Pavlos said. "We must pray for them."

"*You* pray for them, Brother. I teach our boys to shoot straight."

Easter Sunday was sunny and warmer as Thanasis and Yannoula prepared the lambs for roasting, stuffing them with rosemary, thyme, heads of garlic and whole lemons. Village men built a fire in a pit and watched it burn down to hot coals. The lambs were threaded onto spits positioned over the coals and two men at a time turned them slowly while brushing them with bunches of rosemary dipped in lemon juice and red wine. The air became so savory that you could taste it. In the meadow, Takis and the other boys went on with their target practice while I helped some of the women peel and quarter potatoes in the same house we'd been in the first night. Yannoula and the others gathered greens on the mountainside.

"Are you spoken for?" asked the woman who'd fed us that first day. Though we'd mentioned Stelios then, we hadn't talked about any connection between him and me. There'd been no particular reason to do so. "We see how our young men look at you," she said.

"I haven't noticed that," I said. I usually tried to keep my eyes lowered around the village men.

"They burn for you," the woman said. "It's in their eyes. You could choose one, stay here, make babies. Why not?" She said this lightly as if the decision to marry someone unknown and start a family in a place that, only a little while earlier, I'd never heard of was an ordinary thing to do.

"I'm sure there are already worthy young women here," I said.

"But what kind of life is it for you, traveling through these mountains? Anything could happen."

The other women peeling potatoes all nodded and repeated, "Anything, anything." Then the crone asked me what kind of dowry I had. I thought of my father's house so far away and felt a pang for it. Was it still standing? Would I ever see it again? But I didn't want to mention it as that might be laying a card on the table.

"Alas, I have no dowry," I said.

"Ah, such a pity, but never mind. A woman's good name is always the best dowry. I myself could help you. I've arranged many matches."

"You honor me with your offer, but I . . ."

"The honor would be mine. You can ask anyone about the matches I've made." She waved her arm at the other women, who giggled like schoolgirls. Then she covered my right hand with her own, which was gnarled with arthritis, a claw. I didn't like the direction of all this and took my hand away.

"You see, there's already an understanding," I said.

"Oh?" She drew back her own hand. "You should have said so."

"I'm doing so now."

Her tone grew sharper. "Well, I'm surprised. Your fiancé allows you to travel around the countryside with a merchant and only the old one as chaperone? And that boy? What sort of man would permit such behavior?"

I looked around for an escape from this conversation and was relieved to see Yannoula passing the window with a basket of greens. I called to her and rolled my eyes, nodding sideways at the old woman. Yannoula came inside at once, sized up my companion and said loudly that I must stop this work at once before I accidentally nicked or cut my hands, because then how would I work the puppets?

"Come look at the greens we've gathered," she said, taking me by the arm and steering me out the door.

"They're trying to marry me off," I whispered.

"I know," she said once we were outside. "The others were talking about it on the hillside over there. Apparently there's a dim young man here that none of the village girls will have, so an outsider will do nicely. They actually said that though he's not so bright and does drool a bit, he'll inherit two fields and is said to have a big *thing*. Can you imagine?"

"I'd rather not."

"And I think he's provided the potatoes from one of his family's fields. He hopes to impress you and put us under an obligation. As if potatoes would do it. In any case, we're artistes. We pay with our art and *nothing else*."

We walked over to watch the men basting the lambs as they sizzled and spat over the coals. The women had finished carrying the pans of potatoes in oil and lemon to the central clay oven fired with brushwood. The crone glared at us as she passed on her way back to the house. So Yannoula and I went to the meadow to watch the boys at their target practice. Taking turns with Vasili's pistol, each fired at pinecones of various sizes tossed into the air one at a time by another boy. Those who could hit only the larger ones were jeered at by the others and lost their chance to shoot again. Takis was so excited that when Vasili's gun was passed to him, he hopped around at first, causing the other boys to step back as if the gun might go off accidentally. But as cones of ever smaller sizes were thrown up, he picked off even the smallest. Yannoula and I looked at each other.

"This won't end well," she said.

"Well, but look, he has skill. If he could just find some other use for it. And he's made some friends. I don't think he's ever had any before."

I looked at him over there with the others taking on the swagger of those boys who, along with him, were the best shots. Takis and

Mitso were acting like men, or at least like imitations of them. They had the walk, the bearing of fathers or older brothers but not their gravity. And especially not their faces full of deep lines etched there by bad times and sharp weather. And while I hated seeing Takis with a pistol, I hoped that, with friends, he was moving beyond the call of imagined voices. Beyond danger.

When the lambs were done, Vasili extracted them from their spits and carved them on a table the women had brought outside. We speared the meat from platters and spooned out the roasted potatoes and boiled greens. Takis and his new friends joined the crowd filling their plates. Vasili's pistol was tucked into the sash around Takis's waist. I tried to catch his eye, but he was talking excitedly with the others, telling them about Patroclus from *The Iliad*, I supposed, because he was saying, ". . . and he speared him just like a fish and flipped him out of his chariot!"

We all sat on sheepskins on the ground in a circle, washing the succulent meat down with strong retsina dipped from a pine cask. Across the circle I caught the glance of what must have been the young man with the two fields. His face looked as if it had slid down on one side, which I now know was probably a birth defect or the result of a slight stroke. Then, I knew from my own village that such a flaw was often taken as a result of the evil eye. Aside from his face, he was probably all right but doomed to be treated otherwise. He had a shy but steady gaze.

Yannoula followed the direction of my glance. "No matter what's wrong with him," she said, "if he owns two fields, sooner or later someone will have him."

After the meal, one of the men took out a clarinet and played a wild and mournful melody while someone else thudded on a drum. Did we know the Cretan dances, Vasili called out, oh, never mind, he would teach us. We were pulled to our feet and into a line that included the whole village: crones and children, young housewives, men in their jackboots and sashes. The musicians led the way, followed by a young man holding a handkerchief, then Vasili, Thanasis, Yannoula and me and the rest of the village. Takis and the other boys were at the end.

The long line swayed forward and back, dipping suddenly as dancers made abrupt little jumps and skips. The steps were not so different from ones I'd learned from my father. The young man first in line leaped high enough to slap the heels of his boots in midair. He and the two musicians led us around the village lanes between the stone houses, beside the little church and out into the olive grove nearby. The musicians in front wove in and out of the olive trees as flocks of blackbirds swept up from the branches, cawing. At the edge of the grove we could see far down a craggy slope. Miles away, a valley opened out to the blue-green sea.

Through the grove and out the other side we danced. Those of us in the first half of the line had just danced back toward the church. As we approached the bed of still-glowing coals, we stopped suddenly at the sight of two strangers removing the remains of the roasted lambs from the table where they'd been carved. To one side were a half dozen others, bearded, in shaggy clothes, some with machine guns. As they saw us, they turned their guns in our direction. The music stopped. No one spoke for a moment.

"We only want the food," one of them said, apparently the leader.

"It is ours to give, yours to take," Vasili said, his voice controlled and calm. "Good Easter to you."

"And to you."

They could almost have been any two villagers exchanging greetings of the day but for the presence of the guns and the way the carcasses and leftover potatoes were being scooped into a burlap bag. The other guerrillas fanned out over our line, covering us all with their machine guns.

"What else do you have?" the leader asked. A woman farther back in our line moaned softly.

Vasili turned and said to those behind, "Take the children inside."

"Don't," said the leader. "Everyone stays until you've given us what you can."

"Sadly, we have little," Vasili said. "Only our olives . . ."

"Oh? The smoke and smell of your feast traveled far. Even to our caves where we've nothing to eat but the blackbirds we shoot."

He told some of his men to search the houses and take anything edible. They ran into those nearby and dragged out the bags of maize flour Thanasis had brought, along with sacks of lentils and beans, strings of braided onions and peppers, casks of wine and olive oil. While they were doing this, the other guerrillas kept their guns aimed at those of us still behind Vasili. Glancing back, I saw that the last part of the line had melted into the olive grove. Yannoula slipped her arm around my waist and I put mine around hers. We were both trembling. Any minute now they would take the food and go, I told myself. This would be over.

"Where's Takis?" I whispered to Yannoula.

"I don't know."

Into the center of the village the guerrillas herded the village donkeys, including the one-eyed animal from the stable we'd been sharing. The donkeys stood quietly while the guerrillas began to load what they'd taken onto their backs. Vasili said that if they took all that, the village might well starve.

"We take it in return for your protection," the leader said.

"Protection from what?" Vasili asked.

"The government militia."

"They haven't been in these parts."

"Ah, there you see! From that you understand how well we do our jobs. Remember it was we who helped drive the Germans out of these mountains not so long ago. Now we scratch the earth for roots to eat." He spat on the ground at his feet. "Now we fight the fascist militia and police, those collaborators! They hang us. They cut off a head, a hand."

No one said anything for a moment. Then Vasili said, "There have been amnesties."

"Lies, all lies. One of our comrades gave himself up. One from this very village. You would know his name. But days later someone cut his throat."

He turned as if to call out something to his men but then suddenly stumbled and, with mouth still open, slumped to the ground. At first it didn't register that the noise we'd heard—a single shot, which could as easily have been a shutter banging in the breeze—had anything to do with this. His men ran to him as a collective scream went up from some of the women in the line and we broke into flight in all directions. Many of the village men had been unarmed because it was Easter, and who needed a pistol then? But there were others never unarmed who were returning fire. Grabbing Yannoula's hand, I pulled her away and back toward the olive grove, though how we made it there through the firing from both sides, I can't explain.

We came to a tree with low branches so I was able to get a foot up to steady myself and then try to pull Yannoula up behind me. "I can't," she said. "My old knees . . ." I kept pulling her up, anxious that our legs not show below the tree branches. When I got her up beside me, I saw the blood on her right arm just below her shoulder.

"I didn't feel anything," she said. "Just a little burn."

But there was quite a lot of blood now; it had soaked the sleeve of her blouse. Holding on to the trunk of the tree with one hand, I got her to give me a handkerchief and together, with her one free hand and mine, we managed to tie it above the bleeding. Then we clung to the tree and each other, looking back toward the village through branches and leaves. There was still sporadic shooting but single shots only, not machine gun fire. It looked as if the remaining guerrillas were pulling the food supplies off the donkeys and throwing them into the bed of Thanasis's truck beside the church. The guerrillas evidently hadn't noticed it before this. They half carried, half dragged the bodies of their dead and wounded and loaded them too.

Then we heard Thanasis himself, though we couldn't see him. His voice was raised in argument about his truck with one of the men until a short burst from a machine gun brought silence. Yannoula and I looked at each other in horror. Was it possible? We were to find out that not only was it possible but that one of the guerrillas was rummaging through Thanasis's pockets for his keys. In a few minutes, the truck coughed into life and, with a grinding of gears, drove off. Yannoula and I didn't move for some time, unsure if they were really gone.

"Thanasis," she said. "Thanasis, Thanasis."

She let herself down to the ground, trembling and weeping, and began to make her way back toward the village, dripping blood as she went. I followed, full of dread as I tore a sleeve off my shirt, calling out to Yannoula to let me rewrap her arm. As we came out of the grove near the church, there were a half dozen villagers on the ground. I stepped forward to help and nearly tripped over Vasili's body. Kneeling beside him, I could see that he was still breathing. His eyes were open but unfocused. Then Takis was standing over us. Where had he come from?

"*Your* pistol, Vasili," he said proudly. "Did you see how well I shot?"

"He can't hear you. Help me hold up his head."

But it was too late. Vasili's eyes had become fixed and a trickle of blood ran from his mouth.

"Is he . . . ?" Takis asked.

I nodded.

Takis knelt and touched Vasili's face. "He can't be," he said.

"Well, he *is*, poor man."

"But his eyes are still open. Vasili, can you see me? It's me, Takis. I've brought your pistol back." He put it down beside Vasili.

I stared at it and then the thought hit me. "It was *you*, wasn't it? You who had the first shot? Where *were* you?"

"Over there." He pointed to the church. "Just inside the door. They didn't see us." He and the other boys had been at the back of the line and had run off when they'd heard Vasili and the guerrilla leader talking.

"They might have left with just food," I said, "if you hadn't fired at them. Vasili might still be alive. And these others."

Takis knelt beside me, astonished. "You mean I wasn't supposed to shoot?" He put his face close to Vasili's and said, "But you gave me your pistol. What's a pistol for if not to shoot?"

With my hand, I closed Vasili's eyes. By then the unharmed villagers had come running from their hiding places and were bending over the wounded and the dead, calling out to them, tearing strips from their clothing to bind wounds and stop the bleeding. The man with two fields was on the ground with the others. Someone ran to use the single village phone in Vasili's house. Beside me, Takis stood up.

"I was just trying to help."

I could see Yannoula, who'd gone to the place beside the church where Thanasis's truck had been parked. She was standing motionless. As I stood to go to her, Takis said, "When they drove off, did you see . . . ?"

But I was running to Yannoula, who stood quite still, staring down at Thanasis lying on his face in the dirt. In death, he looked smaller. It seemed impossible that this ordinary figure on the ground had been a bear of a man with so much energy.

"Come away," I told her. "We have to do something about your bleeding."

"Bleeding," she repeated, dazed.

I took her to the village well and helped her wash her wound, which looked as if a bullet had just grazed her. I was still carrying the sleeve I'd torn off my shirt and I used it to rewrap her wound and looped it into a makeshift sling. When I looked up from what I was doing, I saw again the bodies on the ground along with Vasili. And I remembered those in my own village, and Chrysoula and Sophia. My legs failed me and I sat down hard on the ground. Yannoula tried to pull me to my feet with her one good arm, but she couldn't manage it and we both collapsed beside the well. A terrible noise came from her, choking and sobbing.

The old woman who'd wanted to marry me off rushed over to us, her arms full of what looked like bedsheets. She dumped them on us, telling us to tear them into strips for bandages. How long did we do this? It's hard to say. No matter how many sheets we tore up, we were always given more. Time had slowed down and was measured out in bandages.

Eventually two Red Cross ambulances arrived, along with a truckload of militia. Some of them spread out beyond the village while others stayed behind and questioned individuals in front of the church. The boy Mitso said that he and Takis and the others had hidden in the church while Vasili was talking to the guerrilla leader. Mitso had seen Takis shoot Vasili's pistol.

"He's a hero," Mitso said. "He killed that bastard."

A hero? I thought. Vasili dead and Thanasis dead and all these others killed or wounded, and Takis was a *hero*? What about the other village men who'd shot some of the guerrillas? Mitso grabbed Takis's hand and raised it in the air. Word went around among the militia that Takis had fired the first shot after only just learning how. There was much hand shaking and slapping of his back the rest of the day. But the surviving villagers and the doctors who'd come with the ambulances didn't even look up as they went on helping the wounded.

As the darkness of evening came on, the bodies of Vasili and Thanasis and the others were brought into the big house and some of the women washed and prepared them for burial. Candles were put at head and foot and one of the women began to ululate and the others joined in. The eerie sound of their voices rose and fell as the mountain wind nosed around the outside of the house as if trying to get inside. Yannoula and I sat in a corner. She was still dazed and I felt myself driven by the high voices of the women into a kind of dream once again without really being asleep. My father was complaining again, saying the newly dead were always so much trouble. *They don't want to settle down, Aliki, with the rest of us. They won't accept what's happened to them and keep hearkening back.* He fished his usual cigarette out of the shirt pocket near the bullet holes and lit up. *Unfinished business lasts forever here so there's no rush. By the way, did you ever find the ax I left in the woods, or that hammer . . . ?*

Then I was again in the dark room with the light from behind the partly opened door. What was it; what did it mean? And what was this other sound so loud it had to be coming from my own mouth? It circled round inside me and formed words, something about trees and a river. Yannoula would tell me long after that it had gone something like this:

We are Thanasis and Vasili,
Trees brought down by lightning
Our limbs broken and burned, our leaves scattered
In the river,
Taken to the sea.
To the sea,
Taken away by the sea.
We are Thanasis and Vasili,
We are gone,
As smoke is gone,
As dust is gone,
Taken by a breeze,
Taken away by a breeze.

There was more to it than that, something about *the wing of death.* "Aliki, Aliki," Yannoula said, gently shaking me with her good arm. I looked around and saw the villagers staring at me. "I didn't know you could lament," she said. "You never said so."

"It started back in my own village where so many were killed by the Germans," I said. "But I don't understand why or how it comes over me."

The old woman who'd given us the bedsheets to tear into bandages came over to us and said, "We don't want your laments. You can stay tonight, but tomorrow morning, take your foolish puppets and go, all three of you." Behind her scowled some of the other women I'd peeled potatoes with earlier in the day. "You've brought misfortune on us and we don't want you here," she said. "You dishonor our dead."

Yannoula and I looked at them without speaking. It was true that if Thanasis hadn't brought the lambs, we might not have attracted the attention of the guerrillas. And if Vasili hadn't given Takis the pistol, wouldn't he still be alive? And Thanasis and my would-be suitor? But I could have gone backward with this line of thought forever: if my father hadn't been executed, if my mother hadn't left my father, if Germany hadn't wanted the whole world. There was no end to these ifs just as there was no undoing any of it, ever.

"We've lost someone too," Yannoula said to the woman. "You don't own all the grief."

But they'd all turned and walked away. Yannoula was talking to herself, muttering something I couldn't catch. I went to find Takis. Would he leave with us? Did we want him to? Was this finally and at long last the place, the time, to cut him loose from my life? There was nothing more I could do for him, nothing he could do for me.

A large tent had been erected next to the church, just there where the guerrillas had taken Thanasis's truck. I could hear talk, laughter from inside. I pushed back the flap and stepped in. Folding tables had been set up and the militia soldiers were eating and drinking, though the village now had neither food nor drink. At a central table with soldiers on either side sat Takis wearing one of their caps. I remembered him that day in Halandri, riding in the British jeep as the crowd cheered and threw flowers. So here we are again, I thought, another massacre with Takis at its center and again he is surrounded by soldiers. Cups were raised to him. Then he noticed me.

"Oh, Aliki," he said, surprised. Everyone turned in my direction. I felt their stares travel over me.

"Let's go outside," I said to Takis. He didn't move for a moment and seemed unsure about leaving his new friends to talk with me. One of the soldiers gave him a nudge and said something I couldn't make out. Everyone laughed.

Once outside the tent and before I could tell him about leaving, Takis said, "I saw *him*. I tried to tell you earlier, but you ran off. He was right here, don't you see, right where we're standing now." I must have looked blank so he added, "Stelios. He was the one who drove Thanasis's truck away with the guerrillas. At least, I *think* it was Stelios. He has a beard now so I'm not sure, but otherwise it looked just like him."

CASSETTE 4 • Side 2

Yes, yes, that noise you hear comes from the women all worked up again, and gathered at my door as usual. They're like crows on a fence waiting for the last of us old ones to be on our way so they can get into our houses the way we got into Zephyra's. Well, there can't be much of interest in Aphrodite's house and she's the one they've come about. If the filth of your house could do you in, she would have died long ago. The doctor who comes here from the nearby town talks endlessly about cleanliness, as if we keep livestock in our parlors. It's insulting. But looking at Aphrodite's house through his eyes, I understand.

The last time the doctor visited her uninvited, Aphrodite put a curse on him, waving burned herbs in his face and telling him that his wife would always be barren. The doctor just laughed so she went on to say that all his children would be stillborn, which, as the doctor pointed out, was unlikely with a barren wife. It was quite a show for the women who were hanging around outside listening.

I'm reluctant to visit because when I was last there, she said my arrival meant death was at hand. This time it might be true. Still, I don't want my face in her doorway to scare her out of this life. It wouldn't be the first time that's happened. Perhaps it's a gift to someone suffering, but relatives do not always see it this way. Everyone has their ideas about exits, even more than entrances. But one thing certain is that the world is a revolving door, swinging babies in one side and the dead out the other.

"You must go to her," one of the women says through my window.

"It's her time," says another.

"How do you know?" I ask.

"Her nails have turned black."

"Her face is gray."

"She may be in a trance," I say. "I've seen her like that."

"She's been so for days."

"She's a healer," I say. "She'll heal herself. She's done so before."

They insist that Aphrodite has lost her powers. Just a month ago, she used homemade oil of mouse to treat a cut on a small boy from another village. It didn't stop the bleeding so the doctor was brought in. But Aphrodite said she'd made the remedy as always, drowning a pink and hairless baby mouse in a bottle of olive oil, which she then left out in the sun for a year or more, the longer the better. Such a stink came out as the bottle was opened, but when Aphrodite brushed the oil on a wound and said her special words, it always stopped any bleeding. When she heard it hadn't worked this time with the boy, she blamed the mouse.

"You can't count on anything these days."

But the women say now that the real problem is Aphrodite herself, whose powers are waning.

"She can't heal anyone, not even herself."

"Her hour is near."

"And she may have things to say to you."

"About Zephyra."

"About your father."

Oh, dear, do I really want to know more about his nighttime trysts or about Zephyra's infernal goat noises? What the dying have to say is worth hearing and it's an honor to listen, but sometimes I've heard more than enough. One old shepherd told me that he'd cared more for one of his sheep than for his wife. He'd moved the sheep into his house after the wife died. Oh, my. And remember Zephyra and her goat noises? But Aphrodite? It won't be a matter of sheep or goats, of that I'm certain. I still can't lament for her until asked by her or her relatives, and she has no living ones, as far as we know. I remind the women that my calling is only to compose the lament for the wake.

Stelios once said that our stories never finish. They just get braided with those of others into some larger strand that only later generations can understand. Yes, I know, that doesn't really sound much like him, does it? But he started to say that kind of thing after he returned from the mountains. We didn't know what to make of it at first. But then, we were still stunned by what had happened in that village—the deaths of Vasili and Thanasis. Especially Yannoula, who was growing more glum and unresponsive.

The militia allowed her and Takis and me to ride with them in the back of a troop truck to a place where we could catch a bus to Heraklion. Wedged among soldiers who sat on wooden benches on either side, we tried to stay dry. But rain leaked through the canvas tarp above and blew into the opening in back. With Yannoula positioned between us, her arm in a Red Cross sling, Takis and I took turns holding an old jacket over her head.

She seemed dazed and didn't notice the weather. She didn't respond when Takis told us that he'd heard from the soldiers that the guerrillas who'd raided the village had already been caught. Their mistake had been to panic and take Thanasis's truck rather than returning on foot to their hideout. The truck was well-known in these parts. With militia blocking most roads, there'd been little escape for a known vehicle loaded with stolen provisions, not to mention the bodies of the guerrillas' fallen comrades. Those still alive had already been arrested and taken to Heraklion to be turned over to the police there for questioning.

"Does that mean they have Stelios too?" I asked Takis, leaning over Yannoula. "Was he really the driver?"

"They just said they'd caught them all." His expression didn't give away how he felt about any of this. "But I did see him drive away. Mitso and I were still inside the church at the window."

"Did you tell them that he isn't a guerrilla, that he was abducted? They'll believe you since they think you're such a *hero*."

"I *did* tell them. And I *am* a hero. They don't blame me the way you do." He turned away and stared out the back of the truck into the rain.

I didn't say anything, as I felt too empty to argue. And what individual soldiers thought about Stelios wasn't going to matter much anyway. The lines of authority among local police, government militia and the shadowy groups called security committees—which took the place of courts—would be confused and confusing. People were arrested, then freed, then rearrested. It didn't make sense. But the Heraklion police captain knew us all. Could we rely on him to help Stelios?

The troop truck stopped at the side of a meadow and there sat the dilapidated country bus with a spray of bullet holes along one side. Half the windshield was a spiderweb of splintered glass. On top of the bus were so many bundles, suitcases and boxes that the bus sat low to the ground. Milling around the bus were passengers and soldiers smoking and talking. We'd heard this was the only bus of the week through this remote area. And it wouldn't go back to Heraklion the way we'd come with Thanasis, but instead would travel there by backroads, stopping at every village along the way.

Inside it so many passengers were standing that the seated ones weren't even visible. A pair of armed soldiers stood in front, one of them paring his fingernails with a knife, the other reading a comic book. They were there for our protection, I assumed, because guerrillas had been known to stop buses to rob passengers or take hostages. But they didn't make me feel any safer.

Village women with black head scarves pulled across their noses and mouths sat with baskets of cabbages or potatoes wedged between their legs. One woman had two live chickens trussed at the feet and hanging from a rope tied around her waist. Sweat stains blotched everyone's clothes; the weather was clearing and turning warm. In the back of the bus a baby was squalling while on the floor two boys punched one another between passengers' feet. As the bus started off, an old man tilting up a wicker-covered demijohn of wine for a drink spilled it over people near him. A woman told him he was not fit for human company and he said, well, he'd never cared much for humans anyway since all they did was kill each other.

Before long I felt a hand sliding up under my skirt. We were packed so tightly I couldn't turn to confront the person so I reached down, got hold of one of his fingers and bent it back as hard as I could until I heard a cry of pain. The hand dropped away.

"I'm dying," Yannoula said. "I can't stand this." It was the first time she'd spoken all day. After the next stop, Takis found a vacated seat for her, but then a young shepherd got on with a goat, which promptly wet her shoes and then began to nibble the hem of her skirt. The smell of the goat was overwhelming, but the shepherd looked away.

"Here you are, dear," said a plump woman in a flowered head scarf next to Yannoula, handing her a bunch of herbs. "Hold this under your nose. It'll revive you." While Yannoula was sniffing it—strong mountain sage—the woman took off her shoe and gave the goat a crack on its head with the heel. "That'll turn out his lights," she said as it stumbled to its knees. The shepherd turned on her and accused her of trying to kill his animal that he was taking to market; it was all he had left to sell. The woman said she'd only been protecting the old one there, indicating Yannoula. The shepherd fired back a stream of curses and so did the woman. On and on they went.

It was already night when we dragged ourselves and our luggage from the Heraklion terminal to the boardinghouse. How much warmer it was down here near the sea. In the chill of the mountains, it was easy to forget that it was late spring here down below. As we rounded the corner, we saw a figure standing in the shadows in front of the entrance. The streetlight lit him from behind, a gaunt man with a scraggly beard. When he turned and saw us, I couldn't tell if his smile was really that or only a shadow across his face. Stelios.

He hurried toward us with difficulty—there was a limp—and Yannoula gave a little cry as he tried to gather all three of us in his arms. His face was wet and his beard scratchy, but my knees weakened and I fell against him. All in a huddle, we made our way into the lobby. He glanced around the room, saying, "I didn't expect I'd ever see this place again. Nothing has changed."

"Except for you," Takis said.

"Yes, well."

In ordinary light, Stelios looked not so much older as weathered down. Burned dark by the sun, his face was a map of tiny creases. Sharp cheekbones emphasized sunken eyes that held a tiredness beyond sleep. And the remnants of his clothes hung from shoulders that looked no stronger than a wire coat hanger.

"They let you go?" Takis asked. "Just like that?"

"It was the captain of the police here," Stelios said. The militia had brought him and the others to the police station and the captain recognized him at once. But he sent for Theo to identify him as the abducted puppeteer and, after that, released him. "I guess I have you to thank, Takis. Thank God you saw me and spoke up to the militia in that village." He collapsed onto the old sofa next to Yannoula.

"So it *was* you driving the truck?" Takis asked, looking pleased with himself. He glanced at me as if to say, *See.*

"Yes. But what were all of you doing there? You were actually in that village? Hard to believe."

I explained about our travels with Thanasis in search of him. Stelios had been posted as a lookout at the edge of the village, so he hadn't seen the villagers and certainly not us. He'd just heard the shooting.

Then there'd been this argument between the guerrillas and the owner of the truck.

"Thanasis," I said, interrupting. "He was the one who brought us to the village."

"I'm sorry about him. I didn't see who shot him exactly, but someone threw me his keys."

"That's when I saw *you*," Takis said. "You were starting the truck."

It had all been chaotic, Stelios said, with the loading of the stolen provisions and the bodies of the dead and wounded. Then, only a few miles outside the village, the militia blocked the road, arrested them and brought them back here to Heraklion. The militia soldiers told the captain that the boy, Takis, who'd shot the guerrilla leader had identified the driver of the stolen truck as the abducted puppeteer everyone had been looking for.

"But it's not over," Stelios said, sighing. "They could still charge me with something, I don't know what."

The other guerrillas had already been sent to Agios Nikolaos, a town we'd passed through with Thanasis. The security committee for the area was at a detention center there. But what had happened the night he left the boardinghouse?

"I went across the street to think things over," Stelios said. While he was sitting there in the empty café, an old rattletrap truck drove by and then came back and stopped. He stood up and started back across the street. The next thing he knew someone grabbed him from behind and pressed a wet cloth into his face.

"It smelled sweet, but that's all I remember. When I came to, I was lying in a dank cave somewhere cold and had a terrible headache. Worse than that was to come, because I . . ."

"Ah, my little cabbages," Theo said, walking into the lobby with a basket of food: warm cheese pies, bread and a demijohn of wine. "All together again, yes? Thanks be to God." He embraced us one by one, kissing us on both cheeks, and we caught him up on what we'd been saying. The captain had already told him about Thanasis.

"Ah, my poor friend. They buried him there, yes? May the earth rest lightly on him." He tapped his head in thought. "Everyone around here knew him and the sad story of his wife. He was the best of men."

"Thanasis?" Yannoula said. It was the first she'd spoken since we arrived. She'd apparently missed other mentions of Thanasis. Her face was flushed and her eyes darted feverishly from one of us to the other. "Isn't he here yet?"

In our excitement at being together again, we hadn't paid much attention to her. Theo felt her forehead. "She's burning up," he said, then pointed to her sling. "What happened to her arm?" I told him and he said, "We need to get her to the clinic near the *plateia*."

He and Stelios helped Yannoula to her feet, but Stelios was unsteady too so Theo said no, Stelios should rest and have something to eat. "Takis and I can manage."

"Where are we going?" Yannoula asked.

"For a little walk."

"Too tired to walk."

"We'll help. Takis, take her other arm. That's it."

When they were gone, Stelios and I sat on the sofa with the basket between us, not talking much, breaking off chunks of bread to eat with the little pies. I got some glasses and we drank quite a bit of Theo's wine. Stelios looked so much like the shaggy guerrillas who'd raided the village that I felt a little shy with him. There was a lot I wanted to ask, but I didn't know how to begin. I became aware of one thing strongly.

"What would you think about having a bath?" I asked.

"How did you know?" We both laughed. "There was this mountain stream we used when it wasn't frozen. That was it."

I ran up the stairs to turn on the wheezy old water heater in the bathroom. When I came back, I helped him up the stairs and asked about his limp. He said the guerrillas moved camp regularly to avoid discovery and often treated him like a pack animal. They called him a city boy because he wasn't used to climbing over rocks and boulders like those that littered the icy mountain passes. His shoes were soon shredded by the sharp stones and he fell repeatedly, dumping the rolls of bedding, pots and pans and other gear. He'd had to crawl around gathering them up only to fall again later.

"It was always my left leg that got hurt," he said. "I'd get it wedged between stones. It never gets better now."

"Let me look at it," I said when we were in the bathroom. He seemed so weak, propping himself against the wall. While the bathtub was filling, I knelt and tried to roll up his pant leg, but it was so filthy it stuck to the skin. His shoes were just strips of rubber cut from old tires, tied to his feet with rope and rags. I got him out of them while he fumbled with his belt buckle, the only part of his clothing I recognized. Any shyness I'd felt faded as I helped him. Together we peeled his pants off and I helped him out of his shirt.

"Aliki, are you sure you . . ."

"Shh, just get in."

I knelt beside the tub and worked shampoo into his hair and beard.

"I feel like a child," he said.

"Close your eyes so you don't get soap in them." I had him stand up and I soaped him all over. I could feel each of his ribs and his pelvic bone jutting out, his badly bruised and swollen leg. Putting my arms around him, I soaked my blouse, so I took it off, along with my other clothes. When he sat back down in the water, I climbed in, facing him.

"Well," he said, and he said it again. Then he began to soap me as I'd done him: my hair, my breasts, my legs. He made me stand too and stood beside me, rinsing me with water poured from his cupped hands. Then, sitting down again, he put his head up against my belly and kissed me there and also *there* until I was moaning softly. We stepped out, dried each other and wrapped ourselves in our damp towels. After I'd helped him down the hall to what had been his room, we slid under the clean sheets. With his head resting on my chest and my hand stroking the long line of his back, his breathing slowed into sleep and I soon followed. Sometime in the night, I woke to feel his mouth on my left breast, his beard tickling my skin, and I felt a rush of heat everywhere.

It became stronger as he went on exploring me with hands and tongue. Soon his palms were beneath my lower back, pulling me up toward him. Where had this strength come from in a man who'd seemed so frail just a few hours earlier? I asked. Who knows, he asked, or cares? I helped him in, my old friend, my companion, my love. How much time had seemed to pass in our lives before we'd come to this wonder, this return.

When we lay still at last, we drifted in and out of shallow sleep and then, as the sun lit the window, he began to talk in a rambling way, how the first cave was a dreary place with water dripping onto heads and smoky brushwood fires that reddened the eyes. Lice and other vermin infested everyone's clothing. At the cave mouth, a stack of brush covered the entrance, where a shepherd in a homespun cape stood guard. Outside it was raining and wind blew into the cave, rippling a tattered banner with hammer and sickle hanging against one of the cave walls. Voices rose and fell as men argued about what to do with Stelios and other captives.

"One of them was saying it would come to no good, this kidnapping of civilians. I think some had escaped and gone to the police, those lucky ones. They'd betrayed hiding places, I guess, so the group had to move regularly. But others said their group was too small now; many comrades had been killed or captured. They needed more men."

They talked openly about all this, paying little attention to the new arrival. Stelios came to understand that there were other such groups in the mountains, but they were fighting among themselves over territory.

"It was always the same; nobody could agree on anything and every group was out for itself. There didn't appear to be any overall plan except to harass the government militia and local police. They killed them and left their bodies as warnings; sometimes mutilated. The right hand—they took it as proof of the kill. Or the head."

They'd interrogated Stelios to find out if he had a family able to ransom him, but after he'd convinced them that he didn't, they told him he'd have to work if he expected to get fed. That meant carrying heavy loads of supplies up mountain trails, leaping from boulder to boulder. Food was often little more than wild greens or snails boiled over a campfire or eaten raw when the smoke from a fire would have betrayed their location.

"The stupid thing was that they took from villagers who had little to give. And then called this *liberating* them."

They hadn't allowed Stelios to go with them on village raids until the last big one on Easter Day, which had been unplanned. The scent of the food had been irresistible. And they thought they might need extra help as the whole village would be gathered. Other times, usually he and the recent arrivals weren't trusted enough and were left behind with an armed guard. They were supposed to be "educated," but only one of the guards had a book, the teachings of Marx. The guard didn't know how to read and no one else had much interest. Sometimes the others returned with a stolen sheep or goat, which they slaughtered and roasted. Every bit was devoured: entrails, brains, eyes. After a raid, there was constant arguing over spoils.

"They fought over guns and boots. They fought over everything."

"Did they fight over your tweed jacket?" I told him about the three hanged people.

"It disappeared one night while I was asleep. I never knew what became of it." The leader of the group, Stephanos, treated Stelios "like some kind of insect at first," he said, "something he could crush if I tried to escape. At those heights, it was easy enough to lose your footing. A nudge with the butt of a rifle could do the trick."

I asked what Stephanos looked like, remembering the guerrilla who'd argued with Vasili. When Stelios told me, I said, "I think he's the one Takis shot."

"Did he really do that? I heard the soldiers tell the captain that. But it didn't seem possible."

I told him about Vasili and target practice with the village boys. Stelios climbed out of bed with a sheet wrapped around him and walked back and forth.

"*Was* Takis the first to shoot?"

"I don't know. It happened so fast. But Mitso, one of the other boys, said he'd seen it." I thought back on it and added, "If he hadn't shot at all, maybe no one else would have. And no one would have died."

"But then I wouldn't be here, Aliki. I'd still be . . . out there." He paced some more and then started talking rapidly about Stephanos, how his attitude toward Stelios had changed when he found out about Stelios's knowledge of the Karagiozis plays.

"Ah, this is excellent," Stephanos had said. "Nights are long and we love stories, even ones for children. But stories must have messages, good messages. Do your stories have messages?"

"You can decide for yourself," Stelios had told him. He'd set about making crude figures out of pine bark, the way he'd done in Chrysoula's basement. In the light of a campfire where lentils or beans were boiled for meals, Stelios made shadows dance on cave walls. Stephanos and the others were delighted, laughing and clapping like boys. Here were these hardened mountaineers, as tough as wild goats, reduced to children by Karagiozis and company. Stephanos declared that Karagiozis was a true communist, fighting for the rights of the working class against the sultan and his armies.

"You can read anything into Karagiozis," Stelios told him. "That's why he's lasted so long. He'll be anything you want."

"Then this is what I want," Stephanos said. "Karagiozis, man of the people!"

Some nights, lying awake with the others on the floor of one lair or another, Stelios told stories to them from *The Iliad* to pass the time. Of course Stephanos said the rage of Achilles against the Trojans was class warfare. It hadn't done any good for Stelios to point out that the kings and warriors on the Greek side were hardly exploited peasants.

"Never mind," Stephanos told him later out of earshot of the others. "Some of my men, they know little of these histories. I teach the good lesson when I can in order to give them courage. They need it because we *will* lose, you know, in the end. The government militia, the fascist police in the towns, they are too many for us. But we stay the course. Someday others will follow. We're like early Christians spreading their new religion, but we're superior to them because we don't expect a reward in the afterlife."

There was a knock on the bedroom door just as Stelios was saying that what he'd learned from Stephanos was that "people fighting for a cause that's mostly wrong can still sometimes be right."

From the other side of the door, Takis said, "Aliki, are you in there?" I wrapped a sheet around me, went to the door and opened it a crack. "I'm going to the clinic to see Yannoula," he said. "Want to come?"

"Yes, yes," I said, embarrassed that since the night before I hadn't thought of her even once. "How is she?"

"Her wound is infected." Takis tried to peer around me.

"I'll just be a minute," I said, closing the door. "Meet you downstairs."

I had no clothes in the room, but I opened the closet and Stelios's suitcase was just where I'd left it before we'd gone off with Thanasis. While I was pulling on some of Stelios's old clothes, he got up and opened the door and blurted out, "Takis, is it true that you shot Stephanos?"

Takis must have been partway down the stairs by then, but I heard him ask, "What? Who's Stephanos?"

Stelios, now out on the landing in his bedsheet, explained, and Takis said, "Yes. Yes, I did do that." Neither of them said anything for a moment and then Takis asked, "Was that a bad thing to do? Aliki thinks it was a bad thing to do. But everybody else says it was a good thing."

"It was a good thing, Takis. But I'm sorry it had to be you who did it."

Takis didn't say anything for a moment and then he asked, "Why are you and Aliki wearing sheets?"

Stelios didn't answer but came back into the room and I, now in his clothes, went out and down the stairs to Takis.

"You look silly," he said.

"They're Stelios's clothes. Let's go." We went outside and started toward the square.

"He thinks it was a good thing," Takis said.

"I heard him."

"And . . . ?"

"I guess I can change my mind if I want to."

"*Are* you changing your mind?"

"I'm thinking about it. Tell me about Yannoula."

Takis walked on in silence, then said, "Why were you and Stelios wearing sheets?"

"Tell me about Yannoula."

"Tell me about the sheets first."

"You wouldn't understand."

"Why?"

"You're not old enough."

He stopped walking, turned on me and said, "I'm old enough to kill a man. Old enough to speak up for Stelios. I *saved* him. Isn't that old enough for *you*?"

Well, no, I thought, not at all; though I was glad there seemed to be some sort of bond between the two of them over Stelios's release. I suspected this wouldn't last, but before I could answer Takis's question, he walked ahead of me, saying over his shoulder matter-of-factly that

Yannoula had a high fever by the time he and Theo got her to the clinic the night before. I hurried to keep up with him as he said that her wound was turning septic. I didn't know what that meant and he said he understood it to be blood poisoning, a serious condition. A nurse had cleaned it out and packed rolled-up towels filled with ice around Yannoula's head to lower her fever.

I followed Takis to her room, where Yannoula was sitting up in bed just inside the door. Her wounded arm was heavily bandaged and in a clean, new sling. With her other hand, she was fanning herself with a folded newspaper. She didn't look as if she was suffering from a serious condition.

"Well, I thought I'd been abandoned," she said. "I don't even remember coming here. Did you two bring me? *They* tell me I was off my head." She pointed to the two other beds with patients in the room. "I must have said something embarrassing because everyone giggles when they pass my bed. Thanks to God I'm almost well, but it's so warm in here I could die."

The warm May sunshine was pouring in the curtainless window. Yannoula did look much better than the day before but was so talkative that I wondered what they were giving her.

"Now, is Stelios back or did I just dream that?" she asked.

"He's back," we said.

"He and Aliki stayed in the same bedroom last night," Takis said. Yannoula and I exchanged glances.

"Well, thank you for that information, Takis," she said, winking at me as I colored. "But that really isn't your business, is it?"

Takis didn't say anything.

"Someday up ahead you might want to be private with someone too, and it won't be anybody else's business either."

"I'd like to be private with Aliki," he said.

"Takis!" I said.

"I think maybe you and I should have a little talk, Takis," Yannoula said.

"I wish I hadn't saved Stelios."

"You saved him?" she asked. "How was that?"

Clearly she didn't remember much from the last few days. Before we could fill her in, Theo arrived, and just after him, Stelios. Yannoula threw her good arm around Stelios's neck and said she hadn't expected ever to see him again, and yes, her other arm was much better. But the nurse had told her they were going to keep her there for another day, just in case. And she'd have to come back from time to time to make sure the wound was healing properly.

"But here we are all together again," Yannoula said, "like a family, right, Aliki?"

I nodded but thought that though we were all here, the nature of our family was changing now that Stelios and I were together again and Takis thought he was both grown up and a hero.

"And how would this family feel," Theo said, "about shadow theater again at my café? When you've had a chance to settle down, Stelios, and rest, of course."

"I thought your customers were tired of it," Stelios said.

"Yes, but some of the families nearby, they ask about it for their children." He tapped the side of his head rapidly. "They bring them for the fruit-flavored ices now the weather is warm. With Karagiozis, I can sell more."

"I don't know," Stelios said. "I've been thinking of something new, but I don't have much energy yet."

"Of course not. You'll rest, then we'll see."

"*I* can do it," Takis said. Everyone looked at him; Theo raised an eyebrow. "I can, I really can. I mean, Aliki and I. We've done it all over the area."

"It's true?" Theo asked.

"Yes," I said. "In Ierapetra, the villages. He's good."

"He *is*," Yannoula said.

Theo still looked dubious. "Your mind," he said to Takis, "it is, well, clearer than it used to be?"

"What do you mean, *clearer*?" Takis asked.

"I mean no *talking to fish*."

"*They* were talking to me, not the other way around."

"Oh, that makes all the difference." Theo laughed.

"When he's working with the puppets," I said quickly, "Takis is fine. He puts himself into them and he's better all around. And anyway, I've been doing it with him and that seems to work okay."

"Aliki's right, Theo," Stelios said. "Give him a chance. And to tell the truth, I've lost interest in Karagiozis and those patriotic histories. There are better stories to tell."

"Such as . . . ?"

"I don't know exactly yet. I've been working it out in my mind."

Theo looked hard at Takis, took a deep breath and said, "All right. We'll try you. For the sake of the sales of ices."

"Without Stelios?" Takis asked.

"Without Stelios."

Takis glanced quickly at me as he said maybe we should practice for a while. It was one thing to perform for village children, but maybe here in the city expectations would be higher. And the puppets needed repairs. Theo said there was no rush; the warmer the weather, the better the sales of ices. So the first week of June was set for Takis's debut solo performances.

Back at the boardinghouse, we took the puppets out of their battered suitcase and they did look rather sad. After all, they'd been dragged all over eastern Crete and were tattered and faded. The three of us, with glue, tape and paint pots, spent the day touching up their faces and costumes, patching tears, making joints swing freely and strengthening the hinges attaching the puppets to the poles that controlled their movement. The white screen was nearly gray with dirt so I washed it and mended places where it had ripped. Mostly it was pleasant for the three of us to be working so well together. We spent the rest of the month in this happy work while Takis and I practiced.

"Are you sure you don't mind?" Takis asked Stelios.

"Not at all. I've been thinking up a different story."

"What kind?"

"I'm not sure how to describe it."

He'd spent a lot of time thinking about it in the mountains, he told me at night when we lay awake. Our pattern had become to sleep, to make love, to talk and then do it all over again. His work in the mountains, he said, had mostly been forced labor, drawing water from mountain streams, setting traps for hares or wild ibexes, digging for edible roots and bulbs, carrying supplies on his back. Stelios said he had tried to free his mind so as not to trap it in the guerrilla cycle of violence and drudgery, "which," he realized, "is a story itself, but only one kind." There were, after all, so many others besides the ones about war and madness. There were the grand ones, the movements of peoples.

"I remembered my father telling me how the Jews wept in exile beside the waters of Babylon when they remembered Zion. And all those other Old Testament stories." And there were the intimate stories of love and its end, like *The Count of Monte Cristo*. There were stories that began with a stranger coming to town or the tale of a journey and the return, ". . . which is the story of us all."

"Tell me a story," I'd say in the dark.

And he'd say, "What would you like? Hector's farewell to his wife, Andromache, before Achilles killed him? Or something more Old Testament—Ruth saying, 'Whither thou goest, I will go'? Or Esther saving her people?"

As he talked, he smoothed out the bedclothes in front of us as if clearing a place for the story to happen, his fingers with their cracked and broken nails patting down here a battle plain, there a meadow.

"I used to tell myself about the courtship of my parents," he said, "what I can remember of what they told me long ago. But do you know the plot of that movie where Charlie Chaplin as the little tramp is so hungry he has to eat his own shoe boiled? It still makes me smile." When I thought I'd heard all his stories, he'd come up with others, some of them quite silly. "This is the story of Aliki's right breast, so jealous of her twin sister to the left who gets more attention, or so she thinks. And it's also the story of a journey into the velvet underworld that begins"—his hand slid from my breasts down my belly and between my legs—"right here."

Some nights I heard footsteps and wondered if it was Takis moving around in the hall, listening. But I put him out of my mind. I did all I could for him in the daytime as we rehearsed together. He barely needed rehearsal, he was so good. But he rarely met my eyes anymore. And the nights belonged to Stelios and me.

I came to understand that Stelios was an altered version of the man who'd disappeared that night, though often he was just like the boy I knew who said the kinds of things I'd expect to hear. But other times, especially when we were alone at night, he was a voice in the dark that sounded like him and yet not like him. His experience in the mountains seemed a kind of prism through which he now saw everything. Our pleasure together was all the richer for it.

On the night of the performance at Theo's café, the usual old men sipping ouzo and fingering their worry beads had moved to tables outside across from the harbor. Inside, it was all families, young couples with children and grandparents. It was chaotic with children chasing each other around the tables and playing hide-and-seek, boys pulling the braids of girls and being smacked by parents. Theo's face was tomato red as he rushed around serving brightly colored ices and the sodas he made from sweet syrups and bubbly water. At the side of the room, Takis and I set up the screen and when Theo had sold as much as he could, he stood in front of our stage and clapped his hands, but no one paid any attention. So he shouted at the adults please to control their children so the performance could begin.

I took his place in front of the screen to sing the opening. Poor Yannoula had wanted to do it, but she seemed to drift between being clear of mind and foggy. The doctor said she needed some of a new kind of drug called antibiotics, which we'd never heard of, and none of it was available on Crete at that time.

I stood there trembling. Being behind the screen was one thing, but it was entirely another to be in front. My singing voice wasn't strong and I knew Stelios was in the audience somewhere. I wanted to do well for him as it was the first time he'd just watched in a long time. I warbled the little verse and finished with:

And I'll tell a tale to you,
to all this noble company,
and may the time pass pleasantly.

Then I ducked behind the screen and we began the fastest performance ever. Takis had developed wonderful timing. But he didn't wait for the children to stop laughing at one line before sprinting into another. The laughter came in bursts and explosions and the children called out to the puppets.

"Don't trust her!"

"Knock him down!"

"Look behind you!"

When we'd finished, they applauded a long time and then called out for us to do it all over again, which we did. At the end, Stelios came up to Takis and said, "You're better than I ever was."

"Really?" Takis beamed.

"You love it, don't you? It shows."

"Yes! Yes!"

They shook hands. Stelios said he needed to borrow the puppets the next day to rehearse something he'd been working out in his mind.

"Borrow?" Takis said. "But they're yours."

"Not anymore. They're yours now by right."

I'd never seen Takis look so happy. Stelios too seemed pleased and relaxed.

The next day, he worked constantly, painting new backdrops, making new puppets, scribbling in a notebook furiously. All he would tell us was that he was going to perform a new play in two parts over two nights and Theo had agreed to this. Working in a corner of the lobby, Stelios asked us to stay away and not to look at anything. When he took a break, I told him I missed the times when we read together and how I'd carried his copy of *The Iliad* with me everywhere.

"I'd rather tell stories," he said, "than read them. You hold on to my copy for the time being, all right?"

He worked all of the next few days too. On the day of the first of his two performances, I went to the clinic to see Yannoula but was startled to find her bed empty. She was having tests, a nurse told me. Tests for what? I asked. The nurse didn't know and said I should come back the next day. I didn't like the sound of that and went to find a doctor. But there never seemed to be one around. Who was treating her? Who was making decisions? I found the office of the manager on the first floor, but he wasn't in, either. I waited for what seemed like hours until it was time to go to Theo's and meet Takis for Stelios's first performance of his play.

The audience that evening was a mixture of old men with some parents and children who probably thought they were going to see more Karagiozis. But there was no opening song, no title or idea of what was to come. What we saw first were the shadows of a woman and boy crossing the screen. From behind the screen, Stelios raised his voice to be the woman.

WOMAN: *Remember all this one day*
when you return by this path,
when you have grown into yourself.
Listen, in spite of what we've seen,
the world is going on.
A twig snaps, the leaves whisper.
At a turn we see threads of cloud,
the wings of a hawk.
Now in a valley of olives,
smoke floats from chimneys.
BOY: *We must stop. You are ill.*

The shadow of a village woman in an apron appeared on the left of the screen.

VILLAGE WOMAN: *It is good that you have come.*
WOMAN AND BOY: *It is good that we have found you.*

There was a second boy here, small and jumpy, hopping around the new arrivals. And an older girl.

SMALL BOY: *There's a ghost with orange hair*
downstairs in the basement.
Do you play cards?
BOY: *Do you read books?*

The girl shook her head and put a finger to her lips.

SMALL BOY: *She hasn't talked since her father died.*
She's my friend.

"It's about *us*," Takis whispered to me.

"Sort of," I said. "But so much is left out." And where was it going? I wondered. Up to the real events of that night, events that Takis had never faced? What was Stelios trying to do? He and Takis had been getting along reasonably well, so what was this about? As the play went on, Takis shifted in his chair and kept glancing at me to see my reaction. I was trying to keep my face blank and stay calm, but I worried that Takis could tip into one of his states.

"I don't think I want to see any more," he said.

But already puppets wearing swastikas were on the screen. Then a placard dropped down with the words TIME PASSES. When it was pulled back, we could see the outline of a house. In the windows were tufts of red cellophane flames. The three children were leaving.

BOY: *Death follows as shadows*
fixed to our heels.
Terror is the white bone
we found on the shore,
washed hollow by time.
We see at a turn threads of cloud,
the wings of a hawk,
now a city beside the sea,
the lost home found.

I was relieved. Takis had not been implicated in what happened. Was that what Stelios now believed or was it just a matter of keeping the story moving? But I couldn't see where Stelios could take this—after all, our stories had no end yet. We were still living them.

Takis had gone quite still in his chair, but the other customers in the café looked puzzled—this wasn't the kind of performance they were used to. I was looking around when I noticed the police captain come in the front door. He said something to Theo, who pointed at the screen. The captain walked through the tables to the front and behind the screen. The play stopped while he and Stelios talked. The audience grew restless.

"What's going on?" someone called out.

"Continue the show!"

"Or give us our money back."

Theo rushed back toward the screen, but just then the captain and Stelios emerged. Stelios looked flushed and angry. He was still holding the pole with the girl puppet when the captain told the room that the security committee in Agios Nikolaos had ordered the arrest of Stelios for collaboration with the guerrillas. There was a collective gasp, then customers began to mutter. One booed the captain, and some shook their fists at him. Someone else smashed a plate against a wall. Hands were waved in the air, insults were shouted about the mother of the captain, about Theo, about God and the Virgin Mary. But the captain moved calmly through the angry customers, holding Stelios by the arm.

As they neared us, Takis jumped up and said, "It's a mistake. I was there; I saw what happened."

"I was there too," I said, though I hadn't seen Stelios with the other guerrillas.

"I'm sorry," the captain said. "I have orders."

Stelios handed the puppet to me as he said to the captain, "But no one has asked *me* what happened," he said. "Can't I talk to that committee?"

"It's in Agios Nikolaos. That's where we're going."

And they were gone. It was fast and there was nothing to be done about it. We stood with Theo outside watching the taillights of the captain's car disappear, thinking about the rumors of life in the detention camps.

"Is there a bus to Agios Nikolaos tomorrow?" I asked Theo.

"Yes," he said, "but if you're thinking of going there, don't." Stelios might well be back in a few days anyway. It was all probably just a misunderstanding and meanwhile the captain, when he returned, would let us know what was going on. "A detention camp is not a place for a young woman."

"I'll go with you, Aliki," Takis said. "I'll protect you."

"No, no," Theo said. "I've advertised more children's performances this week and next. If all my puppeteers are in Agios Nikolaos, what'll I do?"

"What do *you* want me to do, Aliki?" Takis asked.

"Stay. This is your time. You'll have to work alone, though. Can you do that?"

"Stelios did it, didn't he?"

What I'd heard about any kind of arrest was that detainees who had relatives or friends to inquire after them and bother authorities, well, they seemed to do better than those who had none. When I stepped off the bus in Agios Nikolaos the next day, I recognized it as one of the places where Thanasis had stopped with us to sell his produce. The town itself seemed pleasant enough, built around a curving bay. There was a lagoon that stretched into the middle of the town, with cafés and restaurants around it. It didn't seem like the sort of place to have a detention center. I asked for directions to it and made my way to the outskirts. The detention center looked more like a warehouse, which was probably what it had been before the war. Barbed wire had been thrown up around it, but people were coming and going through the main gate casually. I would come to learn that disorganization was the rule in such places.

The officer at the gate couldn't find Stelios's name on a list but said it wasn't up-to-date because it changed throughout the day. I'd have to look for him myself, he told me, waving me through. Inside, several hundred men were lying on the floor on blankets. I supposed the women were in another part of the building. Many prisoners had their heads shaved. I asked one what this meant and was told that they were to be shipped to prison camps on islands. Half-eaten loaves of bread and plates of food lay here and there among the men who were reading newspapers or playing cards or chess. Family members came and went while children chased each other around the walls of the huge room. Among the prisoners and their families moved armed guards singling out certain men and leading them outside. Others brought new captives in, though there was really no space for them.

I worked my way along one side of the room, stepping over people, but couldn't see Stelios among them. Then I did the other side with the same result. Some of the men made lewd gestures as I passed and one caught my hand and tried to pull me down beside him. I gave him a kick and went to the exit, where a family group of visitors was leaving. Mixing in with them, I was waved outside by the guard.

The prisoners who'd been singled out inside, a half dozen of them, were now lined up and guarded in the open space in front of the warehouse. Townspeople stood around watching. Then, from the prison, an equal number of soldiers emerged and lined themselves up, each with a rifle, facing the prisoners. I realized with a start that an execution was about to take place just as I noticed that one of the prisoners did resemble Stelios—that same shaggy beard. There was a shouted command, the soldiers fired in unison and the prisoners pitched over backward or sideways. The townspeople applauded.

I found I couldn't move. The speed of the execution and its almost routine, matter-of-course feeling froze me in place. Had those inside known that the men led out were to be shot? Had the men themselves known? There hadn't been any tearful farewells that I'd noticed, no wailing women or children, no attempts to escape. And the crowd outside had watched with the same level of interest they might have brought to one of our Karagiozis performances. The soldiers then marched back inside and the crowd broke up and trailed away. No one approached the bodies; no one claimed them. They didn't even look much like bodies now; they could have been piles of soiled laundry.

Looking around, I wondered if anyone else had grasped the horror of what had just happened. But there was no one there until two more soldiers appeared leading a horse-drawn cart. Moving from body to body, one soldier would take hold of the feet while the other took the arms. They'd swing each body back and forth between them for momentum, then sling it onto the cart. When it was full, it passed by me and I saw that the bearded one wasn't Stelios. But he might as well have been. He was the same age and build, his sharp cheekbones and sunken eyes still open, an expression of surprise on his face.

When my legs began to work again, I stumbled back into town, where I immediately got lost in a tangle of narrow streets. I came out at the waterfront and sat on a bench there, trying to collect myself. It was a sparkling day; light dazzled on the surface of the water and people strolled past racks of drying fishnets as if nothing had ever happened—war, executions, guerrilla raids. I put my face in my hands and tried to decide what to do next. It was the chief of police who coordinated these matters in any town, I reasoned, so the captain from Heraklion would probably have taken Stelios to the local police station.

After asking around, I found the place, a renovated two-family house with a wraparound porch and a Greek flag, facing a square. There they did have Stelios's name on a list but would give me little information since I wasn't a relative. What they did tell me was that the newer detainees were being housed in an old cinema because of overcrowding at the detention center. When I found the place, I saw the tattered movie posters were still on display, stars whose names I'd barely heard of then: Clara Bow, John Gilbert, Leslie Howard. The lightbulbs around the posters had all been broken.

Inside, it was much like the detention center with people coming and going. The seats had been removed and men sat or lay on the floor on blankets. When I asked a sentry about Stelios, he waved his hand at someone standing on the other side of the room. I could see from there that his head had been shaved. But was it Stelios? I hoped not, knowing what a shaved head meant. He turned as I came toward him.

"Aliki!" he said, putting his arms around me. "Aliki."

His scalp was a mess. There were nicks and scabs among a few remaining tufts of hair. Worse were his eyes, which had taken back the look of exhaustion they'd had when he first returned from the mountains.

"I'm to be sent away. Exile, three months, maybe more. It's an open-ended sentence, like most these days."

"Oh, no. How do you know? You've only been here overnight."

The police had told him that the security committee understood he'd been abducted, but it was their understanding that Stelios had cooperated with the guerrillas. He'd driven the getaway truck after the driver had been murdered.

"It was decided before I even got here." He sighed. "They wouldn't see me or hear what I had to say." His voice thickened and he put his hands over his face for a moment, saying behind them, "And there's no way to appeal." He didn't know exactly what exile meant, but he'd learned from some of the other detainees that it was not the same as the dreaded prisons or the so-called reeducation camps, where torture took place. Exiles were detainees—people that the security committees thought should be "banished temporarily for the good of the body politic." Stelios was to be sent to an island, where he and other detainees would have to work for the local community under supervision of local authorities. He might or might not be released in a few months.

"It could be worse," he said. "I suppose."

I took him into my arms. "Yes. I saw an execution," I said. "Six men; and afterward people applauded. One of the men looked like you. I thought it *was* you at first."

"*Theo mou.* Where?"

I told him about the detention center. He'd been brought straight to the cinema and had never seen the center. But he'd heard that guerrillas accused by witnesses of murder were being executed without any kind of trial.

"Where are they sending you?" I asked. "And when?"

"I don't know. The one decision came fast so the other is sure to be slow. Some of these men here have been waiting for months."

He stood back from me and we sat down on the blanket on the floor. No one had told him anything more.

"I want to go with you," I said.

"Only relatives can go; at least that's what I hear. I didn't expect to see you again and didn't know how to get a message to you." He paused and then gave me a little smile. "So I couldn't tell you that in fact, there is a way."

"A way?"

"Wives can go with the exiles. They can't live with them, but they can see each other and, you know, be together sometimes."

"Wives?"

"A wife. You could become mine."

He glanced over my shoulder as he said this. I turned to see what he was looking at, but the room was no different. Up front, the red curtains across the stage hung in tatters. Above, a pair of plaster cupids flanked the masks of drama, one smiling, the other frowning. They might as well have been the faces of fate, uninterested in who lived, who died.

"I already am your wife," I said. "In fact if not in name. Of course I'll go with you, my dear."

Stelios took my hands in his and said softly that the guards were open to bribes and for a certain sum, they would file marriage papers for us at the town hall and pay a priest to sign them. There weren't civil marriages in Greece then, only religious ones. So a church document with a priest's signature had to be forged as if a church ceremony had actually taken place.

"My Jewish ancestors might rise out of their graves if I married in an actual church. Funny, my parents weren't observant at all; we didn't even go to synagogue. And then my father and uncle were taken just because they were Jewish. Why? Why not Catholics or Orthodox? Not that I'd wish ill on any of them. But, I mean, why Jews?" He'd heard that on the other side of the island, near the city of Chania, the entire Jewish population had been herded onto German troop ships for deportation. But somewhere in the Mediterranean, the ship had been torpedoed and no one survived.

There was a commotion on the other side of the room and we looked in that direction. One of the guards was shaving the head of a detainee, who'd begun to cry, saying he wasn't supposed to be sent, it was all a mistake, leave my hair, oh, please.

Stelios turned back to me. "Humans! Look how *vile* we can be. I think war's just an excuse for everyone to lower themselves into their barbaric roots. I mean, both sides are mostly Christian—love thy neighbor and all that—but it hasn't stopped the killing."

He shook his head then pulled me to him and whispered into my ear that with a little bribe, we'd have the paperwork and be legally married. "Let's make something *good* out of all this, Aliki. Some of the families will even leave on the same boat with us detainees."

"Is that what you want?" I asked.

"No, in many ways, I don't. It would be selfish of me to take you with me. It'll probably be awful. But how can we know?"

He glanced away again and didn't say anything for a moment. Then he waved his hand at the others in the theater. "Some of these have done the same thing. Been married, I mean. Look, I know it's probably not the way you ever expected it might be. But, I mean, well, this is our life now, isn't it?"

The captain had given him some money because he'd thought the decision of the committee unfair and he felt bad about what was happening. He'd told Stelios that he'd probably have to pay for his own food and shelter in exile. Stelios could pay him back when he returned. And then he could finish performing the play that had been interrupted that night in the café.

With several new scenes, I thought, maybe including this one.

"So what do you think?" Stelios asked.

"Yes," I said simply. Then, "Yes and yes and yes." I could feel the strength of the two of us together, even if physically apart. "You're my good return," I said.

"What do you mean?"

"When I'm with you I feel as if I've returned from a long journey. You are my way of returning. We're home now wherever we are."

"Yes, Aliki, yes, that's so."

We stood in each other's arms and I felt strength pour through me, strength that could get us through anything, could cope with the new place we'd be going to and everything that would come to pass after it. I thought of Chrysoula and her advice, but I wouldn't have to learn to love the one I was marrying because I was marrying the one I loved.

"We're going to be all right," I said. "I just know it."

"If *you* believe it," Stelios said, not looking so convinced, "then I believe it."

We didn't say anything for a few minutes and my mind started racing through what I'd have to do before leaving. I needed to go back to Heraklion to collect our things and see how Yannoula was doing. I told Stelios how she hadn't been there on my last visit to the clinic. And how I didn't know what would happen to her now.

"That's strange," he said, "her not being there. Could she have walked out?"

"But she's too sick. And where would she go? I'll talk to Theo about looking after her. And Takis too. I don't like to think what he'll be like on his own." I'd made a choice, the only I could have made, and I'd made it happily. But there would be consequences and Takis was the main one. "I don't know how to tell him I'm leaving."

"Maybe you shouldn't. You'll have to go back to Heraklion and wait until the captain lets you know that we're leaving. Then just grab our things and get on the bus. Let Theo tell Takis you're gone. If you tell him yourself, there's bound to be a scene or worse. Anyway, you'd have to face leaving him eventually. He *is* capable of good things—after all, he did stand up for me about what happened there in the mountain village. So I'm indebted to him for that, I guess. But maybe he'll grow up faster if he's on his own, not always looking to you for help and sympathy. Anyway, we won't be gone forever."

I knew he was right, but I was going to put Takis out of my mind for the present, along with Chrysoula's words, *Treat him like a brother always.* Well, even brothers had to grow up, didn't they? As for now, I was a bride and that was what mattered.

We'd probably have to get the marriage papers first just in case Stelios got shipped out right away. If that happened before I got back from Heraklion, I could follow after him.

"But you don't know where you're going," I said.

"The captain will let you know."

We sat silently for a while. He pressed some folded bills into my hand and said this was for the small hotel down the street. Why didn't I spend the night there; I must be exhausted. Maybe after he'd done his time in exile, maybe then we could have a proper ceremony of some kind, if I'd like that. But it didn't really matter to me. I'd never imagined myself in one of those big white dresses that made brides look like enormous cakes.

The hotel turned out to be full of wives, children and soon-to-be brides. I had to share a room with one of them, Froso, who was going to have an actual church ceremony the next day.

"What do you think?" she said, trying on a dress she'd rented from a photographer who specialized in weddings and rented out the same bridal dress several times a month. She was too plump for its tight satin bodice. "I can't breathe," she said. "And I can smell the perfume of the last bride. But who cares? Just so I step on Dimitri's foot before he does mine."

It was the custom that when the priest led the bride and groom around the altar the traditional three times in what was called the

Dance of Isaiah, the first one who stepped on the other's foot would dominate the marriage.

"Like my mother says," Froso told me as she preened in front of the mirror, "life is short, but marriage is long. My Dimitri, he's a nice boy, but no one's going to tell *me* what to do."

She'd warned him not to get involved with those crazy communists, but had he listened to her? Some of the nationalist troops had tried to seize land owned by his mother. So his communist friends, ". . . they hanged two of the nationalists from the old plane tree in the meadow," she said. "Not Dimitri himself, you understand, but it was his family land, his meadow, his tree. So they took him too. You know how it goes."

The result was this hurry-up wedding and detention in some probably dreadful place. But she and Dimitri were going to build a house in their village near Ierapetra.

"It's my dowry that'll pay for it," she said, "and it'll stay in my name. Dimitri, he'd give everything to the poor if he had the chance. So, what's your fiancé like?"

I hadn't yet thought of Stelios as a fiancé, but I supposed he was then. I had a flush of pleasure at the thought as I answered her question.

"A puppeteer?" Froso asked. "He can make a living at that? Well, I hope you have a good dowry, that's all I can say. My mother says that most men are useless when it comes to money."

In a couple of days the wedding papers had come through. It was official and again I felt my conviction that Stelios and I would get through anything life threw at us. Back in Heraklion, I went straight to the clinic. I found Theo and Takis there, standing in the hall outside Yannoula's room. I avoided meeting Takis's eyes, thinking of what I was going to do. But from his and Theo's faces, I could see something was wrong. I asked them what was going on, and they explained that, shortly after I'd left for Agios Nikolaos, Yannoula had been found in the basement of the clinic, muttering among the brooms and mops. No one knew how she'd got down there and no one mentioned her having any kind of tests. Theo said her infection had returned.

"She has full-blown septicemia now," he said. "Or that's what they say, the doctors. But what do they know, bah!"

Yannoula still needed medicine not available on Crete. Couldn't the nurses just clean the wound and patch it up the way they'd done before? I asked. Theo didn't see why not. Yannoula was a tough old bone, as we'd always said. She could get through anything.

"She keeps singing the same song," Takis said. "About a carriage."

He and Theo had to get back to the café for the evening's performance so I went in to see Yannoula alone. She seemed to be talking to the wall and went right on as I stood beside her bed.

". . . my second husband, Manolis, in the river wading toward me. But no, it was—guess who—Karagiozis. He said he'd carry me across; I should just hop on his back. So, fool that I am, I did it. Partway across, just as we got into water over his head, he said he'd forgotten to tell me he couldn't swim. When I said we'd both drown, he told me no, only I would, because he was just cardboard and would float downstream."

She looked at me then and raised an eyebrow as if trying to remember who I was. "And here you are," she said. "But why? Did you come to rescue me? A little brandy might keep me afloat. If you could just look in my suitcase . . ."

"It's probably at the boardinghouse," I said.

"Oh?" She glanced around the room as if surprised to find herself in it. She looked as thin as a twig under the covers. Closing her eyes, she turned away from me toward the wall.

"What's this I hear about a carriage?" I asked.

The word seemed to rouse her. She turned back to me and sang tunelessly in a croaky voice.

See how the carriage passes by
with you and your love inside?
It passes by, it passes by.
How the carriage passes by.

"Do you know who I am, Yannoula?" I asked.

"Of course, Aliki, why wouldn't I?"

"You've been very sick, I hear."

"I fell down, that's all, in the basement. I was just trying to organize things down there. I don't know why everyone got so upset. No one has a sense of humor anymore. Where've you been?"

I told her about Stelios, how he was being sent into exile on an island still unnamed. She looked puzzled for a minute, but then something of her old self came into her eyes. "Oh, that's right. They took him away right in the middle of the performance. Theo told me."

"We're, well, married now."

"What? Whatever for?"

"So I can go with him."

"Go where?"

"We don't know yet."

"Doesn't sound like a good idea to me." She glanced at my hand. "In any case, you're not wearing a ring."

Rings! She was right. We'd forgotten to get them.

"We'll buy them later."

"Not possible. They're part of the Orthodox ceremony. You couldn't have gone through it without them." I'd never been to a wedding so I didn't know that. She studied my face. "So, are you married or not?"

I explained.

"Oh, well, what does it matter? You two have been married for a long time as far as I'm concerned. But where will you go? That reminds me of the time when Manolis—he was my second husband, you know—took a salesman's job and went off somewhere . . . now where was it? And what was he selling, do you remember?"

I said I hadn't been around then, probably hadn't even been born, but she paid no attention and rambled along, lost the thread of the story, doubled back, then trailed off and closed her eyes. I wasn't sure what to think. She seemed herself and not herself by turns. I wanted to talk to a doctor. When I leaned over to kiss her forehead, which was hot, her good arm suddenly shot out and she grabbed my wrist.

"Don't tell Takis," she said.

"Don't tell him what?"

She squeezed my wrist hard. "He comes to see me every day, poor boy." She let go of my wrist and turned back to the wall. "He talks only of you," she mumbled.

CASSETTE 5 ✦ Side 1

I **sit here** now at the kitchen table thinking of poor Yannoula, who was so gallant and carried her misfortunes so lightly. She told me once that we—Stelios, Takis and I—were a kind of gift to her, a bit of new life. But it was really *she* who was our gift, with her lightness, her silliness, her advice, her strength. She leavened those bad times for us. And of course they were also good ones because they kept us together and, though we didn't understand it then, taught us to rely on each other, because what else could we do? Resentment would have burned us up. We saw enough of that in the towns and villages we'd passed through, people consumed in the slow fires of the soul. They were still walking around, but to look into their eyes was to peer down empty hallways.

I could fill this new cassette just with my thoughts of Yannoula, but I suppose I should move along. One of these days you're going to show up, my scholarly friend, to listen to the laments I've recorded, not to mention everything else I've babbled about. Oh, before I go any further, I should tell you that eventually—sorry to be so inexact, but you'll be like this when you're my age—the British announced they could no longer afford to aid Greece. They'd been supplying arms and men to the royalist government (returned from exile in Cairo, remember?), which was chasing the communist guerrillas in just about every corner of the country. The king himself would finally return after a positive referendum only to find, a year later, that the Brits were pulling out. Well, who could blame them? They'd been bombed flat by the Germans and had their own country to glue back together.

And in time, your old Harry Truman over there in the Land of Big Radios would decide to rush in to replace the Brits with American weapons and aid? I'm not sure, but what I remember was that he and his Congress feared that the communists might win here and install Stalin in the Parthenon. Who could imagine such a thing? Well, Harry could, I guess. So before long you Yanks were everywhere, like ants. Tall, well-fed young men with *miles* of very white teeth. First it was just tanks and weapons. But before long they were joined by engineers, architects, nutritionists, road builders—the whole lot. Everything from medicine to mules. You Americans, you tend to go too far—I hope I can say that to you without offense, my friend. You wouldn't have been born yet, of course. But it was as if your Mr. Truman thought he would not only defeat communism but drag Greece and the rest of Europe into the twentieth century. Ha. Our Byzantine ways and snaky politics were not so easily untangled.

Well, that was the beginning of our love-hate affair with you all. Like most affairs, it began with lilacs and roses (roads, housing and weapons). The end would be another story entirely. Still, the effort would be enough for old Harry to get his own statue in a public *plateia* in Athens. More about that later. I'm rambling again and I'm sure I've got way ahead of myself. Where was I? Oh, yes, Yannoula.

At least I should record her lament, as much as I can remember of it. There's no need for a lament for Aphrodite just now. She's improved, or so the women have told me. She may be having that burst of clarity that the nearly dead often have. They come back to themselves a bit and then they're gone, as if Death gave them one last look, home before dark.

I sat with Yannoula the night I got back from Agios Nikolaos.

Takis was there too, after he'd finished his performance at Theo's café. I looked at him, his sadness at what was happening to Yannoula, and wondered how he would cope with my leaving in addition to what he was already feeling. A doctor came—plump, balding, with flat, lifeless eyes—and listened to her chest, saying only that her infection was advanced and would soon take her. She'd also contracted pneumonia, he said, maybe from other patients in the clinic.

"It's in the air," he said. "Anyway, she's old."

"What do you mean?" Takis said. "Can't you make her well? What kind of doctor are you, anyway?"

"What kind do you want? I'm the one you've got. If you'd like to move her to one of the big hospitals in Athens, and can afford it, then do it. But seas are high; there'll be no ship for a while."

"Isn't there anything you can give her?" I said. "Just something. She's usually very strong. We've been traveling and she's just worn down."

He put his stethoscope back in his bag and went to the door, saying, "I'll send the women shortly."

We didn't know what he meant, but the talking brought Yannoula around.

"Oh, how lovely," she said, sitting up, eyes glistening. "There's someone at the door. I don't recall his name, but he's the gentleman who . . ." She stopped and glanced around her at us. "Aliki, Takis, could you bring him around here? I feel, oh, I don't know how to say it, a little *ethereal*. Is that what I mean? No, more like *ephemeral*. As if I might float up to the ceiling like a balloon and bob around there."

A spasm of coughing convulsed her and she fell back on the pillow. When the coughing had stopped, she lay exhausted.

"What are we going to do?" Takis asked. "We have to do *something*." The words caught in his throat and his eyes were filling. I could think of only one thing.

"There's no point in her being in this useless place any longer," I said. "Let's see if we can find a stretcher and get her back to the boardinghouse. At least she'll be more comfortable there."

But though we searched up and down the hall, we couldn't find one. We tried other floors but with no luck. And I wondered if Yannoula would even know where she was. Were we doing this for her or for ourselves? When we got back to the room, two women in black were there, each carrying a small ceramic incense burner.

"The doctor sent us," one of them said.

"But what do doctors know?" the other said. "They only turn to us when they've failed."

They lit small cones of piney church incense in the burners and waved them back and forth over Yannoula, muttering something that Takis and I couldn't make out. Then the first woman took a handful of cloves and dropped them on the two cones of glowing incense. A spiral of spicy smoke rose and perfumed the area, then drifted away. Yannoula shifted in the bed and seemed to relax. All tension went out of her and she smiled as she closed her eyes, as if she had a secret. There was a long exhalation of breath and her breathing stopped.

"May the earth rest lightly on her," the first woman said, crossing herself.

"One door closes and another opens," the second said, crossing herself too.

They left the room.

"Is she . . . ?" Takis asked.

I lifted one of Yannoula's arms, but it was limp. I kissed her hand.

Then the women were back with a basin of water and a clean white towel, which they put down beside Yannoula. This was for St. Michael, they said, who comes to collect the soul.

"He'll need to wash his sword and dry it."

"What nonsense," I said, as they turned to leave.

"We'll be back for the basin," one said from outside the door.

All I wanted was to be alone with Yannoula. I needed to say

good-bye to her in my own way, which would involve washing and dressing her so I could let go. I asked Takis to go back to the boarding-house and see if he could find her luggage, still unpacked since our return from the mountain village. She'd once said she wanted to be buried in her yellow gown, but I didn't know if she'd brought it from Athens.

"I don't want to leave," he said. "I don't want to find that dress. I know why you want it."

"Please, Takis. I need a few minutes alone with her. I'll be here when you come back."

He stood for a minute or two, shifting weight from foot to foot, but then he left. I removed the basin and towel and rested my head on Yannoula's still-warm chest and felt all energy drain out of me. I slid my feet into her slippers on the floor beside the bed and after a while I drifted away to that familiar room with the door ajar. Amber light came from beyond. And I felt as always that behind the door was some kind of true thing. It would have explained everything, but I couldn't get near it, no matter how I walked in that direction. I heard a sound, words coming from somewhere outside, but I couldn't make them out at first. And then I could.

I was Yannoula.
Will you sing the verse of me
waiting at the top of the stairs
for you to take my arm and
lead me down into the time
of being old, of being dead?
Here in this theater
where the play that was mine
finished before I could take the roses
you passed to me when
my last lines went unspoken.
Sing to me, Manolis, the song of us,

the song of our leaving and returning
as the painted moon behind us
sails through painted clouds.

The words repeated themselves until I recognized my own voice and felt Takis shaking me.

"You're talking in your sleep, Aliki."

"It wasn't sleep," I said.

"What, then?"

"I don't know."

He'd found Yannoula's yellow gown so I . . . Oh, but you know, I can't bear to talk about this even after all these years. Yannoula is in the earth in her long box and will be there for all time, turning as the earth turns, each day and night the same forever. It's more than anyone can comprehend. We live our lives like termites inside a fallen tree, feeling our way along in the dark, blind and unknowing of any universe outside.

Takis was unhinged by Yannoula's funeral and burial; he couldn't seem to recover from it—and who ever does recover from that? At least he was distracted from what was happening with Stelios, so I spent as much time as I could comforting Takis and encouraging him to continue his performances at Theo's café without giving in to grief. Then I realized it had been a couple of weeks and more, so I was afraid Stelios had already been taken to the island of exiles and I wouldn't know how to find him. But when I went to see the captain, he told me that no, Stelios was still there in Agios Nikolaos. There'd been no available troop ships to transport prisoners and there wouldn't likely be any until late August. I don't know how I dragged myself through that long summer of waiting, but there was no choice.

But during that time Takis finally seemed to find himself through the shadow puppets; he turned to them more than ever now. So when the captain finally told me I should get to Agios Nikolaos as soon as possible, I told Theo I was leaving, wonderful Theo, who'd taken care of the funeral arrangements for Yannoula and stood by Takis and me through it all.

"Go with Stelios," he said. "You must. Takis, well, I don't understand him. But the town children, they love his Karagiozis. He has to stay for them; they'll be his life. I'll talk to him, explain everything so he understands. But you're right, best just to go. Then I'll tell him."

He was giving me the coward's way out. But Stelios was right in saying I couldn't protect Takis forever. I packed my bag and took it along with Stelios's bag to the bus terminal without seeing Takis. All the way to Agios Nikolaos, I tried not to imagine Takis's reaction when he realized I'd gone. But I did have a clear sense of relief, the feeling of a burden lifted, one I'd carried ever since that terrible night in our own village. I wouldn't have to think about what I said to him. I wouldn't have to worry. I was on my way to Stelios and that was what I wanted. I was returning.

"Thank God," Stelios said when I arrived. "I thought I was going to miss you. We leave tonight."

"Yannoula."

He looked at me hard. I'd held myself together until then, trying to manage everything, with Theo's help. But finally the tears came. Stelios didn't say anything, but he looked stricken. He opened his mouth to speak then closed it. On the stage in front, an official announced that all relatives accompanying detainees were to leave the theater and present themselves in the harbor with their papers. I kissed Stelios quickly as guards moved among the men, shouting at them and herding them to one side of the theater with the butts of rifles.

In the harbor, the sun was going down as wives and children milled around with luggage and bundles of belongings. Froso waved me over to her, saying, "Have you heard? The island camp may be changed to a real prison camp. Not at all what we were told. Our men are supposed to be exiles—detainees—not prisoners."

How did she know this? I asked. Her Dimitri had told her. It was a rumor passing among the guards. "But as my mother says, rumors are like cats. They follow you home; they eat your heart."

Froso said that the island had produced marble from quarries in ancient times. Now the old quarries were being reopened and the detainees would be expected to work in them. It would be backbreaking and the length of time they'd be doing this was completely open. The only other thing anyone knew about the island was that it had a miracle-working icon of the Virgin in the Church of the Dormition. Many people with illnesses came there seeking cures during the Feast of the Dormition in mid-August. The detainees from the labor camp were obliged to help prepare the island for the event. But this year's ceremonies had been poorly attended because of the difficulty of traveling for anyone other than troops.

"My Dimitri," Froso said, "he isn't strong. I don't know how much work he'll be able to do. And I don't expect any icon to take an interest."

For that matter how would Stelios manage this new ordeal? His leg hadn't healed properly and he hadn't gained back the lost weight. He and the other detainees were a sad lot when they arrived in the harbor about an hour later. They'd been issued drab gray uniforms and, with their shaved and scabby heads, they looked miserable. Once the detainees had boarded and were standing at attention on deck, the families were allowed to show our papers and board. We went belowdecks where a long, low-ceilinged room was filled with bunk beds with bare mattresses. There was a smell of mildew and of the toilets in the stern.

"It's only for a night," Froso said. "I can stand anything for a night."

I went back on deck. The ship's horn blasted its three mournful cries as the ship pulled out of the harbor. Standing at the railing, I was watching the harbor fall away when I noticed a small figure with suitcases run out to the end of the quay. Something about him made me think of Takis. But could it be? Surely not. And yet there was this boy with suitcases, waving both arms wildly. Daylight was nearly gone and it was hard to make him out. But whether or not it was Takis, I was suddenly overwhelmed by what I'd done. How could I have abandoned him? It was almost as if I'd severed a piece of myself. Looking after him in spite of whatever he'd done had been part of me for so long. Would he recover from my desertion? Would I? But I was right, *right* to be leaving with Stelios; he was my good return, my home. I'd made a choice.

"Do you know him?" Froso asked beside me. I hadn't noticed her come up to the railing.

"Yes," I said. "I mean no. Oh, I don't know."

"Hmm, sounds . . . difficult." Just then the wind off the water slammed waves against the left side of the ship and the shattering spray drenched us all but especially the detainees. The guards had been trying to play cards under a tarp, but the wind and spray snatched them away, sending the men scrambling. I went over to talk with Stelios while Froso went to the other side of the deck to talk to her Dimitri, a slight young man with sunken cheeks. I couldn't imagine him taking part in a hanging. He looked like a schoolboy who should be learning his multiplication tables.

Stelios asked about Yannoula and I told him the details.

"I can't remember a time when she wasn't part of my life," he said. "I don't know how old I was when Mother hired her. She's just always been there. Almost more mother than Mother." He looked out across the slate-colored sea in the half-light of evening. A wind was stirring the waves, slapping them against the side of the ship. We stood for a long while and then he said, "We only have each other now. Well, that's how it should be, isn't it? But what about Takis? Did you get away without him knowing?"

I didn't mention the boy on the dock but told Stelios what Theo had planned and Stelios said, "Oh, poor Theo. I wouldn't like to be him when Takis finds out."

Sea spray burst over us and again ripped some of the cards away from the guards. The hot, dry wind of August called the *Meltemi* was battering the ship. The guards swore at it while the other men laughed. Stelios said he'd got to know many of them when they were in the theater in Agios Nikolaos. Most were communists and the guards were almost certainly nationalists. Others probably wouldn't be able to tell you exactly what they were. But most were being burned up by one kind of hate or another and the stories they'd told Stelios were bitter.

"The nationalists are really fascists who hate the communists, who hate one branch or another of themselves. They're split over loyalty to Moscow or to their local leaders. They can't agree on anything except how they hate the British. The royalist government likes them, of course, since it's being propped up by them. Then there's the military, gaining ground against the guerrillas everywhere." He threw his hands in the air. "But even they have their purges and divisions."

One of the stories he'd heard was about a village in the mountains that had been too friendly with the Germans. Some villagers had invited them into their houses and maybe even some of the women had taken them into their beds. Who could say if it was true or just rumors spread because of old resentments? But after the Germans moved on, a few men from the next village came in the night and burned down houses, two or three, no more. In return, men from the burned village came and shot up the people of the first village, killed their livestock, threw lye down their wells.

"One act like this always makes a bigger one. Finally no one from either village had anything, not sheep, not crops, not even their lives. When the Germans passed through again, there was nothing there, I mean, just charred remains." He ran his hand back and forth over the stubble that had begun to grow on his scalp and said, "When they heard what happened, the Germans thought it was funny. Two villages were wiped out and they hadn't had to lift a finger."

In the countryside everything was personal. If you hated your cousin and he became a communist, you became the opposite. "It's nothing to do with ideas, nothing to do with books. I think it's probably not just the countryside but the whole country. I don't see how we'll ever get ourselves straightened out."

The wind was picking up and the guards began handing out thin blankets to the detainees for the night. They probably wouldn't need more because it was so hot. They were to bed down on deck. I went below, where Froso was pouring lilac cologne on a handkerchief.

"Do you want some?" she asked. "If you put it over your nose when you sleep, it might help." But the sweetish aroma along with the foul odors of the room made me queasy so I took Stelios's mother's coat from my suitcase and came back on deck to one of the ship's stationary benches.

Uncomfortable as the bench was, it seemed only minutes later when the blast of the ship's horn startled me awake. We were heading for a gray smudge of land just as the big yolk of sun was rising behind it. The island slowly grew into an imposing brown rock with not much green on it. Sailing alongside, we looked up at high cliffs plunging down straight as a curtain to half-submerged boulders where waves shattered into foam. Some of the cliffs were streaked with white, the island's famed marble, someone said, jutting out in places like bones. Then the ship turned left and made its way into a little horseshoe-shaped harbor with a scattering of cement buildings, all cubes so brightly whitewashed that they dazzled in the morning sun. Passengers were to disembark there and the ship would sail on to the labor camp, which had its own small harbor on the other side of the island where the detainees would disembark.

"I'll come find you as soon as I can get a place to stay," I told Stelios. There was no hotel or inn on the island, I'd heard, but villagers rented out rooms in their houses. Stelios looked alarmed now that we were going to separate.

"Come with other women," he said. "Don't come alone. I don't know how safe it will be. And keep asking fo me if I'm not there." Fear flickered in his eyes as he added, "Don't let me disappear."

"Don't even think it," I said, though I was frightened too. I'd be his only link to the outside in this tiny place where we knew no one. But what was I to do here when I wasn't visiting him? It startled me that I hadn't thought of this sooner. I'd been so intent on getting away from Heraklion and to Agios Nikolaos before Stelios left that I hadn't thought further than that. For once, I didn't have a plan.

We held each other as long as we could. I didn't want to let go of him and I didn't want to be alone. Ashore, I looked around at the little port. There wasn't much there: yellow nets drying in the sun, local children gaping at us new arrivals, a café where old men played backgammon at outside tables. To one side were a few blocks of marble each the size of a small car. A crane was loading them one by one onto fishing boats, which ferried them to a freighter I could see a mile or so out. Had these been chiseled out by detainees? Was that what Stelios would be made to do?

Some of the families from the boat started out among the harbor houses, knocking on doors, looking for rooms. But I couldn't seem to make myself do that or do anything at all. This was the first time I'd been entirely on my own. A chilly wind blew off the sea and I felt I'd come to the edge of the earth.

"Let's do it together," a voice said behind me. Froso shoved her suitcase along with her foot until it was next to mine. "Not exactly the place you'd choose for a holiday, eh? What do they do for fun on Saturday nights, shoot each other?"

We left our suitcases at the waterfront café and walked to the outskirts of the village, the side closest to the camp. The houses there were also white cubes, like the buildings in the harbor. Behind them were what appeared to be well-tended vegetable gardens with orange and lemon trees and arbors of grapevines. Doors and shutters of the houses were painted bright primary colors and women opened them to look at us, new strangers in town, as we passed. They called out.

"I have a room. Very nice. Come and see."

"Very cheap, my house. Best in the neighborhood."

"Here with me you'll be closest to the camp."

We looked at some of the offered rooms, which were plain but tidy and clean. While showing us around, the women tried to get our stories out of us with questions about our relatives in the labor camp: what they'd done, how long they were sentenced for, how much we had to spend on a room. The island, we were told, had been all but forgotten by the world until the camp was built with prison labor.

"What can we do?" an elderly woman named Stavroula asked. She was tiny, shrunken with age, but her eyes never stopped sizing us up. She raised her hands in the air as if there was no choice but to take whatever the situation offered. "Such are our lives." She had a room for rent in her house next to the abandoned village schoolhouse. Her spare room was sunny and clean with its own bathroom and entrance. It was the best we'd seen but only big enough for one. Froso decided to take it once Stavroula had agreed to let Dimitri squeeze in when he was released, until they could return to Crete. But what about the schoolhouse? I asked, thinking maybe I could get it for nothing as it wasn't being used.

"Oh, it's been closed since before the war," Stavroula said. "The Ministry of Education in Athens, they stopped sending teachers. Our children grow up not reading or writing." She raised her hands in the air again. "It's not right, but what can we do?"

I went next door and peered through a dirty window at one large room with shadowy shapes of student desks piled on top of each other. I wondered again if I could have this for no or low rent if I offered to clean it up and do something with it. I had an idea so when I went back to Stavroula's, I asked if she thought the village might be persuaded to let me live there for the time being. I could fix it up a bit and get it ready to reopen, which was sure to happen eventually, wasn't it?

Froso took a look and said, "But it's so primitive, Aliki. And dirty."

"With only an outside toilet," Stavroula said. "And it's not good for a young woman to live alone. No one would have a good opinion of this."

I insisted it would be fine for me until I had a better idea how long my husband would be at the camp. It was the first time I'd used the word *husband* and as it came out of my mouth, I tripped over it. Stavroula raised an eyebrow and glanced at Froso, who hadn't seemed to notice. Stavroula went on tut-tutting about the schoolhouse, but in the end she phoned her cousin, the mayor of the village, who also turned out to be the local official in charge of the camp. Camps as small as this one, I gathered, often did not have commandants assigned to them but only guards who reported to a local person, in this case, the mayor. Stavroula said that although her cousin, the mayor, was very busy with important duties, he would try to make time to see me.

After two hours of waiting around for him outside Stavroula's house, the mayor arrived in a long white car with a driver who must have been a detainee, as he wore the same drab uniform. The mayor himself, a plump, middle-aged man in a rumpled brown suit, climbed out of the car, apologizing for the delay.

"It's a new group, you know, just arrived today." He pulled a handkerchief from his breast pocket and wiped his forehead. "Such a confusion. Well, it's always the same, getting them to understand how we do things here." There was a long-suffering tone to his voice and he looked at us with sad eyes as if he actually expected expressions of sympathy.

When I told him what I proposed about the schoolhouse, he said that yes, Stavroula had told him, but no, the place wasn't suitable for a young woman. What would everyone think? I should find a place in a house with a nice family.

"I could pay a little," I said.

"No, no, it would not be correct. We must be respectable here, where we have the holy icon. What would Our Lady think?"

He then went on about the history of the island and the marble quarries. All this seemed to have little to do with anything, especially considering that he was supposed to be so busy, but he clearly enjoyed the opportunity to give a little lecture. As he was describing "the exquisite, translucent quality of our marble," he got back into the car and his driver started the engine. I had to say something, anything, so I blurted out, "Look, I'll teach the children. Then it'll be a real school. No one could object to that, could they?"

He told his driver to turn off the engine. "*Are* you a teacher?" the mayor asked out the car window. "You didn't mention it before. And at *your* age? What experience do you have?"

"Well, I'm not a proper teacher with papers from the ministry," I said, unsure of how to continue. And then I knew. "But then, you don't have a proper school. Your children are growing up ignorant. I can read and write." I felt the color come into my face as I spoke, knowing I could barely read and the only book I had was Stelios's well-worn copy of *The Iliad*. But Stelios once said that whole generations had learned history and language from it. And it had worked with me, sort of. As I talked on, I felt myself growing into the argument I was making. I concluded firmly, "Why not let me try and see how it goes? What's there to lose? Only your children's ignorance."

The mayor looked me over while asking questions: where was I from, who were my people, why had I been on Crete, who was it that I had in the camp here? When I'd told him, he said, "Seems to me he made a good choice in you, young lady. Well, let me think about it." He nodded to the driver and the car drove off.

"That was quite a performance," Stavroula said behind me. "I'm sure your, uh, *husband* would be proud."

"Can you really teach?" Froso asked.

"We'll see," I said, and I went next door to the schoolhouse. I nudged the door and it opened. "Well, he didn't say yes, but then, he didn't say no," I said aloud as I went in. Pushing the student-sized tables and chairs to one side, I laid out my belongings on the floor and made a list of the cleaning supplies I would need. Then I walked back to Stavroula's house, where she was talking to Froso, and suggested we walk out to the camp. Where was it exactly?

"Oh, I wouldn't go today," Stavroula said. "It's too early."

"Too early for what?" we asked.

"For visits."

"I want to see my Dimitri," Froso said. "And I'm going to."

"My cousin won't like it," Stavroula said. "And just when you've made a good impression, Aliki."

"But we're only here because of our men."

As we walked, Froso said that Stavroula was "all talk, talk, talk. She and that mayor—already I know more about this place than Crete, where I've lived my whole life."

Outside the town, the island was barren. Sails of whitewashed windmills stood motionless beside the dusty road in the late-summer heat. We passed a village where most of the houses were abandoned, roofs fallen in, shutters ripped off windows, weeds everywhere. A dead plane tree stood in what must have been the *plateia*. I supposed the marble in nearby quarries had been exhausted and the workers had moved their families. In ancient times, the mayor had said, thousands of slaves worked the quarries.

"As far as I'm concerned," Froso said, "a rock is just a rock."

Chips and chunks of marble were everywhere. I picked up one the size of a lemon and held it up to the sun. The light seemed to be inside the stone, which almost glowed with it. The mayor had been right about its translucence. A rock was not just a rock. A truck passed us heading back to town with blocks of it in its bed. I supposed they would be loaded onto boats in the little harbor.

As we neared the camp, other women who'd been on the ship had already gathered there. We exchanged greetings and talked about the places we'd found to live. There was a sisterly sense among us, as we traded names and stories and our reactions to the dismal camp on a stony hillside with only a guardhouse and lots of ragged tents. They trailed down into a huge cave that was the entrance to one of the quarries. The other side of the hillside dropped into another quarry, a deep pit that held a small lake far below. The near side of the quarry lake was on camp grounds and the fence ran up to it. The far side was outside the grounds, but there was no way to cross to that side. It was said that seawater seeped into the abandoned quarry through underground caves. No one knew how deep the lake was, but there were rumors that sea creatures had been trapped there by currents long ago and bred in the dark water.

"These people here, they believe anything," Froso said.

The guardhouse was built entirely out of chunks of the crudely cut, unfinished stone. There was a wire fence around the camp, but it didn't look substantial. I supposed that, as we were on an island in the middle of the sea, there wouldn't be much point in escape attempts. There was no one in the guardhouse and no visible detainees so we stood around in the sun waiting for someone to appear. The women were all from Crete, of course, strong women who'd tilled fields and raised families. I wondered if they'd been among those who'd attacked the first German parachutists with scythes and pitchforks.

Finally a guard with a rifle came out and shouted at us, "Not today! Go home. The new arrivals have duties to learn."

There was a moment of astonished silence then a low grumble started up from those of us who'd been standing in the heat. Some of the women tried to argue with the guard, saying how long we'd waited and that we had a right to see our men. The guard just repeated what he'd said before. A few of the women in front hissed at him and spat on the ground at his feet. There were about twenty of us and we moved forward as a group. The guard shouted a command and at once a good dozen or so others came running and aimed their rifles at us. Was the mayor inside? I wondered. Would he appear?

The women became enraged; some of them picked up shards of marble from the ground. This was all happening so fast; surely it couldn't be like this every day. In my memory flashed the night in my own village, the women throwing handfuls of pebbles at the Germans. And everything that followed.

Then Froso said, "Let's go, Aliki. We'll be back tomorrow." She took my arm and we started to walk away. This seemed to break the tension and some of the other women followed us, tossing their stones to the ground, cursing. "Well, we see how it is here," Froso said. "None of this 'a few months in exile, helping out the happy villagers.'"

"We'll be here every day," one woman said.

"We'll make those guards miserable at the sight of us," another said.

Some of the others joined us in agreement, saying: We have our rights; those guards are born of women like everyone else. Who are they to aim rifles at us? I liked these strong-minded women with their ferocity and their warmth. They were different from the local women I met the next morning when I went to the general store to get the items on my list of cleaning supplies. Stavroula had told me when I got back from the camp that the mayor had phoned to say I could use the schoolhouse for the time being and we'd just see how it worked out (or not).

The store was a jumble of a place, just one large room and a little storeroom in back. It reminded me of the store in the mountain village on Crete. Canned goods were mixed in with farm implements and baskets. Fresh fruit and vegetables were next to brooms, mops and lightbulbs; pickaxes and jars of pickles were stacked with boxes of screws and rolls of bandages. Women exchanged gossip in the crowded aisles and men stood out front talking about crops and tools. The women questioned me about my husband, my family, my place of birth. Nothing went unremarked in some way: everything I said was greeted with nods, clucking noises or sidelong glances. Although they were curious, the women showed little warmth. I thought of telling them I was a teacher, but I didn't have the courage. It was a relief to step outside with my purchases.

Passing the harbor, I noticed that the morning ship had docked. There were no new detainees getting off this time, just a few passengers. But there was a small group of detainees boarding the ship to leave the island. They were laughing and joking with each other, clearly delighted to be going home. At least no one's here forever, I thought. Some do go home, just as Stelios and I would be going home sometime soon. And then I noticed the small figure standing there with his suitcases among the passengers and realized that he had indeed been the boy waving on the dock. Takis hadn't yet seen me and for a few seconds I had conflicting urges; the first was just to walk on. But he looked so lost and helpless, a truly motherless child standing there. Still, I was angry that he'd followed me and now he'd probably be angry at my desertion. But he *is* here, I thought, and this is an island. There's no escape.

I went over and stood near him until he noticed me. His face lit up but quickly turned into a scowl.

"How could you *do* that?" he asked.

"I had to," I said. "Stelios needs me."

"And I don't? I thought we were a family. You always said we were. Don't you want me in it anymore?"

His eyes and voice were full of hurt. He was again the old Takis, the pouty boy of the British barracks, but the pout only partly covered the anger. He scuffed his right foot along the ground.

"You had no right to follow me," I said. "You should have stayed at Theo's. You know you've got a chance for a new life there."

"But I don't want a new life if it means being alone. I start to, well, you know."

"I thought you were beyond all that."

"Sometimes. Sometimes not." There was an awkward silence. I didn't want to think what *sometimes not* really meant. I said that Theo wasn't supposed to have told him about my leaving until after the performance.

"There wasn't one," he said. "I went looking for you because I missed Yannoula. I was so sad I didn't know what to do. When you weren't there, I asked Theo, and do you know what he said? He said I should leave you alone, let go once and for all. 'What do you think you're going to do?' he asked me. 'Marry her someday?' I hit him. Blood came out his nose. He threw me out of his café."

"Oh, no, Takis." I stepped back from him, almost afraid he might hit me too. "Poor Theo. He's been such a good friend to us."

"Not anymore."

"No, I expect not." I supposed that was the last we'd see of Theo, even if we ever went back to Crete. But was Takis likely to hit anyone else? I changed the subject.

"How did they let you on the ship? You're not a relative of a prisoner."

"No one asked me anything; they just took my money after I got a ride to Agios Nikolaos on a truck. What about you? You're not a relative either."

"No one asked for papers." This was partly true. I didn't say that they'd only glanced to see the marriage papers in my hand. Withholding truth—it was easier than lying but amounted to the same thing, I supposed. But I didn't want to risk his anger now that he'd taken to hitting people.

"How's Stelios?" Takis asked. "How long's he going to be here?"

"I don't know. They wouldn't let us see any of the detainees yesterday."

There was a long pause. The ship's horn blasted three times. It was time for it to depart. I couldn't let it go without him.

"Listen, Takis, you'd better get right back on board. You can just make it. There's nothing for you here. I didn't ask you to come and I don't want you here."

His head jerked back as if I'd slapped him. He put his hand over his mouth while his eyes, full of hurt, looked at the ship in the harbor. He's leaving, I thought. I've hurt him that much. But instead he stood there in silence and then the ship's horn blasted once more. We could hear the announcement that all nonpassengers must go ashore. I reached out to him, intending, or so I thought, to give him a nudge on his way. But instead I pulled him to me and held him. By then the ship's engines had begun churning and the space between the ship and the quay widened slowly. There was now no chance of him leaving that day. I'd wavered, and there was nothing more to be done about it. Where would he go here and what would he do? If he stayed more than a day or two, how would I tell Stelios? They'd been getting along much better back in Heraklion, but that didn't mean Stelios would want him here with me.

I sighed and picked up one of his suitcases and started the walk back to the schoolhouse. He followed along in silence. As we approached, I saw Froso ahead waiting for me. We'd planned to return to the camp together that day. I whispered to Takis that I was going to introduce him as my brother and he should play along. I didn't know how else to explain his presence.

"Oh, the boy on the dock in Heraklion," she said, giving me a look. I'd forgotten that she'd been with me at the railing when the ship pulled away from Crete. "You didn't say he was your brother."

"Sometimes I wish he weren't."

Takis glared at me, but Froso said, "That's the way with brothers. I've got one too."

I told her that Takis and I needed to talk for a minute and then I'd go with her to the camp. I took him into the schoolhouse.

"All right, you can stay a day or two, but that's it," I said. "There's nothing here for you, Takis."

"*You're* here. And you don't seem to know whether you want me or not so I might as well stay until you decide." He looked around the room at the cracked blackboards, the broken desks. "*Theo mou*, what a place!" he said. "You really live here? It's so dirty. Where do you sleep?"

I'd made a pallet on the floor out of my coat and other clothes. It wasn't much, but considering that we'd lived in stables and even outdoors, it could have been worse.

"It's so uncomfortable," he said.

"Look, I didn't ask you to come."

"Okay, it's okay. I guess."

"A day or two, that's all."

"I can't go back. Theo said he never wanted to see me again."

"I don't blame him."

"That's mean. Why are you being so mean?"

"Oh, Takis, I don't know what to *do* with you. But I can't think about it now."

On the way to see Stelios and Dimitri, Froso said, "It's good he's here. Now you won't be living alone, which might give a wrong idea. As my mother says, men in small places are worse than ones in cities."

"How does she know?"

"She knows everything."

Froso said this with no trace of humor. We walked on.

At the camp, women were passing in and out of the blockhouse. When we went inside, we saw a wooden wall with open windows. Detainees sat on one side of the windows and visitors on the other. I gave Stelios's name and waited. When his face appeared at the window, something in me turned over. Even before he spoke, I could see the change. There was no expression in his voice or face. His eyes had a flat, dull look as he slumped against the frame of the window.

"I'll never get out of here," he said. "I'll die here."

"What's happened?"

"Some of these men, they've been here for a year or longer. When I told them I'd only been sentenced for a few months of exile, they laughed." He sighed and ran a hand across the stubble on his scalp. "We carry stone up the hill near the quarry lake, then carry it back down again. The pointlessness is worse than the labor." The mayor had given the new arrivals a talk outlining camp rules and regulations. He'd promised that after a few weeks of pointless work to break them in, they'd begin the real work of cutting stone with special saws and chisels for commercial use, the kind of work the other detainees were already doing. "He said it as if that would be our reward."

Some of the other detainees told Stelios they'd heard of much worse in other camps, where the prisoners were beaten and sometimes tortured until they signed a paper renouncing old partisan loyalties. But the guards here were bad enough, expecting bribes for leniency as they controlled supplies of food and water. Toilets were just fly-and-maggot-infested ditches at the side of the camp. And the tents were flimsy and offered little protection from weather. At that time, this didn't much matter. But just wait until the winter wind and rain, the others said. Stelios hadn't expected to be there then.

"My life is over," he said.

"No, no, don't say that. This won't last. I saw detainees leaving on the ship this morning. No one's here forever."

"Oh? I've heard some stories."

He looked around at the guards, who were mostly talking to each other.

"From time to time, bodies are found. Sometimes along the shore; other times in that quarry with the water at the bottom. Anyone the guards don't like, they just disappear."

I remembered what Froso had said about that quarry. There didn't have to be sea creatures in it for it to be a watery gravesite.

"But the relatives, don't they cause a lot of trouble?" I asked.

"Not everyone has relatives here. That's why you have to come every day, Aliki. Those here inside with someone on the outside survive better. That's what they all say. Just keep asking for me. Insist."

I thought that Takis could be another visitor asking for him, but I was still hoping to get Takis off the island somehow and soon. Could I bring some paper and pencils? he asked. Detainees were allowed to write letters, but what he really wanted the paper for was to write down a few more ideas for the rest of the play he'd performed that night at Theo's. And maybe some of the stories he was hearing.

"It will keep me from going crazy when I carry the stone."

I wanted to tell him about my plan to teach and maybe to use *The Iliad*, but the guards called out rotation time, which meant that new visitors and detainees replaced those of us still at the windows.

On the way back to town with the other women, Froso said, "My Dimitri, he's ill already. Such a cough he has, and no doctor in the camp." I mentioned Stelios's bad leg and his weight loss, which was worsening.

"And no hospital or clinic on the island," someone else said.

"What's to be done?" asked another.

"What's ever to be done?"

That was the question. It would always be so as long as we were on the island. I went back to the general store to buy paper and pencils for Stelios. But there wasn't much left of the money he'd given me in Agios Nikolaos. It was possible that he still had some, but I didn't want to ask. He'd need it to bribe the guards. As I returned to the schoolhouse, I was thinking again about how to get started teaching. And what to do about Takis. And then I had an idea.

"Did you bring the puppets with you?" I asked. He'd dragged one of the desks out to the middle of the room and was just sitting there.

"Yes, everything; screen and backdrops. But why? You want to give shows here?"

"Not exactly. But I need money."

"I have some from what Theo paid me for Karagiozis."

"Hang on to it." I told him about my conversations with the mayor and that I'd been wondering if I could teach a few simple things, like numbers and the alphabet and some practical reading skills. I didn't know much, but then the children knew nothing. I figured I could stay a step or two ahead of them. But maybe *The Iliad* wouldn't be best right at the start. Now that Takis had brought the shadow puppets, I could start by making up little scenes. Just ordinary conversations about going shopping, talking to a friend, making dinner, greeting people. Karagiozis and the other puppets would act these out and then the children would repeat the phrases. I'd write the words out for them and help them copy them down, sounding out each word, syllable by syllable. "It'll seem like a game, but they'll learn."

"Sounds kind of boring," Takis said.

"Does it? Well, it has to be simple at first."

"Why not just do the plays?"

"Because once they've seen them, that's that. This way, they'll go on learning. And their families will pay whatever they can pay."

He tilted his head as if thinking all this through, then said, "So, does this mean you want me to stay? Or isn't it more that you want the puppets, but you'd just as soon I go back to Crete? Or somewhere."

He looked hard at me and I paused before speaking. He had a point, of course. I couldn't very well talk him out of the puppets and then tell him to leave. And maybe Froso was right that it would be better to have him living with me. And he was talented with the puppets. I felt myself sliding down an old familiar hill. He was Chrysoula's boy and she wanted me to look after him. Oh, God. Here we were again.

"If you want to stay, you'll have to help me so we can help Stelios."

"You keep changing your mind. Did you tell him I'm here?"

"Not yet. He was too upset when I saw him." I described the camp and its ways.

"*Theo mou!* Let me out there. I saved him once—well, briefly, anyway. I can do it again."

I looked at him, unable to decide if he really cared at all what was happening to Stelios or if he just liked the thought of being a hero again. "You don't know what it's like, Takis. I don't see how you could do anything. And anyway, we don't know how long he'll be there."

I could sense Takis thinking it over, perhaps working out that once Stelios was free, there'd be no need for him anymore. So was helping Stelios, even if such a thing were possible, a good idea? As the next few weeks became months and summer turned to rainy autumn, Takis and I slid back into our old ways with each other, like brother and sister. At least there seemed to be no more romantic notions on his part. But he was much more secretive, disappearing for long amounts of time, evading my questions about where he'd been. I'd catch him looking at me sideways when he thought I wasn't paying attention, just as I went on watching him for signs of any downward mood shifts. We'd nearly run through the money from Theo that he'd brought with him. They were giving me credit at the store, but we'd need to start teaching soon. But it was increasingly difficult to keep Takis's attention on the task and so it was taking us longer to prepare.

At the camp, I'd been telling Stelios about my preparations for teaching, but I hadn't mentioned the puppets since I didn't want to explain how they'd come to be there.

"I still don't understand what you'll teach, Aliki," he said. "Words from *The Iliad*?"

He looked a little worse every time I saw him, thinner, his face narrow and pinched, his uniform tattered.

"No, not classical words," I said. "Parents want their children to be able to read directions on tins of food. Or on medicine bottles. Or to read newspapers from the mainland. I'm working on it, making lists and plans."

He'd been telling me that the men were organizing themselves.

They assembled at dawn and did exercises for a half hour, led by one who'd been a fitness instructor. Then they sang the national anthem and broke into groups, each with a leader who recommended work assignments—the cutting and carrying of the stones—to the guards, depending on strength and general health of the other men. The guards seemed to accept this, as the detainees were making the guards' jobs easier. After all, there was no disobedience involved.

"In this way we keep some pride," Stelios said. But there was a rumor that guard reinforcements had been requested. Stelios lowered his voice and said that detainees like himself had not been released at scheduled times. I knew this, of course, but didn't know if anything could be done about it. "There might just be a hunger strike," he said.

I didn't like the sound of that. Wouldn't there be reprisals of some kind? "If we can just wait this out," I said, "maybe we can go home."

"We are home. We're here together."

"Yes, but you know what I mean. We can't stay on this island forever, camp or no camp."

But where would we go when all this was over? His family house in Athens? Back to my father's house in the village? Soon we would have been on the island longer than the original sentence of three months. Winter was here with its winds and rain, and still there'd been no indication how much more time Stelios would have to serve. What if a strike brought on an additional sentence?

"If you could see how it is here from the inside, you'd understand better."

This was probably true, but I was too frightened by the thought of a strike to care. I distracted myself by putting up posters in the general store about lessons in reading and writing for village children. I offered to teach for one week with no fee. If at the end of that time, the parents or children weren't happy with my teaching, that would be the end of it. Otherwise, the lessons would continue for whatever the families could manage to pay.

"What am I supposed to do in all this?" Takis asked. "Anything?"

"Be the puppet master."

"I can't teach anything because I don't know anything."

"I don't know much either. Just do these little sketches and leave the rest to me. We'll see how it goes."

When we'd first unpacked the shadow puppets, we noticed that they included the ones Stelios had been using at the last performance at Theo's café, the ones of all of us; there were also others we'd forgotten about, soldiers with swastikas on their uniforms.

Takis had looked startled. "I don't remember these."

"Oh? They were in his play that night in Heraklion."

"I didn't watch that part."

He turned away from me but not before I'd caught the slight glazing of his eyes, that telltale loss of focus.

"Oh, well," I'd told him, "we don't need them."

He tossed them in the corner.

Our first students were a brother and sister, a shy and undernourished-looking pair about six years old, along with an older boy who said he was a cousin. Takis and I had placed the best of the old desks in a semicircle facing the puppet theater. We turned out the lights and used kerosene lamps to create shadows on the screen. The first lesson was learning the numbers one through twenty, in numerals and words, but the three students had never seen shadow puppets before so Takis first introduced Karagiozis the baker dancing and counting his fingers. We'd worked out this song for him:

Trin, trin, trin,
I can count to ten.
But what happens then?

Do I start again?
Ten fingers, ten toes,
And this bread, how many loaves?
Who knows, who knows?

We got the three students to sing along the second time around and then Karagiozis counted out his pies, cakes and loaves of bread while making silly mistakes. *Two pies or ten? Count again!* I wrote the numbers on the blackboard in numerals and words as he talked, and then I got the students to sound everything out and copy from the blackboard. Their shyness dropped away as they laughed and called out to Karagiozis, "Count again! Count to ten!" We sent them home with their drawings of the puppets and lists of numeral words.

They must have told their parents good things about us because after a few days, more students came. Takis and I quickly learned to plan everything carefully in advance, working out the little conversations and scenes for the next day so the students would always be busy. Any lull in activity meant trouble.

"Catch, Takis!" one of the boys said, after he'd leaned out the window and pulled an orange from a tree. It went flying across the room and Takis tried to catch it, but it burst against the opposite wall. The boy's sister brought a pair of scissors from home and, when no one was looking, cut letters of the alphabet out of her dress or anything else she could find: my scarf, her brother's jacket, pages of an old textbook.

At first they treated Takis as an equal since he was only a few years older. He would move among them, taking away oranges and scissors, correcting written work if he knew the answers. Sometimes he got into pinching and poking contests with the boys and I had to shoo them all outside for a break.

"We have to make them respect us," I told Takis after class. "You can't act like one of them and expect that to happen. Grow up."

"I think I'm growing *down*."

"Try sideways. This will never work unless you act like a real teacher."

"I've never had a real teacher."

"Well, all I had was the old schoolmaster back in the village before the war. Remember Petros? He used a stick to keep us quiet."

I shouldn't have said it. Takis brought a stick to class and smacked it loudly against the blackboard to startle students into silence. He liked doing this and did it regularly, making them jump in their seats. One morning a girl burst into tears and had to be calmed with sweets.

"You're frightening them," I said.

"Good," Takis said. "It keeps them quiet."

"I don't want them quiet. They have to speak to learn."

"You know what, Aliki? I like this. Do you think I could be a real teacher one day? In a real school?"

"Well, I don't know. You'd have to go to school yourself for many years."

"But you'd come too, wouldn't you?"

"Oh, Takis, I don't know. We'll have to see about that."

At least we were being paid a bit, mostly in produce from gardens, and from the shops—lentils, beans and rice along with yogurt and cheese. The food at the camp was minimal—day-old bread, and onions and rubbery potatoes made into thin soup—hardly enough to sustain men who worked at hard labor in the cold wind. The guards charged ridiculous prices for the sparse food. So I'd taken to bringing Stelios extra produce.

"My Dimitri, he has such a terrible cough," Froso said. "No one does anything for him except your Stelios, who tries to keep Dimitri warm by giving him his own blanket." There was little shelter for the men in the quarries. Stelios had torn apart an old tent and made floppy canvas hats for Dimitri and himself. When I handed the bag of produce through the window to Stelios, he said, "I'll give it to the others, those not going on the hunger strike."

It was to begin the next day, he said, and last as long as necessary, a protest against delayed releases mostly but also the poor food, the lack of sanitation and the heavy work. The men wanted to be able to form classes and teach one another skills they could use after their sentences were finished. There were many trades represented: tailoring, plumbing, carpentry and others.

"We're supposed to be in a camp for exiles, not prisoners. That's what they told us in Agios Nikolaos. We're supposed to do service to the community. But the guards and that mayor, they treat us like slaves." About one-third or so of the men were going to strike, he said. The others were too afraid of reprisals.

"And you?" I asked. "Aren't you afraid?"

"Yes, yes, of course. But our fear, it's all we really own here. We have to do something with it before it swallows us. I learned that much from Stephanos in the mountains. Remember me telling you about him? He was wrong, but right to fight for his wrong."

At least Stelios had lost that defeated look he'd had at first. He was still as gaunt as he'd been when he came back to Heraklion, and he said that his leg wasn't much better, but there was this new conviction in him. I told him that I'd heard how some newspapers from Athens were saying that guerrilla fighters all over the country were losing ground, but other papers said just the opposite. Who knew what to believe? We hoped it would all soon be over. "A strike right now could make everything worse, couldn't it?"

"It's going to get worse anyway." He glanced around, but the guards, as usual, were talking to each other. In a whisper, he told me there was a rumor that the camp was going to become like ones on other remote islands, where prisoners were tortured until they signed papers denouncing any past political loyalties and swearing an oath to the government. I remembered Froso telling me about this before we left Agios Nikolaos. So it was really happening?

"We hear that those who don't sign just disappear."

"Then don't strike," I said again.

"Some men are already starving; others are sick. There's tuberculosis here and pneumonia. We have to do what we can."

The next day we heard that the camp had been closed to visitors. Barricades were put up around the perimeter and the guardhouse remained shut. No one knew what was going on inside, but it was rumored that some of the detainees were refusing food. Apparently there'd never been a hunger strike at the camp before and the customers in the general store were talking about it. Some thought the detainees were right, but others worried what this might mean for the future of the camp. The island economy was dependent on it; the land for the camp was rented from the township and island food was purchased. Why should the men there expect to have rights? There was also the worry that if word of the strike got out, there might be inspectors from the International Red Cross, who had been known to close down camps. Though usually they reopened later after the inspectors were gone. We heard that more camps were opening all the time on other islands.

There was nothing Takis and I could do about any of this so we tried to get on with our lessons for the children, and every day one or two more students joined the group. We divided them into two sections because we needed to start all over for the new ones while moving ahead with the others. Takis loved it all.

"Teach me, Aliki, so I can teach them. I want to learn *everything*."

We prepared in the afternoons for the next morning's lessons and Takis worked hard. When he wasn't preparing or teaching, he roamed. I didn't know exactly where, but the camp was closed so there was no way he could see Stelios. He must have been out that way, though, because he said once that he went to the far side of the quarry lake and stared down at the water for a long time, hoping to see one of the rumored sea creatures.

"Do you know how to swim?" I asked. Funny—I'd known him all his life but didn't know a little detail like that.

"No."

"Then you'd better stay away from there."

"There's not much to do here, as you might have noticed."

He sometimes told me stories about people in the village and I worried that he was lurking around, spying, maybe. He seemed to know things he shouldn't have known—who had visitors late at night when the village was asleep, who had a bag of sovereigns under the kitchen floorboards, which husbands beat their wives or children. When I asked how he knew such things, he was evasive, repeating that old opening line of folktales: "Maybe it's true and maybe it isn't."

But what was true about the strike at the camp? At first we couldn't get any news at all and I was lying awake at night wondering how long poor Stelios could survive without food. Then, in the general store on the third day of the strike, Takis heard about the forced feeding of detainees at the camp. I don't know how the news made its way there, but perhaps the mayor had said something to his cousin, Stavroula, who wasn't known for keeping secrets. Froso seemed to hear about it at the same time, probably from the same source. She and Takis came running over to the schoolhouse late in the afternoon.

"Can you imagine?" Froso said. "The guards hold a prisoner down and put a tube through his nose and slide it down into his stomach. Then they pour in milk."

"There's a lot of choking," Takis said. "And gagging and bleeding. Sometimes they don't put the tube in correctly. Milk went into the lungs of one man and it was like drowning. That's what someone said, anyway. He drowned even though he was on dry land. Is that possible?"

"What it *is*, is disgusting," Froso said. "Most throw up afterward so what's the point? I'm going out there and not leaving until they show me that my Dimitri is all right."

No one had heard any names of those who'd been force-fed. The three of us walked to the edge of the village where the road to the camp began and saw Cretan women coming from all directions, talking angrily. As we passed the abandoned village, a cold wind was stirring up little whirlwinds of dust and leaves.

"Let's let them know we're coming," someone said and began a song. Others joined in.

Make sure in this life
You get what you want.
The years fly off like birds.
The first wind lifts them and they're gone.

At first it seemed an odd song to sing, but then it didn't. There were a lot of verses and Takis picked them up right away, but I didn't feel like singing. I kept imagining Stelios being fed that way and what it would feel like to have the tube pushed through your nostril and down inside you. When we got to the guardhouse, there was no one around, but the metal barricades stretched out on either side of the guardhouse. The absence of anyone at all made us uneasy. Then Froso called out Dimitri's name. And the others began to call out the names of their own men, repeating them.

"Vangelis! Soterios! Aris!"

Takis and I called out for Stelios, but the sound was just one of so many in the air that it was impossible to make out individual names anymore. Some women were shrieking as if in pain and others began to pull their hair, keening as if there'd been a death. "Ooo, loo, loo, loo, loo, oo loo, oo, loo . . ." The sound surged and fell and surged again like a living thing with a momentum of its own.

The door of the guardhouse flew open and a uniformed guard with a rifle stepped out and shot once over our heads. The screaming and shouting stopped and there was a long silence. Beside me, Takis snapped to attention; I'd almost forgotten his reaction to military uniforms. The women in front of the crowd pressed forward and the guard said something to them that we in the back couldn't hear. But the women turned and passed the word along: finished, the hunger strike was finished. Go home, the guard told us, no visits until tomorrow.

The women in front hissed at the guard and jeered.

"Son of a whore!"

"Sperm of the devil!"

"Eater of men's souls!"

He turned and went inside. We sat down on the ground. And then the calling out of names began again.

"Andonis! Stamatis! Pavlos! Dimitri! Stelios! Lambros! Haris! Sotiris! Aris! Michaelis! Vangelis!" Some of the women called on saints too.

"Agios Georgios!"

"Agios Panteleimon!"

"Agios Polycarp!"

Others called out the names of long-dead relatives or of God Himself or Panayeia, Mother of God. There was no movement in the guardhouse.

"This is great!" Takis said. "Let's do some more."

"It's not a game, Takis."

The women were roaring again anyway and continued until throats grew raw and voices hoarse. And then we roared some more.

Finally the door to the guardhouse flew open again and out came two guards dragging the slumped body of a prisoner. They pitched him forward into the mud in front of the barricade. From the rear of the crowd we couldn't make out who he was, but as he fell, I saw that his hands were tied behind his back. He lay still on the ground.

"If you don't leave at once," one of the guards shouted at us, "there'll be others." Then the pair went back inside.

The women in front surged toward the body on the ground as Takis pushed through the crowd. One woman seemed to be propping the body up, pinching his nostrils closed while breathing into his mouth. Another splashed his face with water from a flask and then slapped his cheeks. But he slumped back into the dust. Then there was a scream and it took me a few seconds to realize that Froso wasn't with us, that she'd got to the front and the scream was hers. By the time I made it there, the other women were pulling her off the body, which stank of the sour milk that saturated his clothes. Takis was staring in rapt wonder.

There were no marks on Dimitri that we could see, no bullet holes in his clothes, no signs of a beating. Froso had begun rending her face with her nails until the other women pulled her hands behind her back and propped her up between them. We made a kind of loose stretcher out of blouses and shawls and lifted Dimitri into it. With two of us carrying at either end, we all began to make our sad way back to the village. Froso shrieked most of the way until she collapsed, and the women made another kind of sling out of scarves so she could partly walk and partly be carried.

Stavroula let us use her house for the wake, though she wasn't sure her cousin would approve. "It's the decent thing to do for the husband of my poor tenant." She even donated one of her late husband's old suits and she and two of the other women washed and dressed Dimitri in a room next to the one Froso had rented. The village coffin maker donated a pine box and, once Dimitri was in it, we all filed past tossing flowers onto him. In death, he looked more a boy than ever.

In the room with the amber light words still flowed, or so I was told afterward. I said something like this:

In the hills above our village,
I trapped hares with my brother,
and later trapped the men who took our mother's land.
We hanged them in the orchard by the old fence

that needed the repairs it never got
because we were taken, first my brother,
then Mother and finally me.
The soldiers took us all,
away from the hills above our village.

There was a lot more of it, Stavroula told me afterward, but I didn't remember anything else. The next morning, I returned to the camp with a bag of bread and other food. Everything looked normal again with no sign of what had happened the day before. When Stelios came to the window, his face was so thin and drawn as to be almost skeletal and his voice was flat and without expression. He wheezed a bit when he said, "May the earth rest lightly on Dimitri."

After the first few days of the strike, he told me, the guards chose men for forced feeding, picking out mostly the younger, weaker ones who'd been fainting from lack of food in the cold. A pair of guards tied each one to a chair with hands behind the back and one guard held the prisoner's head while the other inserted a rubber tube into one of his nostrils.

"We were made to stand and watch. Some of us, we begged to take Dimitri's place, but they wouldn't listen. He fought, *Theo mou*, how he fought! Who would have supposed the boy had such strength? The milk was coming out everywhere. It went on and on. He was choking and it looked like he couldn't breathe, but they kept on, those *malakes*, until Dimitri turned blue. Only then they took the tube out. But it was too late."

Stelios rubbed tears from his eyes as he talked. He pounded the window frame with his fists and swore. A coughing spasm shook him. It was wet and awful. He had to hang on to the sill to steady himself. Water streamed from his red-rimmed eyes. I tried to hold him, but the guard came and pulled Stelios to his feet.

"He's ill," I said. "He needs a doctor." But the guard, whose eyes had the look of the island lizards, shrugged and took Stelios away.

Back in the village, Takis and I walked with Froso to the ship for Crete. Some of the village men carried Dimitri's coffin. We all shuffled along behind it. Froso's grief seemed to have turned to anger. She muttered as she walked and kicked stones in the road. "Now I have to grow old alone," she said, "a widow pitied by everyone, living with my know-it-all mother."

CASSETTE 5 • Side 2

No one in the village talked much about what had happened at the camp in the months afterward. Even Stavroula, cleaning out Froso's room for whoever would be the next tenant, said, "Well, it's too bad what happened, but that's all over now."

But it wasn't. I was sure the command for the forced feeding had come from her cousin, the mayor, so no wonder she didn't want to talk about it. In the streets and the general store, the townspeople tried not to meet our eyes when we, the camp women, passed them. It seemed to me that in some way the village felt shamed by what had happened at the camp and this was mixed with worry that it might be closed. The fighting on the mainland went on through the next spring and summer and seemed without end. There'd been huge battles won by government forces in the north of the country and in the Peloponnese region, as well as southwest of Athens. Many of the guerrilla forces were imprisoned or forced into exile. At least, that was what newspapers from Athens were saying, and by Easter of that year, many people uprooted by fighting in those areas were on the move. That would have been in, let's see, '46, was it, or '48? Sorry to be so muddled about dates. Looking back, it seems that one year ran into another without a break in the national misery. Anyway, by that midsummer we started to see the arrivals on the island of many of the wounded and maimed, hoping for miraculous cures from the holy icon during the festival of the Dormition of the Virgin. The festival had been small the previous summer because of the difficulty of travel to the island. It wasn't much better this year, but people seemed determined to come; a lot of rooms had been reserved in village houses. So a general sprucing up was taking place all over the village. Men from the camp had been brought into town to scrub the pavements and storefronts with bleach and water.

"We must provide a nice clean face for our visitors," Stavroula said, pausing while whitewashing the street side of her house. It was as if things that had happened at the camp could be whitewashed too.

"And if we clean our face for our visitors, we do it for ourselves too. This is how it is every year—our new beginning. You women and your men, you'll be leaving, but we're here for life. It's different for us." She turned back to her whitewashing and said over her shoulder, "We won't even remember you."

"But we'll remember *you*," I said. "And your cousin."

Her brush slapped whitewash fiercely onto the wall.

And suddenly he was everywhere—the mayor—directing the repair of broken roof tiles on the church, the filling of potholes in streets where the church procession would pass, the planting of red and white oleanders around the *plateia*.

It was ridiculous, Stelios said the next time I brought him a bag of food, that the kind of work they'd been supposed to do as exiles—work to benefit the local population—was what they were now being told they had to do to prepare for the holiday.

Tasks were being handed out to prisoners depending on their skills: painting, carpentry, masonry and so forth. Stelios's only skill was with the shadow puppets and because he was always coughing, they didn't really know what to do with him. But he'd volunteered to put on a Karagiozis performance so he supposed he'd have to make some puppets out of bark again. He was already working on one but asked me if I knew where I could find more bark as there were few trees around the camp and quarries.

"I keep making them," he said, "first at Chrysoula's then in the mountains. And now here. This time I'd better save them."

I couldn't keep from him the fact that the actual puppets, the ones he'd had from childhood and the new ones he'd made on Crete, were here on the island.

"What? You mean . . . ?"

"Yes. He followed me. The next boat the next day."

"Takis has been here all this time?"

I nodded. But I couldn't say anything else for a moment as the shame of not telling Stelios sooner began to consume me. I felt as hot as the sun, radiating embarrassment. When I could speak again, I told him about how we'd been using the puppets in the classroom. And what an enthusiastic teacher Takis had become. Stelios didn't say anything for a moment and seemed to be having trouble taking in this information. He started to cough but put his hand over his mouth and choked it off.

"You didn't tell me," he said. "Where's he staying?"

"At the schoolhouse."

"With you? All this time?"

"Yes."

A tiredness came into his eyes beyond what had already been there. The coughing started up again.

"I'll get you the puppets," I said.

He turned away and muttered, "I'll make my own."

I couldn't stand the dejection in his voice and told him how sorry I was not to have told him sooner. But the first time I'd seen him at the camp, he'd been so unhappy. I hadn't wanted to make things worse by telling him about Takis. The two of them had got along much better in Heraklion before Stelios's arrest, but I'd sensed that telling him about Takis on one of my visits to the camp would be a mistake. At least, at first when he was so unhappy. And as time went on, it became more difficult to tell him.

Stelios was still looking away without saying anything so I said that maybe he should have something to eat. I'd already passed him the shopping bag, but he hadn't taken anything out of it, saying then only that he'd share it with some of the others. I took from my pocket a bar of chocolate I'd half eaten and passed it to him. He took it but just looked at it.

"Please eat something. You look like you might faint."

"So how *is* the little devil?"

"Actually he's been a great help. And he hasn't had any of those spells." I tried to explain how Theo had said he'd keep Takis in Heraklion. But Takis had Chrysoula's strong will; there was no doubting that. And now I didn't really know what to do about him. I didn't add that although I'd been angry that he followed me, it had been good to have his company these past months. I also didn't mention that Takis had punched Theo so there wasn't much chance of him going back there.

"If only that doctor in Heraklion had worked out something for him," Stelios said. "If only I hadn't been . . ." He trailed off.

I stood there, growing annoyed to think that putting Takis away somewhere would have been Stelios's answer. "Well, to be fair," I said, "Takis did stand up for you back in that mountain village."

"Yes, I know. And I'm grateful, though little good it did me in the long run. But he does have courage, that's for sure. It's just that we keep coming back to the beginning with him and here we are once again. I don't dislike him, but are we going to have responsibility for him forever?" He moved away from the window, saying over his shoulder that he'd just had an idea for a new puppet and had better get on with it.

As I walked home, I wondered whether Takis could possibly stay there on the island and run the school after Stelios and I had gone. It didn't seem likely since his own reading skills were even poorer than mine. I'd begun to teach him months ago, but I still had to go over everything with him first before he could work with the children. And when peacetime came, maybe the Ministry of Education in Athens would send a real teacher again. So what would become of Takis if he stayed?

When I got back to the schoolhouse, Takis told me how some houses near the center of the village had converted their front rooms into shops that sold *tamata*. These were miniature body parts: symbolic hearts, limbs or anything else afflicted. They were made of metal, usually tin or silver but sometimes even gold. "If your foot hurts, you buy a foot *tama*, give it to the icon of the Virgin and, presto, your foot's okay! Isn't it funny?" Also for sale were miniature houses, cars, boats and other items that visitors could present to the icon in hopes that she might be moved to arrange the real thing for them. "Maybe she could give me a new head. I could use one."

I did later see a whole rack of miniature heads—male, female, adults, children—in front of one of the houses. But I would have settled for freedom for Stelios. I doubted there was a *tama* for that. The irony was that many of the visitors were victims of one side or another of the civil fighting. If the icon could heal the nation's warriors, couldn't it heal the nation itself? Much of the fighting was over, but the bitterness it spawned lived on. There was no *tama* for that either.

The next day a poster went up in the *plateia* advertising a Karagiozis performance on Sunday before the church procession. After the performance, the icon was to be carried on a platform around the village, accompanied by a band, the priest, acolytes and local dignitaries. Takis was puzzled by the poster and said that no one had asked him to give a Karagoizis performance.

"It's Stelios," I said. "It's something he's been told to do."

Takis looked startled. "He's going to be here in the village?" I nodded. "But we have his puppets. And we need them for classes. And anyway . . ." He looked down at his shoes. "*I'm* the puppet master now."

"He's making his own."

"What? Out of bark? Ha. We're not in Mother's basement. He needs the real things. But I should be the one giving the performance, not him."

"As I say, he has to."

"I'll go see him."

I said nothing, but the thought of the two of them together for the first time in all these months alarmed me.

"You don't want me to, do you?" Takis asked. "Does he even know I'm here?"

"He knows. Oh, go if you want."

What was the point of trying to keep them away from each other? They were going to have to work something out and maybe it was better if I stayed away. Takis gathered all the puppets, including the ones with swastikas he'd thrown to one side months before, put them into a suitcase and left for the camp.

I paced around the schoolhouse trying to imagine what they would say to each other after all this time. After about forty-five minutes, I could stand it no longer and started the walk to the camp.

As soon as I arrived I could see how things were going. Takis was standing there holding the puppets in his arms and shaking his head with impatience, saying, "*What* doctor?"

"The one who gave you an injection in Heraklion to calm you down," Stelios said. "The day I was kidnapped."

"I don't remember that."

"He knew of a place for boys with problems, so Aliki and I, I mean, well, we thought . . ."

"*You* thought, Stelios," I said from behind Takis, who turned around, surprised to see me. "And Theo thought so too."

But why was Stelios telling Takis this? Just to be mean to make Takis feel how precarious his life with us had been? And still was?

"I don't understand," Takis said. "A place? Where? Why?"

A series of coughs tore through Stelios so he couldn't speak for a few minutes. Takis turned to me. I told him that Theo had said that there was a doctor who might be able to help him. There was a kind of hospital for boys with problems. But then everything had changed because Stelios disappeared.

"Help me? How? Like that place in Kifissia? That woman with the . . . tubes?"

"No, of course not. We were only going to talk to this doctor."

"You didn't say anything to me."

"We were going to, Takis. Believe me, we wouldn't have made any decisions without you."

"You thought I was crazy," Takis said, his eyes wide.

"You were talking to *fish*!" Stelios blurted out between bouts of coughing. "And trees!"

"No, you don't understand," he said, shaking his head. "They were talking to *me*. It's not the same. For me, they were real. I don't know how to explain it. You hear a voice that's yourself but comes from outside yourself. And it's as clear as either of your voices here and now."

I thought of my laments, how they too came both from me and from outside me. And I understood a bit of what Takis was saying. But my laments grew out of my feeling for the dead somehow, though I'd never understood how it happened or why I seemed to end up in the room with the amber light. I'd never thought to question it since it was like an unasked-for gift. But was my gift really another kind of madness, akin to his? Did it matter? It certainly didn't to the dead, nor to their living relatives, who've been comforted by laments all these centuries.

"But what if the voices wanted you to hurt someone, Takis?" Stelios asked. "Or yourself? I mean, you could have drowned that day in the Heraklion harbor."

"They never told me to hurt anyone. And I'm better now, I think.

Making the puppets talk for me, that helped." He paused and then said in a choked voice, "But I'd be better off drowned than in a place like that one in Kifissia."

He tossed the suitcase of puppets on the ground and walked away.

"Why did you tell him that?" I asked Stelios. "It was unkind."

"I know. I know it was."

"Then why?"

"I'm sorry. I was thinking about what we'll do with him when I get out of here. When we leave the island."

A flush of anger passed through me, maybe because I'd been wondering the same thing but didn't want to admit it. "He even brought you the puppets," I said, though that had nothing to do with it.

"I know. I know. Could you pass them to me?"

I picked up the suitcase and brushed the dust off as I passed it to Stelios. He opened it and turned them over in his hands.

"I've had these so long, almost my whole life. Except for the ones I've made."

"But you gave them to Takis."

"I think we could say he's given them back."

A guard said our time was up. Just as I was leaving the camp, I saw Takis sitting there on a rock, waiting.

"He hates me," he said as I came up to him. "I helped him on Crete, but he still hates me."

He stood and walked with me in silence. "I don't think he does," I said. "But do *you* hate him?"

Takis didn't say anything at first. "Well, not exactly. I mean, yes, sometimes. The trees, they used to warn me about him—how he would take you away from me. They said they were my only friends."

"Maybe they were right." He said nothing and we walked on in silence. Then I was the one who had to stop and sit on a boulder by the side of the road. I thought that maybe the truth was that Stelios and

Takis actually *liked* each other but would never understand that as long as I was around. A wave of sadness washed through me and for just a moment I thought of throwing myself in that quarry lake back behind the camp. It was then that Takis said maybe he should drown himself so Stelios and I would be rid of him.

"I was just thinking of doing the same thing with myself."

"Oh, no," he said, alarmed. "You can't leave me. You can't *ever* leave me." His tone was so desperate that it frightened me.

"It's *you* who have to leave. You need a life of your own."

He began walking in a wide circle around me. He was passing behind me when he said, "A life without you and Stelios, that's what you mean, isn't it?"

"Well, if you really want to be a teacher, you'll go to school and you'll meet other people who want that too. Maybe there'll be someone you like more than others. I think that's how it's supposed to work."

"What do *you* want?" He stopped in front of me.

"I want Stelios to be free. I want you to have your own life, and I want . . . well, I want to have a *place*, a place in the world. Everyone else seems to have one except the three of us. A place to go to and stay without moving all the time. But I'm not sure where that would be."

His eyes widened. "We could do it, Aliki. We could go back to our village, couldn't we? And live in your father's house? Why don't we, you and me?"

"And leave Stelios here by himself? Absolutely not. And anyway, are you sure you'd want to go back? Don't you remember what happened there? What happened that night?"

I stood up and went on walking. I'd just been standing up for him with Stelios, but now I felt myself turning against him. What was wrong with me? I was letting the two of them pull me back and forth and I'd had about enough of it. I'd gone only a few steps when I realized he wasn't following me. When I looked back at him all the color had gone out of his face. He was staring at me with this bleached expression. Then he caught up with me.

"No," he said. "No, I don't remember. I try to. I try to get to it, but I can't. I just remember going outside the house. It was a clear night and the stars were all out. Then the soldiers were there. But there must be more." He paused and then his voice hardened. "But I'll bet that's why you and Stelios want to put me away, isn't it? You two remember what I can't."

"That's not how it is, Takis."

"How is it then?"

He practically snarled the question at me and I flushed with anger. We were just by the abandoned village, where I stopped walking and faced him.

"Now listen, Takis, it's time to grow up and understand a few things." I could feel something inside me beginning to tear. But like Stelios, once I'd started, I had to go on. "Stelios and I will be starting a family one day and while you'll always be welcome wherever we are, well, we have to be on our own because, you might as well know, we're . . . married."

He didn't say anything but just stood there, still looking at me. "But . . . but . . ." he sputtered, "that means you can't marry *me*."

I couldn't speak for a moment. He couldn't be serious, I thought, but looking at his face, his astonished expression, I could see that he was.

"Of *course* I can't marry you. Even if I were free. You're still a boy, Takis, and . . . I can't . . . I mean . . ." I walked back to him and tried to put a hand on his shoulder. He gave me a push. So I turned and walked on. Then he ran up behind me and gave me another push, harder this time.

"Stop that!" I said over my shoulder as firmly as I could. But the astonishment in his face had turned to anger and it frightened me. I realized I was trembling and I didn't want him to see that so I moved along faster. We passed the abandoned village where the hot wind was rolling dried brushweed through the *plateia*. I didn't want to look back, but his footsteps continued. We walked on without speaking until we came back into town and arrived at the schoolhouse.

Our students were inside, some throwing paper planes, others waiting. Takis caught up with me but didn't look directly at me. I reminded him that we'd have to teach without the puppets for a while. He went ahead of me into the classroom and began to draw a simple Karagiozis on the blackboard, as a baker with a stack of pies.

I handed out paper and pencils as Takis started reviewing numbers. He was going too fast for the students, whacking the blackboard with his stick as he called on students to spell out the corresponding word for each numeral. I shook my head at him, but he still wouldn't meet my gaze. He went on hitting the blackboard until finally the end of the stick, a couple of inches, snapped off and flew at a boy sitting in front, hitting him in the eye. At first the boy was too startled to grasp what had happened, but then he cried out and ran from the room, covering his eye with his hand.

Takis stood still in front of the blackboard with everyone staring at him. "It was an accident," he said. "I didn't mean to."

I went after the boy to see if he was all right, but he'd disappeared. When I came back, Takis was gone too. The other children stared at me without speaking. I didn't think I could go on with the lesson. A feeling of foreboding had come over me, so much so that my limbs felt like stone and my mouth dried out.

Shortly after I sent the children home, a few mothers appeared at the door, including the one of the boy who'd been hurt. I remembered her from the day when she'd first brought her son. She'd been pleasant enough then, a small woman with a worried face and hair in a tight bun. But now she was furious.

"My Andonis, his eye will be blind!" she said.

"Oh, I hope not," I said. "But it was an accident." My voice sounded small to me, not much above a whisper. Why couldn't I speak? I took a deep breath and tried to push words out until, almost shouting, I said, "It could happen to anyone."

"It happened to *my son*," she said. Her face had grown red. "Takis should be locked up."

The others joined in, calling out, "Something's wrong with him."

"Snooping around all the time."

"Stealing secrets. Talking to himself."

"He should be put away."

"It was an accident," I repeated, but my voice cracked. "I'm so sorry. How can we help your Andonis?"

"Help him? Takis almost killed him!"

"Get Takis out of here," another woman called out. "He's not to be around children."

I just stood there, thinking that she was no doubt right and nothing I could say was going to help. I went inside and closed the door behind me. There was a lot of angry conversation outside, but after a while, everyone left. I sat on one of the student desks and tried to clear my mind. But all I could do was remember Yannoula saying, *Don't tell Takis.* At the time I thought she didn't want me to tell him that she was dying. Now I knew better.

He didn't come back that night. The next day when my legs seemed to be working again, I walked through the village looking for him among the strangers who'd come to the island for the celebration. Most were gathered in the center of the village where some of the detainees were doing a last-minute sweeping of the street that led from the church, past the *plateia* next to it, and on through the village. The visitors were on crutches or in wheelchairs, a few even on stretchers. With nurses or relatives to get them from one place to another, they bought *tamata* from the local housewives, who'd also rented them rooms. Takis wasn't anywhere, but I went into the church where the sick and wounded knelt—those able to—in front of the icon of the Virgin. Her pinched face was all that was visible. The rest of her had been covered by heavy silver plating probably made from melted-down *tamata*, the gifts of years of pilgrimages. With a Byzantine frown, she glared out of her silver wrap as if she'd had a headache for centuries.

I circled the village, avoiding any of the women who'd been outside the school the night before. But there was no Takis. I wondered if he'd possibly gone back to the camp, but when I got there, a solitary guard said everyone was in town for the church procession. When I got back to the *plateia* beside the church, I saw that Stelios had started his Karagiozis performance in the dark shade of some ilex trees, where he was using candles to make shadows on the screen. It was the first time I'd seen him outside the camp since we'd come to the island. I stood off to the side so I could watch him working behind the screen, making the children laugh and call out to the puppets. The boy who'd been hit by the end of Takis's stick, Andonis, was in the audience. With a bandage over his eye, he was standing with his mother. They hadn't noticed me.

I looked back at Stelios, who was trying to make use of his terrible cough as if the sultan was hacking and coughing in evil glee. But how graceful Stelios was, I thought, in spite of everything. Though gaunt and ill, he expertly controlled the puppets on their poles. Even the slightest movements of his hands caused them to react and brought forth laughter from both children and adults on the other side of the screen. I remembered how we'd stayed awake at night while he told me stories he'd told himself in the mountains, or stories we'd read together of Achilles and Hector and Priam. He would have had another kind of life entirely but for the events of the times. But here he was now, doing his best at what he knew best, telling a story that made children laugh.

When he'd finished and was taking his bow in front of the screen, I went over and kissed him on the cheek, forgetting that the women I wanted to avoid would see me. He turned and put his arms around me, holding me to him as the audience applauded. It seemed to me that this was how it should be, a sun-splashed day with smiling children, Stelios and I holding each other in the applause, as if *we* were the play, characters in our own stories. I told him that as we bowed, hands over hearts.

"Yes, of course. All this around us," he said, standing and waving at the trees, the people, the church, "maybe it's just painted scenery, just some kind of backdrop. And we're the shadows on the screen. We can't grasp the actual lives we're shadowing, not now, not while we're living them. So how do we know what they're really about?"

"Maybe that's what laments try to tell us," I said.

It must have been nearly time for the procession from the church, as a few of the parents were taking their children over to the side of the *plateia*, where they waited, looking expectantly at the church. In front of it, four men in dark suits were hoisting a platform covered with flowers onto their shoulders. The street was lined on both sides with guards from the camp, visitors in wheelchairs or on stretchers and others leaning on canes or crutches.

"Wait!" Stelios told the audience. "There's more!"

He dashed back behind the screen and pulled out other puppets, attaching them to poles. They were the ones he'd made in Heraklion, the ones based on all of us in Chrysoula's house.

"You want to do that now?" I said. "Here?"

"Yes, yes, let's tell them our story, what we can know of it, anyway, just its shadows. I've been thinking about it all this time and I've made some changes. Stand over there, Aliki. Tell me what you think of it. Where's Takis, by the way?"

I said I didn't know. What I know now is that Stelios was probably aiming this performance at least partly at Takis, hoping to upset him just as he'd done in telling him about the place for disturbed boys. I started to tell Stelios what had happened at the schoolhouse, but he was ready to begin. So I stood beside one of the ilex trees to watch. Some of the parents and children who'd started toward the church paused to see what Stelios would do next. The play began exactly as it had that night in Theo's café. The Sophia puppet spoke.

Remember all this one day
when you return by this path,
when you have grown into yourself.
Listen, in spite of what we've seen,
the world is going on . . .

The play progressed more or less the same as in Theo's café, but at the point where the Chrysoula puppet said, "It is good that you have come," I heard a noise behind me and turned to see a barefoot girl half-hidden behind another tree. I turned away, but, struck by something familiar about her, looked again and realized it was Takis, in a green dress. His eyes were glazed; either he hadn't noticed me or he hadn't taken in who I was. I said his name, but it didn't seem to register. I went over to him and put my arms around him. He looked directly at me but seemed unsurprised, as if I'd been there all along.

"It's the same play," he said.

"Where've you been? And why the dress?"

"Oh. It was on someone's clothesline."

"What happened to your own clothes?"

"I don't remember." He pointed at the screen. "That's me again."

There's a ghost with orange hair
downstairs in the basement.
Do you play cards?

"Takis, let's get you home and cleaned up and into your own clothes."

"But what happens next in the story?"

"You know what happens next. Let's go."

"I don't remember. Oh, that's me again! And you."

She hasn't spoken since her father died.
She's my friend . . .

After a few more scenes, a new puppet appeared, made of bark. It had to be the one Stelios had made at the camp. I couldn't tell who it was supposed to be at first until I saw the crudely carved swastika. The Takis puppet was talking to him.

They're in the basement,
the two of them.
Strangers from Athens.
Hiding.

Colonel Esterhaus. And a soldier was there in front of the house backdrop with its windows full of red cellophane flames. Stelios had added the scene on purpose—Esterhaus must have been the new puppet he'd said he had an idea for.

Now, beside me, Takis was shaking his head, saying, "I never said that, never told him that." Then he shouted at Stelios, "It's not true!"

Everyone turned to look at him, this shouting boy in a green dress. Stelios peered over the top of the screen. There was a moment of silence and then the mother of Andonis called out, "That's him—the one who tried to blind my son! Look what he did." She pointed to the bandage over Andonis's eye. "And that teacher there, she protects him." Several village men gathered around her, listening to her story, and turned to stare at Takis and me.

"We need to get out of here," I said, grabbing Takis's hand.

From the church came the blare of trumpets as the band started its march up the street past the *plateia*. Following it were a half dozen white-robed acolytes carrying the silk banners of the church on tall poles. Next came the bearded priest in a billowing golden cape. Leading other local dignitaries, the mayor walked after him in a crisp blue suit and tie with a sparkling stud. Behind them was the flower-covered platform carried on the shoulders of the four men in suits. It was like a wooden house of flowers open on each of its four sides so everyone could see the icon propped up inside. Its silver plating threw ovals of reflected sunlight over the crowd as it neared the *plateia*. The sick and wounded lined each side of the street, reaching out to the icon with one hand while crossing themselves with the other.

Suddenly Takis pulled away from me and ran into the crowd. Several of the men who'd been talking to Andonis's mother ran after him. There were screams in the crowd as people in wheelchairs or on crutches tried to get out of the way. Someone collided with one of the men supporting a front corner of the platform and that corner dipped. Though the other three men struggled to keep the platform upright, the icon fell clattering into the street in front of an old man on a stretcher.

A gasp went up from the crowd as the procession halted and the band stopped playing. No one said anything for a moment while everyone stared down at the icon, its silver still gleaming in the sun, the Virgin now glaring straight up at the sky. Then the old man rose from his stretcher, crossed himself three times and picked up the icon.

"He walked!" someone nearby shouted. "It's a miracle!" The word passed through the crowd as hundreds of hands crossed hundreds of chests.

"No. No, you fools," the old man said. "There's nothing wrong with my legs. I'm here for my migraines." He handed the icon to the priest, who'd come fluttering up in his robes like a golden butterfly. From the church came the shouts of the village men and camp guards who'd apparently cornered Takis inside and now marched him out, holding his arms behind him. I ran over to them. His eyes were full of terror.

"Stop it!" I said. "He's done nothing wrong."

Stelios was there beside me still holding his Takis and Esterhaus puppets on their poles. "It's my fault," he said with a troubled look. "My play upset him."

The priest rushed over to us and said, "The boy caused the icon to fall. It's a bad omen for the village."

"And he hit my son with a stick," the mother of Andonis called out, trying to get through the crowd to us. "My Andonis may be blind now."

"The stick broke," I said. "It wasn't . . ."

"And just look at him wearing a dress," the mother said, now beside me. "Something's wrong with him. My neighbor saw him peeking in her bedroom window."

"Who are you, boy?" the priest asked. "Where are you from?"

Takis couldn't speak. His eyes darted from one to the other of us and his mouth opened and closed, but no sound came out.

"He's my brother," I said.

"And you are . . . ?" the priest asked.

"My wife," Stelios said. "Leave them alone." He brandished the puppet poles as if about to strike the priest. "Let go of him."

One of the guards lunged at Stelios, but the mayor bustled up, waving him away.

"So, it's you," he said to me. "Our little teacher." His eyes slid over Stelios and he frowned but made no comment, probably remembering him among the men in the strike. Then he noticed Takis in the dress and asked, "And what in creation is *this*?"

The mother started to talk about what Takis had done and I was saying it wasn't true while the priest was insisting that the procession must go forward with the icon in place. The mayor cut us all off, saying the priest was right. He called over some of the camp guards and told them to take all detainees back to the camp.

"And this one too," he said, nodding at Takis. "We'll straighten all this out later. We can't hold up the procession. We must consider our visitors." He waved an arm at the crowd of people now gathered around us, the sick and the lame, the blind and crippled. Then he took his place in the street and the priest returned the icon to its platform, which was then righted. There was a clash of cymbals and the procession started up again.

Takis looked wild-eyed as they took him away, but Stelios had an arm around his shoulder and seemed to be trying to comfort him. Stelios had tossed his two puppets to the ground. I went over to pick them up, but instead I just looked down at them. They lay together, limbs splayed, Takis and Colonel Esterhaus, always with us. Only minutes earlier Stelios and I had had a bit of near bliss, but we couldn't hang on to it anymore. It was almost as if we were trying to drive Takis into one of his states. And maybe we were meaning to without directly meaning to—was that possible? Stelios had told him about the doctor in Heraklion and I'd told him we were married. The anger and despair Takis felt led him to slamming the stick in the classroom, which injured Andonis. Then Stelios had played the scene of Takis betraying him and his mother to the colonel. Were we as awful as this place was awful—the camp, the townspeople, the church and its icon, the false promise of cures? There was no cure for anyone, not for war or its miseries or anything else; it was all a fraud.

"It's not right," one of the Cretan women said, coming over to me. It was as if she'd been reading my thoughts, but she was talking about Takis. "He's just a boy."

Several other camp women joined us and said they'd been talking to some of the wounded visitors to the island who had themselves been former inmates of such camps elsewhere and had been released because of their medical conditions. They were surprised that the same thing wasn't happening here and that detainees at our small camp hadn't had their sentences reviewed and in some cases reversed. But official news of anything like this hadn't reached here as far as anyone knew. Or had it? Maybe such possibilities were being suppressed by the mayor to benefit the local economy as long as possible.

"We should be out there at the camp," one woman said.

"Who knows what might happen?" asked another. She repeated the rumors that some of the staff in mainland camps had been torturing prisoners. And there were even worse rumors that guards had been getting rid of prisoners who might likely testify after they'd been released.

More women joined us and agreed that it was best to go out to the camp to see what was happening and try to find what they'd done with Takis and the others. And we should go right then, when most everyone else was still occupied with the church procession. Yes, I thought, yes, we must. These women seemed at that moment outside the ugliness of the world, of this place and of myself.

As we passed the abandoned village, some said it was foolish for us to go just as we were, as we had done in the past. We should have something to show we were serious this time. Did we want to be just a bunch of angry women with empty hands? We fanned out in the empty village, some wrenching out fence posts or lintels from collapsed doorways. One woman found an old rusted scythe; others pried shards of glass from broken windows and gathered up scattered pieces of old silverware in abandoned kitchens—dull forks and spoons.

As we continued walking, the women talked about what their husbands or brothers would do when they were free and everyone could go back to Crete. Where would I go when the time came? they asked. I assumed Stelios and I would return to Athens and maybe one day go back to my village to see if my house was still there. But it was hard to imagine what kind of life we would have. In a way, the war and the civil fighting that followed had been a kind of temporary answer. Everything had been postponed until later.

When we got to the guardhouse, no one was there. We called out but got no response.

"Let's see if we can force the door and go onto the grounds," one said.

"Who's to stop us?" asked another.

He was—the guard who opened the door of the guardhouse at that moment. He was young, probably younger than most of the prisoners. In a voice attempting gruffness, he told us not to go any farther. What did we want? Visiting hours were not until the next day. The guards had just brought the prisoners back from the procession.

"We want to see them now!" we said, and we told him that this camp should close as others were doing.

"What?" he asked. "I know nothing of this."

We said we wouldn't leave until we saw that our men were okay. And what about the boy, Takis? What had become of him? The guard closed the door and we sat on the ground and started calling out the names of our men again. After a few minutes of this, the door opened once more and another guard came out. He was an older, much larger version of the previous one but with a dark beard. Walking among us and shoving his rifle at us, he told us to leave or else our men would not fare well. It was up to us, he said, what happened.

"That's right," a crone in black replied, and she rammed a fork into the calf of his right leg. He screamed and fell to the ground, holding his leg. The crone quickly climbed on top of him, pulled off her head scarf and stuffed it in his mouth. The women nearby also threw themselves onto him and held him down while one grabbed his rifle. It all happened so fast and with no plan on our part, so that we looked at each other, astonished. We had a detainee of our own. Some of the women were so excited that they looped arms over each other's shoulders and drew themselves into a line for a little victory dance in front of the guardhouse, blocking the view of anyone inside. Humming tunelessly, they took a dozen or so steps counterclockwise and two back, then a little leap for the joy of it.

We almost didn't hear the old truck wheezing its way toward us. With a squeal of brakes, it stopped. The driver was one of the men from the harbor who hauled blocks of marble down to the boats. He paused, looking us over, and honked his horn to get us out of the way. He didn't appear to see the guard on the ground with the women sitting on him. He was choking by then and someone took the head scarf out of his mouth.

"Murderers!" the man on the ground shouted. "Assassins!" But he was barely audible above the ratchety engine of the truck. The crone stuffed her scarf back in his mouth.

The young guard opened the gate beside the guardhouse and signaled the truck to enter. The dancing women parted for it, but, as it passed, some of us ran behind. One jumped up onto the bed of the truck and pulled others up until several of us were on, including the woman who'd taken the rifle. She was figuring out how to fire it when the young guard saw us on the back of the truck and ordered us to get down. The rifle went off; he grabbed his shoulder and fell.

Inside the camp, we could see that the other guards and prisoners were a way off down a slope among the white tents. But at the sound of the shot, some of the guards turned and came running in our direction. We scrambled off the truck and scattered. The guards tried to chase us, but there were more of us than them so although they caught some of us, others ran off toward our men, who were laughing at this spectacle of women and guards. But seeing the guards so distracted, they soon began to scatter back up the hillside at the rear of the camp. I couldn't see either Stelios or Takis, but I ran toward the backs of the running men and tripped on one of the chunks of marble that littered the ground and fell on my face. Maybe I knocked myself out just briefly, I don't know, but the next thing I saw was that most of the men had got to the top of the hill. And then I saw them, Stelios and Takis, up there too. It seemed at first that they were holding hands, but from the glint of metal, I realized that they'd been handcuffed together, left wrist of Takis to right wrist of Stelios.

Neither could make much progress because of the other, though they were trying to run in unison, Stelios limping badly. He fell and Takis helped him up. I called out to them, but they couldn't have heard me. I ran on, realizing that they had to be close to the edge of the quarry lake. Then I saw that they'd stopped. Stelios had something in his hand—a rock?—that he was raising in the air with one hand and bringing down hard. There was a sudden blast of gunshot behind me and I looked over my shoulder to see complete chaos, women on the ground but also guards. When I turned back, Stelios and Takis were gone.

CASSETTE 6 • Side 1

When I first came back to this village in the 1960s, it seemed that I'd just imagined the life I'd lived away from here. Even the ruin of Chrysoula's house with its chimney sticking out of the undergrowth—a burned shell of the house I'd lived in—didn't shake the feeling that I'd never gone away. My own house was still standing though badly disintegrated. It hadn't burned that night, but in the many years since then, the windows had been smashed out and part of the roof had collapsed. The rooms were full of fallen plaster, leaves and dirt. As I touched the moldy walls and warped floorboards, I remembered the morning we set out from here for Athens, Stelios limping and Takis completely unhinged. Since then the house had sat here empty and eyeless. My return was empty too with nothing of Stelios in it. But at least it was a place, *my* place.

The very last of the sporadic fighting didn't end until—What year was it?—1949, I think, give or take a year. How time punches holes in my memory. Some of the camps like the one on the island had closed before that, but others—really unspeakable ones such as Makronisos—stayed open well into the fifties. All those dollars that your Harry sent from the Land of Big Radios, where did they go? The ones that didn't find their way into the pockets of politicians and government officials did provide some new highways and schools, a bit of rural electrification and indoor plumbing. But only a bit. Much of the country remained in ruins from the fighting, the railroads destroyed, the bridges blown up, a nearly worthless currency and a demoralized people. We'd done more damage to ourselves than even the Germans had done to us.

True, foreign tanks and weapons helped end the war in the government's favor, but, as they say, a war never truly ends. Even the decade of recovery that followed didn't stop the resentments left over from the civil war. Old grudges and hatreds kept bubbling up like some nasty stew. And the divided country, with a new government every time we sneezed, became an excuse for the military dictatorship of the colonels in the sixties. By then the Land of Big Radios, thoroughly mired in our politics, ended up actually supporting that regime, with its censorship, election rigging and torture of those who dared to speak out. Shame on you! Well, not *you* personally. You know what I mean. It seemed like half the youths of Athens lined up to dump successive buckets of red paint on that statue of old Harry, who wasn't even around anymore. Later they bombed it, pulled it down and smashed it, a symbol of the beginning of the end of our love affair with you all. Well, the statue is back in place now, or so I understand. Everything circles back, given enough time.

Eventually we ran into the troubled arms of the European Union. Again all lilacs and roses to start, but even it was unable to save us from the folly of our leaders, with their secret bribes, payoffs and borrowing, taxes going mostly into the pockets of tax collectors, everyone cheating everyone, mortgaging the future for the present. I once heard that one of our ancient writers, this man Hesiod, said that you shouldn't relieve yourself in a river upstream if you plan to drink from it downstream. Now, no one can doubt the wisdom of that advice. But that's just what our governments did—left, right, or center. And that, I think, brings us more or less to now. The irony is that here we are stuck with Germany again, but in an economic occupation this time around. And after your Land of Big Radios and its allies meddled in the Middle East, we here in our nearly bankrupt state have had to deal with the river of damaged humanity, so many poor and desperate souls, flowing into Europe through our back door.

Oh, yes, I know that's a huge simplification of a lot of tangled history, but those are stories for other days, other cassettes. Are you still with me? I'm off the rails again, but I *will* get back to those laments that interest you, I promise.

Just after I came back here to the village, I thought I glimpsed a bit of my father's shirttail as he rounded a corner into the kitchen. But no one was there. I risked the rickety stairs down to the basement where I'd first met Stelios and his mother. Standing on the dirt floor in the dark, I heard the rustle of what was probably a rat in the wall. Except for that, the house seemed as empty as a shell scoured out by sand and sea.

I'd saved some money from my work in Athens after I left the island and there also were the proceeds from Stelios's house in Kolonaki. So I restarted my life here in the village by trying to get my house renovated around me while living in only one room—a good way to lose your mind. Unlike the rest of the country, the village seemed much more prosperous in general because the quality of the local olive oil had been discovered by the world outside. A processing plant and bottling works stood near the place where I used to hop around showing Takis how my father made charcoal. No one made it here anymore. We who'd survived the war years had become like charcoal ourselves, burned down to a dark core that glows for a long time before becoming ash.

The old dirt road into the village had been widened and paved and a few of the villagers even had cars. They drove them back and forth on the new pavement, honking horns constantly to let us all know who could afford them. Everyone had running water indoors so women no longer gathered at the fountain outside Chrysoula's house. The fountain itself wasn't even there anymore and neither were the women, a fact that startled me at first.

What had I expected, that those who were the grown-ups when I was young would still be here to greet me? In my mind I'd carried them along through the years just as they'd always been. When I got off the bus with my suitcase in the *plateia* under the tall plane trees, it was a shock to recognize no one. And of course no one recognized me. Then I felt foolish not to have realized sooner that the generation of women with their wisecracks and leathery old faces was mostly over in the cemetery with my father, Chrysoula and Sophia. Children I'd gone to school with before the war had grown up and were already growing old, like me. When I explained to them who I was, they said they'd heard of my family but thought us all long dead. And I might as well have been, because for the first few days back here, I felt like a ghost flitting around looking for signs of the life I'd once lived.

Could I become part of this place again? Did anyone still want laments? Well, I needn't have worried about that. Aphrodite was here in the next village where she's been since we were children, my sister in dread. Even now the other women our age sit on my front steps waiting for a sign so we can all rush to her hut to be part of her last hour. Yes, there are always more of the dead. And they remain as busy as ever, whining and complaining to me almost as if I were already one of them. Some mornings, trying to persuade my ancient bones to rise from bed, I think maybe I've joined them in the night. Considering all the things that want you dead in this world, it's improbable to be alive at all. No wonder I can't let go of the dead, who are often more real to me than when they were living. It's the loving that does it, I suppose, keeps them tied to us in a kind of half life. We keep dragging them back with all this love, everyone loving someone, even when they're dead. Death and love—they're braided together so tightly they can't ever be combed out straight.

Take Stelios, who still touches my shoulder in sleep when I whisper, "Tell me a story." How did it finish, I ask him, your play with all of us in it? I'd seen the beginning twice but no middle and no end. *How does any story end?* he says. *It just turns into the beginning of another one, the one about us all.*

The dead say things like that. But I wanted details, the kind I eventually got from Takis about what happened at the camp and quarry before I got there that day. The story came out in pieces and in no order. He was incoherent at first and confined to the camp. I wasn't so coherent myself, weighed down by grief as surely as if I carried one of those blocks of marble. Raising an arm or leg, opening my mouth to speak—it all took effort. But I forced myself out to the camp again, forced myself to sit there in the unreality of him on the other side of the window instead of Stelios. I had to know.

"Get me out of here!" was all Takis would say at first. I told him I couldn't. The mayor had ordered him held for the time being. It was probably the safest place for him, considering that the mother of Andonis, along with some of the other mothers, was still saying that Takis was disturbed and should be put away. The priest too spread tales about Takis, how he'd brought a curse to the village when the icon fell to the street. Then there was the question of what exactly had happened in the quarry. Other detainees had talked about the way he and Stelios argued all the way from the *plateia* back to the camp. How was it that the boy had survived and not the man? everyone was asking.

What I pieced together out of his rambling was first that the voice of the wind had told him to run from the *plateia*. That would have been when the guards were leading him, Stelios and the other detainees away.

"The wind in the trees," he said. "I heard it as clearly as I hear you, Aliki."

How reliable was what he said if he thought wind was the source of trouble? But that had often been the way with him. He'd tried to obey and run off, he said, but one of the guards handcuffed him to Stelios in the hope of calming him. The other men were no help, laughing at his green dress and asking if he was a boy or a girl. By the time

I talked to him, he'd exchanged it for one of the drab camp uniforms way too large for him. I was reminded of his huge British Army uniform at the barracks outside Athens. We seemed to have come round to that again.

"It was all Stelios's fault," Takis said. "Everything. I shouted at him that I didn't want to be one of his puppets anymore. Not ever. Not a bad puppet in a stupid, untrue play." Stelios was coughing so hard he could barely speak but managed to say that the play was just a story. A story that didn't have to be true. "But I said that *he* thought it was what really happened with the Germans back then. And you do too, don't you, Aliki?"

"I don't know what else could have happened, Takis." The words came out of my mouth slowly, as if I had pebbles under my tongue.

"That doesn't mean it was my fault. Just because I can't remember."

There was no point in going over this again. It wasn't why I'd come. I wanted to know what else happened on the way to the camp.

"I kept telling him that he'd put it in the play on purpose."

Takis was probably right about that. Stelios would most likely have decided on it the day I told him Takis had been on the island all along. Stelios went off to work on a new puppet, probably of Colonel Esterhaus. What had Stelios wanted to do, drive Takis away or just drive him crazy or both? Well, it was true that Stelios and I both, in our ways, wanted Takis out of our lives. But that wasn't what we'd got.

"We were all right, weren't we, Aliki, before Stelios ever came along? Back in the village, I mean." Takis gripped the edge of the window frame and his voice went up. "That's what I told Stelios, how we were just fine without him and his mother. Why did they have to come to *our* village anyway?"

Stelios told him it hadn't exactly been a matter of choice; the partisans had brought them. Takis tried to pull away from him and Stelios yelled for him to stop. The handcuffs were cutting into both their wrists.

Takis ignored this, saying, "We played cards and we laughed and Aliki showed me about making the charcoal and . . ."

Stelios had begun coughing again so hard he stumbled and fell to his knees. Takis was pulled down with him and they sprawled together in the dust until the guards hauled them to their feet. At the camp, the detainees assembled below the tent area. It was said that the mayor would join them after the procession to administer the dreaded loyalty oath that no one wanted to sign. But what were the consequences of not signing?

"What did I care?" Takis said. "All I could think about were the things you and I did together in the village before Stelios came and how much better everything was back then. Except for that girl who hated us—what was her name? Started with *Z*."

"You mean Zephyra?"

"That's the one. She hated us. Well, she hated me, anyway. She wanted your friendship and didn't want me to have it. Her mother was a real witch too."

Now, remembering what he said then, I'm reminded of the goat noises Zephyra made when I visited her just before she died. I must ask Aphrodite more specifically about them before she dies too.

Takis said Stelios was so exhausted from coughing spasms that he lay down in the dust again, forcing Takis down with him. "I knew he was sick, but there was nothing I could do about it. He wasn't listening to me anyway. He just went on coughing over the top of everything I said. He was doing it on purpose. I couldn't stop talking."

"About . . . ?"

"You, you, always you, Aliki."

I can see the look in his eyes still, as ardent as any lover. I felt sick at the thought that his feelings for me had helped bring us to this point: Stelios dead, Takis detained in the camp. It was my fault; I should have cut myself loose from Takis long before. If only we'd been able to arrange something on Crete with that doctor, awful though it might have been.

It was while he was sitting on the ground with Stelios coughing, Takis said, that they heard the rifle shot from the entrance and turned to see us women there. The guards stopped what they were doing and ran toward us as the detainees scattered. Stelios stumbled to his feet, pulling Takis up with him and saying something about finding a sharp rock. "I didn't know what he meant but he was limping along, pulling me, and I had to go with him." They climbed the hill together, as I'd seen them doing from afar. Takis said he was still talking, saying how he and I had never needed anyone else. And we were both going back to the village soon, where everything would be just the same.

"It's true, Aliki, isn't it? We will now, won't we?"

All he could talk about was resuming our childhood as though nothing had happened at all. But Stelios was gone and the life he and I had hoped for was gone with him. I tried to keep my voice level as I asked Takis just to tell me what happened next.

At the edge of the quarry, Stelios found a rock with a sharp edge and tried to position Takis opposite him with a block of marble in between. Pulling tight the links that bound them together, Stelios raised the stone in his free hand.

"I thought he was going to kill me and throw me into the quarry. That's what he wanted, I'm sure. But I guess he changed his mind because he slammed it onto the links. Over and over again." He told Takis to pull the chain tight so the stone would come down on the same link each time, weakening it. "Then one broke and I pulled my hand free. But I stumbled backward and lost my balance. He reached for me and caught my hand, but I was already falling. I took him down with me. I didn't mean to, Aliki. It was just what happened."

Takis gave me a sharp look as if trying to figure out if I believed him or not and then rushed on. "He fell on top of me. I couldn't breathe and the water was cold. We sank. And came up and sank again. I thought I was going to die."

That was what I saw as I reached the edge of the quarry: two figures thrashing in the dark water below. I was trying to get to them, scrambling down the half-chiseled marble blocks that jutted from the sides of the quarry while shouting for help. I saw Stelios surface, gasping, but Takis was flailing and hitting him in the face, yelling that he couldn't swim. Above them, I had to turn away to watch where I put my feet or else I would have fallen too. When I looked back, Stelios had struck out for the flat rocks at the side of the water, swimming weakly with one arm and pulling Takis with the other. But I could see that Takis was going under. Stelios turned and put Takis's arms around his neck, trying to swim with Takis on his back, but the weight seemed to push them both under. Stelios had been ill, of course; he wouldn't have been strong enough for this, especially with Takis hanging around his neck. Gravel skidded out from under my shoe and I had to flatten myself against a boulder to remain upright. Below, they were close to the side of the quarry.

"I jumped off and touched rock bottom," Takis said. "I thought Stelios had too. Then you were there."

Takis was collapsed on the ground, panting and spewing. But Stelios was facedown in the water, not moving. I ran in and pulled him ashore, thumping on his chest, blowing into his mouth while holding his nose. I didn't know what I was doing. I called his name over and over. Then I started shaking him as if that would bring life back into the limp body. Takis was no help, lying there semiconscious.

It was a while before anyone saw us down there or heard my cries for help. Back at the entrance of the camp, we heard later, the guards had finally subdued the other women, but it was only when they tried to round up the scattered detainees that they realized Stelios and Takis were missing. In time they found us, and men lowered themselves down with ropes and stretchers.

"Now you hate me, don't you?" Takis said, tears starting to flow. "I'm alive and he isn't and you wish it was the other way around."

I have to stop the tape here.

All right, back again. It's an hour later. I've poured myself a raki (or two). While I was drinking and trying to raise the strength to go on, the village women here gathered outside to gossip about Aphrodite, who seems to be worsening. She's been asking for me and I'll go to her soon, as I have a question of my own for her. But I want to tell you the rest quickly now while I can bear it and while the raki gives me its false strength.

I seemed to be in a kind of trance those first few days after Stelios died. Not the kind where I end up in the room with the door and the light beyond. I couldn't lament, couldn't think or sleep. You don't lose a person all at once. It happens in stages. Every time you remember something else you'd almost forgotten, the old misery starts up again. It sickened me to recall my thinking in Agios Nikolaos that Stelios and I would be able to survive anything yet to come and that Takis might grow up and grow away. Except for him, Stelios would have been alive. But it wasn't really drowning that killed Stelios so much as war and imprisonment and stupidity and being in the wrong place in the wrong life, in the wrong century even. And maybe some of it was that he died of my loving Takis sometimes more than him, or at least so it must have appeared to him. In the night I know that's so, and in the morning when I rise. I'd lost my good return.

When they brought in the coffin for the wake, I asked them to take off the lid so I could see him one last time. He'd gone all gray and his hair was oiled down on his skull so you could see its whole shape. Gravity had tugged down the corners of his mouth as if in disapproval and I thought how death had aged him already. There he was, the bald and crabby old man he might have become, the one I loved. I'd asked one of the Cretan women to read a short passage Stelios had once pointed out to me in *The Iliad*, about one of the ships leaving for Troy.

Dawn came early, a palmetto of rose,
Time to make sail for the wide beachhead camp.
They set up mast and spread the white canvas,
And the following wind, sent by Apollo,

Boomed in the mainsail. An indigo wave
Hissed off the bow as the ship surged on,
Leaving a wake as she held on course through the billows.

So Stelios had a kind-of lament by none other than Homer himself. Maybe that's what *The Iliad* is, after all, one long lament for the dead. It could as well be for all of us, dying on a dusty plain of our own making, wherever that turns out to be, with or without the futility of war.

A while back, someone told me about another one of these ancients, this man Herodotus, some kind of historian, I guess. Anyway, he insisted that Helen was never in Troy in the first place. She and Paris were blown off course when they sailed from Sparta and ended up in Egypt. There, the pharaoh, enraged that Paris had stolen his host's wife, allowed only Paris to sail on to Troy and kept Helen until after the war, when she was returned to her husband, Menelaus. At Troy, the Trojans kept telling the Greeks that they didn't have her, but the suspicious Greeks wouldn't believe them. Well, she was probably just a pretext for a war as heartless as our own civil struggle. But as Homer knew, it made a better story if Helen was there. And, in the end, we become the stories we tell, as Stelios once said.

The story of Takis was in question; he was too young to remain in such a place. What would they do with him? My state was still so vague and meandering that I was only dimly aware that some officials from the Red Cross had arrived to investigate what had taken place here. Then the mayor told everyone with any connection to the camp to clear out immediately. All the guards except one (for Takis) left the island and the loyalty oath was never administered. The remaining detainees were taken to a holding camp somewhere to await notification of any further penalties. No charges were to be brought against the Cretan women and myself if we would leave the island at once. We were being erased, or whitewashed, the way the village had erased the forced feeding and death of Dimitri.

Well, there was no reason for me to return to Crete. I had to wait for a ship to Piraeus and could get a trolley from there to Athens. The Cretan women and their men—those well enough to travel—gathered in the harbor. I stood with Stavroula and other islanders to watch them board the ship back to Crete.

"Now we'll be nothing again," Stavroula said. "The world will forget us here."

I didn't care. I just wanted to get out of there and I couldn't bear to see Takis again. But Stavroula told me that the mayor wanted me to come to his office in a building on the other side of the *plateia* from the church. Inside it reminded me of the office of the police captain in Heraklion, the framed photograph of the king on the wall behind his desk. Here too a boy was sent to the café to bring back coffee. The mayor seemed a bit deflated, as if he'd shrunk inside his suit. He no longer had the camp, its staff and detainees to command so maybe that was why he seemed as diminished as his role. What did the mayor of such a small place so far away from any other have to do anyway? I supposed that was why he now had time for me. Or did he understand his part in what had happened? If he hadn't sent Takis and Stelios off to the camp together so the precious parade could proceed, would the worst have happened? But if that was on his mind, he made no direct mention of it.

"It's not up to me," the mayor said, "what happens to your brother. He is your brother, isn't he?"

I nodded. I couldn't change my story at this point.

"He's underage, and probably not responsible for his behavior. But what to do with him? I'm waiting for word from a government social service agency in Athens." Of course everything was still chaotic; the fighting had ended, but the government was all upside down and it wasn't clear who was in charge of what, or which agencies were actually functioning.

"It will take some time. Everything takes some time."

He looked out the window. I followed his gaze to the *plateia* and was startled to see that Stelios's shadow puppets and his screen, also the suitcase we carried them in, were all stacked under one of the ilex trees. I'd forgotten about them.

"I hear that you did a good job at our little school," the mayor said, "until the unfortunate accident with Andonis. So I wanted to tell you how sorry I am about the man who drowned, your husband?" Was it a question? I didn't answer. He stood up behind his desk, a signal for me to go.

I collected the suitcase and puppets from the *plateia* and left for Piraeus the next day. From the deck of the ship leaving, I said good-bye to Stelios again, buried forever in the heart of the island in the heart of the sea. I remembered him talking about *The Count of Monte Cristo* and the idea that only someone who experienced deepest grief could know the greatest happiness. But some people don't get out from under grief or are permanently numbed by it, or so it seemed to me on board the returning ship. And happiness—wasn't it just a giddy idea?

In Piraeus, construction was under way all over the port. I dodged cement mixers and scaffolding to find the trolley to Athens. With a pang, I realized that I was passing the café where we'd performed *The Hero Katsondonis* in another time. Above the café were the rooms where Yannoula had told me about her music hall career while we listened to the *rat-a-tat* of gunfire outside. Now only the noise of jackhammers pounded through my longing for those days and nights. Then we'd wanted the fighting to be over and now I understood that it was what held us together.

In Athens, I walked through Syntagma Square in front of Parliament, where crowds had gathered to celebrate the liberation on the night Stelios and I arrived from the village on the back of a truck. As I neared Kolonaki, I felt my life was running in reverse so that I might at any minute turn into my younger self when I opened the door of the house. But it was hanging on its hinges. The house had been broken into and ransacked. Even the light fixtures were gone. In the parlor where Yannoula brought me chicken soup that first night, I sank onto the bare floor and leaned against the wall in exhaustion.

At least it was still standing, I thought, more than could have been said for me. I didn't know then how long I'd stay in that run-down house—right through the fifties—while the city rebuilt itself around me. Stelios's father never returned to read whatever his son had written in the letter left for him, which had, of course, disappeared. I heard that Greek Jews had been taken mostly to Auschwitz, where they were considered too disruptive for any kind of work detail so they were sent straight to the gas chambers. I knew it had happened; there were the photographs taken when the camps were liberated. But part of me never accepted the truth of anything that monstrous. Stelios's father and uncle would have been among those who perished. I couldn't bring myself to imagine them in those awful piles of lost humanity.

I found work at one of the switchboards of the telephone company, specializing in—what else?—long distance. People all over the country were trying to trace relatives they hadn't heard from since the German invasion. When I connected multiple callers, I couldn't help eavesdropping. There were the calls of the three sisters in Crete whose father turned out to be one of the unidentified bodies in the Athens morgue. And the woman who traced her soldier husband to a prisoner-of-war camp in Italy. The people of a village on the island of Samos, who thought their men had been executed, found that they were living in caves on another island. Their lives with guerrilla comrades had made them lose interest in returning home. Well, at least they were alive. For a while, there seemed to be weekly discoveries of more mass graves on Mt. Hymettus, just behind Athens and elsewhere, followed by the agonizing phone calls of officials to relatives.

When I took off the headphones at the end of a day I felt that a large measure of the national grief had washed through me. Sometimes I wished for someone I could phone with my own story: Once a girl and her father lived in a village . . . That had been the story of Stelios's play without an ending.

Eventually I was promoted to supervisor and, with the extra salary, was able to make a few repairs to the old house. But living alone in the place I thought I'd be sharing with Stelios was hard. At first I thought it might get easier in time, but it really didn't. So I finally decided to sell the house and go back to my father's house in the village. But before I could do this, I received a letter from the director of a place called St. Elena School for Boys, out in Peristeri, a poor suburb of Athens. Takis was there—would I please contact them about him? I didn't respond. Then another message came.

I knew that there were a lot of unclaimed children moving across the country. During the civil war years, we found out afterward, communist partisan fighters had taken children from rural families and given them to families in Eastern Europe to protect them from fighting, or so they said. But it was widely assumed they would get political indoctrination there. Whether they did or didn't, some were now returning, but in many cases, their families had died or disappeared. On the other side of the struggle, the queen of Greece had set up boarding schools for nationalist children where indoctrination also took place and those children too were now released. Institutions run by the church and government agencies were taking in the refugee children, but they seemed to be mixed in with all other kinds of children damaged by the war in one way or another. That would have included Takis.

When I finally phoned from the switchboard, I was told that he'd been passed from one institution to another because of behavior problems before arriving at St. Elena. But they had few of his original records so they weren't sure how he'd come into the system in the first place. It was the same with so many of their boys. They were hoping to apprentice him in a trade, plastering maybe, or plumbing, something he could use after completing his military service. But they were desperately overcrowded and couldn't house him much longer now that he'd medically stabilized, whatever that meant. Could I help?

No, I said. I couldn't explain why, but taking him back was unthinkable. Wasn't I his sister, the only living relative? they asked. It's hard to escape your own lies, though they later turn out to have been true. Even if I couldn't take him, there were papers to be signed and I'd need to go there.

Well, anyway, he already had a trade, I thought, and pulled out the suitcase of puppets. He might be able to make some sort of living with them. He'd been so good with them; even Stelios had said so. That was all I was willing to do for him.

St. Elena was a ramshackle place, a two-story, gray stucco building with sprays of bullet holes still in its facade. A high fence of metal spikes surrounded it. I pressed a button beside a gate to ring a bell, but there was no sound and no one came. I called out to a boy in the yard, who went inside and came back with an old man who said he was the janitor. He showed me into a shabby lounge, where I put the suitcase next to an armchair and asked to see the director. I planned just to leave the puppets for Takis, sign any necessary papers and then go. At least, that was what I told myself. I didn't really want to see him, but had I been firm about that, I probably wouldn't have come at all. In any event, only a few minutes later, there he was in the doorway and a slight chill ran through me. He'd grown taller, leaner and was a young man, altogether more poised and collected than the rambling boy I'd last seen in the detention camp. Outside the school, I might not have recognized him. From the way he looked at me, I thought I must have changed too.

"I've never had a visitor," he said.

"How are you, Takis?"

"I told them where to find you. I was sure that was where you'd be."

He seemed cool and contained, standing there in the doorway. I didn't know what to say.

"You left the island without even saying good-bye," he said. His tone was flat and matter-of-fact.

"I was too upset about Stelios."

He didn't say anything for a full minute or more and I expected him to ask if I still blamed him. And to tell me that nothing had been his fault, that it all had to do with wind in the trees. But instead he said mildly, "Would you like me to show you around?"

There didn't seem to be anything else for us to do so I said yes. He took me to a dining hall, a clean but spartan room with rows of trestle tables. It smelled of cooked cabbage. Then a dormitory with dozens of bunk beds, all neatly made. The windows were high up and barred. In general, St. Elena seemed to be a clean and well-organized place, though in poor repair. As we walked and talked, he relaxed a little. In a hallway with classrooms on either side, he said, "I know how to read and write now, probably better than you. I can even spell. Say a word, any word, and I'll spell it for you." A bell rang just then, doors opened and the hall was full of boys.

"Should you be in class?" I asked.

"They gave me a pass because of you. I've never had a visitor before."

"So you said."

"I don't know anyone except the people here. They're all right, I guess. I've been in a few of these places. Some are worse than others. They don't beat us here, anyhow." There was an edge of bitterness in his voice but no self-pity.

"They beat you? In some other place?"

"Only when I got, well, you know. Here they just give us pills that make us feel stupid."

I supposed this was what was meant by medically stabilized. I thought of the purges at that place in Kifissia. St. Elena was at least an improvement on that.

"And they lock us in at night." He paused, then asked, eyes downcast, "What did they say to you about me on the phone?"

When I'd told him, he said, "Well, what do you think?"

"About your coming to live with me?" I wavered and couldn't get anything out. His poise had slipped away and he looked earnest and lost. He didn't act crazy. He was Takis from my village; I'd known him all my life. He was as close to a brother as any I was likely to have. His eyes were filling slowly. How could I not do something for him?

"I can give you some money," I said, though that wasn't what I'd thought to say. It had just come to me that when I'd sold the house, I'd be able to afford something, maybe a monthly stipend. "If that will help you make a new start. But you can't live with me again."

His face fell and he wiped his eyes. "I wasn't asking for money."

"I'll talk to them in the office. Try to set up something for you. I'll sign papers as your sister, but you know I'm not really a relative of yours. And I don't want to be contacted again."

I could see in his face the struggle to control his emotions, sadness giving way to anger. He took a few seconds to collect himself, then narrowed his eyes as he said, "You've changed, haven't you? You're cold and hard. I should have guessed."

His tone was spiteful, like that of a child not getting his way. But he was right: I *had* changed. The years alone scraping by in the old house, with little to look forward to other than trudging off to work, had thinned down my ability to see or take any pleasure in life. A kind of numbness of the senses had set in. My face in the mirror had taken on a pinched look with the mouth set in a line. It was mostly because I didn't care much for this person I saw each morning and night, that I'd decided to go back to my village. No matter what had happened there, it was where I was from. I felt pulled back to my father's house.

Takis turned abruptly and started walking me back toward the lounge. He didn't speak until we were there, and then, in a voice full of bravado, he said, "Well, I've changed too. I don't care anymore. I don't care about anything."

I ignored the bravado and said, "I just think you'll be better off here. And they'll help you find a place in the world, a trade perhaps." We were back in the lounge and I noticed the suitcase. "Oh, I almost forgot. I brought you these."

I picked up the suitcase of puppets and handed it to him. Takis looked surprised but then seemed to recognize it and frowned.

"What would I want with those?"

"You were always good with them so I thought that maybe . . . Well, it's a kind of trade, isn't it? Better than plastering or plumbing."

His face contorted and he dropped the suitcase on the floor. "Don't you remember the last time Stelios used them?" His eyes blinked rapidly and his voice went up. "How could you forget?"

"I didn't forget, I just thought . . ."

He glared at me for what must have been a full minute, then turned to leave the room. But partway to the door he turned back and said, "Listen, you might as well know this—I held his head under the water."

"What?"

"Stelios. The fall knocked the breath out of him. He was weak and struggling. When I was on his back, I just pushed his head under and held it there. You were only halfway down the side of the quarry and you didn't see, did you? I did that for *you*, Aliki. I thought we could be together someday. But now I see we can't. So you might as well know."

He was so calm as he said all this that it took me a few seconds to take it in. Then rage rose through me fast and my hand flew out almost of its own accord and slapped him hard. It echoed in the lounge and I went for his throat with both hands. He just stepped back and laughed.

"You believe me, don't you? Ha. I just said that to hurt you. Don't worry, Stelios drowned without any help from me."

I stormed past him to the door, but as I left he called out with heavy sarcasm, "Oh, and thanks for the puppets." I found the director's office and signed papers giving up any responsibility for Takis. I didn't make any financial arrangement.

I'm stopping the tape here once more.

Now it's weeks later. Sorry to have let so much time pass. I'm sitting here with the reel turning these last few minutes thinking how to continue. Nothing has changed, yet everything has changed. The day I last talked into this machine, the women went with me to Aphrodite's hut but stayed outside the door as I went inside. The place had been cleaned. No chicken feathers, no musty rugs, even the bunches of herbs had been taken down and stacked to one side. You could walk about without them hitting you in the face. I supposed the other women had done it and I supposed rightly that Aphrodite wasn't happy about it.

"Crows, that's what they are," she said, muttering from her mat in the corner. The women must also have perfumed the air with church incense as there was a sweetish scent that couldn't have come from Aphrodite. "They're worse than death. Make them go away. They'll listen to you."

But they wouldn't. It's the custom to gather round at such a time and there's no changing this. Aphrodite knew that, of course, but what she did and didn't know had already begun to blur. I couldn't always tell if she was talking to me or to the icon of St. Athanassios on the wall above her. Her mind seemed to have turned into a kind of swamp, but here and there were islands of sense where she'd speak distinctly.

"There's no turning back, no going forward or anywhere at all. And what of it?" She laughed, a long, wheezy kind of laugh, and reached for one of the crumpled handkerchiefs around her, all spotted with blood.

"Now, listen," I said. "You can't die yet. There's something I want to know." Who was I, she asked, thrashing from side to side. I'd brought a little flask of raki with me and got her to drink some. This calmed her and she fell asleep. I waited a few minutes, then nudged her awake. She began to ramble about various villagers, probably running through things she'd learned about the people she'd treated through the years. Disputes over dowries and property lines, the baker who mixed sawdust into his dough to bulk it up, the bribes for illegal building permits. I interrupted her.

"Do you remember Chrysoula's boy, Takis?"

"I remember everything. It's a curse."

"Tell me."

"Not right in the head, that one."

"He used to say how Zephyra hated him because she was so jealous of his friendship with me."

"Of course. She was like that, lonely and bitter. Nothing is as hateful as a bitter child."

She told me all over again about Zephyra and the goat stealing, how her mother had put her up to wearing the skin to calm the goats she stole from the Germans (who'd stolen them from the villagers in the first place). And I remembered again the poor soul just before her death lying in bed making that sound, *Maaahhh, maaahhh.*

Now Aphrodite said the goats Zephyra had stolen weighed on her so much because of their connection to other worse things she'd done. When the Germans posted a sentry to prevent the thefts, that was the end of Zephyra's stealing. She and her mother had to go back to eating snails and grass, like everyone else. Except of course for us at Chrysoula's house where, thanks to Sophia's gold sovereigns, we were eating much better. But the generosity of Sophia was apparently well-known.

"Zephyra had worked it out those nights when she was stealing goats," Aphrodite said. "Ha! Something she saw or heard. Something. Maybe a person passing a window in Chrysoula's house, maybe sounds from inside. And probably more than once. Zephyra put it together: there were more people living there than just Chrysoula and you and Takis."

I remembered Chrysoula warning us when we wanted to put on shadow puppet plays, *You will make a lot of noise and get us all shot.*

Zephyra told her suspicions to her mother, Aphrodite said. She and others had already noticed that we of that house looked fairly healthy when everyone else was nearly starving. And this had to mean that whoever was in the house with us could afford to buy black market food.

"That's why she got Zephyra to do it," Aphrodite said. "That's what she told me."

"What *who* told you?"

"Zephyra. Before she died."

"Told you that . . . ?"

"Her mother made Zephyra lead that German back to Chrysoula's house."

It was a moment before I could understand. What she said was clear enough, but somehow I wasn't sure what she was talking about.

"What do you mean? Brought him when?"

"That night."

What was wrong with me? I couldn't understand her. She repeated herself.

"That night—the night of the killing."

Then I got it.

"Zephyra?" I said. "It can't be."

"It's what she told me."

"Zephyra brought the colonel that night?"

"Was he a colonel? Who cares? Zephyra brought the German."

Take care of your own mice that they don't get us all caught, Zephyra's mother had told Chrysoula when we were looking for snails and bulbs. And Zephyra herself had said at the end, *Not my fault.* But it *was* her fault, wasn't it, the terror of what happened? And the mother who put her up to it. I clapped my hand over my mouth.

"But why?"

"Ha! Envy. Spite. You were eating and they weren't. Hunger does such things. Well, you know. Those times, they made us that way. And Zephyra was always jealous of that boy. It weighed on her. That's why she made goat noises at the end. When she could no longer speak, it was a kind of truth. A goat truth."

Aphrodite began to laugh in little explosions. She'd quiet down and then say "a goat truth" again and start all over. Tears were running down her face.

I couldn't speak for a moment as I tried to piece it together. Takis had left the house in a fit of bad temper and jealousy of Stelios. But of course we never knew what he did outside. Maybe he'd stormed around kicking stones in anger. Maybe he'd thrown himself down on the ground and screamed. It wouldn't have been the first time. It was just our—Stelios's and my—guess that he'd marched off to the colonel. We'd never thought that it could have been someone else, least of all Zephyra. Then we were all outside and there he was. The horror of seeing his mother shot before his eyes would have fallen on Takis and undone his already poorly hinged mind, shrouding that night from him for the rest of his days.

When I'd referred to it at the Zappeion, he'd asked, *What happened? Something happened, didn't it?* And when he'd later come to Stelios's house on New Year's Eve, he broke down, saying, *I want my mother. I don't know what happened to her.* Each time he fell into what Yannoula called one of his spells, it was usually due to either jealousy of Stelios or a reference to the events of the night his mother was killed. Or both. We'd all blamed him and he'd had to live under the weight of that blame and that would have led him where it did. *That doesn't mean it was my fault,* he'd said in the camp on the island. *Just because I can't remember.*

"But why?" I said. "Why could Zephyra tell *you* about this but only make noises with me?"

"Do I know? That's often the way. Clouds of the mind parting just a little before the end. But not much. You must have seen such things."

"But what I don't understand," I said, "is why her mother sent Zephyra to the colonel. Why didn't her mother go herself?"

"The German liked children. That's what everyone said."

Villagers had seen Colonel Esterhaus talking to Takis. And the mother wouldn't have been able to make the German understand without old Petros to translate. But Zephyra just took his hand and led him. His men followed.

"That's what she told me," Aphrodite said. But she began to drift off. She slumped back on the mat as I recalled how poor little Zephyra had wanted to come live with me and my father, but that wasn't possible. And later she'd been so jealous when I moved in with Takis and Chrysoula.

"So it wasn't Takis?" I said. "Even Takis believed it was Takis. So did we all."

"What? What?" Her eyes jerked open. "Oh, that. The mother died long ago while you were away. So only Zephyra lived on, carrying her little secret."

"Not so little. It ruined Takis." But that wasn't it, I thought. It was we who'd ruined him by believing him guilty and treating him as if he were. Until he'd become guilty in deed of other, larger things. Leading me to abandon him at that school in Peristeri. What if Zephyra had kept her suspicions to herself and the Germans had left the village at the end of the war without incident, as they had in so many other places? How our small universe had turned on the jealousy of a child. And the envy of her mother.

Aphrodite fell back again before she could say more and the women, peering through the door, apparently thought she'd died. They rushed into the hut shrieking and tearing at their hair, snatching up blankets and saucepans, smashing a spindly chair and a washbasin. Aphrodite's eyes flashed open and, grasping my shoulder, she actually managed to get to her feet.

"Out!" she said. "All of you, out!"

The women flapped around, dropping things they'd picked up, pots and pans, and rushed for the door. Aphrodite handed me a bunch of dried herbs—it looked like oregano, thyme and rosemary—along with a box of matches. "Burn it," she said. "Wave it around. Smoke out those crows."

The herbs were so dry that they flared up at once and burned themselves down. The thick herbal smoke filled the room and made me start coughing.

"Wave them here at the saint." She pointed to the icon of St. Athanassios sitting in the mouth of a cave. "He knows all our secrets. Let's see if he has another."

She was mumbling at the icon as if in conversation with it. It seemed all nonsense words or some strange language I couldn't follow. And then the nonsense turned to sense, something about my father and Chrysoula after my mother left the village. How Chrysoula's husband wouldn't have understood it, crazy as he was, always accusing people of plotting against him.

What was he to understand exactly? Then I recalled the other women saying my father had been like a bee gathering nectar from other flowers. Was this what they meant? Aphrodite said there'd come a time when Chrysoula and her husband went away to a clinic for treatment for him. A place near Athens. Kifissia, it was.

Kifissia? Could it be the same place? Chrysoula had put her own husband there? Surely there weren't two such places in the same suburb of Athens.

"She came back alone months later," Aphrodite said. "With a baby. Let's see, you would have been about what, seven or so? Didn't you ever notice that you and Takis had the same nose, eyes and hair?"

"What do you mean? We certainly did not."

She teetered around the room, surprisingly agile for someone who'd been near death only minutes before.

"What are you saying?" I asked.

"It's what Zephyra also told me," Aphrodite said. "But what did she know, that old goat-thief?"

"Told you what exactly? That my father . . . ?"

"Oh, you work it out. I'm too tired." She flopped back down on her rugs, wheezing. Then she added, "Chrysoula told everyone that her husband was in no state to care for their new child; she'd do it alone until he came back. But he never did."

"I don't believe it. And how would Zephyra know anyway? She would have been little when all this happened. If it did."

"Her mother, of course. She knew everything." Aphrodite paused and then asked, "Well, isn't half a brother better than none?"

So my lie was not an untruth after all. The last call I'd had from St. Elena came a few years after my visit, when the school was closing. The caller told me that my brother had stayed until he'd joined the army, but he'd left a suitcase behind. Did I want to claim it? I didn't and heard nothing more about him until one day, sometime in the sixties, old Stamatis in our village store showed me a newspaper with a photograph of some military men. He told me that the article said that one of the men was from here, our very own village—did I recognize anyone? I looked closely at the photo and, matching it to the names beneath, I realized that, sure enough, the third one in was Takis, grown to manhood and looking spiffy but stern in his crisp uniform.

Well, well, I thought, he finally got one of his own and at least this one fits. But when I looked even more closely, I saw the insignia of the dreaded military police. This was during the years of the junta dictatorship in the sixties and seventies when military police persecuted and arrested leftists along with any other real or imagined critics of the right-wing regime. It saw plots and enemies behind every lamppost, under every stone. I was sickened to think that Takis was part of that national paranoia. Could I have saved him from it if I'd taken him in? I tortured myself with this question for some time but thought finally that maybe he'd been on that path most of his life. When the regime fell in 1974, many of the military police were tried and imprisoned; others simply disappeared in acts of retribution by relatives of the previously persecuted or murdered. I never heard anything more about Takis. But I worried that he might still turn up one day. And now was I to believe that he was in fact my brother?

Suddenly I was angry at Aphrodite, the wheezy old know-it-all, waiting to tell me things that could no longer be proven true or not. "Oh, really, how can we believe this?" I said. "It's old gossip. Deathbed chatter, nothing more."

"Suit yourself. Maybe it's true; maybe it isn't. Do I care? Not when I really can't breathe. Help me; there's no air in here."

I tried to fan her with the stub of the burned bunch of herbs I was still holding, but I was paying little attention. Maybe it was the smoke in the room, or, as she said, the lack of air, but I felt detached suddenly, drifting. Chrysoula had once said that Takis was so strange and unpredictable that he certainly didn't take after her. I hadn't thought much about it at the time, but that didn't sound like my father either. Of course in those times there was so much intermarriage between families and even between relatives that there was often no sure way of knowing who was really whose. Any shame was quickly covered up. The truth is that the baby Chrysoula brought back to the village—if that's what she did—could have been anybody's. Poor Takis with such a clouded inheritance, though he never knew it. I thought of Yannoula that night in the mountain village saying that he would always be a boy hearing voices; he wouldn't grow out of it. Perhaps he never did.

I seemed to be above Aphrodite, looking down on her wretched old head, her matted hair, the mess that she was and maybe we all were. Such messes we made of our lives. Such messes the times made of us. I felt sick and dropped the burned herbs in Aphrodite's lap. I was back beside her.

She shrieked and said, "Now can everyone please let me get on with dying?"

The women in the doorway rushed back into the hut. They moaned and pulled their hair, all the while casting their eyes around at Aphrodite's few possessions, the ones they hadn't grabbed before. Here was another woman without family, but there wasn't much to bother with, it seemed. I walked out.

I didn't even take a pair of her shoes to help me with a lament. In fact, no lament came to me at all. It was not a matter of deciding against it but rather that, for the first time, I had no urge to do it. My lament for Zephyra had been my last. I think it's because I no longer end up in that room with the open door and the amber light beyond. How can there be any kind of a truth behind that door? And why did I think so for so long? Maybe the fact that there isn't one *is* the truth itself. When I realized that, the vision stopped coming to me, and the laments.

It's awful to have lost that vision after so many years. But gone it is and with it the voices of the dead; they speak to me no more. It's like losing all your friends at once. Even my father has stopped complaining, though I must say I miss him turning up in my back garden for a smoke. I'd like to ask him: So was Takis really your son and my brother? And his madness didn't come from Chrysoula's mad husband? From you, then? Or from Chrysoula herself, with her stories of wild chickens and her curious advice to other villagers? Does my abilty to lament come from the same place? What gets passed on through families and what is learned? Do you know?

The question is too simple, I imagine him saying, *and the answer too complicated.* He fishes for a cigarette in his breast pocket. I can see through the bullet holes where his heart once was. But he has nothing more to say.

So in the telling of my story, it has changed. Or is it I who have changed? I just listened to the beginning of the first cassette and can hardly believe that chirpy old bird is me. And here is this letter from you, my little scholar, which came a while back, between cassettes four and five. I didn't open it when it arrived, expecting that you would want to know how the lament cassettes were coming along—and what could I say? That I've used up all the cassettes for my own purpose? When I did finally read the letter, I understood it to say that you're coming back here to see me and as it turns out, this is the day. Well, here are the cassettes and maybe in fact they do contain what you asked for. A record of a life nearly complete could also be said to be a lament for that life, couldn't it? When I started, I wanted to keep these cassettes to remind me of, what, myself? But in the telling, I've worn myself out, and grown tired of my own voice, tired of this story. So take them!

But it does seem to me too bad that you're spending your youth on such a project, listening to an old woman with what is probably my last lament for another time, for the lives of Stelios and Takis. There was so much I didn't know then, such as how days get used up and are irreplaceable. Like lives. Sometimes when I watch the village children playing, I think that they're like messengers into a time to come. And I wonder if I should send a message with them. But what one? Love one another? Something like that? But they'll probably learn enough of that sort of thing, learn it and forget it on the way to war.

A while back I saw on that television in Stamatis's shop that the Land of Big Radios had sent some kind of device out there among the planets and stars. Not a satellite exactly, the newsperson said, but a kind of voyager that might sail on through the blackness forever, if such a thing is possible. Inside it is, well, I don't know, a sort of phonograph record with information about us earthlings in all our languages. Can you imagine? Everything about what we eat and wear, the music we listen to, the gods we worship and I don't know what all. Maybe all our stories from the Trojan War to the Germans here in Greece and, who knows, maybe even Karagiozis—why not? Ah, humans, I thought. We can be such barbarians and then turn around and act like children hoping that among the stars, someone or something might care about our yearnings, our stories. Hope, that's all we've got, isn't it, our most important word?

There's a word for Takis's illness now and maybe that's on the record too. I've heard it but can't at the moment remember it. He could probably get medication these days and not remain a person as divided as this country. But his shadow puppet self lives on, as do Stelios's and mine.

I know because just after Aphrodite died, a puppet master touring the provinces came to our village and set up his shadow theater under the plane tree where my father was executed. Working at night with battery-operated lamps to make the shadows, he performed the comedies at first on successive nights. I could hear the children screaming with laughter all the way to my house. When I heard that he was to perform *The Hero Katsondonis*, I waited until the play was well under way then stood at the back of the crowd.

It was the scene where Katsondonis was dying. But I was shocked to see that at one side of the screen stood Stelios's old Takis puppet reworked as a shepherd, and the Stelios and Aliki puppets, dressed as the priest and the wife of Katsondonis, weeping and lamenting for the dying hero. Oh, no, I thought, the puppeteer, could he possibly be Takis, who'd survived in spite of everything? When the performance was over and the puppet master came from behind the screen to take his bow, I saw he was a tiny old man hardly bigger than a child. His white hair was so curly he looked as if he'd been electrocuted. I waited until he was packing everything up to ask how he'd come by the set of puppets. He'd bought them, he told me, at a sale of the contents of an old school in Peristeri. It was closing down and anything left there by former students had been for sale. Most of the puppets were too old and damaged to be of any use and he'd thrown them out.

"But these handmade ones," the puppeteer said, holding up the ones of Stelios, Takis and me, "they're so beautifully done."

"I knew the man who made them."

"Really? Was he a puppeteer too?"

"Oh, yes, a good one."

"Ah, there aren't many of us left. Television and computers, they've stolen our audience. And our stories."

But we were still characters in a larger story, as Stelios had said we were, like extras in a movie—people at the edge of a scene that you barely notice, though important enough to share the stage with the hero, all our shadows on the screen. I imagine them now when my last hour has come, Karagiozis and the others dancing around, tearing their make-believe hair. They lift glasses of raki and drink to me. The goose that escaped returns and volunteers itself for my funeral feast. Katsondonis speaks.

I say good-bye to you, tall hills, and to you, rocks on high.
You are my witnesses . . .

And I think of that night before Stelios's funeral when I was sitting by myself in the schoolhouse and felt as if someone had come in the door. There was a sheen of light across my eyes that blurred the room. I knew at once that it was Stelios, his spirit. I reached for his hand and saw us walk together along a street in Athens then up the hill behind Chrysoula's house outside my village. And we were in other places I didn't recognize. We grew up. We had a son and a daughter. We became middle-aged and our children had children too. We were on a ship and then on a plane and then we were coming home again. We argued and drank too much and got fat and fell down stairs and made money and lost it. We grew old together. He became bald and nearsighted and crabby. Then all over the room his light dimmed and began to fade. *Good-bye,* he called over his shoulder. *Good-bye.*

Oh, but there's the knock at the door. I gather myself and glance out the window to see you, still with that eggbeater hair. *Theo mou!* I stand up to open the door and as I do, I press the button to turn off this little red light, my life.

AUTHOR'S NOTE

The period covered by Aliki's story is still a polarizing one for both those who survived it and those who've had to live with its repercussions, which have helped shape the present. This narrative is in no way meant to be a definitive account or explanation of those awful years but rather an imagined story in turbulent times. In order to suit the larger purposes of the narrative, the actual years of civil fighting have been telescoped to a more condensed time frame. For anyone wishing for more information on the period, the craft of shadow theater or the art and practice of lamenting, I suggest the following books, to which I'm indebted.

Alexiou, Margaret. *The Ritual Lament in Greek Tradition* (Cambridge: Cambridge University Press, 1974).

Andrews, Kevin. *Greece in the Dark* (Amsterdam: Hakkert, 1980) and *The Flight of Ikaros* (London: Weidenfeld and Nicolson, 1959).

Beevor, Antony. *Crete: The Battle and the Resistance* (London: John Murray, 1991).

Carabott, Philip, and Thanasis D. Sfikas. *The Greek Civil War: Essays on a Conflict of Exceptionalism and Silences* (Burlington, VT: Ashgate, 2004).

Cockburn, Patrick, and Henry Cockburn. *Henry's Demons: Living with Schizophrenia: A Father and Son's Story* (New York: Scribner, 2011).

Danforth, Loring M. *The Death Rituals of Rural Greece* (Princeton, NJ: Princeton University Press, 1982).

Danforth, Loring M., and Riki van Boeschoten. *Children of the Greek Civil War: Refugees and the Politics of Memory* (Chicago: University of Chicago Press, 2012).

Herodotus. *The Histories,* translated by Aubrey De Sélincourt (London: Penguin Books, 1972).

Hesiod. *Theogony, Works and Days,* translated by M. L. West (New York: Oxford University Press, 1988).

Holst, Gail. *Road to Rembetika* (Athens: Anglo-Hellenic Publishing, 1975).

Homer. *The Iliad*, translated by Robert Fagles (New York: Penguin Books, 1990); Richmond Lattimore (Chicago: University of Chicago Press, 2011); Stanley Lombardo (Indianapolis, IN: Hackett Publishing, 1997); and Stephen Mitchell (New York: Free Press, 2011).

Janes, Colin. *The Eagles of Crete: An Untold Story of Civil War* (n.p.: CreateSpace Independent Publishing, 2013).

Matthews, Kenneth. *Memories of a Mountain War: Greece 1944–1949* (London: Longman, 1972).

Mazower, Mark. *After the War Was Over: Reconstructing the Family, Nation, and State in Greece, 1943–1960* (Princeton, NJ: Princeton University Press, 2000) and *Inside Hitler's Greece: The Experience of Occupation, 1941–44* (New Haven, CT: Yale University Press, 1995).

Myrsiades, Linda S., and Kostas Myrsiades. *Karagiozis: Culture and Comedy in Greek Puppet Theater* (Lexington, KY: University Press of Kentucky, 1992) and, as translators, *Karagiozis: Three Classic Plays* (New York: Pella Publishing, 1999).

Oswald, Alice. *Memorial: An Excavation of The Iliad* (London: Faber and Faber, 2011).

Psychoundakis, George. *The Cretan Runner: His Story of the German Occupation*, translated by Patrick Leigh Fermor (London: Penguin Books, 2009).

Seremetakis, C. Nadia. *The Last Word: Women, Death, and Divination in Inner Mani* (Chicago: University of Chicago Press, 1991).

Spatharis, Sotiris. *Behind the White Screen* (New York: Red Dust, 1976).

Voglis, Polymeris. *Becoming a Subject: Political Prisoners during the Greek Civil War* (New York: Berghahn Books, 2002).

Woodhouse, C. M. *Modern Greece: A Short History* (London: Faber and Faber, 1991).

ACKNOWLEDGMENTS

I'm grateful to the Boston Athenæum for its solitude and grace: much of this work was written and revised there. I also want to thank Tom Jenks of *Narrative* magazine for his close reading of and suggestions on an early draft of the manuscript. On later drafts, Thomas H. McNeely of GrubStreet made countless invaluable and perceptive comments. I also thank my agent, Susan Golomb of Writers House, for her belief in the story and my editor, Claire Zion, and her staff at Berkley for their enthusiasm and careful work at all levels. I'm forever indebted to my wife, Jane McLachlan, my first and most tireless reader, for her belief from beginning to end.